英文
閱讀技術

Advanced English Reading Skills

全MP3一次下載

http://booknews.com.tw/mp3/9789864542581.htm

iOS 系統請升級至 iOS 13 後再行下載，下載前請先安裝ZIP解壓縮程式或APP。

此為大型檔案，建議使用 WIFI 連線下載，以免占用流量，並確認連線狀況，以利下載順暢。

作者序

　　對大部分台灣的學生來說，學習英文很多時候其實就是在背單字。每次上英文課好像都是在學單字，每位學生都花費相當長的時間在背單字，彷彿誰能背得更多，英文就會更好。有些學生甚至相信只要將所有英文單字背完的那一天，自己的英文就天下無敵了。然而，理想往往很美好，現實卻很骨感。不但單字永遠都背不完，而且辛辛苦苦背下來的單字，往往無法幫助自己在閱讀長篇文章時，有效提升自己的閱讀理解力。

　　為什麼會這樣呢？這是因為不論是利用字根、字首、字尾或其他的記憶巧門，其目的都是希望能夠在最短的時間內，牢牢記住最多數量的單字。但是，對於每一個死背或是利用其他技巧記下來的單字，常常只是一知半解，對其正確的使用方式更幾乎是一無所知，這樣符號式的單字記憶其實無助於閱讀理解力，因為單字是單字，句子是句子，文章是文章，對我們大腦來說，單字就像是化學符號那樣，不容易直接聯結到我們的生活經驗，導致我們流失這些單字的速度常常比南極冰川融化的速度更快。最後，只好重頭再「練單」，只是仰賴各種記憶單字的方式來精進英文常常會有做白工感覺，努力學習英文十幾年的時間，程度卻是原地踏步，經不起實戰閱讀的考驗。付出了努力，卻得不到相對應的收獲，是台灣莘莘學子普遍的心聲。

相同字首一起背	相同字尾一起背	相同字根一起背	易混淆字一起背
mis<u>judge</u>	ed<u>ible</u>	xeno<u>phobia</u>	adapt vs. adept
mis<u>match</u>	cred<u>ible</u>	hydro<u>phobia</u>	lessen vs. lesson
mis<u>behave</u>	afford<u>able</u>	arachno<u>phobia</u>	desert vs. dessert
mis<u>understand</u>	predic<u>table</u>	claustro<u>phobia</u>	expensive vs. expansive

·符號式的單字記憶無助於閱讀理解力

　　也就是說，如果學習的方法不正確，再多的努力也只會是「事倍功半」。本書的宗旨是幫助讀者建立更有效率的閱讀方式，在閱讀長篇文章之中，自然地從上下文的脈絡學到單字的意思，並體驗單字正確使用的情境。由於文章出現的每一個單字都有特定的情境，所以容易留下深

> "Reading is to the mind what exercise is to the body."
> Joseph Addison, essayist

刻的印象，故對我們的大腦來說，從文章中所學到每一個單字將不再只是一個符號而已。而是一個真真實實的「經驗」。

在這個素養教育的時代，閱讀素養的重要性不言而喻，舉凡國內外的各項英文考試，從大學入學學科能力測驗到多益等國際語言檢定測驗，「素養題」已成為重要的命題方向，最明顯的變化就是閱讀理解的題型大幅增加，不只題目變長，閱讀測驗的字數也明顯變多，十分考驗學生閱讀長篇文章的理解力。很明顯地，知道很多單字的意思，已不足以應付新時代的閱讀素養考題。在國內 108 課綱推出以來，已經有不少家長與學生覺得英文考試好像在測驗考生的「速讀」能力一樣。然而，很多學生一看到長文就容易放棄，因為長篇閱讀的訊息量龐大，不會抓重點的學生不容易知道作者想表達的重點是什麼。缺乏組織分析能力的學生在考場上佔盡劣勢。因此閱讀能力較差的學生幾乎無法在素養教育的時代，取得理想的分數。另一項國際測驗的趨勢是「跨領域整合」能力，許多閱讀測驗幾乎都是跨領域的主題，以前的教育強調「專才」，現在則強調「通才」，因此，廣博的知識、跨領域整合及演繹歸納的能力，已成為現今英文閱讀測驗的一個潛規則。

本書使用知名語言學和英文閱讀的理論，以宏觀閱讀與微觀閱讀兩階段式的閱讀方式，有效提升讀者對於長篇閱讀的理解力。本書共收錄由作者親自撰寫的 24 篇文章，涉及八大主題，分別是世界旅遊、藝術歷史與文化、新冠疫情與保健、人物傳記、經濟與財經、資訊與科技、社會議題和自然科學。故本書的閱讀練習能夠幫助讀者增廣見聞，除了知識層面的提升之外，每一篇閱讀文章皆由六種不同面向的閱讀方式，包含掃讀、略讀、細讀、高理解速讀、跟讀、聽讀，有系統地帶領讀者增強自己的閱讀理解力。市面上初階的閱讀書籍已經很多，本書適合程度中上的讀者挑戰自己，更上層樓。由於本書步驟清楚，也能帶領程度較弱的讀者一步一步地加強自己的閱讀實力。藉由大量且系統化的練習，讀者的英文實力將能夠「有感」提升。

周昱翔　2022 年於台北

How to use this book
使用說明

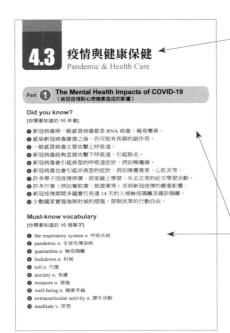

跨科目、跨領域取材：

本書因應國際化教育方針、核心素養的閱讀命題趨勢，閱讀內容囊括最新取材的主題，包括旅遊、藝術歷史與文化、疫情與健康保健、人物傳記、經濟與財經、資訊與科技、環保與社會議題、科學、自然與動植物等領域。

閱讀前的熱身：

本書第四章閱讀訓練的實地演練中，首先提供讀懂文章所需的背景知識，以及必須知道的 10 個字詞，讓你有「先睹為快」的感覺，接下來在閱讀過程中更能夠掌握各段主旨，而不會看完一篇文章還是似懂非懂、抓不到重點。

6D 閱讀法之「掃讀」訓練：

根據一開始提供的 10 個 must-know vocabulary 在文章中快速找到這些字詞，目標是在文章中搜尋特定的人名、時間、地點，或相關詞語，就像是在電話簿中搜尋某人的電話號碼一樣，其他內容完全不看，最後再給自己一個小小測試吧！

6D 閱讀法之「略讀」訓練：

訓練讀者用 30 秒的時間讀過各段第一句，並對照頁面右側的中文解說，粗略了解文章結構與每一段大意。最後再確認自己是否了解各段的大意。

STEP 2 略讀 Skimming

針對剛才的文章，用 30 秒鐘瀏覽各段的第一句，粗略了解文章結構與大意即可。

The world's first vaccine was developed in 1796 by Edward Jenner, a British physician whose seminal work led to the development of the smallpox vaccine and helped eradicate smallpox from the world. A variety of other vaccines have also been developed to date, saving many lives each year. Before each vaccine is approved for mass production, it undergoes clinical trials that are rigorous and time-consuming. Despite these efforts, vaccines are not perfectly safe since people have different reactions to vaccines. Common side effects include, for example, swelling, muscle pain, tiredness, and fever. In some rare cases, negative reactions can be severe and even result in death.

歷史上首支成功的疫苗

In 2020, people once again pinned their hopes on vaccines in the wake of the outbreak of SARS-CoV-2, aka COVID-19. Up until the end of. 2022, COVID-19 has killed more than 6.5 million people worldwide, with over 650 million infected, according to the World Health Organization. In an effort to reduce the death toll, pharmaceutical companies rolled out COVID-19 vaccines in less than

人們也希望利用疫苗結束新冠疫情

■ 回答以下問題，確認自己是否正確理解整篇文章的大意：

Q1. _____ Vaccines have been around for a long time. (T/F)

Q2. _____ There are no smallpox patients today. (T/F)

Q3. _____ The smallpox vaccine protected people from COVID-19 in 2020. (T/F)

Q4. _____ The unvaccinated people have been bullied. (T/F)

Q5. _____ Voluntary consent to vaccination is a human right. (T/F)

▶▶ 解答請見 p.256

6D 閱讀法之「細讀」訓練：

讀者逐字讀文章的特定部分。這部分又稱為「重點區域細讀」訓練，就像是合約中最重要或特別重要的部分。然後再測試自己是否了解這個段落的文意。

STEP 3 細讀 Close reading

請用 60 秒的時間仔細閱讀以下內容，並回答問題。

In an effort to reduce the death toll, pharmaceutical companies rolled out COVID-19 vaccines in less than one year. Accelerated from development to deployment, COVID-19 vaccines were the fastest vaccines that had ever been developed. These vaccines have been authorized under an Emergency Use Authorization (EUA) by the Food and Drug Administration (FDA), which claims that the benefits outweigh risks.

_____ Q1. According to this passage, which of the following is correct?
(A) The risks of COVID-19 vaccines are well known.
(B) The FDA has authorized COVID-19 vaccines.
(C) Accelerated vaccines are the best vaccines.
(D) COVID-19 vaccines have no risks.

_____ Q2. According to this passage, why have COVID-19 vaccines been authorized under an EUA?
(A) There wasn't enough time for the development of these vaccines.
(B) EUA authorized vaccines are the same as fully authorized vaccines.
(C) These vaccines have been perfectly developed.

6D 閱讀法之「高理解速讀」訓練：

這是重點中的重點訓練了！訓練每一眼看到的都是一個個「有意義的群組」（不是一個字、一個字看）。作者提到英文中有 3 大意義群組：WHO/WHAT 群組（像是人物或是抽象概念等）、ACTION 群組（表示動作的動詞）、CIRCUMSTANCE 群組（表示狀態的副詞或介系詞片語）。同樣地，最後再搭配實戰練習，不必理會艱深難懂的字彙也能快速理解文章。

STEP 4 高理解速讀 Speed Reading with Greater Comprehension

請用 90 秒的時間，看完整篇文章。然後跟著每一個有意義的色塊，提升理解的速度。（請盡量試著不查自己不認識的字，利用前後文去推測意思。）

The world's first vaccine was developed in 1796 by Edward Jenner, a British physician whose seminal work led to the development of the smallpox vaccine and helped eradicate smallpox from the world. A variety of other vaccines have also been developed to date, saving many lives each year. Before each vaccine is approved for mass production, it undergoes clinical trials that are rigorous and time-consuming. Despite these efforts, vaccines are not perfectly safe since people have different reactions to vaccines. Common side effects include, for example, swelling, muscle pain, tiredness, and fever. In some rare cases, negative reactions can be severe and even result in death.

`歷史上首支成功的疫苗`

In 2020, people once again pinned their hopes on vaccines in the wake of the outbreak of SARS-CoV-2, aka COVID-19. Up until the end of 2022, COVID-19 has killed more than 6.5 million people worldwide, with over 650 million infected, according to the World Health Organization. In an effort to reduce the death toll, pharmaceutical companies rolled out COVID-19 vaccines in less than one year. Accelerated from development to deployment, COVID-19 vaccines were the fastest vaccines that had ever been developed. These vaccines have been authorized under an Emergency Use Authorization (EUA) by the Food and Drug Administration (FDA), which claims that the benefits outweigh risks.

`人們也希望利用疫苗結束新冠疫情`

● 讀回答以下問題：

_____ Q1. Which of the following is NOT a common side effect of vaccination?
(A) swelling (B) tiredness (C) death (D) fever

_____ Q2. Which description of vaccines is incorrect?
(A) Vaccines save many lives each year.
(B) Vaccines are perfectly safe for everyone.
(C) Vaccines undergo time-consuming clinical trials.
(D) Vaccines can prevent people from being hospitalized.

6D 閱讀法之「跟讀」+「聽讀」訓練：

每一篇文章皆由外籍專業人士以正常速度錄製跟讀與聽讀的音檔。讀者可透過手機掃描 QR 碼，隨時隨地訓練自己的口說及聽力。亦可於本書第一頁下方掃描 QR 碼下載全書 MP3 音檔，不需註冊會員，或額外安裝自己不熟悉的播放 APP 才能聽，更省去每次聽音檔都要掃描、耗費流量等的麻煩！

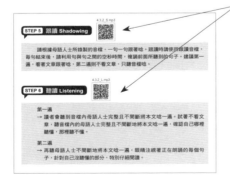

STEP 5 跟讀 Shadowing　　4.3.2_S.mp3

請根據母語人士所錄製的檔。一句一句跟著唸。跟讀時請使用跟讀音檔，每句結束後，請利用句與句之間的空秒時間，複誦前面所聽到的句子。建議第一遍，看著文章跟著唸。第二遍則不看文章，只聽音檔唸。

STEP 6 聽讀 Listening　　4.3.2_L.mp3

第一遍
→ 讀者會聽到音檔內母語人士完整且不間斷地將本文唸一遍。試著不看文章，聽音檔內的母語人士完整且不間斷地將本文唸一遍，確認自己哪裡聽懂、那裡聽不懂。

第二遍
→ 再聽母語人士不間斷地將本文唸一遍。眼睛注視著正在朗讀的每個句子，針對自己沒聽懂的部分，特別仔細閱讀。

單字 Vocabulary

❶ seminal [ˈsɛmɪnl̩]	adj. 有深遠影響的 She wrote a seminal article on linguistics ten years ago. 她十年前寫了一篇對語言學有深遠影響的文章。
❷ eradicate [ɪˈrædɪket]	v. 根除 Scientists hope to eradicate this disease. 科學家希望根除這種疾病。
❸ outbreak [ˈaʊtˌbrek]	n.（疾病、戰爭等的）爆發 There has been an outbreak of war in Ukraine. 烏克蘭爆發了一場戰爭。
❹ rollout [ˈrolˌaʊt]	n. 首次推出 The iPhone has been a huge success since its rollout in 2007. iPhone 自從 2007 年首次推出以來一直相當成功。
❺ lift [lɪft]	v. 撤銷（法令等） Vaccine mandates have been lifted in many countries. 在許多國家，疫苗強制令已經被撤銷了。
❻ incriminating [ɪnˈkrɪmɪnetɪŋ]	adj. 指控他人有罪的 He made some incriminating statements last week. 他上週發表了一些指控他人有罪的言論。
❼ pharmaceutical [ˌfɑrməˈsjutɪkl̩]	adj. 製藥的 She is trying to buy a pharmaceutical company. 她嘗試要買下一家製藥公司。
❽ consent [kənˈsɛnt]	n. 同意、允許 Preschoolers need to have the consent of their patents to be vaccinated. 幼兒園學童須家長同意之後才可以施打疫苗。

延伸學習 — 單字：

　　除了一開始提供與背景知識相關的 10 個字詞，每一篇文章最後還提供加碼學習的單字，包含本篇文章以外的單字意義，再搭配例句。讓你不但懂還能舉一反三。

慣用語和片語 Expressions and Phrases

❶ in (the) wake of　在⋯發生之後
Gun control laws have been tightened in (the) wake of mass shootings.
在發生大規模槍擊案件之後，槍枝控管的法律一直是很嚴格的。

❷ on the other end of the spectrum　在另一個極端
Some people do not finish the food on their plates. On the other end of the spectrum, many die of famine.
有些人沒將自己的食物吃完，而在另個極端世界裡，許多人卻死於飢荒。

❸ turn a blind eye to　對⋯視而不見
The President turned a blind eye to the demands of the people.
總統對於人民的訴求充耳不聞。

❹ at odds with　與⋯不同
She was at odds with her colleagues on the issue of gun control.
她與她的同事在槍枝管控的議題上意見相左。

延伸學習 — 慣用語、片語：

　　片語及慣用語是增添文章精采與豐富度的利器！無論是在寫作或口說能力的展現上，都能為自己再加分！尤其是口說方面，若刻意用艱澀字彙不僅讓人聽起來很不自然，且容易用錯情境！事實上，慣用語才是老外日常用語，且為口說檢定「詞彙豐富度」加分的重要項目。

模擬測驗：

在「6D 閱讀」訓練以及「延伸學習」之後，緊接著還有讓你小試身手的檢定考試擬真試題，且皆附上正確答案，精準掌握重點核心概念！讀者可從練習中漸漸成長、複習，往後碰到英文閱讀測驗，既能加快閱覽題目的速度，亦能敏捷地找出正確答案！

STEP 8 模擬測驗

A. Fill in the blanks with suitable words or phrases 將適合的字詞填入空格中

ⓐ pharmaceutical ⓑ in the wake of ⓒ at odds with ⓓ turn a blind eye to

1. Many people have had the habit of wearing masks ____________ the COVID-19 outbreak.
2. The mayor ____________ widespread corruption in the city.
3. Sanofi is a famous ______ company, having manufactured many vaccines to date.
4. His conclusion was ______ that of the original paper.

B. Multiple choice questions 選擇題（可利用此題型熟悉多益、英檢考試）

______ 1. This electric vehicle has attracted much attention since its ------- last year.
(A) rundown (B) rollout (C) runaway (D) roll-up

______ 2. Thanks to the successful invention of vaccines, the disease had finally been -------.
(A) eradicated (B) abdicated (C) chastised (D) mandated

解答＋解析＋翻譯篇：

全書包含第四章所有小測驗以及模擬試題等的解答與部分解析。因此在您進行閱讀、口說、聽力訓練時一本就夠，不必分成題本與解答本耗時費力地反覆對照。解答篇的「高理解速讀」部分，逐題清楚標示每一題的答案及說明，並清楚告訴您這一題的答案在文章中的哪個位置，以及為什麼這個選項是錯誤的，可以從文章中哪一句得知。另外，「細讀」與「高理解速讀」的題目以及整篇文章，也提供中文翻譯，比起市面上類似書籍，擁有難以比擬的超豐富、超紮實內容，讓讀者每訓練一篇都真實感受到實力提升！

4.3 Part 2 - Controversies over COVID-19 Vaccine Mandates

Step 1 掃讀 Scanning

- 選擇正確的意思

B A B A A B B A B A

Step 2 略讀 Skimming

T T F T T

- 答案解析

Q1. (T) 由首段第一句可知，人類從 1796 年就開始研究疫苗了。
Q2. (T) 由首段第一句可知，天花病毒已絕跡。
Q3. (F) 由第二段第一句可知，新冠病毒所使用的疫苗是 2020 年開始研發的新疫苗。
Q4. (T) 由第四段第一句可知，未施打新冠疫苗的人受到網路霸凌。
Q5. (T) 由第四段第一句可知，施打任何疫苗都是一種基本人權，需要徵求個人的同意。

Step 3 細讀 Close reading

B A

- 答案解析

Q1. 根據這段短文內容，以下何者是正確的？
(A) 新冠疫苗的風險是眾所皆知的。
(B) 美國食品藥物管理局（FDA）已授權新冠疫苗的使用。
(C) 加速完成的疫苗是最好的疫苗。
(D) 新冠疫苗沒有風險。

解析 由第三句可知，美國食品藥物管理局已給予新冠疫苗緊急許可證，並聲稱新冠疫苗利大於弊，所以正確答案是 (B)。

Q2. 根據這段短文內容，為何新冠疫苗獲得緊急許可證？
(A) 沒有足夠的時間開發這些疫苗。
(B) 緊急許可的疫苗與正式許可的疫苗是相同的。
(C) 這些疫苗已經完美地研發出來了。
(D) 這些疫苗已經研發很久了。

解析 由第一句和第二句可知，為了盡快減少死亡人數，藥廠在不到一年的時間內就研發並製造出新冠疫苗，所以正確答案是 (A)。

Step 8 模擬測驗

- 解答

A. 1. in the wake of 2. turned a blind eye to 3. pharmaceutical 4. at odds with
B. 1. (B) 2. (A) 3. (C) 4. (A) 5. (D)

文章中譯

世界上第一支疫苗是在 1796 年由英國的醫師愛德華・詹納（Edward Jenner）所開發，他這項創舉促成了天花疫苗的開發，並幫助天花從這世上絕跡。如今，其他各種疫苗不斷被開發，且每年拯救了無數生命。在每一款疫苗獲准量產之前，都要經過嚴格且耗時的臨床試驗。儘管做出了這些努力，疫苗並不是絕對安全的，因為人們對疫苗會有不同的反應。常見的副作用包括，例如，腫脹、肌肉疼痛、疲倦和發燒。在一些極少數案例中，可能會有嚴重的不良反應，甚至導致死亡。

Contents
目錄

Contents
目錄

第一章

影響英文閱讀理解力的重要因素

1 影響英文閱讀理解力的重要因素

　　英文閱讀理解力是一種認知上的預測能力。比方說，當看到作者在文章一開始談論南極冰川融化的現象，讀者便可以預測接下來作者可能會討論氣候變遷的議題。然而影響閱讀預測能力的因素有很多，本課討論尤其重要的三個因素：背景知識、跨文化的視野、和思辨能力（critical thinking）。

1.1 背景知識

　　很多時候看不懂英文閱讀，問題除了出在英文理解力不足之外，另一個關鍵因素就是缺乏所需的背景知識。在素養教育的趨勢之下，閱讀測驗的特色之一為「跨領域、跨學科」，因此，讀者是否能夠融會貫通，整合所學過的知識，將會直接影響閱讀理解力。若缺乏相關背景知識，即使看得懂題目，也未必能夠順利作答。

　　但由於每個人的背景知識量並不相同，英文閱讀對於每個人來說並不是完全公平的。英文閱讀能力想要進步，必須要有廣博的知識。然而，單單熟記大英百科全書是不足夠的，因百科全書更新的速度遠遠慢於日新月異的知識爆炸時代。知識跟英文單字一樣是無邊無際的，舊的單字可能會被賦予新的意思，全新的單字也不斷地被創造出來。同樣地，現有的知識隨時可能會被更新，甚至被推翻。在此趨勢之下，想要提升英文閱讀能力，就必須跨出自己的「知識舒適圈」。

　　舉例來說，一直以來許多人都認為股票市場和債券市場都是反向的關係，當股市下跌的時候，債市通常能夠抗跌，或甚至逆風上漲。所以每當股市走跌的時候，許多人會轉而去購買債券作為避險的手段。然而，在各國央行陸續推出量化寬鬆的貨幣政策之後，股市和債市明顯已成了相同方向的趨勢，債券不再能夠有效地避險。舉例來說，在 2020 年 3 月股市因為新冠疫情崩盤時，債市也同樣地崩跌，隨後因為各國央行的量化寬鬆政策，股市全面的上漲，同樣地，債券市場也隨之上揚。

　　另外一個顛覆認知的例子是人體的免疫系統，一直以來科學家都認為先天免疫系統不具備免疫記憶的能力，也就是說，先天免疫系統的免疫細胞無法記住過去交手過的病毒或細菌，故無法針對特定的病原體產生相對應的免疫反應。免疫記憶能力是後天免疫系統獨有的特色能力，然而，最新的研究發現，隸屬於先天免疫系統的自然殺手細胞，竟也能夠展現出免疫記憶的能力，此一發現跌破科學家的眼鏡，也重新修正了我們對於先天免疫系統的認知。

最後一個例子是浩瀚宇宙中的神祕黑洞，長期以來，科學家已經知道黑洞會吞噬所有靠近它的物質，行星、恆星、甚至是宇宙中速度最快的光，都無法逃脫黑洞強大的引力。科學家也知道黑洞並不是只有單向吸入靠近它的物質，當黑洞吞噬一個天體之後，有時候黑洞隨即會「吐出」一些剛剛才被吞噬的天體殘餘物。然而這個「知識」卻在 2022 年被改寫了，哈佛大學的天文學家在 2022 年驚訝地觀測到離地球 6.65 億光年以外的一個黑洞，竟然「吐出」了一堆在三年多前曾經被它吞噬進去的那顆行星的殘餘物質，天文學家從來不知道黑洞竟然能夠在這麼長的時間以後，才吐出行星的殘餘物質，此一發現徹底顛覆了天文學家對黑洞的認知，也改寫了所有天文學的課本。

在這個資訊爆炸的時代，「博識」變得更重要了，我們必須抱持著開放的心態，面對隨時可能會顛覆我們既有認知的新知識，只有持續更新自己的知識庫，並將新的知識與自己已經建立的知識體系融會貫通，才能夠強化英文閱讀即戰力。

1.2 跨文化的視野

第二個重要因素就是跨文化的視野，不同的文化對於相同的事物常常會有不同的認知、聯想與意涵。舉例來說，中文形容一個人冥頑不靈，會用牛來比喻，例如：牛牽到北京還是牛。然而，同樣頑固的概念，英文所聯想的動物卻是驢，而不是牛，因此英文會說 as stubborn as a mule。此外，中文用「雞皮」疙瘩來形容我們皮膚上面因為緊張或興奮而產生類似雞皮的小顆粒，同樣的現象，英文卻是用鵝來形容，而非雞，所以雞皮疙瘩的英文是 goosebumps。

另一個文化差異是冠夫姓的文化，在台灣，冠夫姓的女性寥寥可數，不但是一個非主流的文化，有時候甚至還會給女性負面的感受。然而，冠夫姓的文化在英文中卻相當常見，例如美國前國務卿希拉蕊柯林頓，即是用她先生的姓氏「柯林頓」作為自己的姓氏。美國前眾議院議長南希佩洛西，也在婚後使用她先生的姓氏「佩洛西」作為自己的姓氏。冠夫姓的文化在英文中不但沒有明顯對女性負面的意涵，更持續地存在於英文的主流文化裡。

此外，中英文對於顏色的聯想也不盡相同。東方以紅色象徵喜氣與幸運。西方卻認為紅色是危險的意思。以股票市場的漲跌顏色為例，在台灣，股票上漲是用紅色表示，當股票下跌的時候，則是用綠色來表示。然而，美國的股市漲跌顏色跟台灣卻是完全相反的，美國用綠色代表股票上漲，用紅色代表下跌，所以當美股一片綠油油的時候其實是股票大漲的意思，這是因為在英文裡，綠色通常代表安全，紅色卻是危險的。

1.3 思辨能力（critical thinking）

只要英文讀得多，閱讀理解能力就一定可以提升嗎？答案是不一定。雖然大量閱讀絕對是好事，但實際上，「閱讀理解力」跟「大量閱讀」這兩件事情並不完全相同。除了大量閱讀之外，提升閱讀理解力很重要的是「思辨能力」。

所謂思辨能力，不是隨波逐流地跟風同意或反對，而是對於同一件事情，能夠有不同的詮釋角度和立場。舉例來說，當一位媽媽苦勸小孩多吃青菜，看到小孩的排便是一顆一顆的形狀時，就跟小孩說，你就是青菜吃太少了，所以排便才像羊咩咩那樣一顆一顆的。沒有思辨能力的小孩可能會回答，喔，那我以後會多吃青菜，這樣才不會像羊咩咩那樣一顆一顆的。然而，有思辨能力的小孩則可能會回答：可是，羊咩咩吃很多青菜耶，為什麼排便還是一顆一顆的呢？

當看見西漢古裝劇裡面的人在紙上書寫文字，我們便要質疑其合理性，因為紙張是在東漢以後才出現的。或是，當尋找地外文明的研究中心（the SETI Institute）積極找尋地外文明的時候，知名的物理學及宇宙學家霍金就曾經提出警告，認為此舉對人類文明恐怕不會有好結果，霍金認為當人類文明遇上地外文明時，結果很可能會像是北美的印地安人遇到哥倫布那樣的結局。雖然 SETI 前中心主任 Jill Tarter 表示她不同意霍金的看法，但是她並沒有也無法證明她自己的觀點是正確的，而霍金的是錯誤的。SETI 至今仍舊堅持己見地代表全人類文明積極尋找地外文明，希望能與其進行接觸，彷彿認定地外文明必然會友善地回應人類文明的邀請，然而，思辨能力告訴我們，在能夠客觀評估所有可能的利益和風險之前，SETI 任何的探索恐怕都是一廂情願的。

此外，在閱讀文章時必然會遇到自己不認識的單字，但會發現大部分生字的意思都能夠從上下文的脈絡中推敲出來。舉例來說，在閱讀金庸的《書劍恩仇錄》之前，應該沒有人知道「回龍壁」是什麼意思，因為這是金庸在小說裡面自己創造出來的詞，雖然讀者從沒有聽過「回龍壁」這個詞，但是從小說情節中其實很容易知道，「回龍壁」是一種暗器。正因為文章前後的脈絡，這些陌生的字詞並不會成為我們閱讀金庸的絆腳石。同樣地，在英文閱讀遇到不認識的單字怎麼辦？以下面的句子為例：

John was reading a **gripping** story last night. He could not move his eyes away from the book for a second.

即便不知道 gripping 這個單字的意思，從句子前後的脈絡很容易可以得知 gripping 是一個正面的字，因為 John 連一秒鐘都不願意將目光從書上移開，並且可以合理推斷 gripping 正是這個故事很吸引 John 的原因。

本書長篇閱讀的獨特設計可以培養讀者不去查出每一個陌生單字的「良好習慣」，即便在文章中遇到不認識的單字，讀者也能夠利用本書系統化的閱讀步驟，整合上下文的訊息，利用「語境」推斷出單字的意思，並理解文章的意思。廣義來說，每篇文章都是一個「故事」，重要的是了解語意邏輯和情節發展，並思考文章背後的意義。閱讀本身是一個思辨的過程，利用自己的背景知識和跨文化的經驗，去思辨文章的觀點就是一種培養思辨能力的方式。由於文章的弦外之音常常需要間接推論出來，如果沒有思辨能力，便無法輕易推理出文章的弦外之音，因此邏輯推導的過程很重要，如何依據線索做出合理的推斷和結論，都需要讀者的思辨能力。

第二章
英文閱讀與語言學理論

2.1 認知基模理論（Schema Theory）
2.2 文體結構理論（Genre Theory）
2.3 功能語言學理論（Functional Linguistic Theory）

2 英文閱讀與語言學理論

　　本書的理論基礎來自於知名的閱讀理論與語言學理論。由於閱讀是一種認知行為，本書的設計奠基於知名心理學家 Jean Piaget 與 Richard Anderson 的認知基模理論（Schema Theory）。本書閱讀步驟的設計則是依據著名語言學家 John Swales 與 Michael Halliday 所分別提出的實踐方法。

2.1 認知基模理論（Schema theory）

　　心理學家 Jean Piaget 是認知科學的泰斗，在該領域有相當卓越的貢獻，他所提出的「認知發展理論」中指出，知識的擷取取決於大腦對於這個世界的認知，他認為大腦內建了一個龐大且複雜的資料庫，大腦會將所有學習到的新知識轉換成為心理圖像，分類存放於大腦的資料庫中，故吸取新知識的認知能力與這個資料庫有著密不可分的關係。

　　Jean Piaget 的觀點隨後由教育心理學家 Richard Anderson 發揚光大，將其發展成為英語教學中最重要的閱讀理論之一「認知基模理論」。此理論指出，在閱讀的時候，大腦會利用既有的背景知識、經驗、各種認知與抽象概念，幫助我們去理解書中的新知識，並將新知識分類歸納，存放於大腦的相關資料庫中。也就是說，當一個人的背景知識與經驗越多，他所能夠產生的心理圖像就越多，便更容易將新知識與大腦的資料庫做有效率的連結。因此，在本書的每一個閱讀練習開始之前都會幫助讀者喚起相關的背景知識與經驗，啟動所需要的「認知基模」。

利用既有的背景知識、經驗、各種認知與抽象概念去理解書中的新知識，將新知識分類歸納，並存放於大腦的相關資料庫中。

2.2 文體結構理論（Genre theory）

　　語言學家 John Swales 從宏觀的角度出發，認為每種文體都可以被劃分為不同的區塊，這些區塊可能剛好就是一個段落，也可以短於或長於一個段落，這些不同的區塊組成了一篇有組織、前後連貫的文章。因此，掌握文體結構便能夠幫助讀者了解作者在文章各區塊的核心宗旨。以下面這篇人體神經系統的文章舉例：

> It is not an overstatement to say that the nervous system is one of the most complex parts of human body. Controlling what we think and feel as well as what our body can do like walking and running, the nervous system is a network of nerves sending signals throughout the body. Thanks to the nerves all over our body, we are able to feel sensations, such as pain. Specifically, our body has two nervous systems that work in tandem with each other: the central and peripheral nervous system.

> The central nervous system is made up of the brain and spinal cord. The brain, in particular, is the command center for our body, controlling body functions by receiving and sending signals through nerves. The largest part of our brain can be divided into left and right halves. The left side is considered logical and rational, in charge of skills such as math and science. The right side is thought to be more creative and artistic, involving subjects like art and music. On the other hand, the spinal cord serves as the bridge that connects the brain to the peripheral nervous system. Both the brain and spinal cord can send signals via motor nerves to the rest of the body, telling the body what actions should be taken.

> The peripheral nervous system is like two-way traffic. Sensory nerves of the peripheral nervous system constantly receive information from the eyes, ears, mouth, nose, and skin, and relay it back to the central nervous system. Motor nerves then take orders from the brain and spinal cord to take actions such as eating and swallowing. In addition to these voluntary actions, the peripheral nervous system has another card up its sleeve—involuntary actions that operate independently of conscious awareness. These involuntary actions, such as heartbeat and breathing, continue even when we are asleep.

本文章三個段落的核心宗旨也可以理解為下面三個區塊：

第一區塊（第一段）：
人體神經系統的功能

第二區塊（第二段）：
中樞神經系統

第三區塊（第三段）：
末梢神經系統

在閱讀完本文章的三個段落之後可知，作者在每一個區塊都有一個核心宗旨，掌握這些核心宗旨便可以讓讀者對於整篇文章有較為宏觀的理解力。

2.3 功能語言學理論（Functional linguistic theory）

從微觀的角度看每一個英文句子，可以看到不同的組成和功能。語言學家 Michael Halliday 將這些組成稱為元語言（metalanguage），而其功能稱為元功能（metafunction），功能語言學理論詳細分析了英文中各種元語言和元功能，並且凸顯元功能與句意的直接關聯。以下面的句子舉例：

Jim was reading a book in a public library.

傳統英文的閱讀方式著重於每個單字的文法詞性，也就是名詞、動詞、介系詞、副詞、形容詞、冠詞、連接詞、代名詞等文法單位。但是，由於文法詞性本身是沒有實質意義的，因此用這樣的方式閱讀時，我們無法直接理解句意。如下表：

以詞性為基本理解單位								
Jim	was	reading	a	book	in	a	public	library
Noun	Verb	Participle	Article	Noun	Prep.	Article	Adj.	Noun

由於句意的組成並不是一個字一個字分開來理解的，英文的元功能可以幫助我們看見句中的意義群組與其功能，因此可提升閱讀理解力。英文中的意義群組包含 WHO、WHAT、ACTION、WHEN、WHERE、HOW。因為元功能本身是有實質意義的，用這樣的方式閱讀時，我們能夠更直接地理解句意，上述的句子便可以簡化成為四個意義群組，如下表：

以意義群組為基本理解單位			
Jim	was reading	a book	in a public library.
WHO	ACTION	WHAT	WHERE

第三章

6D 閱讀法

3 6D 閱讀法

3.1 掃讀（Scanning）

　　掃讀是一個相當實用的閱讀方法。掃讀即是在文章中搜尋特定的字詞（就如同在電話簿中搜尋某個人的號碼一樣），其他內容完全不看。這個閱讀方法尤其適合在長篇閱讀或考試中用來迅速鎖定欲仔細看的文章部分時使用。舉例來說，如果希望在下面的文章內找尋 acquired immunity 這個詞的話，則需要從第一段開始，逐句從頭到尾掃描一次，直到找到目標字詞 acquired immunity 為止。

第一段

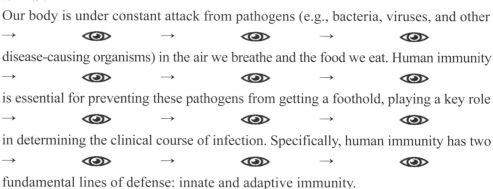

如此方式接續掃描第二段與第三段。

第二段

　　Present from birth, innate immunity serves as the first line of defense against any intruder, reacting almost instantly to prevent pathogens from making their way to our body. For example, a cut on the skin or a breach of the mucosal surface of our nose, throat, or intestines can result in redness and swelling, many immune cells immediately recruited to the site of infection. In most cases, innate immunity alone is capable of clearing the infection. Provided that the invader slips through, the innate immune system calls for help from the adaptive immune system. This is where adaptive immunity comes into play.

第三段

The adaptive immune system is the second line of defense, capable of differentiating between different types of pathogens and producing millions of antibodies to ward off the enemy. However, the adaptive immune system is slower in response and can take a few days or even weeks before it kicks in. This adaptive immunity is built up as we are exposed to diseases or are vaccinated. It is therefore also called acquired immunity for this reason.

3.2 略讀（Skimming）

在英文閱讀中，最常使用的閱讀方法之一就是略讀。略讀即為快速地綜覽各段的第一個句子[1]，用以粗略了解文章的結構，但是對於全文未能夠有深入的理解。依據文體結構理論，讀者能夠以略讀的方式，預測段落的主要目的或功能。下面用三個段落舉例：

第一段

Our body is under constant attack from pathogens (e.g., bacteria, viruses, and other disease-causing organisms) in the air we breathe and the food we eat. Human immunity is essential for preventing these pathogens from getting a foothold, playing a key role in determining the clinical course of infection. Specifically, human immunity has two fundamental lines of defense: innate and adaptive immunity.

讀者從第一段的第一個句子能夠合理預測，本段落應會談論各種病菌不斷侵害人體健康的相關過程、結果、或人體防禦機制。

---

1 有時候，一個段落的前兩句才是一個完整的概念，在這種情況下，應將該段落的前兩句視為略讀的目標範圍。

第二段

Innate immunity serves as the first line of defense against any intruder, reacting almost instantly to prevent pathogens from making their way to our body. For example, a cut on the skin or a breach of the mucosal surface of our nose, throat, or intestines can result in redness and swelling, many immune cells immediately recruited to the site of infection. In most cases, innate immunity alone is capable of clearing the infection. Provided that the invader slips through, the innate immune system calls for help from the adaptive immune system. This is where adaptive immunity comes into play.

讀者從第二段的第一個句子能夠合理預測，本段落應會談論作為人體第一道防線的先天免疫系統。

第三段

The adaptive immune system is the second line of defense, capable of differentiating between different types of pathogens and producing millions of antibodies to ward off the enemy. However, the adaptive immune system is slower in response and can take a few days or even weeks before it kicks in. This adaptive immunity is built up as we are exposed to diseases or are vaccinated. It is therefore also called acquired immunity for this reason.

讀者從第三段的第一個句子能夠合理預測，本段落應會談論作為人體第二道防線的後天免疫系統。

3.3 細讀（Close reading）

細讀是對於文章中特定的區域逐字閱讀，這種方法在閱讀長篇文章時尤其重要，因為當文章較長時，讀者有時候會需要再次確認自己剛才所理解或記憶的文章內容是否正確，因此需要回顧文章中某個特定的片段，再仔細閱讀一遍。除了字面上的意涵，細讀還能夠幫助讀者理解言外之意，因此也需要讀者的思辨能力，以剛才那篇文章的第三段舉例：

The adaptive immune system is the second line of defense, capable of differentiating between different types of pathogens and producing millions of **antibodies** to ward off the enemy. However, the adaptive immune system is slower in response and can take a few days or even weeks before it kicks in. This adaptive immunity is built up as we are exposed to diseases or are vaccinated. It is therefore also called acquired immunity for this reason.

　　若題目問 innate immunity 不稱為 acquired immunity 的可能原因，讀者則需要細讀本段的最後一句話來推斷出其原因：

This adaptive immunity is built up as we are exposed to diseases or are vaccinated. It is therefore also called acquired immunity for this reason.

　　由本段最後一句話得知，adaptive immunity 是從罹患疾病或是施打疫苗而產生的，由於 innate immunity 與 adaptive immunity 是兩種不同的免疫系統，故讀者可以合理推斷 innate immunity 並不是從罹患疾病或是施打疫苗而產生的，而可能是從出生便與生俱來的。

　　此外，細讀也可以幫助我們臆測文章中陌生單字的意思。以本段第一句的 antibodies 為例，假設不認識 antibodies 這個字，讀者至少可以從前後文的脈絡中得知兩件事情，第一件事情是 antibodies 是被 the adaptive immune system 製造出來的東西。第二件事情是數以百萬計的 antibodies 能夠抵禦來犯的病菌。因此，即便讀者不知道 antibodies 是「抗體」的意思，依然能夠清楚知道 antibodies 的來源與功能，所以閱讀理解力不至於受到 antibodies 這個陌生單字的阻礙。在面對英文閱讀時，即便遇到陌生單字，我們依然能夠利用細讀的方式與前後文的脈絡來輔助我們去理解文章中陌生單字的意思。

3.4 高理解速讀（Reading with greater comprehension & speed）

　　高理解速讀即是用較短的時間，完整閱讀並充分理解文意。根據功能語言學的理論，意義的產生並不是侷限於每一個單詞，而是在於具有功能意義的群組（或字群）。以下面的句子作為示範：

Our body is under constant attack from pathogens (e.g., bacteria, viruses, and other disease-causing organisms) in the air we breathe and the food we eat.

傳統閱讀
（以每個單字作為基本的理解單位）

Our body is under constant attack from pathogens (e.g., bacteria, viruses, and other disease-causing organisms) in the air we breathe and the food we eat.

Our **body** is under constant attack from pathogens (e.g., bacteria, viruses, and other disease-causing organisms) in the air we breathe and the food we eat.

Our body **is** under constant attack from pathogens (e.g., bacteria, viruses, and other disease-causing organisms) in the air we breathe and the food we eat.

Our body is **under** constant attack from pathogens (e.g., bacteria, viruses, and other disease-causing organisms) in the air we breathe and the food we eat.

Our body is under **constant** attack from pathogens (e.g., bacteria, viruses, and other disease-causing organisms) in the air we breathe and the food we eat.

Our body is under constant **attack** from pathogens (e.g., bacteria, viruses, and other disease-causing organisms) in the air we breathe and the food we eat.

Our body is under constant attack **from** pathogens (e.g., bacteria, viruses, and other disease-causing organisms) in the air we breathe and the food we eat.

Our body is under constant attack from **pathogens** (e.g., bacteria, viruses, and other disease-causing organisms) in the air we breathe and the food we eat.

Our body is under constant attack from pathogens (**e.g.,** bacteria, viruses, and other disease-causing organisms) in the air we breathe and the food we eat.

Our body is under constant attack from pathogens (e.g., **bacteria**, viruses, and other disease-causing organisms) in the air we breathe and the food we eat.

Our body is under constant attack from pathogens (e.g., bacteria, **viruses**, and other disease-causing organisms) in the air we breathe and the food we eat.

Our body is under constant attack from pathogens (e.g., bacteria, viruses, **and** other disease-causing organisms) in the air we breathe and the food we eat.

Our body is under constant attack from pathogens (e.g., bacteria, viruses, and **other** disease-causing organisms) in the air we breathe and the food we eat.

Our body is under constant attack from pathogens (e.g., bacteria, viruses, and other **disease-causing** organisms) in the air we breathe and the food we eat.

Our body is under constant attack from pathogens (e.g., bacteria, viruses, and other disease-causing **organisms**) in the air we breathe and the food we eat.

Our body is under constant attack from pathogens (e.g., bacteria, viruses, and other disease-causing organisms) **in** the air we breathe and the food we eat.

Our body is under constant attack from pathogens (e.g., bacteria, viruses, and other disease-causing organisms) in **the** air we breathe and the food we eat.

Our body is under constant attack from pathogens (e.g., bacteria, viruses, and other disease-causing organisms) in the **air** we breathe and the food we eat.

Our body is under constant attack from pathogens (e.g., bacteria, viruses, and other disease-causing organisms) in the air **we** breathe and the food we eat.

Our body is under constant attack from pathogens (e.g., bacteria, viruses, and other disease-causing organisms) in the air we **breathe** and the food we eat.

Our body is under constant attack from pathogens (e.g., bacteria, viruses, and other disease-causing organisms) in the air we breathe **and** the food we eat.

Our body is under constant attack from pathogens (e.g., bacteria, viruses, and other disease-causing organisms) in the air we breathe and **the** food we eat.

Our body is under constant attack from pathogens (e.g., bacteria, viruses, and other disease-causing organisms) in the air we breathe and the **food** we eat.

Our body is under constant attack from pathogens (e.g., bacteria, viruses, and other disease-causing organisms) in the air we breathe and the food **we** eat.

Our body is under constant attack from pathogens (e.g., bacteria, viruses, and other disease-causing organisms) in the air we breathe and the food we **eat**.

高理解速讀
（以意義群組作為基本的理解單位）

Our body is under constant attack from pathogens (e.g., bacteria, viruses, and other disease-causing organisms) in the air we breathe and the food we eat.

Our body **is under constant attack** from pathogens (e.g., bacteria, viruses, and other disease-causing organisms) in the air we breathe and the food we eat.

Our body is under constant attack **from pathogens** (e.g., bacteria, viruses, and other disease-causing organisms) in the air we breathe and the food we eat.

Our body is under constant attack from pathogens (**e.g., bacteria, viruses, and other disease-causing organisms**) in the air we breathe and the food we eat.

Our body is under constant attack from pathogens (e.g., bacteria, viruses, and other disease-causing organisms) **in the air** we breathe and the food we eat.

Our body is under constant attack from pathogens (e.g., bacteria, viruses, and other disease-causing organisms) in the air **we breathe** and the food we eat.

Our body is under constant attack from pathogens (e.g., bacteria, viruses, and other disease-causing organisms) in the air we breathe **and** the food we eat.

Our body is under constant attack from pathogens (e.g., bacteria, viruses, and other disease-causing organisms) in the air we breathe and **the food we eat**.

3.5 跟讀（Shadowing）

　　跟讀利用聽覺與口說的雙重感官來加強自己的英文認知理解力。跟讀時，不須看任何文字內容，只要專注聆聽播放出來的句子，以「模仿」與「重複」的方式掌握英文的「節奏」，即聽到什麼，就像影子般如影隨行地跟著複誦一遍。

　　在「跟讀」訓練的音檔中，音檔在播放一句英文之後，即會在句子與句子之間提供 5 秒左右的靜默空檔，讀者在靜默的 5 秒鐘空檔內，心裡重複默念一次，並以「幾乎同步」的速度「模仿」自己所聽到的句子唸出來。這種如同全民英檢口說「複誦」題目的訓練，可以讓自己的理解力更加流暢，因為有空秒的設計，讀者不需要麻煩地按暫停鍵，如此便可以在有時間限制的壓力下，更加專注於耳聽跟口說的練習。

　　只要確實做到以幾乎同步的速度將自己所聽到的內容複誦出來，即使剛開始可能會感覺有點跟不上，但是經過反覆聆聽與複誦的練習，便能夠練出直覺性的英語語感，讓自己的認知理解力跟上口說朗誦的速度。

3.6 聽讀（Listening）

　　有些語言測驗，例如托福測驗等，會綜合考察閱讀和聽力，全面性地測驗考生的認知理解能力，故在本書「聽讀」訓練的音檔中，讀者會聽到音檔內的母語人士完整且不間斷地朗讀文章。

第一遍

　　→ 試著不看文章，只聽音檔內的母語人士完整且不間斷地將文章唸一遍，專注聆聽播放出來的內容，確認自己聽懂了多少，如果還有聽不太懂的地方，可針對文章該處加強學習。

第二遍

　　→ 再聽母語人士不間斷地將文章唸一遍，此次在聆聽的同時，眼睛注視著正在朗誦的每個句子，針對自己沒有完全聽懂的部分，特別再仔細閱讀一遍。

第四章
主題練習

4.1 國外旅遊趣
Traveling Abroad

Did you know?
[你需要知道的 10 件事]

❶ 紐西蘭是位於南太平洋的一個狹長型島國。

❷ 紐西蘭最大城市是奧克蘭（Auckland）。

❸ 奧克蘭人口約 150 萬，佔了紐西蘭總人口的 30%。

❹ 紐西蘭的首都威靈頓（Wellington）是世界上最南的首都。

❺ 紐西蘭由「北島」及「南島」組合而成，國土面積與英國相近。

❻ 紐西蘭面積約為台灣七倍大。

❼ 紐西蘭人口只有四百多萬人，約為台灣的七分之一。

❽ 八成旅居海外的紐西蘭人生活在隔壁的澳洲。

❾ 紐西蘭地形樣貌多元，有火山、平原、瀑布、湖泊等自然景觀。

❿ 紐西蘭位處南半球，氣候與北半球相反，所以十二月並不是冬天。

Must-know vocabulary
[你需要知道的 10 個單字]

❶ island nation *n.* 島國

❷ the southern Pacific Ocean *n.* 南太平洋

❸ Auckland *n.* 奧克蘭

❹ International Date Line *n.* 國際換日線

❺ intra-day weather *n.* 日內天氣

❻ exaggeration *n.* 誇大

❼ kiwi *n.* 奇異鳥

❽ national bird *n.* 國鳥

❾ nocturnal animal *n.* 夜行性動物

❿ kiwifruit *n.* 奇異果

> 　掃讀的目標是在文章中搜尋特定的人名、時間、地點，或相關詞語，就像是在電話簿中搜尋某人的電話號碼一樣，其他內容完全不看。

■ 請於 **30** 秒內在以下文章中找出下列文字並畫線，不要閱讀內容或嘗試理解文章。

❶ island nation　　　　　　　❷ the southern Pacific Ocean
❸ Auckland　　　　　　　　　❹ the International Date Line
❺ intra-day weather　　　　　　❻ exaggeration
❼ kiwi　　　　　　　　　　　❽ national bird
❾ nocturnal animals　　　　　　❿ kiwifruit

New Zealand

（423 words）　　　　　　　　　　　　　　　　　　　　　　　By Yushiang Jou

　　About the same size as the United Kingdom, New Zealand is a mountainous island nation in the southern Pacific Ocean. Built around two harbors, Auckland is the largest city in New Zealand, sitting on seven hills which were formed 50,000 years ago by volcanic activities. Since the International Date Line is to the east of the country, New Zealand is the first place on earth to see the sunrise every morning. Many tourists may be surprised by the fact that the intra-day weather in this neck of the woods changes dramatically and it is no exaggeration to say that one can experience spring, summer, fall, and winter within one single day. It can be sunny in the morning but cold in the afternoon.

　　New Zealand has no dangerous wild animals, snakes or insects, except for one rarely seen poisonous spider. This makes New Zealand a safe place to go walking in the forest anytime a day. Unique to its forests is the national bird of New Zealand, the kiwi. The name kiwi comes from the sound the bird makes: "ki-wi". They repeat this funny sound frequently. They are nocturnal animals, often living in the forests far away from people. The kiwi is about the size of a chicken and has soft brown feathers. Their food is mainly insects and worms as well as berries and

4.1

國外旅遊趣 Traveling Abroad

31

seeds. Kiwis are unusual birds because, like many other native birds in New Zealand, they cannot fly. Before humans and their accompanying pets explored New Zealand, these birds had no enemies to fly away from. As a result, Kiwis lost the ability to fly, with a pair of wings all but useless today.

Interestingly, the word kiwi can mean other things as well. The word kiwi was first used in the army by New Zealand soldiers fighting in wars overseas. After that, the people of New Zealand started to call themselves Kiwis. In other words, the Prime Minister of New Zealand is also called the Kiwi Prime Minister. Another widely known meaning of kiwi is kiwifruit, often shortened to just "kiwi" in many other countries. Kiwifruit in fact is a native of northern China and was brought to New Zealand in 1904 by a visiting school teacher. The fruit grew well in New Zealand. When it began to be exported, it was named kiwi because it resembled the kiwi bird. Now, there are several varieties of kiwifruit but the most common one is about the size of a large egg, with a brown skin and a soft green center.

■ 請選擇正確的意思

_____ ❶ island nation　(A) 陸地 (B) 島國

_____ ❷ the southern Pacific Ocean　(A) 南太平洋 (B) 太平洋

_____ ❸ Auckland　(A) 威靈頓 (B) 奧克蘭

_____ ❹ the International Date Line　(A) 國際換日線 (B) 國際標準時間

_____ ❺ intra-day weather　(A) 日內天氣 (B) 跨日天氣

_____ ❻ exaggeration　(A) 低估 (B) 誇大

_____ ❼ kiwi　(A) 奇異鳥 (B) 禿鷹

_____ ❽ national bird　(A) 國定假日 (B) 國鳥

_____ ❾ nocturnal animals　(A) 日行性動物 (B) 夜行性動物

_____ ❿ kiwifruit　(A) 奇異果 (B) 百香果

▶▶ 解答請見 p.322

針對剛才的文章，用 30 秒鐘瀏覽各段的第一句，粗略了解文章結構與大意即可。

About the same size as the United Kingdom, New Zealand is a mountainous island nation in the southern Pacific Ocean. Built around two harbors, Auckland is the largest city in New Zealand, sitting on seven hills which were formed 50,000 years ago by volcanic activities. Since the International Date Line is to the east of the country, New Zealand is the first place on earth to see the sunrise every morning. Many tourists may be surprised by the fact that the intra-day weather in this neck of the woods changes dramatically and it is no exaggeration to say that one can experience spring, summer, fall, and winter within one single day. It can be sunny in the morning but cold in the afternoon.

紐西蘭
地理
資訊

New Zealand has no dangerous wild animals, snakes or insects, except for one rarely seen poisonous spider. This makes New Zealand a safe place to go walking in the forest anytime a day. Unique to its forests is the national bird of New Zealand, the kiwi. The name kiwi comes from the sound the bird makes: "ki-wi". They repeat this funny sound frequently. They are nocturnal animals, often living in the forests far away from people. The kiwi is about the size of a chicken and has soft brown feathers. Their food is mainly insects and worms as well as berries and seeds. Kiwis are unusual birds because, like many other native birds in New Zealand, they cannot fly. Before humans and their accompanying pets explored New Zealand, these birds had no enemies to fly away from. As a result, Kiwis lost the ability to fly, with a pair of wings all but useless today.

紐西蘭
野生
動物

4.1

國外旅遊趣 Traveling Abroad

Interestingly, the word kiwi can mean other things as well. The word kiwi was first used in the army by New Zealand soldiers fighting in wars overseas. After that, the people of New Zealand started to call themselves Kiwis. In other words, the Prime Minister of New Zealand is also called the Kiwi Prime Minister. Another widely known meaning of kiwi is kiwifruit, often shortened to just "kiwi" in many other countries. Kiwifruit in fact is a native of northern China and was brought to New Zealand in 1904 by a visiting school teacher. The fruit grew well in New Zealand. When it began to be exported, it was named kiwi because it resembled the kiwi bird. Now, there are several varieties of kiwifruit but the most common one is about the size of a large egg, with a brown skin and a soft green center.

kiwi
的意思

■ 回答以下問題，確認自己是否正確理解整篇文章的大意：

Q1. _____ New Zealand is larger than the U.K. (T/F)

Q2. _____ New Zealand is located in the Northern Hemisphere. (T/F)

Q3. _____ We can climb mountains in New Zealand. (T/F)

Q4. _____ It is dangerous to go for a walk in the forest in New Zealand. (T/F)

Q5. _____ The word kiwi can only mean one thing. (T/F)

▶▶ 解答請見 p.322

STEP 3 細讀 Close reading

請用 60 秒的時間仔細閱讀以下內容，並回答問題。

Kiwifruit in fact is a native of northern China and was brought to New Zealand in 1904 by a visiting school teacher. The fruit grew very well in New Zealand. When it began to be exported, it was named kiwi because it resembled the kiwi bird.

_____ Q1. According to this passage, which of the following is correct?

    (A) Kiwifruit is a native fruit of New Zealand

    (B) Kiwifruit can grow in northern China.

    (C) Kiwifruit was first grown by a school teacher in New Zealand.

    (D) There is no kiwifruit before 1904.

_____ Q2. According to this passage, what do we know about the color of the kiwi bird?

    (A) black   (B) yellow   (C) brown   (D) white

▶▶ 解答請見 p.322

STEP 4 高理解速讀 Speed Reading with Greater Comprehension

請用 90 秒的時間，看完整篇文章。然後跟著每一個有意義的色塊，提升理解的速度。（請盡量試著不查自己不認識的字，利用前後文去推測意思。）

About the same size as the United Kingdom, New Zealand is a mountainous island nation in the southern Pacific Ocean. Built around two harbors, Auckland is the largest city in New Zealand, sitting on seven hills which were formed 50,000 years ago by volcanic activities. Since the International Date Line is to the east of the country, New Zealand is the first place on earth to see the sunrise every morning. Many tourists may be surprised by the fact that the intra-day weather in this neck of the woods changes dramatically and it is no exaggeration to say that one can experience spring, summer, fall, and winter within one single day. It can be sunny in the morning but cold in the afternoon.

紐西蘭
地理
資訊

4.1

國外旅遊趣 Traveling Abroad

New Zealand has no dangerous wild animals, snakes or insects, except for one rarely seen poisonous spider. This makes New Zealand a safe place to go walking in the forest anytime a day. Unique to its forests is the national bird of New Zealand, the kiwi. The name kiwi comes from the sound the bird makes: "ki-wi". They repeat this funny sound frequently. They are nocturnal animals, often living in the forests far away from people. The kiwi is about the size of a chicken and has soft brown feathers. Their food is mainly insects and worms as well as berries and seeds. Kiwis are unusual birds because, like many other native birds in New Zealand, they cannot fly. Before humans and their accompanying pets explored New Zealand, these birds had no enemies to fly away from. As a result, Kiwis lost the ability to fly, with a pair of wings all but useless today.

紐西蘭
野生
動物

Interestingly, the word kiwi can mean other things as well. The word kiwi was first used in the army by New Zealand soldiers fighting in wars overseas. After that, the people of New Zealand started to call themselves Kiwis. In other words, the Prime Minister of New Zealand is also called the Kiwi Prime Minister. Another widely known meaning of kiwi is kiwifruit, often shortened to just "kiwi" in many other countries. Kiwifruit in fact is a native of northern China and was brought to New Zealand in 1904 by a visiting school teacher. The fruit grew well in New Zealand. When it began to be exported, it was named kiwi because it resembled the kiwi bird. Now, there are several varieties of kiwifruit but the most common one is about the size of a large egg, with a brown skin and a soft green center.

kiwi
的意思

■ 請回答以下問題：

_____ Q1. Which of the following is NOT true about New Zealand?

(A) Being first in the world to see the sun rise each day

(B) About the same size as the United Kingdom

(C) Having many birds that cannot fly

(D) Importing high-quality kiwifruit from northern China each year

_____ Q2. Which of the following NOT a meaning of kiwi?

    (A) large size eggs in New Zealand   (B) kiwifruit

    (C) kiwi bird   (D) New Zealanders

_____ Q3. What can be experienced within a day in New Zealand?

    (A) summer   (B) winter   (C) spring   (D) all of the above

_____ Q4. Which is a feature of kiwi birds?

    (A) flying at night

    (B) having brown feathers

    (C) being dangerous to people walking in the forest

    (D) showing up anytime of a day

_____ Q5. What can be seen in New Zealand?

    (A) volcanic mountains   (B) forests   (C) hills   (D) all of the above

4.1.1_S.mp3

STEP 5 跟讀 Shadowing

    請根據母語人士所錄製的音檔，一句一句跟著唸。跟讀時請使用跟讀音檔，每句結束後，請利用句與句之間的空秒時間，複誦前面所聽到的句子。建議第一遍，看著文章跟著唸，第二遍則不看文章，只聽音檔唸。

4.1.1_L.mp3

STEP 6 聽讀 Listening

第一遍

→ 讀者會聽到音檔內母語人士完整且不間斷將本文唸一遍。試著不看文章，聽音檔內的母語人士完整且不間斷地將本文唸一遍，確認自己哪裡聽懂，那裡聽不懂。

第二遍

→ 再聽母語人士不間斷地將本文唸一遍，眼睛注視著正在朗誦的每個句子，針對自己沒聽懂的部分，特別仔細閱讀。

單字 Vocabulary

❶ **mountainous** [ˈmaʊntənəs]	adj. 多山的 He lives in a mountainous area. 他住在山區。
❷ **volcanic** [vɑlˈkænɪk]	adj. 火山的 Volcanic eruptions are dangerous. 火山爆發很危險。
❸ **intra-day** [ˌɪntrəˈde]	adj. 當日內的 U.S. stocks closed above intra-day lows on Monday. 美國股市週一收盤在當日低點之上。
❹ **beak** [bik]	n. 鳥喙 The beak of the bird is very long. 這隻鳥的喙很長。
❺ **nocturnal** [nɑkˈtɝnəl]	adj. 夜行性的 There are many nocturnal animals in this area. 這個區域有很多夜行性動物。
❻ **overseas** [ovɚˈsiz]	adv. 在國外，去國外 She wants to work overseas next year. 她明年想要去國外工作。
❼ **exaggeration** [ɪɡˌzædʒəˈreʃən]	n. 誇大 He described his experience without exaggeration. 他毫不誇大地陳述他的經歷。
❽ **export** [ɛkˈspɔrt]	v. 出口 Russia exports crude oil to many countries. 俄羅斯出口原油到許多國家。
❾ **resemble** [rɪˈzɛmbəl]	v. 看起來很像 She resembles her mother in appearance. 她長得很像她的母親。

❿ **native**	n. 本地的動植物或人
['netɪv]	This black dog is a native of Taiwan.
	這隻黑狗是一隻台灣犬（台灣土狗）。

慣用語和片語 Expressions and Phrases

❶ it is no exaggeration to say that　說…並不誇張

It is no exaggeration to say that she is the richest person in Taiwan.

說她是台灣最富有的人一點都不誇張。

❷ except for　除了…外

All my friends graduated this year except for Daniel.

除了丹尼爾之外，我的所有朋友今年都畢業了。

❸ far away from...　遠離…

She moved to a city far away from New York.

她搬到離紐約很遠的一座城市。

❹ As a result　因此

He reads a book every day. As a result, he has read more than 300 books this year.

他每天都閱讀一本書。因此，他今年已經讀了超過 300 本書。

A. Fill in the blanks with suitable words or phrases 將適合的字詞填入空格中

a intra-day　**b** resemble　**c** nocturnal　**d** export

1. Taiwan ＿＿＿＿＿ semiconductor chips to the U.S.

2. People were shocked by the ＿＿＿＿＿ volatility of this stock.

3. Bats and owls are ＿＿＿＿＿ animals.

4. His new story closely ＿＿＿＿＿ one of hers.

B. Multiple choice questions 選擇題（可利用此題型熟悉多益、英檢考試）

＿＿＿＿＿ 1. It is no ------- to say that Taiwan Semiconductor Manufacturing
　　　　　 Company is one of the most famous companies in the world.
　　　　　 (A) reason　 (B) exception　 (C) sense　 (D) exaggeration

＿＿＿＿＿ 2. She is working hard on her English because she will study -------
　　　　　 in the fall.
　　　　　 (A) overseas　 (B) at home　 (C) locally　 (D) French

＿＿＿＿＿ 3. Many people came here to see this newcomer, especially its long
　　　　　 -------.
　　　　　 (A) enemy　 (B) history　 (C) beak　 (D) color

＿＿＿＿＿ 4. He had been reading many books. ------- , he did well on this test.
　　　　　 (A) However　　　　 (B) On the contrary
　　　　　 (C) To our surprise　 (D) As a result

＿＿＿＿＿ 5. Mike was ill. So everyone, ------- Mike, went to school on Monday.
　　　　　 (A) including　 (B) except for　 (C) involving　 (D) missing

▶▶ 解答請見 p.324

NOTE

Did you know?

[你需要知道的 10 件事]

❶ 鐵達尼號為早期的大型郵輪之一。
❷ 百年前的鐵達尼號沈船事件在郵輪史上相當罕見。
❸ 現代的郵輪配備有先進的定位和導航系統。
❹ 每艘郵輪上都配備有許多中型的救生艇。
❺ 每天都有數百艘的郵輪在世界各個海域中航行。
❻ 郵輪選擇航行的海域通常比較平穩。
❼ 郵輪有先進的船身平衡器，能夠降低航海時的搖晃感受。
❽ 許多郵輪在旅途中會短暫停靠私人海島或景點。
❾ 郵輪費用不高，每年都有相當多人乘坐郵輪到世界各地去旅遊。
❿ 有許多主題式郵輪，例如，迪士尼郵輪主要搭載有孩童的家庭。

Must-know vocabulary

[你需要知道的 10 個單字]

❶ cruise vacation *n.* 郵輪旅遊假期
❷ floating resort *n.* 海上渡假村
❸ seasickness *n.* 暈船
❹ stabilizer *n.* 船身平衡器
❺ passenger capacity *n.* 載客量
❻ must-see destination *n.* 必訪景點
❼ rough water *n.* 風浪洶湧的海域
❽ medication *n.* 藥品
❾ deck *n.* 船的層面
❿ motion *n.* 搖晃

掃讀的目標是在文章中搜尋特定的人名，時間，地點，或相關詞語，就像是在電話簿中搜尋某人的電話號碼一樣，其他內容完全不看。

■ 請於 **30** 秒內在以下文章中找出下列文字並畫線，不要閱讀內容或嘗試理解文章。

❶ cruise vacation   ❷ floating resort

❸ seasickness   ❹ stabilizer

❺ passenger capacity   ❻ must-see destination

❼ rough water   ❽ medication

❾ deck   ❿ motion

....

Cruise Vacations

(405 words)   By Yushiang Jou

    Cruise vacations are a popular way to unwind and relax. According to the Cruise Lines International Association, around 30 million people worldwide take a cruise vacation each year. Cruise tours usually range from two to six nights. On a cruise, passengers travel internationally on a large ship with thousands of other people. Cruise ships come in all sizes and passenger capacities, large ships capable of accommodating as many as 5,000 people on board. With 24-hour room service, a cruise ship is like a floating resort, offering a variety of dining options, including all-you-can-eat buffets, self-serve salad bars, and late-night bites.

    A cruise ship provides a wide range of entertainment for people of all ages. Passengers may well be dazzled with too many entertainment choices that can spice up their vacation. Most ships are equipped with swimming pools, spas, ice skating rinks, basketball courts, mini-golf courses, rock-climbing walls, and plenty more. Avid runners can opt for in-gym treadmills or outdoor jogging tracks. Nightly entertainment often includes comedy shows, live music performances, and art auctions. Passengers can also sing karaoke, dance in a nightclub, gamble in a casino, watch outdoor movies, or simply chill at the piano bar.

4.1

國外旅遊趣 Traveling Abroad

For those who have been meaning to visit multiple destinations on one single trip, a cruise vacation would fit the bill. A large number of cruises depart from Florida and New England to must-see destinations around the world. While most cruises go to the Caribbean, some sail to Alaska, Spain, Italy, South America, and more. For example, a 12-day Mediterranean cruise would visit such historic cities as Barcelona, Rome, Florence, Pompeii, and Istanbul. On a South America cruise, one can explore rainforests in Costa Rica and enjoy wine tastings in Chile.

However, the fear of being seasick is one of the most common reasons cited by people reluctant to set foot on a cruise ship. Since cruise ships these days are designed to effortlessly sail through the open sea, seasickness is not a given. Thanks to ship stabilizers that help steady the ship, seasickness is in fact a rarity. In rough waters, stabilizers can balance the ship and prevent it from rolling. For those prone to feeling the motion of the water beneath their feet, medications are always available on board for them to get back on their feet. Alternatively, one can choose a cabin on a lower deck in the middle of the ship, where motion is minimized.

■ 請選擇正確的意思

_____ ❶ cruise vacation （A) 郵輪旅遊假期 (B) 國內旅遊假期

_____ ❷ floating resort （A) 海上渡假村 (B) 海灣渡假村

_____ ❸ seasickness （A) 暈車 (B) 暈船

_____ ❹ stabilizer （A) 船舶定位器 (B) 船身平衡器

_____ ❺ passenger capacity （A) 載客量 (B) 旅客名單

_____ ❻ must-see destination （A) 必訪景點 (B) 冷門景點

_____ ❼ rough water （A) 風浪小的海域 (B) 風浪大的海域

_____ ❽ medication （A) 藥品 (B) 毒品

_____ ❾ deck （A) 船身 (B) 船的層面

_____ ❿ motion （A) 平穩 (B) 搖晃

▶▶▶ 解答請見 p.325

針對剛才的文章，用 30 秒鐘瀏覽各段的第一句，粗略了解文章結構與大意即可。

Cruise vacations are a popular way to unwind and relax. According to the Cruise Lines International Association, around 30 million people worldwide take a cruise vacation each year. Cruise tours usually range from two to six nights. On a cruise, passengers travel internationally on a large ship with thousands of other people. Cruise ships come in all sizes and passenger capacities, large ships capable of accommodating as many as 5,000 people on board. With 24-hour room service, a cruise ship is like a floating resort, offering a variety of dining options, including all-you-can-eat buffets, self-serve salad bars, and late-night bites.

郵輪
旅遊
簡介

A cruise ship provides a wide range of entertainment for people of all ages. Passengers may well be dazzled with too many entertainment choices that can spice up their vacation. Most ships are equipped with swimming pools, spas, ice skating rinks, basketball courts, mini-golf courses, rock-climbing walls, and plenty more. Avid runners can opt for in-gym treadmills or outdoor jogging tracks. Nightly entertainment often includes comedy shows, live music performances, and art auctions. Passengers can also sing karaoke, dance in a nightclub, gamble in a casino, watch outdoor movies, or simply chill at the piano bar.

郵輪上
的娛樂
活動

For those who have been meaning to visit multiple destinations on one single trip, a cruise vacation would fit the bill. A large number of cruises depart from Florida and New England to must-see destinations around the world. While most cruises go to the Caribbean, some sail to Alaska, Spain, Italy, South America, and more. For example, a 12-day Mediterranean cruise would visit such historic cities as Barcelona, Rome, Florence, Pompeii, and Istanbul. On a South America cruise, one can explore rainforests in Costa Rica and enjoy wine tastings in Chile.

郵輪
停留多
個景點

However, the fear of being seasick is one of the most common reasons cited by people reluctant to set foot on a cruise ship. Since cruise ships these days are designed to effortlessly sail through the open sea, seasickness is not a given. Thanks to ship stabilizers that help steady the ship, seasickness is in fact a rarity. In rough waters, stabilizers can balance the ship and prevent it from rolling. For those prone to feeling the motion of the water beneath their feet, medications are always available on board for them to get back on their feet. Alternatively, one can choose a cabin on a lower deck in the middle of the ship, where motion is minimized.

暈船
怎麼辦

■ 回答以下問題，確認自己是否正確理解整篇文章的大意：

Q1. _____ Cruise vacations are a popular way to relax. (T/F)

Q2. _____ A cruise ship provides entertainment for adults only. (T/F)

Q3. _____ A cruise ship visits one destination only. (T/F)

Q4. _____ Some people are afraid of being seasick. (T/F)

Q5. _____ Some people are unwilling to be on a cruise ship. (T/F)

▶▶ 解答請見 p.325

請用 60 秒的時間仔細閱讀以下內容，並回答問題。

Since cruise ships these days are designed to effortlessly sail through the open sea, seasickness is not a given. Thanks to ship stabilizers that help steady the ship, seasickness is in fact a rarity. In rough waters, stabilizers can balance the ship and prevent it from rolling.

_____ Q1. According to this passage, which of the following is correct?
      (A) Cruise passengers must feel seasick.
      (B) Most cruise passengers would feel seasick.
      (C) Stabilizers are not important in rough waters.
      (D) Cruise ships a hundred years ago could not effortlessly sail through
          the open sea.

_____ Q2. According to this passage, how common is severe seasickness on a
      cruise ship?
      (A) uncommon
      (B) common
      (C) fairly common
      (D) extremely common

▶▶ 解答請見 p.325

4.1

國外旅遊趣 Traveling Abroad

請用 90 秒的時間,看完整篇文章。然後跟著每一個有意義的色塊,提升理解的速度。(*請盡量試著不查自己不認識的字,利用前後文去推測意思。*)

Cruise vacations are a popular way to unwind and relax. According to the Cruise Lines International Association, around 30 million people worldwide take a cruise vacation each year. Cruise tours usually range from two to six nights. On a cruise, passengers travel internationally on a large ship with thousands of other people. Cruise ships come in all sizes and passenger capacities, large ships capable of accommodating as many as 5,000 people on board. With 24-hour room service, a cruise ship is like a floating resort, offering a variety of dining options, including all-you-can-eat buffets, self-serve salad bars, and late-night bites.

郵輪
旅遊
簡介

A cruise ship provides a wide range of entertainment for people of all ages. Passengers may well be dazzled with too many entertainment choices that can spice up their vacation. Most ships are equipped with swimming pools, spas, ice skating rinks, basketball courts, mini-golf courses, rock-climbing walls, and plenty more. Avid runners can opt for in-gym treadmills or outdoor jogging tracks. Nightly entertainment often includes comedy shows, live music performances, and art auctions. Passengers can also sing karaoke, dance in a nightclub, gamble in a casino, watch outdoor movies, or simply chill at the piano bar.

郵輪上
的娛樂
活動

For those who have been meaning to visit multiple destinations on one single trip, a cruise vacation would fit the bill. A large number of cruises depart from Florida and New England to must-see destinations around the world. While most cruises go to the Caribbean, some sail to Alaska, Spain, Italy, South America, and more. For example, a 12-day Mediterranean cruise would visit such historic cities as Barcelona, Rome, Florence, Pompeii, and Istanbul. On a South America cruise, one can explore rainforests in Costa Rica and enjoy wine tastings in Chile.

郵輪
停留多
個景點

However, the fear of being seasick is one of the most common reasons cited by people reluctant to set foot on a cruise ship. Since cruise ships these days are designed to effortlessly sail through the open sea, seasickness is not a given. Thanks to ship stabilizers that help steady the ship, seasickness is in fact a rarity. In rough waters, stabilizers can balance the ship and prevent it from rolling. For those prone to feeling the motion of the water beneath their feet, medications are always available on board for them to get back on their feet. Alternatively, one can choose a cabin on a lower deck in the middle of the ship, where motion is minimized.

暈船
怎麼辦

■ 請回答以下問題：

_____ Q1. What is NOT available on most ships?
   (A) a swimming pool
   (B) a baseball field
   (C) a basketball court
   (D) a mini-golf course

_____ Q2. What is a nightly entertainment choice on a cruise ship?
   (A) dancing in a nightclub
   (B) watching outdoor movies
   (C) gambling in a casino
   (D) all of the above

_____ Q3. Which of the following is a location a cruise can visit?

      (A) Italy

      (B) Florence

      (C) Istanbul

      (D) All of the above

_____ Q4. How many nights do passengers usually stay on a cruise ship?

      (A) more than twelve nights

      (B) seven to twelve nights

      (C) two to six nights

      (D) one to three nights

_____ Q5. How many people worldwide take a cruise vacation each year?

      (A) 30 million   (B) 40 million   (C) 50 million   (D) 60 million

▶▶ 解答請見 p.326

4.1.2_S.mp3

STEP 5 跟讀 Shadowing

　　請根據母語人士所錄製的音檔，一句一句跟著唸。跟讀時請使用跟讀音檔，每句結束後，請利用句與句之間的空秒時間，複誦前面所聽到的句子。建議第一遍，看著文章跟著唸，第二遍則不看文章，只聽音檔唸。

4.1.2_L.mp3

STEP 6 聽讀 Listening

第一遍

→ 讀者會聽到音檔內母語人士完整且不間斷將本文唸一遍。試著不看文章，聽音檔內的母語人士完整且不間斷地將本文唸一遍，確認自己哪裡聽懂，那裡聽不懂。

第二遍

→ 再聽母語人士不間斷地將本文唸一遍，眼睛注視著正在朗誦的每個句子，針對自己沒聽懂的部分，特別仔細閱讀。

單字 Vocabulary

❶ unwind [ʌn`waɪnd]	v. 放鬆（心情等） Disneyland is a great place to unwind. 迪士尼樂園是一個放鬆心情的好地方。
❷ floating [`flotɪŋ]	adj. 漂浮的 They built a floating bridge over the river. 他們在河上面搭建了一座浮橋。
❸ resort [rɪ`zɔrt]	n. 度假村 There are several ski resorts in Colorado. 科羅拉多州有數個滑雪度假村。
❹ dazzle [`dæzl]	v. 使…讚嘆不已 We were dazzled by her breadth of knowledge. 她的博學多聞讓我們讚嘆不已。
❺ avid [`ævɪd]	adj. 熱衷的 She is an avid reader. 她很喜歡閱讀。
❻ mean [min]	v. 想要 I have been meaning to ask you if you are interested in this research project. 我一直想要問你對這個研究計畫有沒有興趣。
❼ reluctant [rɪ`lʌktənt]	adj. 不願意的，不情願的 Many people are reluctant to talk openly with their parents. 許多人不願意與他們的父母敞開心扉交談。
❽ given [`gɪvən]	n. 必然的事 It is a given that the Fed will combat high inflation. 美國聯準會必然會對抗高通膨。

4.1

國外旅遊趣 Traveling Abroad

❾ rarity [ˋrɛrətɪ]	n. 罕見的事 Snow is a rarity in many countries. 在許多國家，下雪是極其罕見之事。
❿ prone [pron]	adj. 容易⋯的 In the era of COVID-19, people not wearing a mask are prone to infection. 在新冠疫情的年代，不戴口罩的人容易受到感染。

慣用語和片語 Expressions and Phrases

❶ on board 在船／車／飛機上

All the ship's passengers are on board now.
所有乘客都已經上船了。

❷ spice up 增添樂趣

The teacher tried to spice up the class by telling some jokes.
老師試著藉由講些笑話來為課堂增添一些樂趣。

❸ fit the bill 滿足所需，符合期待

They are looking for someone who can speak both English and French. John fits the bill.
他們在找同時會講英文和法文的人。約翰是合適的人選。

❹ set foot on 踏上

He was the first man to set foot on the moon.
他是首位登陸月球的人。

A. Fill in the blanks with suitable words or phrases 將適合的字詞填入空格中

ⓐ resort **ⓑ** prone **ⓒ** unwind **ⓓ** fit

1. She has been working hard and can really use a vacation to _____.

2. There are many ski _____ in Japan.

3. She wants to buy an electric car. A Tesla vehicle _____ the bill.

4. Extremely emotional and sentimental, he is _____ to sadness.

B. Multiple choice questions 選擇題（可利用此題型熟悉多益、英檢考試）

_____ 1. He is never on time. It is almost ------- that he will be late today.
(A) a making (B) a given (C) an inquiry (D) a paradox

_____ 2. She is his type. He has been ------- to ask her out.
(A) posing (B) unwilling (C) annoying (D) meaning

_____ 3. He loves running and is ------- runner.
(A) a resistant (B) a passive (C) an avid (D) an utmost

_____ 4. They have been married for 30 years. They are trying different things to ------- their marriage.
(A) spice up (B) tear down (C) make out (D) split up

_____ 5. Many students are shy and are ------- to speak up in class.
(A) edged (B) eloquent (C) gorgeous (D) reluctant

▶▶ 解答請見 p.327

4.1

國外旅遊趣 Traveling Abroad

Did you know?

[你需要知道的 10 件事]

❶ 南極是全球最冷的地方。
❷ 南極為世界七大洲之一。
❸ 南極冰層的下面是面積廣大的陸地。
❹ 南極雖然是陸地，但不屬於任何國家的領土。
❺ 北極的冰層下面是一片海，沒有陸地。
❻ 除了少數觀光客之外，南極有許多科學研究站。
❼ 阿根廷是距離南極最近的國家。
❽ 郵輪是南極觀光的主要交通工具。
❾ 企鵝是不會飛的鳥類。
❿ 海豹和鯨魚為海洋哺乳類動物。

Must-know vocabulary

[你需要知道的 10 個單字]

❶ continent *n.* 洲，大陸
❷ Antarctica *n.* 南極洲
❸ penguin *n.* 企鵝
❹ species *n.* 物種
❺ destination *n.* 目的地
❻ marine *adj.* 海洋的
❼ mammal *n.* 哺乳類動物
❽ peak time *n.* 尖峰時段
❾ excursion *n.* 短途旅遊
❿ ecosystem *n.* 生態系統

掃讀的目標是在文章中搜尋特定的人名、時間、地點，或相關詞語，就像是在電話簿中搜尋某人的電話號碼一樣，其他內容完全不看。

■ 請於 **30** 秒內在以下文章中找出下列文字並畫線，不要閱讀內容或嘗試理解文章。

1 continent
2 Antarctica
3 penguin
4 species
5 destination
6 marine
7 mammal
8 peak time
9 excursion
10 ecosystem

Antarctica Tours

(405 words)   By Yushiang Jou

Nearly twice the size of Australia, Antarctica is the highest, coldest, driest, and windiest continent on Earth. The lowest temperature ever recorded was in 1983 at -89.2°C. The average temperature of Antarctica's interior is about -57°C. 99% of the continent is covered by ice. Around 70% of Earth's fresh water is locked in Antarctica's ice sheet. Antarctica is in darkness for six months of the year and in constant daylight throughout the Antarctic summer. Home to snow-covered mountains and volcanoes, Antarctica is a large ice-covered desert with no trees or bushes. It is the only continent on the planet with no permanent residents. The Antarctic-Environmental Protocol, signed in 1991, monitors scientific research and commercial tourism in Antarctica, ensuring that all human activity is carefully managed.

Despite the seemingly inhospitable environment, the frozen continent is far from lifeless. Many species thrive here, including a variety of penguins, seals, whales, and seabirds. For those wanting to check this destination off their bucket list, wildlife is probably one of the main reasons for travelling to Antarctica. The penguin is the most common flightless bird in Antarctica. Eight different species of

4.1

國外旅遊趣 Traveling Abroad

penguins can be seen here. In addition to penguins, people may well see marine mammals, such as seals and whales, in their natural environments. There are six species of Antarctic seals. Tourists are likely to witness seals hunting penguins. Another rewarding experience of traveling to Antarctica is whale watching. No less than eight species of whales can be observed in Antarctica. One is likely to spot whales traveling here to feast on krill and feed on seals. Antarctica is also bird-watchers' paradise to see seabirds up close.

The Antarctic travel season lasts from November to March, when the icy ocean starts to thaw. Temperatures range from -10°C to 10°C. The best time for penguin spotting is late December or early January. February and early March are peak times for whale sightings. Approximately 50,000 tourists set foot on Antarctica each year during the Antarctic summer, when there is endless sunlight. Most of the Antarctic cruise ships set sail from the southern tip of Argentina, about 620 miles from Antarctica. Cruise ships will sail past towering icebergs. Weather permitting, tourists can step off the ship for an up-close look at wildlife and take part in excursions. The seventh continent offers a unique off-the-grid adventure. It is imperative that tourists not leave litter behind and make no impact on the ecosystem.

■ 請選擇正確的意思

_____ ❶ continent　(A) 洲 (B) 小島

_____ ❷ Antarctica　(A) 北極洲 (B) 南極洲

_____ ❸ penguin　(A) 海鳥 (B) 企鵝

_____ ❹ species　(A) 物種 (B) 種類

_____ ❺ destination　(A) 出發地 (B) 目的地

_____ ❻ marine　(A) 陸地的 (B) 海洋的

_____ ❼ mammal　(A) 哺乳類動物 (B) 魚類

_____ ❽ peak time　(A) 尖峰時段 (B) 離峰時段

_____ ❾ excursion　(A) 短途旅遊 (B) 長途旅行

_____ ❿ ecosystem　(A) 排水系統 (B) 生態系統

▶▶ 解答請見 p.328

針對剛才的文章，用 30 秒鐘瀏覽各段的第一句，粗略了解文章結構與大意即可。

Nearly twice the size of Australia, Antarctica is the highest, coldest, driest, and windiest continent on Earth. The lowest temperature ever recorded was in 1983 at -89.2°C. The average temperature of Antarctica's interior is about -57°C. 99% of the continent is covered by ice. Around 70% of Earth's fresh water is locked in Antarctica's ice sheet. Antarctica is in darkness for six months of the year and in constant daylight throughout the Antarctic summer. Home to snow-covered mountains and volcanoes, Antarctica is a large ice-covered desert with no trees or bushes. It is the only continent on the planet with no permanent residents. The Antarctic-Environmental Protocol, signed in 1991, monitors scientific research and commercial tourism in Antarctica, ensuring that all human activity is carefully managed.

南極
地理
簡介

Despite the seemingly inhospitable environment, the frozen continent is far from lifeless. Many species thrive here, including a variety of penguins, seals, whales, and seabirds. For those wanting to check this destination off their bucket list, wildlife is probably one of the main reasons for travelling to Antarctica. The penguin is the most common flightless bird in Antarctica. Eight different species of penguins can be seen here. In addition to penguins, people may well see marine mammals, such as seals and whales, in their natural environments. There are six species of Antarctic seals. Tourists are likely to witness seals hunting penguins. Another rewarding experience of traveling to Antarctica is whale watching. No less than eight species of whales can be observed in Antarctica. One is likely to spot whales traveling here to feast on krill and feed on seals. Antarctica is also bird-watchers' paradise to see seabirds up close.

南極的
動物

4.1

國外旅遊趣 Traveling Abroad

The Antarctic travel season lasts from November to March, when the icy ocean starts to thaw. Temperatures range from -10°C to 10°C. The best time for penguin spotting is late December or early January. February and early March are peak times for whale sightings. Approximately 50,000 tourists set foot on Antarctica each year during the Antarctic summer, when there is endless sunlight. Most of the Antarctic cruise ships set sail from the southern tip of Argentina, about 620 miles from Antarctica. Cruise ships will sail past towering icebergs. Weather permitting, tourists can step off the ship for an up-close look at wildlife and take part in excursions. The seventh continent offers a unique off-the-grid adventure. It is imperative that tourists not leave litter behind and make no impact on the ecosystem.

南極
旅遊

■ 回答以下問題，確認自己是否正確理解整篇文章的大意：

Q1. _____ Antarctica is smaller than Australia in size. (T/F)

Q2. _____ The climate of Antarctica is relatively mild. (T/F)

Q3. _____ Animals can hardly survive in Antarctica. (T/F)

Q4. _____ Antarctica is the highest continent in the world. (T/F)

Q5. _____ Tourists can travel to Antarctica anytime they want. (T/F)

▸▸ 解答請見 p.328

STEP 3　細讀 Close reading

請用 60 秒的時間仔細閱讀以下內容，並回答問題。

The Antarctic travel season lasts from November to March, when the icy ocean starts to thaw. Temperatures range from -10°C to 10°C. The best time for penguin spotting is late December or early January. February and early March are peak times for whale sightings. Approximately 50,000 tourists set foot on Antarctica each year during the Antarctic summer, when there is endless sunlight.

_____ Q1. According to this passage, which of the following is incorrect?

    (A) There is no darkness in Antarctica.

    (B) Tourists can see whales in February.

    (C) Temperatures from November to March are mild.

    (D) Tourists can see penguins in early January.

_____ Q2. According to this passage, why does the Antarctic travel season start from November?

    (A) Antarctica is warmer before November.

    (B) Whales come to Antarctica in November.

    (C) Penguins come to Antarctica in November.

    (D) Ships can sail safely starting from November.

▶▶ 解答請見 p.328

STEP 4 高理解速讀 Speed Reading with Greater Comprehension

請用 90 秒的時間，看完整篇文章。然後跟著每一個有意義的色塊，提升理解的速度。（請盡量試著不查自己不認識的字，利用前後文去推測意思。）

Nearly twice the size of Australia, Antarctica is the highest, coldest, driest, and windiest continent on Earth. The lowest temperature ever recorded was in 1983 at -89.2°C. The average temperature of Antarctica's interior is about -57°C. 99% of the continent is covered by ice. Around 70% of Earth's fresh water is locked in Antarctica's ice sheet. Antarctica is in darkness for six months of the year and in constant daylight throughout the Antarctic summer. Home to snow-covered mountains and volcanoes, Antarctica is a large ice-covered desert with no trees or bushes. It is the only continent on the planet with no permanent residents. The Antarctic-Environmental Protocol, signed in 1991, monitors scientific research and commercial tourism in Antarctica, ensuring that all human activity is carefully managed.

南極
地理
簡介

4.1

國外旅遊趣 Traveling Abroad

Despite the seemingly inhospitable environment, the frozen continent is far from lifeless. Many species thrive here, including a variety of penguins, seals, whales, and seabirds. For those wanting to check this destination off their bucket list, wildlife is probably one of the main reasons for travelling to Antarctica. The penguin is the most common flightless bird in Antarctica. Eight different species of penguins can be seen here. In addition to penguins, people may well see marine mammals, such as seals and whales, in their natural environments. There are six species of Antarctic seals. Tourists are likely to witness seals hunting penguins. Another rewarding experience of traveling to Antarctica is whale watching. No less than eight species of whales can be observed in Antarctica. One is likely to spot whales traveling here to feast on krill and feed on seals. Antarctica is also bird-watchers' paradise to see seabirds up close.

The Antarctic travel season lasts from November to March, when the icy ocean starts to thaw. Temperatures range from -10°C to 10°C. The best time for penguin spotting is late December or early January. February and early March are peak times for whale sightings. Approximately 50,000 tourists set foot on Antarctica each year during the Antarctic summer, when there is endless sunlight. Most of the Antarctic cruise ships set sail from the southern tip of Argentina, about 620 miles from Antarctica. Cruise ships will sail past towering icebergs. Weather permitting, tourists can step off the ship for an up-close look at wildlife and take part in excursions. The seventh continent offers a unique off-the-grid adventure. It is imperative that tourists not leave litter behind and make no impact on the ecosystem.

■ 請回答以下問題：

_____ Q1. How many species of penguins can be seen in Antarctica?
(A) seven   (B) eight   (C) nine   (D) none of the above

_____ Q2. Which of the following animals can be seen in Antarctica?
(A) whales   (B) seabirds   (C) seals   (D) all of the above

_____ Q3. Which of the following is possible in Antarctica?

      (A) a temperature at 10˚C

      (B) endless darkness

      (C) constant sunlight

      (D) all of the above

_____ Q4. The Antarctic travel season lasts _____.

      (A) from May to August

      (B) from February to March

      (C) from November to March

      (D) from December to January

_____ Q5. Antarctica is _____.

      (A) a continent

      (B) a desert

      (C) a place where there are no permanent residents

      (D) all of the above

▶▶ 解答請見 p.329

4.1.3_S.mp3

STEP 5 跟讀 Shadowing

　　請根據母語人士所錄製的音檔，一句一句跟著唸。跟讀時請使用跟讀音檔，每句結束後，請利用句與句之間的空秒時間，複誦前面所聽到的句子。建議第一遍，看著文章跟著唸，第二遍則不看文章，只聽音檔唸。

4.1

國外旅遊趣 Traveling Abroad

STEP 6 聽讀 Listening

第一遍

→ 讀者會聽到音檔內母語人士完整且不間斷將本文唸一遍。試著不看文
章，聽音檔內的母語人士完整且不間斷地將本文唸一遍，確認自己哪裡
聽懂，那裡聽不懂。

第二遍

→ 再聽母語人士不間斷地將本文唸一遍，眼睛注視著正在朗誦的每個句
子，針對自己沒聽懂的部分，特別仔細閱讀。

STEP 7 延伸學習

單字 Vocabulary

❶ **continent** [ˋkɑntənənt]	n. 洲，大陸 Asia is the largest continent in the world. 亞洲是世界上最大的洲。
❷ **permanent** [ˋpɝmənənt]	adj. 固定的，永久的 He does not have a permanent address. 他沒有固定的地址。
❸ **protocol** [ˋprotəˌkɑl]	n.（國際的）公約 The Geneva Protocol of 1925 prohibits the use of chemical weapons in a war. 1925 年的日內瓦公約禁止在戰爭當中使用化學武器。
❹ **inhospitable** [ɪnˋhɑspɪtəbl̩]	adj. 不適合居住的 This desert is inhospitable. 這片沙漠不適合居住。
❺ **thrive** [θraɪv]	v. 茁壯成長 Her business thrived before the recession. 在經濟衰退發生之前，她的生意興隆。

❻ **marine** [mə`rin]	adj. 海洋的 Dolphins are marine animals. 海豚是海洋動物。
❼ **rewarding** [rɪ`wɔrdɪŋ]	adj. 有益的，報酬高的 She wants to pursue a rewarding career. 她想追求一份報酬高的職業。
❽ **spot** [spɑt]	v. 看見，發現 They spotted some squirrels in the park. 他們在公園看見一些松鼠。
❾ **paradise** [`pærə͵daɪs]	n. 天堂 This department store is a shopper's paradise. 這間百貨公司是購物者的天堂。
❿ **thaw** [θɔ]	v. 融化 The ice on the lake began to thaw earlier this month. 湖面上的結冰這個月初開始融化了。

慣用語和片語 Expressions and Phrases

❶ bucket list　人生成就解鎖清單，願望清單

Seeing the Northern Lights is one of the things on her bucket list.
親眼看見北極光是她人生成就解鎖清單中的項目之一。

❷ feast on　享用（美食等）

They feasted on free hamburgers.
他們享用了免費的漢堡。

❸ off-the-grid　與世隔絕的

She bought an off-the-grid house in Nevada.
她在內華達州買了一棟十分偏僻的房子。

❹ leave... behind　將…留下，拋下

Navy SEALs will never leave their teammates behind.
海豹部隊絕對不會拋下他們的隊員。

A. Fill in the blanks with suitable words or phrases 將適合的字詞填入空格中

a continent　**b** marine　**c** thrive　**d** feast on

1. Whales are common _____ animals in Antarctica.

2. The bear _____ salmon yesterday.

3. Most plants need sunlight to _____.

4. Greenland is an island, not a _____.

B. Multiple choice questions 選擇題（可利用此題型熟悉多益、英檢考試）

_____ 1. It is impossible to ------- polar bears in Antarctica.
(A) abound　(B) filter　(C) spot　(D) seduce

_____ 2. She is looking for a ------- job, wanting to be financially stable.
(A) permanent　(B) temporary　(C) unpaid　(D) part-time

_____ 3. She wants to teach. She believes teaching is a ------- career.
(A) regrettable　(B) unfortunate
(C) meaningless　(D) rewarding

_____ 4. She wants to be completely independent and has lived ------- for many years.
(A) in a hurry　　　(B) off the grid
(C) on a regular basis　(D) for good

_____ 5. He loves Taiwan. Visiting Taiwan is on his ------- list.
(A) hit　(B) bucket　(C) shopping　(D) set

▶▶ 解答請見 p.330

64

NOTE

4.2 藝術、歷史與文化
Art, History & Culture

Part 1 The Giants of the Renaissance（文藝復興的時代巨人）

Did you know?
[你需要知道的 10 件事]

❶ 文藝復興時期有許多成就非凡的人物。
❷ 文藝復興時期在文學、科學、藝術等方面都引發了巨大變革。
❸ 在文藝復興時期，歐洲許多國家都有代表性的人物。
❹ 英國劇作家莎士比亞為文藝復興時期的代表人物之一。
❺ 達文西為義大利的跨界奇才，是一位藝術家、生物學家、建築師等。
❻ 知名畫作《蒙娜麗莎》即為達文西的作品。
❼ 知名畫作《最後的晚餐》也是達文西的作品。
❽ 忍者龜四位主要角色的名字皆是源自於文藝復興時期的重要人物。
❾ 德國天文學家克卜勒為文藝復興時期知名的科學家之一。
❿ 義大利天文學家伽利略亦為文藝復興時期知名的科學家之一。

Must-know vocabulary
[你需要知道的 10 個單字]

❶ the Renaissance *n.* 文藝復興時期
❷ the Middle Ages *n.* 中世紀
❸ literature *n.* 文學
❹ three-dimensional *adj.* 立體的
❺ fresco *n.* 壁畫
❻ humanist theme *n.* 人文主義的主題
❼ playwright *n.* 劇作家
❽ epic poem *n.* 史詩
❾ the solar system *n.* 太陽系
❿ refracting telescope *n.* 折射式望遠鏡

掃讀的目標是在文章中搜尋特定的人名、時間、地點,或相關詞語,就像是在電話簿中搜尋某人的電話號碼一樣,其他內容完全不看。

■ 請於 30 秒內在以下文章中找出下列文字並畫線,不要閱讀內容或嘗試理解文章。

❶ the Renaissance ❷ the Middle Ages
❸ literature ❹ three-dimensional
❺ fresco ❻ humanist theme
❼ playwright ❽ epic poem
❾ the solar system ❿ refracting telescope

....

The Giants of the Renaissance

(400 words) By Yushiang Jou

Often seen as the bridge between the Middle Ages and the modern age, the Renaissance refers to a period in Europe that took place from the 14th to the 17th century. It started as a cultural movement in Florence and later spread to the rest of Europe. At its core, the Renaissance was about reawakening ideas and cultures of ancient Greece and Rome, particularly in art, literature, and science, among other fields.

Many artists rose to prominence during the Renaissance, including da Vinci, Michelangelo, and Raphael. Da Vinci was an Italian painter, architect, and scientist. He was particularly interested in three-dimensional representations of human beauty. His work *the Mona Lisa* is arguably the most famous painting ever in existence, with over 10 million people traveling to view the artwork in the Louvre Museum in Paris each year. Michelangelo was a painter and sculptor who carved *David*, a sculpture depicting the human form in a true-to-life manner. He is also noted for *the Creation of Adam*, the giant ceiling fresco of the Sistine Chapel in the Vatican. Another famous Italian painter is Raphael. He is best known for *the School of Athens*.

Renaissance literature, too, was characterized by humanist themes, some of the most famous writers including Shakespeare, Milton, and Dante. An English poet, Shakespeare is probably the most famous playwright of all time. He embraced the nature of man, widely celebrated for his plays such as *Hamlet* and *Romeo and Juliet*. Another well-known English poet is Milton. He is noted for his epic poem *Paradise Lost*. Consisting of more than 10,000 lines of verse, his poem tells the story of the creation of Adam and Eve, as well as their failure to resist temptations. Dante was an Italian poet and philosopher. He wrote *the Divine Comedy*, in which he presented the Christian view on the eternal destiny of mankind.

Scientific discoveries during the Renaissance were also nothing short of exceptional. Science took giant strides, particularly in astronomy and mathematics. For example, Copernicus, a Polish astronomer and mathematician, proposed a heliocentric solar system, rightly arguing that the sun, not the earth, was the center of the solar system. Of equal importance was Kepler's discovery of the three principles of planetary motion. He also shed important light on the spatial organization of the solar system. An Italian astronomer and physicist, Galileo boosted the power of refracting telescopes to observe the night sky.

■ 請選擇正確的意思

_____ ❶ the Renaissance　(A) 文藝復興時期 (B) 中世紀

_____ ❷ the Middle Ages　(A) 文藝復興時期 (B) 中世紀

_____ ❸ literature　(A)文學 (B) 學養

_____ ❹ three-dimensional　(A) 平面的　(B) 立體的

_____ ❺ fresco　(A) 油畫 (B) 壁畫

_____ ❻ humanist theme　(A) 人文主義的主題 (B) 功利主義的主題

_____ ❼ playwright　(A) 劇作家 (B) 舞台劇演員

_____ ❽ epic poem　(A) 短篇散文 (B) 史詩

_____ ❾ the solar system　(A) 銀河系 (B) 太陽系

_____ ❿ refracting telescope　(A) 折射式望遠鏡 (B) 顯微鏡

▶▶ 解答請見 p.332

針對剛才的文章，用 30 秒鐘瀏覽各段的第一句，粗略了解文章結構與大意即可。

Often seen as the bridge between the Middle Ages and the modern age, the Renaissance refers to a period in Europe that took place from the 14th to the 17th century. It started as a cultural movement in Florence and later spread to the rest of Europe. At its core, the Renaissance was about reawakening ideas and cultures of ancient Greece and Rome, particularly in art, literature, and science, among other fields.

文藝復興時期

Many artists rose to prominence during the Renaissance, including da Vinci, Michelangelo, and Raphael. Da Vinci was an Italian painter, architect, and scientist. He was particularly interested in three-dimensional representations of human beauty. His work *the Mona Lisa* is arguably the most famous painting ever in existence, with over 10 million people traveling to view the artwork in the Louvre Museum in Paris each year. Michelangelo was a painter and sculptor who carved *David*, a sculpture depicting the human form in a true-to-life manner. He is also noted for *the Creation of Adam*, the giant ceiling fresco of the Sistine Chapel in the Vatican. Another famous Italian painter is Raphael. He is best known for *the School of Athens*.

文藝復興時期知名的藝術家

Renaissance literature, too, was characterized by humanist themes, some of the most famous writers including Shakespeare, Milton, and Dante. An English poet, Shakespeare is probably the most famous playwright of all time. He embraced the nature of man, widely celebrated for his plays such as *Hamlet* and *Romeo and Juliet*. Another well-known English poet is Milton. He is noted for his epic poem *Paradise Lost*. Consisting of more than 10,000 lines of verse, his poem tells the story of the creation of Adam and Eve, as well as their failure to resist temptations. Dante was an Italian poet and philosopher. He wrote *the Divine Comedy*, in which he presented the Christian view on the eternal destiny of mankind.

文藝復興時期知名的文學作家

4.2 藝術、歷史與文化 Art, History & Culture

Scientific discoveries during the Renaissance were also nothing short of exceptional. Science took giant strides, particularly in astronomy and mathematics. For example, Copernicus, a Polish astronomer and mathematician, proposed a heliocentric solar system, rightly arguing that the sun, not the earth, was the center of the solar system. Of equal importance was Kepler's discovery of the three principles of planetary motion. He also shed important light on the spatial organization of the solar system. An Italian astronomer and physicist, Galileo boosted the power of refracting telescopes to observe the night sky.

文藝復興時期知名的科學家

■ 回答以下問題，確認自己是否正確理解整篇文章的大意：

Q1. _____ The Renaissance refers to an art movement in Europe. (T/F)

Q2. _____ The Renaissance refers to a period in Europe. (T/F)

Q3. _____ Many artists became famous during the Renaissance. (T/F)

Q4. _____ Shakespeare was the only famous writer during the Renaissance. (T/F)

Q5. _____ Scientific discoveries during the Renaissance were not significant. (T/F)

▶▶ 解答與解析，請見 p.332

STEP 3 細讀 Close reading

請用 60 秒的時間仔細閱讀以下內容，並回答問題。

Often seen as the bridge between the Middle Ages and the modern age, the Renaissance refers to a period in Europe that took place from the 14th to the 17th century. It started as a cultural movement in Florence and later spread to the rest of Europe. At its core, the Renaissance was about reawakening ideas and cultures of ancient Greece and Rome, particularly in art, literature, and science, among other fields.

_____ Q1. According to this passage, which of the following is correct?

    (A) The Renaissance was mainly about art.

    (B) The Renaissance was mainly about literature.

    (C) The Renaissance affected many different fields.

    (D) The Renaissance started in Greece and Rome.

_____ Q2. The Renaissance as a cultural movement took place in _____.

    (A) Italy   (B) France   (C) The U.K.   (D) all of the above

▶▶ 解答請見 p.332

STEP 4 高理解速讀 Speed Reading with Greater Comprehension

請用 90 秒的時間，看完整篇文章。然後跟著每一個有意義的色塊，提升理解的速度。（請盡量試著不查自己不認識的字，利用前後文去推測意思。）

Often seen as the bridge between the Middle Ages and the modern age, the Renaissance refers to a period in Europe that took place from the 14th to the 17th century. It started as a cultural movement in Florence and later spread to the rest of Europe. At its core, the Renaissance was about reawakening ideas and cultures of ancient Greece and Rome, particularly in art, literature, and science, among other fields.

文藝復興時期

Many artists rose to prominence during the Renaissance, including da Vinci, Michelangelo, and Raphael. Da Vinci was an Italian painter, architect, and scientist. He was particularly interested in three-dimensional representations of human beauty. His work _the Mona Lisa_ is arguably the most famous painting ever in existence, with over 10 million people traveling to view the artwork in the Louvre Museum in Paris each year. Michelangelo was a painter and sculptor who carved _David_, a sculpture depicting the human form in a true-to-life manner. He is also noted for _the Creation of Adam_, the giant ceiling fresco of the Sistine Chapel in the Vatican. Another famous Italian painter is Raphael. He is best known for the _School of Athens_.

文藝復興時期知名的藝術家

Renaissance literature, too, was characterized by humanist themes, some of the most famous writers including Shakespeare, Milton, and Dante. An English poet, Shakespeare is probably the most famous playwright of all time. He embraced the nature of man, widely celebrated for his plays such as *Hamlet* and *Romeo and Juliet*. Another well-known English poet is Milton. He is noted for his epic poem *Paradise Lost*. Consisting of more than 10,000 lines of verse, his poem tells the story of the creation of Adam and Eve, as well as their failure to resist temptations. Dante was an Italian poet and philosopher. He wrote *the Divine Comedy*, in which he presented the Christian view on the eternal destiny of mankind.

Scientific discoveries during the Renaissance were also nothing short of exceptional. Science took giant strides, particularly in astronomy and mathematics. For example, Copernicus, a Polish astronomer and mathematician, proposed a heliocentric solar system, rightly arguing that the sun, not the earth, was the center of the solar system. Of equal importance was Kepler's discovery of the three principles of planetary motion. He also shed important light on the spatial organization of the solar system. An Italian astronomer and physicist, Galileo boosted the power of refracting telescopes to observe the night sky.

■ 請回答以下問題：

_____ Q1. Who pained *the School of Athens*?
   (A) da Vinci   (B) Dante   (C) Raphael   (D) Michelangelo

_____ Q2. Who argued that the Sun was the center of the solar system?
   (A) Copernicus   (B) Kepler   (C) Galileo   (D) Milton

_____ Q3. Who wrote *Paradise Lost*?
   (A) Dante   (B) Galileo   (C) Shakespeare   (D) Milton

_____ Q4. Who carved *David*?

(A) da Vinci　(B) Dante　(C) Raphael　(D) Michelangelo

_____ Q5. Who discovered the three principles of planetary motion?

(A) Copernicus　(B) Kepler　(C) Galileo　(D) Milton

▶▶ 解答請見 p.333

4.2.1_S.mp3

STEP 5 跟讀 Shadowing

　　請根據母語人士所錄製的音檔，一句一句跟著唸。跟讀時請使用跟讀音檔，每句結束後，請利用句與句之間的空秒時間，複誦前面所聽到的句子。建議第一遍，看著文章跟著唸，第二遍則不看文章，只聽音檔唸。

4.2.1_L.mp3

STEP 6 聽讀 Listening

第一遍

→ 讀者會聽到音檔內母語人士完整且不間斷將本文唸一遍。試著不看文章，聽音檔內的母語人士完整且不間斷地將本文唸一遍，確認自己哪裡聽懂，那裡聽不懂。

第二遍

→ 再聽母語人士不間斷地將本文唸一遍，眼睛注視著正在朗誦的每個句子，針對自己沒聽懂的部分，特別仔細閱讀。

4.2

藝術、歷史與文化 Art, History & Culture

單字　Vocabulary

❶ movement [ˋmuvmənt]	n.（文化、思想等）運動 She published a book about the history of the women's movement. 她出版過一本關於婦女運動史的書。
❷ reawaken [͵riəˋwekən]	v. 重新喚起 Writing a memoir will reawaken memories of the past. 撰寫回憶錄會重新喚起過去的回憶。
❸ artwork [ˋɑrt͵wɜk]	n. 藝術品 Her artwork is hanging on the walls. 她的藝術品掛在牆上。
❹ sculpture [ˋskʌlptʃɚ]	n. 雕像，雕刻品 She wanted to see an exhibit of sculpture 她想要去看雕刻展。
❺ fresco [ˋfrɛsko]	n. 壁畫 This church has many ceiling frescoes. 這間教堂許多天花板壁畫。
❻ characterize [ˋkærəktə͵raɪz]	v. 以…作為特色 This school is characterized by its mixed-age grouping. 混齡分組教學是這間學校的特色。
❼ poem [ˋpoəm]	n. 詩 He wrote a poem about his hometown. 他寫了一首關於他家鄉的詩。
❽ temptation [tɛmpˋteʃən]	n. 誘惑 He could not resist the temptation to buy the new car. 他未能夠抗拒購買新車的誘惑。

❾ eternal [ɪˋtɜˋnl̩]	adj. 永恆的，永遠的 He is an eternal pessimist. 他是個永恆的悲觀者。
❿ stride [straɪd]	n. 一大步，闊步 The government has made great strides in controlling inflation. 政府在抑制通膨上已經取得巨大的進展。

慣用語和片語 Expressions and Phrases

❶ shed light on 闡明，說明

These new discoveries have <u>shed light on</u> the origin of the moon.
這些新發現說明了月球的起源。

❷ in existence 存在的

The company has been <u>in existence</u> for 30 years.
這間公司已經開了 30 年。

❸ rise to prominence 崛起，聲名大噪

Tesla has <u>risen to prominence</u> globally as an electric vehicle company.
特斯拉已崛起成為了世界級的電動車大廠。

❹ nothing short of 簡直就是

The show was <u>nothing short of</u> amazing.
這場表演簡直是太神奇了。

4.2

藝術、歷史與文化 Art, History & Culture

A. Fill in the blanks with suitable words or phrases 將適合的字詞填入空格中

ⓐ characterize **ⓑ** to prominence **ⓒ** in existence **ⓓ** nothing short of

1. Electric vehicles have been _____ for many years.

2. This area is _____ by its desert plants.

3. This artist was _____ brilliant and her artwork sold for millions at auction.

4. The Chicago Bulls rose _____ in the NBA in the 1990s.

B. Multiple choice questions 選擇題（可利用此題型熟悉多益、英檢考試）

_____ 1. She always thinks positively. In fact, she is ------- optimist.
(A) a temporary (B) a short-term (C) an eternal (D) an ineffective

_____ 2. She is a functional linguist. Her book ------- different functions of runs out of.
(A) sheds light on   (B) is covered with
(C) looks forword to   (D) runs out of

_____ 3. This company has been successful and has made important -------
in self-driving technology.
(A) failures   (B) strides   (C) setbacks   (D) disappointments

_____ 4. This writing assignment requires that students ------- memories of their childhood.
(A) reawaken   (B) facilitate   (C) legislate   (D) rectify

_____ 5. She was a historian and wrote a book about the civil rights -------.
(A) fiction   (B) fantasy   (C) movement   (D) imagination

▶▶ 解答請見 p.334

NOTE

Did you know?

[你需要知道的 10 件事]

❶ 印象派是第一個現代藝術運動。

❷ 印象派之前的繪畫風格是寫實派。

❸ 寫實派著重於人物的刻畫細節。

❹ 寫實派的畫風細膩，顏色的調配也很細緻。

❺ 印象派畫風與寫實派截然不同。

❻ 印象派的色彩較寫實派更為明亮。

❼ 未經修飾的筆觸為印象派的繪畫技法之一。

❽ 法國畫家莫內為印象派的代表人物之一。

❾ 荷蘭畫家梵谷的畫作也深受印象派的影響。

❿ 世界各地的博物館都有展覽印象派的畫作。

Must-know vocabulary

[你需要知道的 10 個單字]

❶ Impressionism *n.* 印象派

❷ art movement *n.* 藝術運動

❸ leading figure *n.* 主要人物

❹ state-sponsored exhibition *n.* 政府資助的展覽

❺ subject matter *n.* 題材

❻ contemporary *n.* 同時期的人

❼ fleeting effect *n.* 轉瞬即逝的效果

❽ canvas *n.* 油畫布

❾ industrialization *n.* 工業化

❿ satirical review *n.* 嘲諷的評論

掃讀的目標是在文章中搜尋特定的人名、時間、地點，或相關詞語，就像是在電話簿中搜尋某人的電話號碼一樣，其他內容完全不看。

■ 請於 **30** 秒內在以下文章中找出下列文字並畫線，不要閱讀內容或嘗試理解文章。

❶ Impressionism

❷ art movement

❸ leading figure

❹ state-sponsored exhibition

❺ subject matter

❻ contemporary

❼ fleeting effect

❽ canvas

❾ industrialization

❿ satirical review

The Legacy of Impressionism

(414 words)

By Yushiang Jou

Impressionism was the first modern art movement that began in the last quarter of the 19th century in France. Leading figures included Claude Monet and Edgar Degas, among other like-minded painters. Most of their paintings came into conflict with mainstream artistic expectations and thus were rejected by the Salon, the state-sponsored exhibition. These Impressionist painters therefore sought independence, their first self-organized exhibition held in Paris in 1874. Their paintings were characterized by their close attention to color and light, unconventional subject matter, and thick brushwork.

The Impressionists preferred colors brighter than those used in previous art movements. They often used bright colors like red, green, yellow, and orange. Most of their contemporaries, by contrast, tended to prime their canvases with a dark background and use such drab colors as black, gray, and dark brown. Since the Impressionists were preoccupied with the interplay of color and light, they usually opted to paint outdoors. For example, Monet once painted the same place over and over again at different times of day in his efforts to capture the fleeting effects of light before they disappeared.

4.2

藝術、歷史與文化 Art, History & Culture

Their outdoor-oriented subject matter gave us a flavor of what their lives looked like. While the Salon favored such traditional subject matter as historical, biblical and mythological themes, the Impressionists were adept at rural scenes such as landscapes, gardens, and riverbanks. They also embraced modernity and painted cityscapes such as the hectic streets of Paris and increased industrialization around them. As a result, the Impressionists leaned toward using smaller canvases that they could carry around with them outdoors, instead of finishing up a painting from sketches in the studio, a popular approach valued by the Salon.

Just because the Impressionists did not have ample time before the light changed, their paintings were featured by thick and sketch-like brushwork. Unlike clearly portrayed figures found in most artworks of their day, they turned away from fine details and purposely avoided clarity on their canvases. Critics faulted their artworks for a lack of detail. In fact, the term "Impressionism" was born from a satirical review written by an art critic Louis Leroy, who called one of Monet's paintings an "impression." Much to the dismay of Leroy, the Impressionists' unusual taste of art was considered revolutionary in their time. Today, their paintings are exhibited in museums worldwide and have sold for millions of dollars at auction. It is not an overstatement to say that Impressionism has, to a certain extent, shaped the course of modern art.

■ 請選擇正確的意思

_____ ❶ Impressionism　(A) 印象派 (B) 寫實派

_____ ❷ art movement　(A) 藝術運動 (B) 人權運動

_____ ❸ leading figure　(A) 配角 (B) 主要人物

_____ ❹ state-sponsored exhibition　(A) 政府資助的展覽 (B) 私人資助的展覽

_____ ❺ subject matter　(A) 教材 (B) 題材

_____ ❻ contemporary　(A) 同時期的人 (B) 不同時期的人

_____ ❼ fleeting effect　(A) 轉瞬即逝的效果 (B) 持續的效果

_____ ❽ canvas　(A) 油畫布 (B) 油畫框

_____ ❾ industrialization　(A) 農業化 (B) 工業化

_____ ❿ satirical review　(A) 正面的評價 (B) 嘲諷的評論

▶▶ 解答請見 p.335

針對剛才的文章，用 30 秒鐘瀏覽各段的第一句，粗略了解文章結構與大意即可。

Impressionism was the first modern art movement that began in the last quarter of the 19th century in France. Leading figures included Claude Monet and Edgar Degas, among other like-minded painters. Most of their paintings came into conflict with mainstream artistic expectations and thus were rejected by the Salon, the state-sponsored exhibition. These Impressionist painters therefore sought independence, their first self-organized exhibition held in Paris in 1874. Their paintings were characterized by their close attention to color and light, unconventional subject matter, and thick brushwork.

印象派
簡介

The Impressionists preferred colors brighter than those used in previous art movements. They often used bright colors like red, green, yellow, and orange. Most of their contemporaries, by contrast, tended to prime their canvases with a dark background and use such drab colors as black, gray, and dark brown. Since the Impressionists were preoccupied with the interplay of color and light, they usually opted to paint outdoors. For example, Monet once painted the same place over and over again at different times of day in his efforts to capture the fleeting effects of light before they disappeared.

印象派
的色彩
偏好

Their outdoor-oriented subject matter gave us a flavor of what their lives looked like. While the Salon favored such traditional subject matter as historical, biblical and mythological themes, the Impressionists were adept at rural scenes such as landscapes, gardens, and riverbanks. They also embraced modernity and painted cityscapes such as the hectic streets of Paris and increased industrialization around them. As a result, the Impressionists leaned toward using smaller canvases that they could carry around with them outdoors, instead of finishing up a painting from sketches in the studio, a popular approach valued by the Salon.

印象派
的畫作
主題

4.2

藝術、歷史與文化 Art, History & Culture

Just because the Impressionists did not have ample time before the light changed, their paintings were featured by thick and sketch-like brushwork. Unlike clearly portrayed figures found in most artworks of their day, they turned away from fine details and purposely avoided clarity on their canvases. Critics faulted their artworks for a lack of detail. In fact, the term "Impressionism" was born from a satirical review written by an art critic Louis Leroy, who called one of Monet's paintings an "impression." Much to the dismay of Leroy, the Impressionists' unusual taste of art was considered revolutionary in their time. Today, their paintings are exhibited in museums worldwide and have sold for millions of dollars at auction. It is not an overstatement to say that Impressionism has, to a certain extent, shaped the course of modern art.

印象派
的繪畫
技法

■ 回答以下問題，確認自己是否正確理解整篇文章的大意：

Q1. _____ Impressionism was the most recent modern art movement. (T/F)

Q2. _____ Impressionists preferred bright colors. (T/F)

Q3. _____ Impressionists liked to paint outdoors. (T/F)

Q4. _____ Impressionists liked to paint indoors. (T/F)

Q5. _____ Impressionists usually painted very slowly. (T/F)

▶▶ 解答請見 p.335

STEP 3 細讀 Close reading

請用 60 秒的時間仔細閱讀以下內容，並回答問題。

While the Salon favored such traditional subject matter as historical, biblical and mythological themes, the Impressionists were adept at rural scenes such as landscapes, gardens, and riverbanks. They also embraced modernity and painted cityscapes such as the hectic streets of Paris and increased industrialization around them.

_____ Q1. According to this passage, what subject matter would NOT be of
         interest to Impressionists?
         (A) Adam and Eve   (B) Street cafes   (C) Bridges   (D) Mountains

_____ Q2. According to this passage, which of the following is correct?
         (A) Impressionists were innovative.
         (B) Impressionists were conservative.
         (C) The Salon was interested in modernity.
         (D) Impressionists were interested in historical themes.

STEP 4 高理解速讀 Speed Reading with Greater Comprehension

　　請用 90 秒的時間，看完整篇文章。然後跟著每一個有意義的色塊，提升理
解的速度。（請盡量試著不查自己不認識的字，利用前後文去推測意思。）

Impressionism was the first modern art movement that began in the last
quarter of the 19th century in France. Leading figures included Claude
Monet and Edgar Degas, among other like-minded painters. Most of
their paintings came into conflict with mainstream artistic expectations
and thus were rejected by the Salon, the state-sponsored exhibition.
These Impressionist painters therefore sought independence, their first
self-organized exhibition held in Paris in 1874. Their paintings were
characterized by their close attention to color and light, unconventional
subject matter, and thick brushwork.

印象派
簡介

The Impressionists preferred colors brighter than those used in previous
art movements. They often used bright colors like red, green, yellow,
and orange. Most of their contemporaries, by contrast, tended to prime
their canvases with a dark background and use such drab colors as
black, gray, and dark brown. Since the Impressionists were preoccupied

印象派
的色彩
偏好

4.2
藝術、歷史與文化 Art, History & Culture

with the interplay of color and light, they usually opted to paint outdoors. For example, Monet once painted the same place over and over again at different times of day in his efforts to capture the fleeting effects of light before they disappeared.

Their outdoor-oriented subject matter gave us a flavor of what their lives looked like. While the Salon favored such traditional subject matter as historical, biblical and mythological themes, the Impressionists were adept at rural scenes such as landscapes, gardens, and riverbanks. They also embraced modernity and painted cityscapes such as the hectic streets of Paris and increased industrialization around them. As a result, the Impressionists leaned toward using smaller canvases that they could carry around with them outdoors, instead of finishing up a painting from sketches in the studio, a popular approach valued by the Salon.

印象派的畫作主題

Just because the Impressionists did not have ample time before the light changed, their paintings were featured by thick and sketch-like brushwork. Unlike clearly portrayed figures found in most artworks of their day, they turned away from fine details and purposely avoided clarity on their canvases. Critics faulted their artworks for a lack of detail. In fact, the term "Impressionism" was born from a satirical review written by an art critic Louis Leroy, who called one of Monet's paintings an "impression." Much to the dismay of Leroy, the Impressionists' unusual taste of art was considered revolutionary in their time. Today, their paintings are exhibited in museums worldwide and have sold for millions of dollars at auction. It is not an overstatement to say that Impressionism has, to a certain extent, shaped the course of modern art.

印象派的繪畫技法

■ 請回答以下問題：

_____ Q1. What color is often used by most painters of the last quarter of the 19th century?

(A) orange   (B) green   (C) gray   (D) yellow

_____ Q2. Which of the following subject matter is NOT favored by the Salon?

(A) mythological themes

(B) historical themes

(C) biblical themes

(D) landscape themes

_____ Q3. What is the Salon?

(A) the first modern art movement

(B) the exhibition sponsored by Impressionists

(C) the state-sponsored exhibition

(D) a famous barber shop in Paris

_____ Q4. Impressionists were good at paining _____.

(A) riverbanks   (B) gardens

(C) landscapes   (D) all of the above

_____ Q5. How were Impressionists' works perceived by the Salon?

(A) negatively

(B) positively

(C) neutrally

(D) not mentioned in this passage

▶▶ 解答請見 p.336

4.2.2_S.mp3

STEP 5 跟讀 Shadowing

　　請根據母語人士所錄製的音檔，一句一句跟著唸。跟讀時請使用跟讀音檔，每句結束後，請利用句與句之間的空秒時間，複誦前面所聽到的句子。建議第一遍，看著文章跟著唸，第二遍則不看文章，只聽音檔唸。

STEP 6 聽讀 Listening

第一遍

→ 讀者會聽到音檔內母語人士完整且不間斷將本文唸一遍。試著不看文章，聽音檔內的母語人士完整且不間斷地將本文唸一遍，確認自己哪裡聽懂，那裡聽不懂。

第二遍

→ 再聽母語人士不間斷地將本文唸一遍，眼睛注視著正在朗誦的每個句子，針對自己沒聽懂的部分，特別仔細閱讀。

STEP 7 延伸學習

單字 Vocabulary

❶ **brushwork** [`brʌʃˌwɝk]	n. 繪畫技法 The brushwork of his paintings was unique. 他的畫法獨一無二。
❷ **fleeting** [`flitɪŋ]	adj. 轉瞬即逝的 She caught a fleeting glimpse of a meteor the other night. 前幾天晚上她瞥見了夜空中的流星。
❸ **biblical** [`bɪblɪkl]	adj. 聖經的 He likes to read biblical stories. 他喜歡閱讀《聖經》中的故事。
❹ **mythological** [ˌmɪθəˈlɑdʒɪkl]	adj. 神話的 Achilles is a mythological hero. 阿基里斯是神話裡的英雄。
❺ **adept** [`ædɛpt]	adj. 擅長的 He is adept at dealing with difficult customers. 他很擅長應付奧客。
❻ **rural** [`rʊrəl]	adj. 鄉村的 He lives in a rural area. 他住在鄉下地方。

❼ hectic [`hɛktɪk]	adj. 繁忙的 She has a hectic schedule. 她的行程滿檔。
❽ lean [lin]	v. 傾向於，偏好 In the meeting, she leaned toward John's proposal. 在會議上她傾向支持約翰的提案。
❾ sketch [skɛtʃ]	n. 草圖 He drew a sketch of his car. 他畫了一張他車子的草圖。
❿ ample [`æmpl]	adj. 充裕的，足夠的 He has ample time to get to school on time. 他有足夠的時間可以準時到校。

慣用語和片語 Expressions and Phrases

❶ be preoccupied with...　將所有時間投入…，心繫著…

She is preoccupied with preparing for the test tomorrow.
她很專心準備明天的考試。

❷ by contrast　相形之下，對照之下

Inflation in their country is under control. By contrast, inflation in our country seems out of control.
他們國家的通膨已被控制住了。相形之下，我們國家的通膨似乎失控了。

❸ a flavor of　一種…的風味／感受

Her book gives us a flavor of the life in New York.
她的書帶給我們一種紐約生活的風味。

❹ to somebody's dismay　令某人失望的是

To her dismay, she did not keep her job.
令她失望的是，她未能保住工作。

A. Fill in the blanks with suitable words or phrases 將適合的字詞填入空格中

ⓐ lean　ⓑ a flavor of　ⓒ rural　ⓓ preoccupied with

1. Elon Musk is _____ colonizing Mars.

2. She does not like cities. She likes to live in a _____ area.

3. Jean's idea was convincing. Many people _____ toward her idea.

4. Her movie gave us _____ life in Taipei.

B. Multiple choice questions 選擇題（可利用此題型熟悉多益、英檢考試）

_____ 1. He has a ------- schedule because he needs to do many things today.
(A) deadly　(B) hectic　(C) wary　(D) feasible

_____ 2. She is a computer scientist and is ------- computer programming.
(A) adept at　(B) ignorant of　(C) unfamiliar with　(D) new to

_____ 3. Thor is a ------- figure, who does not veally east.
(A) mathematical　(B) scientific　(C) biblical　(D) mythological

_____ 4. She was not under time pressure because she was given ------- time to complete the task.
(A) witty　(B) ample　(C) lavish　(D) insufficient

_____ 5. ------- stories come from the Bible.
(A) Mathematical　(B) Scientific　(C) Biblical　(D) Political

▶▶ 解答請見 p.337

NOTE

Did you know?

[你需要知道的 10 件事]

❶ 利他（有利於他人的行為）是自願性的行為。

❷ 雖然人是自私的，但是幫助別人的「利他」行為也很常見。

❸ 慈善捐款，或甚至幫人開門都可以算是一種利他行為。

❹ 利他的作為不只限於行為，言語上的幫助他人也是一種利他。

❺ 有些文化相信人性本善，有些文化卻相信人性本惡。

❻ 利他不應該有對價的關係或期待。

❼ 感同身受為利他的一種人格特質。

❽ 利他包含同理心、憐憫心和具體的幫助行為。

❾ 研究顯示，幫助他人的時候大腦會感到愉悅。

❿ 研究顯示，人在幼兒時期就能展現一些利他的行為，例如拿餅乾給媽媽吃。

Must-know vocabulary

[你需要知道的 10 個單字]

❶ self-interest *n.* 自利（對自己有利）

❷ voluntarily *adv.* 自願地

❸ self-sacrifice *n.* 自我犧牲

❹ charity *n.* 慈善單位

❺ stranger *n.* 陌生的人

❻ cultural value and norm *n.* 文化價值和行為規範

❼ altruism *n.* 利他（主義）

❽ Daoism *n.* 道家思想

❾ empathy *n.* 同理心

❿ humility *n.* 謙遜

掃讀的目標是在文章中搜尋特定的人名、時間、地點，或相關詞語，就像是在電話簿中搜尋某人的電話號碼一樣，其他內容完全不看。

■ 請於 **30** 秒內在以下文章中找出下列文字並畫線，不要閱讀內容或嘗試理解文章。

1 self-interest
2 voluntarily
3 self-sacrifice
4 charity
5 a stranger
6 cultural values and norms
7 altruism
8 Daoism
9 empathy
10 humility

A Cross-Cultural Perspective on Altruism

(424 words)   By Yushiang Jou

Altruism, in the most general terms, is acting voluntarily in the best interest of others rather than in one's own self-interest, involving self-sacrifice in terms of time, money, or other resources with no expectation of reward. Many people are wired to be sympathetic not just to those they know or relate to but also to strangers. For example, some would give thousands of dollars to a charity or volunteer for overseas duty in the Peace Corps. There are also people who volunteer to undergo major surgery to remove one of their own healthy kidneys and have it transplanted into a complete stranger who is ill and dying.

Many explanations have been offered to explain altruistic acts. Psychologists argue that the answer emerges from a brain sensitive to other people's emotions. This argument suggests that we can feel empathy for other people's distress. On the other hand, social scientists observe that cultural understandings help unlock valuable insights into the emergence of altruism since altruistic beliefs and acts can be motivated by different cultural values and norms.

4.2

藝術、歷史與文化 Art, History & Culture

In Western cultures, people have ingrained tendencies to act altruistically. In particular, equity, diversity, and inclusion are key drivers of their helping behavior. In keeping with the collective moral codes, all are equally worthy of help, and no one should be denied an equal opportunity to thrive due to their ethnicity, nationality, socioeconomic status, sexual orientation, and disability. Since Westerners' altruistic acts are motivated by community values and morals, diversity is embraced and all members of the community should feel welcomed and valued. This community ethos is to create a sustainable climate of inclusion where people care about the welfare of others. As a result, when seeing others in pain or in need of help, they would respond compassionately and would not excuse themselves from stepping in.

Culturally derived altruism can also be observed in Eastern cultures. Daoism and Buddhism, as integral parts of cultural heritage, underscore the importance of compassionate empathy and humility. The teachings of Daoism and Buddhism have been practiced for centuries and have far-reaching implications for Easterners' altruistic behavior. Another worldview that guides their acts of kindness is that all beings are equal and equally worthy. It is therefore imperative to be respectful to not just human beings but also all living beings. While a culture-bound perspective helps paint a rich picture of altruism, the ways to evoke the better angels of our nature vary cross-culturally. Yet, despite these differences, altruism is arguably a positive force within our community and is surely within everyone's reach.

■ 請選擇正確的意思

_____ ❶ self-interest   (A) 他人利益 (B) 自我利益

_____ ❷ voluntarily   (A) 被迫地 (B) 自願地

_____ ❸ self-sacrifice   (A) 自我犧牲 (B) 自我懷疑

_____ ❹ charity   (A) 慈善單位 (B) 營利組織

_____ ❺ a complete stranger   (A) 親朋好友 (B) 陌生人

_____ ❻ cultural values and norms   (A) 法律規範 (B) 文化價值和行為規範

_____ ❼ altruism   (A) 利他 (B) 利己

_____ ❽ Daoism   (A) 道家思想 (B) 儒家思想

_____ ❾ empathy (A) 同理心 (B) 私心

_____ ❿ humility (A) 傲慢 (B) 謙遜

▶▶▶ 解答請見 p.339

STEP 2 略讀 Skimming

針對剛才的文章，用 30 秒鐘瀏覽各段的第一句，粗略了解文章結構與大意即可。

Altruism, in the most general terms, is acting voluntarily in the best interest of others rather than in one's own self-interest, involving self-sacrifice in terms of time, money, or other resources with no expectation of reward. Many people are wired to be sympathetic not just to those they know or relate to but also to strangers. For example, some would give thousands of dollars to a charity or volunteer for overseas duty in the Peace Corps. There are also people who volunteer to undergo major surgery to remove one of their own healthy kidneys and have it transplanted into a complete stranger who is ill and dying.

利他
的定義

Many explanations have been offered to explain altruistic acts. Psychologists argue that the answer emerges from a brain sensitive to other people's emotions. This argument suggests that we can feel empathy for other people's distress. On the other hand, social scientists observe that cultural understandings help unlock valuable insights into the emergence of altruism since altruistic beliefs and acts can be motivated by different cultural values and norms.

利他行
為發生
的原因

In Western cultures, people have ingrained tendencies to act altruistically. In particular, equity, diversity, and inclusion are key drivers of their helping behavior. In keeping with the collective moral codes, all are equally worthy of help, and no one should be denied an equal opportunity to thrive due to their ethnicity, nationality,

西方的
利他文
化

4.2

藝術、歷史與文化 Art, History & Culture

socioeconomic status, sexual orientation, and disability. Since Westerners' altruistic acts are motivated by community values and morals, diversity is embraced and all members of the community should feel welcomed and valued. This community ethos is to create a sustainable climate of inclusion where people care about the welfare of others. As a result, when seeing others in pain or in need of help, they would respond compassionately and would not excuse themselves from stepping in.

Culturally derived altruism can also be observed in Eastern cultures. Daoism and Buddhism, as integral parts of cultural heritage, underscore the importance of compassionate empathy and humility. The teachings of Daoism and Buddhism have been practiced for centuries and have far-reaching implications for Easterners' altruistic behavior. Another worldview that guides their acts of kindness is that all beings are equal and equally worthy. It is therefore imperative to be respectful to not just human beings but also all living beings. While a culture-bound perspective helps paint a rich picture of altruism, the ways to evoke the better angels of our nature vary cross-culturally. Yet, despite these differences, altruism is arguably a positive force within our community and is surely within everyone's reach.

東方的利他文化

■ 回答以下問題，確認自己是否正確理解整篇文章的大意：

Q1. _____ Altruism is motivated by self-interest. (T/F)

Q2. _____ Altruism is voluntary. (T/F)

Q3. _____ Altruism has only one explanation. (T/F)

Q4. _____ Culturally motivated altruism can be observed in Eastern cultures. (T/F)

Q5. _____ Altruism involves material donations only. (T/F)

細讀 Close reading

請用 60 秒的時間仔細閱讀以下內容，並回答問題。

While a culture-bound perspective helps paint a rich picture of altruism, the ways to evoke the better angels of our nature vary cross-culturally. Yet, despite these differences, altruism is arguably a positive force within our community and is surely within everyone's reach.

_____ Q1. According to this passage, which of the following is correct?
     (A) Altruism is a colorful picture.
     (B) Altruism is practiced in the same way cross-culturally.
     (C) Altruism can be practiced by certain people only.
     (D) Altruism can be understood from a cultural perspective.

_____ Q2. According to this passage, how would altruism affect our community?
     (A) positively
     (B) neutrally
     (C) negatively
     (D) unconsciously

▶▶ 解答請見 p.339

STEP 4 高理解速讀 Speed Reading with Greater Comprehension

請用 90 秒的時間，看完整篇文章。然後跟著每一個有意義的色塊，提升理解的速度。（請盡量試著不查自己不認識的字，利用前後文去推測意思。）

4.2

藝術、歷史與文化 Art, History & Culture

Altruism, in the most general terms, is acting voluntarily in the best interest of others rather than in one's own self-interest, involving self-sacrifice in terms of time, money, or other resources with no expectation of reward. Many people are wired to be sympathetic not just to those they know or relate to but also to strangers. For example, some would give thousands of dollars to a charity or volunteer for overseas duty in the Peace Corps. There are also people who volunteer to undergo major surgery to remove one of their own healthy kidneys and have it transplanted into a complete stranger who is ill and dying.

利他
的定義

Many explanations have been offered to explain altruistic acts. Psychologists argue that the answer emerges from a brain sensitive to other people's emotions. This argument suggests that we can feel empathy for other people's distress. On the other hand, social scientists observe that cultural understandings help unlock valuable insights into the emergence of altruism since altruistic beliefs and acts can be motivated by different cultural values and norms.

利他行
為發生
的原因

In Western cultures, people have ingrained tendencies to act altruistically. In particular, equity, diversity, and inclusion are key drivers of their helping behavior. In keeping with the collective moral codes, all are equally worthy of help, and no one should be denied an equal opportunity to thrive due to their ethnicity, nationality, socioeconomic status, sexual orientation, and disability. Since Westerners' altruistic acts are motivated by community values and morals, diversity is embraced and all members of the community should feel welcomed and valued. This community ethos is to create a sustainable climate of inclusion where people care about the welfare of others. As a result, when seeing others in pain or in need of help, they would respond compassionately and would not excuse themselves from stepping in.

西方的
利他文
化

Culturally derived altruism can also be observed in Eastern cultures. Daoism and Buddhism, as integral parts of cultural heritage, underscore the importance of compassionate empathy and humility. The teachings of Daoism and Buddhism have been practiced for centuries and have far-reaching implications for Easterners' altruistic behavior. Another worldview that guides their acts of kindness is that all beings are equal and equally worthy. It is therefore imperative to be respectful to not just human beings but also all living beings. While a culture-bound perspective helps paint a rich picture of altruism, the ways to evoke the better angels of our nature vary cross-culturally. Yet, despite these differences, altruism is arguably a positive force within our community and is surely within everyone's reach.

東方的
利他文
化

■ 請回答以下問題：

_____ Q1. Which of the following is NOT altruism?

(A) to donate a healthy kidney to a stranger

(B) to borrow a book from a library

(C) to engage in volunteer activities

(D) to engage in charitable activities

_____ Q2. What is a possible explanation for altruistic behavior?

(A) a military order

(B) a government mandate

(C) a school requirement

(D) a brain sensitive to others' needs and distress

_____ Q3. Which of the following is NOT motivated by altruism in Western cultures?

(A) equity

(B) diversity

(C) humility

(D) inclusion

_____ Q4. Whether a person deserves an equal opportunity depends on
   (A) ethnicity.
   (B) socioeconomic status.
   (C) sexual orientation.
   (D) none of the above.

_____ Q5. Which of the following can be concluded from the passage?
   (A) Human compassion and empathy exist in both Eastern and Western cultures.
   (B) Altruistic acts in Eastern cultures are necessarily religious.
   (C) People do not donate their healthy kidneys in Eastern cultures.
   (D) Psychologists and social scientists share the same view on altruism.

▶▶ 解答請見 p.340

4.2.3_S.mp3

STEP 5 跟讀 Shadowing

　　請根據母語人士所錄製的音檔，一句一句跟著唸。跟讀時請使用跟讀音檔，每句結束後，請利用句與句之間的空秒時間，複誦前面所聽到的句子。建議第一遍，看著文章跟著唸，第二遍則不看文章，只聽音檔唸。

4.2.3_L.mp3

STEP 6 聽讀 Listening

第一遍
→ 讀者會聽到音檔內母語人士完整且不間斷將本文唸一遍。試著不看文章，聽音檔內的母語人士完整且不間斷地將本文唸一遍，確認自己哪裡聽懂，那裡聽不懂。

第二遍
→ 再聽母語人士不間斷地將本文唸一遍，眼睛注視著正在朗誦的每個句子，針對自己沒聽懂的部分，特別仔細閱讀。

單字 Vocabulary

❶ **charity** [ˋtʃærətɪ]	n. 慈善單位 She gave much of her savings to charity last month. 她上個月捐出大部份儲蓄給慈善單位。
❷ **humility** [hjʊˋmɪlɪtɪ]	n. 謙遜 It is usually good to show humility. 表現謙遜通常是一件好事。
❸ **distress** [dɪˋstrɛs]	n. 悲痛 That he dropped out of school caused his mother great distress. 他退學一事給他母親帶來巨大的悲痛。
❹ **ingrained** [ɪnˋgrend]	adj. 根深蒂固的 It is very difficult to break ingrained habits. 想要改掉根深蒂固的習慣非常困難。
❺ **sustainable** [səˋstenəbl]	adj. 能夠長期維持的 It is central banks' responsibility to achieve sustainable economic growth. 維持長期的經濟成長是中央銀行的責任。
❻ **compassionate** [kəmˋpæʃənet]	adj. 有同情心的 Her response to this shooting was compassionate. 她對這次槍擊事件展現出有同情心的回應。
❼ **integral** [ɪnˋtɛgrəl]	adj. 不可或缺的，完整的 Academic rigor is integral to research at universities. 學術的嚴謹性是大學研究工作不可或缺的一環。
❽ **far-reaching** [ˌfɑrˋritʃɪŋ]	adj. （影響等）深遠的 The Supreme Court of the U.S. issued a far-reaching decision last week. 美國最高法院上週發布了一項影響深遠的決議。

4.2

藝術、歷史與文化 Art, History & Culture

❾ **underscore** [ˌʌndəˈskɔr]	v. 強調 The new President of the University of Pennsylvania underscored in her speech last week the University's commitment to equity, diversity, and inclusion. 賓州大學新任校長上週演講時強調賓州大學對於平等、多元、與共融的重視。
❿ **evoke** [ɪˈvok]	v. 喚起 These photographs evoked memories of my childhood. 這些照片喚起了我的兒時記憶。

慣用語和片語 Expressions and Phrases

❶ in the most general terms　通俗地說

A hostel, in the most general terms, is a hotel in which people need to share bathrooms.

通俗地說，青年旅館是一種需要與他人共用浴室的旅館。

❷ the point of departure　出發點

Semantics is the point of departure for his linguistic research.

語意學是他研究語言學的出發點。

❸ in keeping with　與…一致

In keeping with our family tradition, we get together for breakfast once a week.

為了符合我們的家族傳統，我們每週都會一起吃一次早餐。

❹ within reach　可以做到的，可達成的

With hard work, I feel my goals are almost within reach.

經過努力工作，我覺得我的目標幾乎是垂手可得了。

A. Fill in the blanks with suitable words or phrases 將適合的字詞填入空格中

ⓐ sustainable　**ⓑ** ingrained　**ⓒ** integral　**ⓓ** far-reaching

1. Responsibility is _____ to this position.

2. _____ growth of a company is important to its shareholders.

3. The idea of altruism is _____ in most people in this country.

4. The new policy will have _____ implications for the insurance industry.

B. Multiple choice questions 選擇題（可利用此題型熟悉多益、英檢考試）

_____ 1. This movie ------- our memories of the past.
(A) carped　(B) defied　(C) certified　(D) evoked

_____ 2. She has been working so hard that her goals are -------.
(A) far away　　(B) within reach
(C) from abroad　(D) without exception

_____ 3. She is a woman of great -------, always treating others with respect.
(A) humility　(B) arrogance　(C) paradox　(D) superiority

_____ 4. Students need to show up on time, ------- classroom regulations.
(A) inconsistent with　(B) contrary to
(C) different from　　(D) in keeping with

_____ 5. The President ------- the urgency of gun control legislation.
(A) navigated　(B) underscored　(C) imprisoned　(D) underwent

▶▶ 解答請見 p.341

4.2

藝術、歷史與文化 Art, History & Culture

4.3 疫情與健康保健
Pandemic & Health Care

Part 1 The Mental Health Impacts of COVID-19
（新冠疫情對心理健康造成的影響）

Did you know?
[你需要知道的 10 件事]

❶ 新冠病毒與一般感冒病毒都是 RNA 病毒，極易變異。

❷ 感染新冠病毒康復之後，仍可能有長期的副作用。

❸ 一般感冒病毒主要攻擊上呼吸道。

❹ 新冠病毒能夠直接攻擊下呼吸道，引起肺炎。

❺ 新冠病毒會引起典型的呼吸道症狀，例如喉嚨痛。

❻ 新冠病毒也會引起非典型的症狀，例如嗅覺異常、心肌炎等。

❼ 許多學子因疫情停課，居家線上學習，失去正常的社交學習活動。

❽ 許多行業（例如餐飲業、旅遊業等）受到新冠疫情的嚴重影響。

❾ 新冠疫情期間多國實行長達 14 天的入境檢疫隔離及確診隔離。

❿ 少數國家實施強制封城的措施，限制民眾的行動自由。

Must-know vocabulary
[你需要知道的 10 個單字]

❶ the respiratory system *n.* 呼吸系統

❷ pandemic *n.* 全球性傳染病

❸ quarantine *n.* 檢疫隔離

❹ lockdown *n.* 封城

❺ toll *n.* 代價

❻ anxiety *n.* 焦慮

❼ measure *n.* 措施

❽ well-being *n.* 健康幸福

❾ extracurricular activity *n.* 課外活動

❿ meditate v. 冥想

掃讀的目標是在文章中搜尋特定的人名、時間、地點，或相關詞語，就像是在電話簿中搜尋某人的電話號碼一樣，其他內容完全不看。

■ 請於 **30** 秒內在以下文章中找出下列文字並畫線，不要閱讀內容或嘗試理解文章。

❶ the respiratory system   ❷ pandemic

❸ quarantine   ❹ lockdown

❺ toll   ❻ anxiety

❼ measure   ❽ well-being

❾ extracurricular activity   ❿ meditate

....

The Mental Health Impacts of COVID-19

(411 words)   By Yushiang Jou

COVID-19 can cause a range of known and unknown illnesses. For the most part, discussions surrounding COVID-19 have focused on its impact on the respiratory system and other major organs across the body. Yet, the toll of COVID-19 is not entirely physical. The COVID-19 pandemic has had social and economic consequences in unprecedented ways. Tens of millions of people have lost their jobs and the economy is slowing down. In consequence, the pandemic has been stressful and continues to harm the mental health and well-being of people around the world.

Most people feel frustrated or stressed at this time of uncertainty. According to the World Health Organization, the COVID-19 pandemic has contributed to a significant increase in prevalence of anxiety and depression worldwide. Many people constantly worry about their own health and that of their loved ones who may have been exposed to the virus. Moreover, the measures to break the chain of transmission, such as lockdowns and quarantines, have evoked lingering feelings of frustration. People can also experience loneliness and suffer from depression caused by social isolation. For individuals with pre-existing mental health conditions, their symptoms may well be exacerbated by postponed or skipped doctor's visits.

4.3

疫情與健康保健 Pandemic & Health Care

While all of us have been affected by COVID-19, children and adolescents are particularly vulnerable to disruptions this pandemic has caused. Due to the closure of schools, some of them are left behind. Many have had to shift between online and classroom learning at different stages of the pandemic. According to the United Nations International Children's Emergency Fund, the mental state of children and adolescents has been adversely affected as a result of school closures, the suspension from extracurricular activities, and a lack of interaction with their peers.

To cope with the stress caused by the pandemic, one can try different ways to promote mental well-being. For starters, being unable to get together with family and friends can add to the sense of emotional isolation. To stay connected with them virtually can help combat loneliness. While keeping up with the news can be important, excessive exposure to media coverage of the pandemic can be upsetting and can cause emotional stress. For people who have difficulty sleeping at night, maintaining a regular sleep schedule and avoiding technology for an hour before bedtime can help relieve stress and get better sleep. Taking deep breaths or meditating can be helpful as well. With these recommendations, we may be able to get through difficult times in one piece.

■ 請選擇正確的意思

_____ ❶ the respiratory system　(A) 呼吸系統 (B) 生態系統

_____ ❷ pandemic　(A) 全球性傳染病 (B) 地區性傳染病

_____ ❸ quarantine　(A) 封城 (B) 檢疫隔離

_____ ❹ lockdown　(A) 封城 (B) 檢疫隔離

_____ ❺ toll　(A) 代價 (B) 收穫

_____ ❻ anxiety　(A) 興奮 (B) 焦慮

_____ ❼ measure　(A) 破口 (B) 措施

_____ ❽ well-being　(A) 健康幸福 (B) 萎靡不振

_____ ❾ extracurricular activity　(A) 課業活動 (B) 課外活動

_____ ❿ meditate　(A) 焦躁 (B) 冥想

▶▶ 解答請見 p.343

針對剛才的文章，用 30 秒鐘瀏覽各段的第一句，粗略了解文章結構與大意即可。

COVID-19 can cause a range of known and unknown illnesses. For the most part, discussions surrounding COVID-19 have focused on its impact on the respiratory system and other major organs across the body. Yet, the toll of COVID-19 is not entirely physical. The COVID-19 pandemic has had social and economic consequences in unprecedented ways. Tens of millions of people have lost their jobs and the economy is slowing down. In consequence, the pandemic has been stressful and continues to harm the mental health and well-being of people around the world.

新冠疫情危害身心健康

Most people feel frustrated or stressed at this time of uncertainty. According to the World Health Organization, the COVID-19 pandemic has contributed to a significant increase in prevalence of anxiety and depression worldwide. Many people constantly worry about their own health and that of their loved ones who may have been exposed to the virus. Moreover, the measures to break the chain of transmission, such as lockdowns and quarantines, have evoked lingering feelings of frustration. People can also experience loneliness and suffer from depression caused by social isolation. For individuals with pre-existing mental health conditions, their symptoms may well be exacerbated by postponed or skipped doctor's visits.

危害身心健康的原因

4.3

疫情與健康保健 Pandemic & Health Care

While all of us have been affected by COVID-19, children and adolescents are particularly vulnerable to disruptions this pandemic has caused. Due to the closure of schools, some of them are left behind. Many have had to shift between online and classroom learning at different stages of the pandemic. According to the United Nations International Children's Emergency Fund, the mental state of children and adolescents has been adversely affected as a result of school closures, the suspension from extracurricular activities, and a lack of interaction with their peers.

孩童與青少年受影響的原因

To cope with the stress caused by the pandemic, one can try different ways to promote mental well-being. For starters, being unable to get together with family and friends can add to the sense of emotional isolation. To stay connected with them virtually can help combat loneliness. While keeping up with the news can be important, excessive exposure to media coverage of the pandemic can be upsetting and can cause emotional stress. For people who have difficulty sleeping at night, maintaining a regular sleep schedule and avoiding technology for an hour before bedtime can help relieve stress and get better sleep. Taking deep breaths or meditating can be helpful as well. With these recommendations, we may be able to get through difficult times in one piece.

保持身
心健康
的建議

■ 回答以下問題，確認自己是否正確理解整篇文章的大意：

Q1. _____ We are familiar with health problems caused by COVID-19. (T/F)

Q2. _____ We are equally affected by COVID-19. (T/F)

Q3. _____ Children are least affected by COVID-19. (T/F)

Q4. _____ There is only one way to promote mental health. (T/F)

Q5. _____ Many people do not feel happy due to COVID-19. (T/F)

▶▶ 解答請見 p.343

STEP 3 細讀 Close reading

請用 60 秒的時間仔細閱讀以下內容，並回答問題。

COVID-19 can cause a range of known and unknown illnesses. For the most part, discussions surrounding COVID-19 have focused on its impact on the respiratory system and other major organs across the body. Yet, the toll of COVID-19 is not entirely physical. The COVID-19 pandemic has had social and economic consequences in unprecedented ways. Tens of millions of people have lost their jobs and the economy is slowing down. In consequence, the pandemic has been stressful and continues to harm the mental health and well-being of people around the world.

_____ Q1. According to this passage, which of the following is correct?
     (A) The impacts of COVID-19 are simply physical.
     (B) COVID-19 harms only one organ.
     (C) People have paid less attention to mental health problems caused by COVID-19.
     (D) The mental health impacts of COVID-19 are temporary.

_____ Q2. According to this passage, which of the following is incorrect?
     (A) The pandemic has had social impacts.
     (B) The pandemic has had economic impacts.
     (C) Many people have lost their jobs because of the pandemic.
     (D) The pandemic has been stressful only for those who lost their jobs.

▶▶ 解答請見 p.343

STEP 4 高理解速讀 Speed Reading with Greater Comprehension

請用 90 秒的時間，看完整篇文章。然後跟著每一個有意義的色塊，提升理解的速度。（請盡量試著不查自己不認識的字，利用前後文去推測意思。）

COVID-19 can cause a range of known and unknown illnesses. For the most part, discussions surrounding COVID-19 have focused on its impact on the respiratory system and other major organs across the body. Yet, the toll of COVID-19 is not entirely physical. The COVID-19 pandemic has had social and economic consequences in unprecedented ways. Tens of millions of people have lost their jobs and the economy is slowing down. In consequence, the pandemic has been stressful and continues to harm the mental health and well-being of people around the world.

新冠疫情危害身心健康

Most people feel frustrated or stressed at this time of uncertainty. According to the World Health Organization, the COVID-19 pandemic has contributed to a significant increase in prevalence of anxiety and depression worldwide. Many people constantly worry about their own health and that of their loved ones who may have been exposed to the virus. Moreover, the measures to break the chain of transmission, such as lockdowns and quarantines, have evoked lingering feelings of frustration. People can also experience loneliness and suffer from depression caused by social isolation. For individuals with pre-existing mental health conditions, their symptoms may well be exacerbated by postponed or skipped doctor's visits.

While all of us have been affected by COVID-19, children and adolescents are particularly vulnerable to disruptions this pandemic has caused. Due to the closure of schools, some of them are left behind. Many have had to shift between online and classroom learning at different stages of the pandemic. According to the United Nations International Children's Emergency Fund, the mental state of children and adolescents has been adversely affected as a result of school closures, the suspension from extracurricular activities, and a lack of interaction with their peers.

To cope with the stress caused by the pandemic, one can try different ways to promote mental well-being. For starters, being unable to get together with family and friends can add to the sense of emotional isolation. To stay connected with them virtually can help combat loneliness. While keeping up with the news can be important, excessive exposure to media coverage of the pandemic can be upsetting and can cause emotional stress. For people who have difficulty sleeping at night, maintaining a regular sleep schedule and avoiding technology for an hour before bedtime can help relieve stress and get better sleep. Taking deep breaths or meditating can be helpful as well. With these recommendations, we may be able to get through difficult times in one piece.

■ 請回答以下問題：

_____ Q1. COVID-19 can have an impact on _____.
      (A) the heart
      (B) the upper respiratory system
      (C) the lower respiratory system
      (D) all of the above

_____ Q2. According to this article, the COVID-19 pandemic can cause _____.
      (A) depression   (B) anxiety   (C) pressure   (D) all of the above

_____ Q3. The measures to break the chain of transmission include _____.
      (A) lockdown   (B) quarantine
      (C) self-isolation   (D) all of the above

_____ Q4. What adversely affected the mental state of children and adolescents?
      (A) their return to school
      (B) interaction with their peers
      (C) suspension from extracurricular activities
      (D) all of the above

_____ Q5. What can be helpful for people who have difficulty sleeping at night?
      (A) using their cellphones
      (B) maintaining a regular meals schedule
      (C) meditating
      (D) all of the above

▶▶ 解答請見 p.344

4.3.1_S.mp3

STEP 5 跟讀 Shadowing

    請根據母語人士所錄製的音檔，一句一句跟著唸。跟讀時請使用跟讀音檔，每句結束後，請利用句與句之間的空秒時間，複誦前面所聽到的句子。建議第一遍，看著文章跟著唸，第二遍則不看文章，只聽音檔唸。

STEP 6 聽讀 Listening

第一遍

→ 讀者會聽到音檔內母語人士完整且不間斷將本文唸一遍。試著不看文章，聽音檔內的母語人士完整且不間斷地將本文唸一遍，確認自己哪裡聽懂，那裡聽不懂。

第二遍

→ 再聽母語人士不間斷地將本文唸一遍，眼睛注視著正在朗誦的每個句子，針對自己沒聽懂的部分，特別仔細閱讀。

STEP 7 延伸學習

單字 Vocabulary

❶ **toll** [tol]	n. 代價，喪鐘 The war took a heavy toll and many soldiers died. 這場戰爭的代價慘重，許多士兵都陣亡了。
❷ **physical** [ˋfɪzɪk!]	adj. 身體方面的，生理上的 He has been in physical pain for many years. 他承受肉體上的疼痛很多年了。
❸ **unprecedented** [ʌnˋprɛsə͵dɛntɪd]	adj. 前所未有的 The company is facing an unprecedented challenge. 這間公司正面臨前所未有的挑戰。
❹ **stress** [strɛs]	v. 感到有壓力，擔心 He is stressing about the heavy workload. 沉重的工作量讓他感覺壓力很大。
❺ **evoke** [ɪˋvok]	v. 引起 His speech evoked a positive response from the audience. 觀眾對他的演講反應正面。
❻ **exacerbate** [ɪgˋzæsə͵bet]	v. 使惡化 High inflation is exacerbated by the war in Ukraine. 烏克蘭的戰事更加惡化了高通膨的問題。

❼ disruption [dɪsˈrʌpʃən]	n.（行程等）中斷 The traffic accident caused disruptions in bus service. 這場交通事故中斷了公車的服務。
❽ adversely [ædˈvɝslɪ]	adv. 不利地 The drone was adversely affected by the bad weather. 惡劣天氣對無人機產生了不利的影響。
❾ suspension [səˈspɛnʃən]	n. 中止 Both countries were disappointed by the suspension of peace talks. 兩國對於中止和平談判感到失望。
❿ excessive [ɪkˈsɛsɪv]	adj. 過多的 Excessive exercise can be problematic sometimes. 運動過度有時也會有問題。

慣用語和片語 Expressions and Phrases

❶ contribute to 導致，造成

Heavy drinking contributed to his death.
酗酒造成了他的死亡。

❷ shift between 在…之間交替／更迭

The financial market shifts between good and bad times.
金融市場在繁榮與蕭條之間交替更迭。

❸ get through 渡過（難關等）

They do not know how to get through the winter without the heat.
沒有暖氣，他們不知道該如何渡過這個冬天。

❹ in one piece 全身而退

They returned from the war in one piece.
他們從戰場上平安歸來。

4.3

疫情與健康保健 Pandemic & Health Care

A. Fill in the blanks with suitable words or phrases 將適合的字詞填入空格中

ⓐ evoke   ⓑ in one piece   ⓒ unprecedented   ⓓ exacerbate

1. This political situation is _____. We have never seen this before.

2. The unemployment problem has been _____ by the trade war.
   There are more jobless workers now.

3. Her speech _____ negative responses from the audience. Nobody liked it.

4. They ended the trade war _____.

B. Multiple choice questions 選擇題（可利用此題型熟悉多益、英檢考試）

_____ 1. The death ------- from the earthquake is not yet known.
   (A) toll   (B) scope   (C) quota   (D) woe

_____ 2. Although John was unable to walk, he did not let his -------
   disability prevent him from doing what he wanted to do.
   (A) spiritual   (B) psychological   (C) mental   (D) physical

_____ 3. Unfortunately sales were ------- affected by high inflation.
   (A) beneficially   (B) adversely   (C) harmlessly   (D) fragrantly

_____ 4. ------- drinking is bad for our health.
   (A) Excessive   (B) Insufficient   (C) Irregular   (D) Witty

_____ 5. Her medicine helped her ------- the pain.
   (A) work out   (B) add up   (C) get through   (D) suffer from

▶▶ 解答請見 p.345

NOTE

Did you know?

[你需要知道的 10 件事]

❶ 疫苗幫助人類克服了許多傳染病，例如天花、麻疹、小兒麻痺等。

❷ 疫苗施打在健康的人身上，所以安全性是關鍵考量，因此疫苗的研製曠日經久。

❸ 由於新冠疫情快速蔓延，新冠疫苗研發的時間短暫，多以緊急許可的方式讓民眾接種。

❹ 新冠疫苗為有史以來最快製造出來的疫苗。

❺ 有許多人因為健康因素不適合施打新冠疫苗。

❻ 有許多人因為宗教或政治因素不願意施打新冠疫苗。

❼ 世界各國於 2021 年起紛紛推出疫苗強制令。

❽ 許多不願意施打疫苗的人被迫離職或失去工作機會。

❾ 世界上許多大學反對師生疫苗強制令。

❿ 疫苗與外科手術同是醫療行為，需要自願性的同意。

Must-know vocabulary

[你需要知道的 10 個單字]

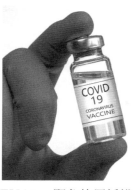

❶ mass production *n.* 量產

❷ clinical trial *n.* 臨床試驗

❸ side effect *n.* 副作用

❹ voluntary consent *n.* 自願同意

❺ incriminating claim *n.* 指控

❻ mandatory *adj.* 強制的

❼ death toll *n.* 死亡人數

❽ Emergency Use Authorization (EUA) *n.* 緊急使用授權

❾ cyber-bully *n.* 網路霸凌者

❿ pharmaceutical *adj.* 製藥的

掃讀的目標是在文章中搜尋特定的人名、時間、地點，或相關詞語，就像是在電話簿中搜尋某人的電話號碼一樣，其他內容完全不看。

■ 請於 **30** 秒內在以下文章中找出下列文字並畫線，不要閱讀內容或嘗試理解文章。

❶ mass production
❷ clinical trials
❸ side effects
❹ death toll
❺ pharmaceutical
❻ Emergency Use Authorization (EUA)
❼ mandatory
❽ voluntary consent
❾ cyber-bully
❿ incriminating claims

Controversies over COVID-19 Vaccine Mandates

(460 words)   By Yushiang Jou

The world's first vaccine was developed in 1796 by Edward Jenner, a British physician whose seminal work led to the development of the smallpox vaccine and helped eradicate smallpox from the world. A variety of other vaccines have also been developed to date, saving many lives each year. Before each vaccine is approved for mass production, it undergoes clinical trials that are rigorous and time-consuming. Despite these efforts, vaccines are not perfectly safe since people have different reactions to vaccines. Common side effects include, for example, swelling, muscle pain, tiredness, and fever. In some rare cases, negative reactions can be severe and even result in death.

In 2020, people once again pinned their hopes on vaccines in the wake of the outbreak of SARS-CoV-2, aka COVID-19. Up until the end of 2022, COVID-19 has killed more than 6.5 million people worldwide, with over 650 million infected, according to the World Health Organization. In an effort to reduce the death toll, pharmaceutical companies rolled out COVID-19 vaccines in less than one year. Accelerated from development to deployment, COVID-19 vaccines were the fastest

4.3

疫情與健康保健 Pandemic & Health Care

vaccines that had ever been developed. These vaccines have been authorized under an Emergency Use Authorization (EUA) by the Food and Drug Administration (FDA), which claims that the benefits outweigh the risks.

In the worldwide battle against this common enemy, how have universities tackled the pandemic with the rollout of COVID-19 vaccines? To prevent people from being hospitalized and dying, most universities in the U.S. require that faculty, staff, and students be fully vaccinated. On the other end of the spectrum, some people are set against the idea of being mandatorily vaccinated for medical, religious, or political reasons. In consequence, there has been heated debate about whether vaccine mandates should be lifted. In fact, COVID-19 vaccination is not mandatory at universities in countries such as the U.K. and Canada.

Although many universities in the world believe that voluntary consent to vaccination, as is the case with all medical procedures, is a fundamental human right, it is not uncommon that the unvaccinated feel bullied for not being vaccinated. Online haters or cyberbullies, for example, often call them names and hold the unvaccinated accountable for spreading the virus and causing others' deaths. Their incriminating claims, however, are not supported by scientific evidence. Researchers at the University of Colorado, the University of California, San Francisco, and the University of Oxford investigated how the vaccinated and unvaccinated were protected against COVID-19 variants. Their studies found no significant differences in the likelihood of being infected, suggesting that both the vaccinated and unvaccinated are likely to be infected and are capable of spreading the virus once infected. Despite these findings, some turn a blind eye to evidence at odds with their deeply held beliefs.

■ 請選擇正確的意思

_____ ❶ mass production　(A) 限量 (B) 量產

_____ ❷ clinical trial　(A) 臨床實驗 (B) 動物實驗

_____ ❸ side effect　(A) 保護力 (B) 副作用

_____ ❹ death toll　(A) 死亡人數 (B) 生還人數

_____ ❺ pharmaceutical　(A) 製藥的 (B) 疫苗的

_____ ❻ Emergency Use Authorization　(A) 正式授權許可 (B) 緊急授權許可

_____ ❼ mandatory　(A) 自願的 (B) 強迫的

_____ ❽ voluntary consent　(A) 自願同意 (B) 強迫

_____ ❾ cyber-bully　(A) 網路執法人員 (B) 網路霸凌者

_____ ❿ incriminating claim　(A) 指控 (B) 讚揚

▶▶ 解答請見 p.347

STEP 2 略讀 Skimming

針對剛才的文章，用 30 秒鐘瀏覽各段的第一句，粗略了解文章結構與大意即可。

The world's first vaccine was developed in 1796 by Edward Jenner, a British physician whose seminal work led to the development of the smallpox vaccine and helped eradicate smallpox from the world. A variety of other vaccines have also been developed to date, saving many lives each year. Before each vaccine is approved for mass production, it undergoes clinical trials that are rigorous and time-consuming. Despite these efforts, vaccines are not perfectly safe since people have different reactions to vaccines. Common side effects include, for example, swelling, muscle pain, tiredness, and fever. In some rare cases, negative reactions can be severe and even result in death.

歷史上首支成功的疫苗

4.3

疫情與健康保健 Pandemic & Health Care

In 2020, people once again pinned their hopes on vaccines in the wake of the outbreak of SARS-CoV-2, aka COVID-19. Up until the end of. 2022, COVID-19 has killed more than 6.5 million people worldwide, with over 650 million infected, according to the World Health Organization. In an effort to reduce the death toll, pharmaceutical companies rolled out COVID-19 vaccines in less than

人們也希望利用疫苗結束新冠疫情

one year. Accelerated from development to deployment, COVID-19 vaccines were the fastest vaccines that had ever been developed. These vaccines have been authorized under an Emergency Use Authorization (EUA) by the Food and Drug Administration (FDA), which claims that the benefits outweigh the risks.

In the worldwide battle against this common enemy, how have universities tackled the pandemic with the rollout of COVID-19 vaccines? To prevent people from being hospitalized and dying, most universities in the U.S. require that faculty, staff, and students be fully vaccinated. On the other end of the spectrum, some people are set against the idea of being mandatorily vaccinated for medical, religious, or political reasons. In consequence, there has been heated debate about whether vaccine mandates should be lifted. In fact, COVID-19 vaccination is not mandatory at universities in countries such as the U.K. and Canada.

大學如何看待利用疫苗對抗疫情？

Although many universities in the world believe that voluntary consent to vaccination, as is the case with all medical procedures, is a fundamental human right, it is not uncommon that the unvaccinated feel bullied for not being vaccinated. Online haters or cyberbullies, for example, often call them names and hold the unvaccinated accountable for spreading the virus and causing others' deaths. Their incriminating claims, however, are not supported by scientific evidence. Researchers at the University of Colorado, the University of California, San Francisco, and the University of Oxford investigated how the vaccinated and unvaccinated were protected against COVID-19 variants. Their studies found no significant differences in the likelihood of being infected, suggesting that both the vaccinated and unvaccinated are likely to be infected and are capable of spreading the virus once infected. Despite these findings, some turn a blind eye to evidence at odds with their deeply held beliefs.

疫苗霸凌屢見不鮮

■ 回答以下問題，確認自己是否正確理解整篇文章的大意：

Q1. _____ Vaccines have been around for a long time. (T/F)

Q2. _____ There are no smallpox patients today. (T/F)

Q3. _____ The smallpox vaccine protected people from COVID-19 in 2020. (T/F)

Q4. _____ The unvaccinated people have been bullied. (T/F)

Q5. _____ Voluntary consent to vaccination is a human right. (T/F)

▶▶ 解答請見 p.347

STEP 3 細讀 Close reading

請用 60 秒的時間仔細閱讀以下內容，並回答問題。

In an effort to reduce the death toll, pharmaceutical companies rolled out COVID-19 vaccines in less than one year. Accelerated from development to deployment, COVID-19 vaccines were the fastest vaccines that had ever been developed. These vaccines have been authorized under an Emergency Use Authorization (EUA) by the Food and Drug Administration (FDA), which claims that the benefits outweigh the risks.

_____ Q1. According to this passage, which of the following is correct?

(A) The risks of COVID-19 vaccines are well known.

(B) The FDA has authorized COVID-19 vaccines.

(C) Accelerated vaccines are the best vaccines.

(D) COVID-19 vaccines have no risks.

_____ Q2. According to this passage, why have COVID-19 vaccines been authorized under an EUA?

(A) There wasn't enough time for the development of these vaccines.

(B) EUA authorized vaccines are the same as fully authorized vaccines.

(C) These vaccines have been perfectly developed.

(D) These vaccines have been developed for a long time.

▶▶ 解答請見 p.347

4.3

疫情與健康保健 Pandemic & Health Care

請用 90 秒的時間，看完整篇文章。然後跟著每一個有意義的色塊，提升理解的速度。（請盡量試著不查自己不認識的字，利用前後文去推測意思。）

The world's first vaccine was developed in 1796 by Edward Jenner, a British physician whose seminal work led to the development of the smallpox vaccine and helped eradicate smallpox from the world. A variety of other vaccines have also been developed to date, saving many lives each year. Before each vaccine is approved for mass production, it undergoes clinical trials that are rigorous and time-consuming. Despite these efforts, vaccines are not perfectly safe since people have different reactions to vaccines. Common side effects include, for example, swelling, muscle pain, tiredness, and fever. In some rare cases, negative reactions can be severe and even result in death.

歷史上首支成功的疫苗

In 2020, people once again pinned their hopes on vaccines in the wake of the outbreak of SARS-CoV-2, aka COVID-19. Up until the end of. 2022, COVID-19 has killed more than 6.5 million people worldwide, with over 650 million infected, according to the World Health Organization. In an effort to reduce the death toll, pharmaceutical companies rolled out COVID-19 vaccines in less than one year. Accelerated from development to deployment, COVID-19 vaccines were the fastest vaccines that had ever been developed. These vaccines have been authorized under an Emergency Use Authorization (EUA) by the Food and Drug Administration (FDA), which claims that the benefits outweigh the risks.

人們也希望利用疫苗結束新冠疫情

In the worldwide battle against this common enemy, how have universities tackled the pandemic with the rollout of COVID-19 vaccines? To prevent people from being hospitalized and dying, most universities in the U.S. require that faculty, staff, and students be fully

大學如何看待利用疫苗對抗疫情？

vaccinated. On the other end of the spectrum, some people are set against the idea of being mandatorily vaccinated for medical, religious, or political reasons. In consequence, there has been heated debate about whether vaccine mandates should be lifted. In fact, COVID-19 vaccination is not mandatory at universities in countries such as the U.K. and Canada.

Although many universities in the world believe that voluntary consent to vaccination, as is the case with all medical procedures, is a fundamental human right, it is not uncommon that the unvaccinated feel bullied for not being vaccinated. Online haters or cyberbullies, for example, often call them names and hold the unvaccinated accountable for spreading the virus and causing others' deaths. Their incriminating claims, however, are not supported by scientific evidence. Researchers at the University of Colorado, the University of California, San Francisco, and the University of Oxford investigated how the vaccinated and unvaccinated were protected against COVID-19 variants. Their studies found no significant differences in the likelihood of being infected, suggesting that both the vaccinated and unvaccinated are likely to be infected and are capable of spreading the virus once infected. Despite these findings, some turn a blind eye to evidence at odds with their deeply held beliefs.

疫苗霸
凌屢見
不鮮

■ 請回答以下問題：

_____ Q1. Which of the following is NOT a common side effect of vacciuation?
(A) swelling　　(B) tiredness　　(C) death　　(D) fever

_____ Q2. Which description of vaccines is incorrect?
(A) Vaccines save many lives each year.
(B) Vaccines are perfectly safe for everyone.
(C) Vaccines undergo time-consuming clinical trials.
(D) Vaccines can prevent people from being hospitalized.

_____ Q3. What is one of the researchers' findings?

(A) The vaccinated are capable of spreading the virus.

(B) The vaccinated are unlikely to be infected.

(C) The vaccinated are unlikely to be hospitalized due to infection.

(D) The vaccinated are unlikely to die of COVID-19.

_____ Q4. Which of the following is true about vaccine mandates?

(A) Some people in the world disagree with vaccine mandates.

(B) All the universities in the U.S. have vaccine mandates.

(C) Universities in the U.K. have vaccine mandates.

(D) Canadian universities have vaccine mandates.

_____ Q5. Edward Jenner

(A) was an American physician.

(B) did important research .

(C) helped eradicate COVID-19 from the world.

(D) died of smallpox.

▶▶ 解答請見 p.348

4.3.2_S.mp3

STEP 5 跟讀 Shadowing

　　請根據母語人士所錄製的音檔，一句一句跟著唸。跟讀時請使用跟讀音檔，每句結束後，請利用句與句之間的空秒時間，複誦前面所聽到的句子。建議第一遍，看著文章跟著唸，第二遍則不看文章，只聽音檔唸。

4.3.2_L.mp3

STEP 6 聽讀 Listening

第一遍

→ 讀者會聽到音檔內母語人士完整且不間斷將本文唸一遍。試著不看文章，聽音檔內的母語人士完整且不間斷地將本文唸一遍，確認自己哪裡聽懂，那裡聽不懂。

第二遍

→ 再聽母語人士不間斷地將本文唸一遍，眼睛注視著正在朗誦的每個句子，針對自己沒聽懂的部分，特別仔細閱讀。

單字 Vocabulary

1 seminal [ˈsɛmɪnəl]	adj. 有深遠影響的 She wrote a seminal article on linguistics ten years ago. 她十年前寫了一篇對語言學有深遠影響的文章。
2 eradicate [ɪˈrædɪket]	v. 根除 Scientists hope to eradicate this disease. 科學家希望根除這種疾病。
3 outbreak [ˈaʊtbrek]	n.（疾病、戰爭等的）爆發 There has been an outbreak of war in Ukraine. 烏克蘭爆發了一場戰爭。
4 rollout [ˈrolˌaʊt]	n. 首次推出 The iPhone has been a huge success since its rollout in 2007. iPhone 自從 2007 年首次推出以來一直相當成功。
5 lift [lɪft]	v. 撤銷（法令等） Vaccine mandates have been lifted in many countries. 在許多國家，疫苗強制令已經被撤銷了。
6 incriminating [ɪnˈkrɪmɪnetɪŋ]	adj. 指控他人有罪的 He made some incriminating statements last week. 他上週發表了一些指控他人有罪的言論。
7 pharmaceutical [ˌfɑrməˈsjutɪkəl]	adj. 製藥的 She is trying to buy a pharmaceutical company. 她嘗試要買下一家製藥公司。
8 consent [kənˈsɛnt]	n. 同意，允許 Preschoolers need to have the consent of their patents to be vaccinated. 幼兒園學童須家長同意之後才可以施打疫苗。

4.3

疫情與健康保健 Pandemic & Health Care

❾ mandatory [ˈmændət(ə)rɪ]	adj. 強制的 Two athletes failed mandatory drug tests before the Olympics game. 有兩名選手在奧運比賽前未能通過藥檢。
❿ bully [ˈbʊlɪ]	v. 霸凌 He was bullied at school. 他在學校遭到霸凌。

慣用語和片語 Expressions and Phrases

❶ in (the) wake of 在…發生之後

Gun control laws have been tightened in (the) wake of mass shootings.
在發生大規模槍擊案件之後，槍枝控管的法律一直是很嚴格的。

❷ on the other end of the spectrum 在另一個極端

Some people do not finish the food on their plates. On the other end of the spectrum, many die of famine.
有些人沒將自己的食物吃完。而在另個極端世界裡，許多人卻死於飢荒。

❸ turn a blind eye to 對…視而不見

The President turned a blind eye to the problem of inflation.
總統對於通膨的問題視而不見。

❹ at odds with 與…不同

She was at odds with her colleagues on the issue of gun control.
她與她的同事在槍枝管控的議題上意見相左。

A. Fill in the blanks with suitable words or phrases 將適合的字詞填入空格中

> **ⓐ** pharmaceutical **ⓑ** in the wake of **ⓒ** at odds with **ⓓ** turn a blind eye to

1. Many people have had the habit of wearing masks _____ the COVID-19 outbreak.

2. The mayor _____ widespread corruption in the city.

3. Sanofi is a famous _____ company, having manufactured many vaccines to date.

4. His conclusion was _____ that of the original paper.

B. Multiple choice questions 選擇題（可利用此題型熟悉多益、英檢考試）

_____ 1. This electric vehicle has attracted much attention since its ------- last year.
    (A) rundown   (B) rollout   (C) runaway   (D) roll-up

_____ 2. Thanks to the successful invention of vaccines, the disease had finally been -------.
    (A) eradicated   (B) abdicated   (C) chastised   (D) mandated

_____ 3. Her ------- book is a must-read for psychology majors.
    (A) malicious   (B) pathetic   (C) seminal   (D) irrelevant

_____ 4. This application is made up of a test and an interview. A written test is ------- before an interview.
    (A) mandatory   (B) optional   (C) selective   (D) competitive

_____ 5. The requirement has been ------- because of some controversies.
    (A) pleaded   (B) praised   (C) implemented   (D) lifted

▶▶ 解答請見 p.349

4.3

疫情與健康保健 Pandemic & Health Care

Did you know?

[你需要知道的 10 件事]

❶ 人體免疫系統是一個複雜的系統。
❷ 免疫力會增強，也會減弱，影響因素眾多。
❸ 嬰兒剛出生時，即帶有來自於母親的先天免疫力。
❹ 先天免疫力為從出生就有的終生免疫防護力，不針對特定病菌。
❺ 後天免疫是在出生之後才獲得的免疫防護力。
❻ 後天免疫機制只能針對某種病菌產生防護力。
❼ 後天免疫能夠維持多久並無定論。
❽ 疫苗提供未染病之健康人施打的醫療行為，能夠提升後天免疫力。
❾ 自然染疫或是施打疫苗都可以產生後天免疫力。
❿ 藥品能夠幫助患者在染病之後減輕症狀。

Must-know vocabulary

[你需要知道的 10 個單字]

❶ pathogen *n.* 病菌
❷ clinical course of infection *n.* 病程
❸ intruder *n.* 入侵者
❹ disease-causing *adj.* 致病的
❺ acquired immunity *n.* 後天免疫
❻ antibody *n.* 抗體
❼ immune memory *n.* 免疫記憶
❽ natural killer cell *n.* 天然殺手細胞
❾ immune cell *n.* 免疫細胞
❿ immune-boosting *adj.* 提升免疫力的

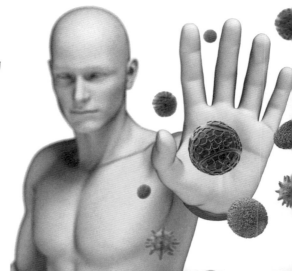

掃讀的目標是在文章中搜尋特定的人名、時間、地點，或相關詞語，就像是在電話簿中搜尋某人的電話號碼一樣，其他內容完全不看。

■ 請於 **30** 秒內在以下文章中找出下列文字並畫線，不要閱讀內容或嘗試理解文章。

1 pathogens
2 clinical course of infection
3 intruder
4 disease-causing
5 antibodies
6 acquired immunity
7 immune memory
8 natural killer cells
9 immune cells
10 immune-boosting

A Close-up of Human Immunity

(442 words)

By Yushiang Jou

Our body is under constant attack from pathogens (e.g., bacteria, viruses, and other disease-causing organisms) in the air we breathe and the food we eat. Human immunity is essential for preventing these pathogens from getting a foothold, playing a key role in determining the clinical course of infection. Specifically, human immunity has two fundamental lines of defense: innate and adaptive immunity.

Present from birth, innate immunity serves as the first line of defense against any intruders, reacting almost instantly to prevent pathogens from making their ways to our body. For example, a cut on the skin or a breach of the mucosal surface of our nose, throat, or intestines can result in redness and swelling, many immune cells immediately recruited to the site of infection. In most cases, innate immunity alone is capable of clearing the infection. Provided that the invader slips through, the innate immune system calls for help from the adaptive immune system. This is where adaptive immunity comes into play.

4.3

疫情與健康保健 Pandemic & Health Care

The adaptive immune system is the second line of defense, capable of differentiating between different types of pathogens and producing millions of antibodies to ward off the enemy. However, the adaptive immune system is slower in response and can take a few days or even weeks before it kicks in. This adaptive immunity is built up as we are exposed to diseases or are vaccinated. It is therefore also called acquired immunity for this reason.

One of the hallmarks of adaptive immunity is the capacity for memory, which can be protective as our body encounters the same intruder a second time. Yet, this immune memory is not always generated. For example, research on COVID-19 patients suggests that only those with severe infection were able to retain immune memory. Scientists have traditionally believed such memory is beyond the reach of the innate immune system and innate immune cells are unable to memorize the same pathogen should the body be exposed to it again. New evidence suggests that natural killer cells of the innate immune system are capable of memory-like responses, something previously thought to be possible only in the adaptive immune system.

To ensure that our innate and adaptive immune systems work effectively and efficiently, we need to give our immune cells the kind of nutrients they need, the most important of which are zinc, vitamin C, and vitamin D. Other daily supplementation such as propolis and echinacea can boost our immunity as well. Yet, boosting human immunity is much more than just taking immune-boosting nutritional supplements. The best way we can boost our immunity is to follow a healthy lifestyle, with a balanced diet, regular exercise, and sufficient sleep.

■ 請選擇正確的意思

_____ ❶ pathogens　(A) 生病 (B) 病菌

_____ ❷ clinical course of infection　(A) 病程 (B) 病歷

_____ ❸ intruder　(A) 來訪者 (B) 入侵者

_____ ❹ disease-causing　(A) 免除疾病的 (B) 致病的

_____ ❺ antibodies　(A) 抗體 (B) 病菌

_____ ❻ acquired immunity　(A) 後天免疫 (B) 先天免疫

_____ ❼ immune memory　(A) 短期記憶 (B) 免疫記憶

_____ ❽ natural killer cells　(A) 癌細胞 (B) 天然殺手細胞

_____ ❾ immune cells　(A) 免疫細胞 (B) 免疫系統

_____ ❿ immune-boosting　(A) 降低免疫力的 (B) 提升免疫力的

▸▸ 解答請見 p.351

STEP 2　略讀 Skimming

> 針對剛才的文章，用 30 秒鐘瀏覽各段的第一句，粗略了解文章結構與大意即可。

A Close-up of Human Immunity

Our body is under constant attack from pathogens (e.g., bacteria, viruses, and other disease-causing organisms) in the air we breathe and the food we eat. Human immunity is essential for preventing these pathogens from getting a foothold, playing a key role in determining the clinical course of infection. Specifically, human immunity has two fundamental lines of defense: innate and adaptive immunity.

各種病菌不斷侵害人體健康

Present from birth, innate immunity serves as the first line of defense against any intruders, reacting almost instantly to prevent pathogens from making their ways to our body. For example, a cut on the skin or a breach of the mucosal surface of our nose, throat, or intestines can result in redness and swelling, many immune cells immediately recruited to the site of infection. In most cases, innate immunity alone is capable of clearing the infection. Provided that the invader slips through, the innate immune system calls for help from the adaptive immune system. This is where adaptive immunity comes into play.

先天免疫是第一道防線

4.3

疫情與健康保健 Pandemic & Health Care

The adaptive immune system is the second line of defense, capable of differentiating between different types of pathogens and producing millions of antibodies to ward off the enemy. However, the adaptive immune system is slower in response and can take a few days or even weeks before it kicks in. This adaptive immunity is built up as we are exposed to diseases or are vaccinated. It is therefore also called acquired immunity for this reason.

後天免疫是第二道防線

One of the hallmarks of adaptive immunity is the capacity for memory, which can be protective as our body encounters the same intruder a second time. Yet, this immune memory is not always generated. For example, research on COVID-19 patients suggests that only those with severe infection were able to retain immune memory. Scientists have traditionally believed such memory is beyond the reach of the innate immune system and innate immune cells are unable to memorize the same pathogen should the body be exposed to it again. New evidence suggests that natural killer cells of the innate immune system are capable of memory-like responses, something previously thought to be possible only in the adaptive immune system.

後天免疫的記憶能力

To ensure that our innate and adaptive immune systems work effectively and efficiently, we need to give our immune cells the kind of nutrients they need, the most important of which are zinc, vitamin C, and vitamin D. Other daily supplementation such as propolis and echinacea can boost our immunity as well. Yet, boosting human immunity is much more than just taking immune-boosting nutritional supplements. The best way we can boost our immunity is to follow a healthy lifestyle, with a balanced diet, regular exercise, and sufficient sleep.

增強免疫力的營養元素

■ 回答以下問題，確認自己是否正確理解整篇文章的大意：

Q1. _____ We are surrounded by different kinds of bacteria and viruses. (T/F)

Q2. _____ Innate immunity responds quickly to invading viruses. (T/F)

Q3. _____ Adaptive immunity can remember the same virus. (T/F)

Q4. _____ Adaptive immunity does not produce antibodies. (T/F)

Q5. _____ Our immune cells do not need any nutrients. (T/F)

STEP 3 細讀 Close reading

請用 60 秒的時間仔細閱讀以下內容，並回答問題。

One of the hallmarks of adaptive immunity is its capacity for memory, which can be protective as our body encounters the same intruder a second time. Yet, this immune memory is not always generated. For example, research on COVID-19 patients suggests that only those with severe infection were able to retain immune memory. Scientists have traditionally believed memory of innate immunity is out of reach, unable to memorize the same pathogen should the body be exposed to it again. New evidence suggests that natural killer cells of the innate immune system can cross over the traditional boundaries between innate and adaptive immunity, with their capacity for memory-like responses, something previously thought to be limited only to adaptive immunity.

_____ Q1. According to this passage, which of the following is correct?
    (A) Adaptive immunity can remember all invading viruses.
    (B) Innate immunity cannot remember invading viruses.
    (C) Adaptive immunity cannot remember COVID-19 variants.
    (D) COVID-19 patients with minor infection may not be able to retain immune memory

_____ Q2. According to this passage, natural killer cells of the innate immune system are capable of _____.
    (A) producing antibodies
    (B) remembering the same virus
    (C) collecting evidence of invading viruses
    (D) causing severe infection

解答請見 p.351

4.3

疫情與健康保健 Pandemic & Health Care

請用 90 秒的時間，看完整篇文章。然後跟著每一個有意義的色塊，提升理解的速度。（*請盡量試著不查自己不認識的字，利用前後文去推測意思。*）

Our body is under constant attack from pathogens (e.g., bacteria, viruses, and other disease-causing organisms) in the air we breathe and the food we eat. Human immunity is essential for preventing these pathogens from getting a foothold, playing a key role in determining the clinical course of infection. Specifically, human immunity has two fundamental lines of defense: innate and adaptive immunity.

各種病菌不斷侵害人體健康

Present from birth, innate immunity serves as the first line of defense against any intruders, reacting almost instantly to prevent pathogens from making their ways to our body. For example, a cut on the skin or a breach of the mucosal surface of our nose, throat, or intestines can result in redness and swelling, many immune cells immediately recruited to the site of infection. In most cases, innate immunity alone is capable of clearing the infection. Provided that the invader slips through, the innate immune system calls for help from the adaptive immune system. This is where adaptive immunity comes into play.

先天免疫是第一道防線

The adaptive immune system is the second line of defense, capable of differentiating between different types of pathogens and producing millions of antibodies to ward off the enemy. However, the adaptive immune system is slower in response and can take a few days or even weeks before it kicks in. This adaptive immunity is built up as we are exposed to diseases or are vaccinated. It is therefore also called acquired immunity for this reason.

後天免疫是第二道防線

One of the hallmarks of adaptive immunity is the capacity for memory, which can be protective as our body encounters the same intruder a second time. Yet, this immune memory is not always generated. For example, research on COVID-19 patients suggests that only those with severe infection were able to retain immune memory. Scientists have traditionally believed such memory is beyond the reach of the innate immune system and innate immune cells are unable to memorize the same pathogen should the body be exposed to it again. New evidence suggests that natural killer cells of the innate immune system are capable of memory-like responses, something previously thought to be possible only in the adaptive immune system.

To ensure that our innate and adaptive immune systems work effectively and efficiently, we need to give our immune cells the kind of nutrients they need, the most important of which are zinc, vitamin C, and vitamin D. Other daily supplementation such as propolis and echinacea can boost our immunity as well. Yet, boosting human immunity is much more than just taking immune-boosting nutritional supplements. The best way we can boost our immunity is to follow a healthy lifestyle, with a balanced diet, regular exercise, and sufficient sleep.

■ 請回答以下問題：

_____ Q1. Which of the following can be inferred from the article?
  (A) Innate immunity does not have any immune memory.
  (B) Adaptive immunity is inherited from parents.
  (C) Bacteria and viruses are all over the place.
  (D) Adaptive immunity responds to intruding viruses almost instantly.

_____ Q2. Innate immunity is capable of _____.
  (A) differentiating between different types of viruses
  (B) reacting instantly to prevent infection
  (C) producing antibodies to guard against intruders
  (D) being activated by vaccination

_____ Q3. Adaptive immunity is capable of _____.

(A) developing over the lifespan of an individual as a result of exposure to pathogens or vaccination

(B) serving as the first line of defense against intruders

(C) reacting instantly to prevent infection

(D) reacting immediately to a cut on the skin

_____ Q4. Which of the following can provide support for human immunity?

(A) zinc   (B) vitamin C   (C) vitamin D   (D) all of the above

_____ Q5. Which of the following is true about natural killer cells?

(A) They cannot be recruited by the innate immune system.

(B) They show characteristics of both innate and adaptive systems

(C) They are able to kill all invading bacteria and viruses.

(D) They are not inherited from parents.

▶▶ 解答請見 p.352

4.3.3_S.mp3

STEP 5 跟讀 Shadowing

　　請根據母語人士所錄製的音檔,一句一句跟著唸。跟讀時請使用跟讀音檔,每句結束後,請利用句與句之間的空秒時間,複誦前面所聽到的句子。建議第一遍,看著文章跟著唸,第二遍則不看文章,只聽音檔唸。

4.3.3_L.mp3

STEP 6 聽讀 Listening

第一遍

→ 讀者會聽到音檔內母語人士完整且不間斷將本文唸一遍。試著不看文章,聽音檔內的母語人士完整且不間斷地將本文唸一遍,確認自己哪裡聽懂,那裡聽不懂。

第二遍

→ 再聽母語人士不間斷地將本文唸一遍,眼睛注視著正在朗誦的每個句子,針對自己沒聽懂的部分,特別仔細閱讀。

單字 Vocabulary

❶ organism [ˋɔrgənɪzəm]	n. 微生物，有機體 Bacteria are single-celled organisms. 細菌是單細胞的微生物。
❷ pathogen [ˋpæθədʒən]	n. 致病體，病原體 Viruses and bacteria are common pathogens. 病毒和細菌是常見的病原體。
❸ foothold [ˋfʊthold]	n. 一席之地 The iPhone has gained a foothold in the global market. iPhone 在全球手機市場佔有一席之地。
❹ clinical [ˋklɪnɪkəl]	adj. 臨床的 Clinical trials of new drugs are often time-consuming. 新藥的臨床試驗通常相當耗時。
❺ swelling [ˋswɛlɪŋ]	n. 腫脹 Bee stings can cause severe pain and swelling. 蜜蜂螫傷能導致劇痛和腫脹。
❻ breach [britʃ]	n. 破口 There is a breach in the wall. 牆上有一個破口。
❼ recruit [rɪˋkrut]	v. 召集，招募（人手等） The basketball team is recruiting players. 籃球隊正在招募球員。
❽ hallmark [ˋhɔlmark]	n. 特點，特徵 Running fast is a hallmark of football players. 跑得快是足球員的特點之一。
❾ nutrient [ˋnjutrɪənt]	n. 營養物 These nutrients are important to a balanced diet. 這些營養物對於均衡的飲食很重要。

4.3

疫情與健康保健 Pandemic & Health Care

| ❿ **supplement**
[ˈsʌpləmənt] | n. 補充品／物
She takes vitamin supplements on a daily basis.
她每天都會補充維他命。 |

❶ Provided (that)...　如果…

He can join us, <u>provided (that)</u> there are enough seats.
如果位子夠的話,他可以加入我們。

❷ come into play　開始起作用

When it comes to election, many factors can <u>come into play</u>.
說到選舉,就有許多因素開始紛擾。

❸ ward off　避開,防止

She took some vitamin C to <u>ward off</u> a cold.
他吃了一些維他命 C 以避免感冒。

❹ kick in　起作用,產生效果

These painkillers do not <u>kick in</u> immediately.
這些止痛藥不會馬上產生效果。

A. Fill in the blanks with suitable words or phrases 將適合的字詞填入空格中

ⓐ kick in   **ⓑ** clinical   **ⓒ** breach   **ⓓ** foothold

1. He wants to work in _____ settings, rather than in lab ones.

2. The pharmaceutical company attempts to gain a _____ in the European market.

3. She felt better after the medication _____ .

4. The company suffered a security _____ that compromised personal information of as many as ten million customers.

B. Multiple choice questions 選擇題（可利用此題型熟悉多益、英檢考試）

_____ 1. Most people get sick because of -------.
     (A) vitamins   (B) medicines   (C) pathogens   (D) belongings

_____ 2. These tribes ------- a common enemy.
     (A) warded off   (B) laid off   (C) took over   (D) assisted with

_____ 3. As the new company is growing in size, it attempts to ------- more workers locally.
     (A) betray   (B) abolish   (C) quench   (D) recruit

_____ 4. Fever is a(an) ------- of infectious diseases.
     (A) ransom   (B) hallmark   (C) exception   (D) experiment

_____ 5. After a week of illness, she felt better after taking some dietary -------.
     (A) developments   (B) experiments
     (C) supplements   (D) compliments

▶▶ 解答請見 p.353

4.3

疫情與健康保健 Pandemic & Health Care

4.4 人物傳記
Biography

Did you know?
[你需要知道的 10 件事]

❶ 馬斯克為 2022 年美國《富比士》雜誌公布的全球第一首富。

❷ 馬斯克創業過非常多次，最成功之一為特斯拉（Tesla）電動車。

❸ 馬斯克說，創立特斯拉電動車的初衷之一為降低地球的碳排放。

❹ 馬斯克的資產多為特斯拉的股票。

❺ 馬斯克喜愛自學，每天閱讀各種主題的書籍, 涉獵領域廣泛。

❻ 馬斯克不只閱讀英文書籍，也閱讀其他語言撰寫的書籍，故對於不同文化的思維有一定程度的了解。

❼ 畢業於常春藤名校，馬斯克說他用人唯才，不在乎幹部員工的學歷。

❽ 馬斯克常常對於時事和政治發表看法。

❾ 馬斯克沒有固定的政黨傾向。

❿ 馬斯克的網路社群有非常多追蹤者，網路聲量大。

Must-know vocabulary
[你需要知道的 10 個單字]

❶ silver spoon *n.* 銀湯匙（比喻「富裕背景」）

❷ serial entrepreneur *n.* 連續創業家

❸ electric vehicle. *n.* 電動（汽）車

❹ carbon emission *n.* 碳排放（量）

❺ long-time proponent *n.* 長期支持者

❻ astronaut *n.* 太空人

❼ high-profile *adj.* 高調的

❽ social media *n.* 社群媒體

❾ censorship *n.*（言論、內容等的）審查（制度）

❿ cryptocurrency *n.* 加密貨幣

掃讀的目標是在文章中搜尋特定的人名、時間、地點，或相關詞語，就像是在電話簿中搜尋某人的電話號碼一樣，其他內容完全不看。

■ 請於 **30** 秒內在以下文章中找出下列文字並畫線，不要閱讀內容或嘗試理解文章。

1 silver spoon
2 a serial entrepreneur
3 an electric vehicle
4 carbon emissions
5 a long-time proponent
6 astronauts
7 high-profile
8 social media
9 cryptocurrencies
10 censorship

Elon Musk

(426 words)
By Yushiang Jou

   Growing up in South Africa, Elon Musk was born with a silver spoon in his mouth. Musk moved to the U.S. after high school and went to the University of Pennsylvania, where he earned a bachelor's degree in physics and another in economics. Shortly after that, he entered a Ph.D. program in physics at Stanford University. However, Musk dropped out of his doctoral program and launched a business career. He became a serial entrepreneur who started several businesses, some of them highly successful. Despite the success he has achieved, his life is full of challenges and the potential for failure is ever present. In addition to being a father of nine living children, he has been wearing many hats, the most notable of which are probably an entrepreneur, rocket scientist, and key opinion leader (KOL).

   Musk is perhaps best known for Tesla, an electric vehicle (EV) company he founded in 2003. Due to heightened worries about increased carbon emissions, the EV industry is booming. In the face of growing competition, he does not live in fear of failure or hardship. Tesla is now a company of roughly 100 thousand employees and the first profitable maker of electric vehicles in the world. Relatedly, Tesla's stock has surged more than 20,000% since it went public in 2010, thereby making Musk one of the world's richest people.

4.4

人物傳記 Biography

Being a physicist by training, Musk has also been a long-time proponent of colonizing Mars. He is deeply invested in rocket science and founded SpaceX, a rocket company that has been in the vanguard of commercial space exploration. Having successfully launched two NASA astronauts into space, SpaceX is aggressively moving forward with its plans to develop reusable rocket technology. As Musk is defining space travel on his terms, his contributions have been recognized. In 2022, Musk was elected to the National Academy of Engineering for his accomplishments.

A high-profile influencer who has made his mark on social media, Musk has over 120 million followers on Twitter. He is vocal about politics, education, and space exploration, just to name a few. Every time he tweets, hundreds of thousands of his Twitter followers would "like" his tweet and retweet his post. His tweets about Tesla's stock can easily trigger a rally or sell-off. He also has enormous influence on cryptocurrencies like Bitcoin and Dogecoin. Active on social media, Musk once blasted Twitter for its censorship, calling for a major overhaul of its speech policies. In an unexpected turn of events, Musk bought Twitter in 2022.

■ 請選擇正確的意思

_____ ❶ silver spoon (A) 富裕背景 (B) 貧窮背景

_____ ❷ a serial entrepreneur (A) 單次創業家 (B) 連續創業家

_____ ❸ an electric vehicle (A) 電動工具 (B) 電動汽車

_____ ❹ carbon emission (A) 碳排放 (B) 二氧化碳

_____ ❺ a long-time proponent (A) 長期反對者 (B) 長期支持者

_____ ❻ astronaut (A) 創業家 (B) 太空人

_____ ❼ high-profile (A) 低調的 (B) 高調的

_____ ❽ social media (A) 廣播電台 (B) 社群媒體

_____ ❾ cryptocurrency (A) 加密貨幣 (B) 央行發行的貨幣

_____ ❿ censorship (A) 言論審查 (B) 言論自由

▶▶▶ 解答請見 p.355

針對剛才的文章，用 30 秒鐘瀏覽各段的第一句，粗略了解文章結構與大意即可。

Growing up in South Africa, Elon Musk was born with a silver spoon in his mouth. Musk moved to the U.S. after high school and went to the University of Pennsylvania, where he earned a bachelor's degree in physics and another in economics. Shortly after that, he entered a Ph.D. program in physics at Stanford University. However, Musk dropped out of his doctoral program and launched a business career. He became a serial entrepreneur who started several businesses, some of them highly successful. Despite the success he has achieved, his life is full of challenges and the potential for failure is ever present. In addition to being a father of nine living children, he has been wearing many hats, the most notable of which are probably an entrepreneur, rocket scientist, and key opinion leader (KOL).

馬斯克的成長背景

Musk is perhaps best known for Tesla, an electric vehicle (EV) company he founded in 2003. Due to heightened worries about increased carbon emissions, the EV industry is booming. In the face of growing competition, he does not live in fear of failure or hardship. Tesla is now a company of roughly 100 thousand employees and the first profitable maker of electric vehicles in the world. Relatedly, Tesla's stock has surged more than 20,000% since it went public in 2010, thereby making Musk one of the world's richest people.

馬斯克與特斯拉

Being a physicist by training, Musk has also been a long-time proponent of colonizing Mars. He is deeply invested in rocket science and founded SpaceX, a rocket company that has been in the vanguard of commercial space exploration. Having successfully launched two NASA astronauts into space, SpaceX is aggressively moving forward with its plans to develop reusable rocket technology. As Musk is defining space travel on his terms, his contributions have been recognized. In 2022, Musk was elected to the National Academy of Engineering for his accomplishments.

馬斯克與火星殖民

4.4

人物傳記 Biography

A high-profile influencer who has made his mark on social media, Musk has over 120 million followers on Twitter. He is vocal about politics, education, and space exploration, just to name a few. Every time he tweets, hundreds of thousands of his Twitter followers would "like" his tweet and retweet his post. His tweets about Tesla's stock can easily trigger a rally or sell-off. He also has enormous influence on cryptocurrencies like Bitcoin and Dogecoin. Active on social media, Musk once blasted Twitter for its censorship, calling for a major overhaul of its speech policies. In an unexpected turn of events, Musk bought Twitter in 2022.

馬斯克
與社群
媒體

■ 回答以下問題，確認自己是否正確理解整篇文章的大意：

Q1. ＿＿＿＿ Musk was born in a poor family. (T/F)

Q2. ＿＿＿＿ Musk became famous as the founder of Tesla. (T/F)

Q3. ＿＿＿＿ Musk is not interested in the outer space. (T/F)

Q4. ＿＿＿＿ Musk is high-profile on social media. (T/F)

Q5. ＿＿＿＿ Many people are interested in Musk. (T/F)

▶▶ 解答請見 p.355

STEP 3 細讀 Close reading

請用 60 秒的時間仔細閱讀以下內容，並回答問題。

Musk moved to the U.S. after high school and went to the University of Pennsylvania, where he earned a bachelor's degree in physics and another in economics. Shortly after that, he entered a Ph.D. program in physics at Stanford University. However, Musk dropped out of his doctoral program and launched a business career. He became a serial entrepreneur who started several businesses, some of them highly successful. Despite the success he has achieved, his life is full of challenges and the potential for failure is ever present.

_____ Q1. According to this passage, which of the following is correct?

(A) Musk has two bachelor's degrees.

(B) Musk earned a Ph.D. degree at Stanford University.

(C) Fear of failure prevented Musk from building up his business.

(D) Musk lived in the U.S. before high school.

_____ Q2. According to this passage, what do we know about Musk?

(A) He entered a Ph.D. program in the University of Pennsylvania.

(B) He finished his Ph.D. program.

(C) He took courses in economics.

(D) He is a serial entrepreneur whose businesses are all highly successful.

▶▶ 解答請見 p.355

STEP 4 高理解速讀 Speed Reading with Greater Comprehension

請用 90 秒的時間,看完整篇文章。然後跟著每一個有意義的色塊,提升理解的速度。(請盡量試著不查自己不認識的字,利用前後文去推測意思。)

Growing up in South Africa, Elon Musk was born with a silver spoon in his mouth. Musk moved to the U.S. after high school and went to the University of Pennsylvania, where he earned a bachelor's degree in physics and another in economics. Shortly after that, he entered a Ph.D. program in physics at Stanford University. However, Musk dropped out of his doctoral program and launched a business career. He became a serial entrepreneur who started several businesses, some of them highly successful. Despite the success he has achieved, his life is full of challenges and the potential for failure is ever present. In addition to being a father of nine living children, he has been wearing many hats, the most notable of which are probably an entrepreneur, rocket scientist, and key opinion leader (KOL).

馬斯克
的成長
背景

4.4

人物傳記 Biography

143

Musk is perhaps best known for Tesla, an electric vehicle (EV) company he founded in 2003. Due to heightened worries about increased carbon emissions, the EV industry is booming. In the face of growing competition, he does not live in fear of failure or hardship. Tesla is now a company of roughly 100 thousand employees and the first profitable maker of electric vehicles in the world. Relatedly, Tesla's stock has surged more than 20,000% since it went public in 2010, thereby making Musk one of the world's richest people.

Being a physicist by training, Musk has also been a long-time proponent of colonizing Mars. He is deeply invested in rocket science and founded SpaceX, a rocket company that has been in the vanguard of commercial space exploration. Having successfully launched two NASA astronauts into space, SpaceX is aggressively moving forward with its plans to develop reusable rocket technology. As Musk is defining space travel on his terms, his contributions have been recognized. In 2022, Musk was elected to the National Academy of Engineering for his accomplishments.

A high-profile influencer who has made his mark on social media, Musk has over 120 million followers on Twitter. He is vocal about politics, education, and space exploration, just to name a few. Every time he tweets, hundreds of thousands of his Twitter followers would "like" his tweet and retweet his post. His tweets about Tesla's stocks can easily trigger a rally or sell-off. He also has enormous influence on cryptocurrencies like Bitcoin and Dogecoin. Active on social media, Musk once blasted Twitter for its censorship, calling for a major overhaul of its speech policies. In an unexpected turn of events, Musk bought Twitter in 2022.

■ 請回答以下問題：

_____ Q1. What does it mean by "being a father of nine living children"?

(A) Musk has nine children so far.

(B) Musk has adopted nine children.

(C) Musk does not recognize some of his children.

(D) At least one of his children passed away.

_____ Q2. Why did Musk drop out of Stanford University?

(A) He wanted to start his own business.

(B) He did not study hard enough.

(C) He did not do well on exams.

(D) He did not have enough money to pay for his tuition.

_____ Q3. What made Musk one of the richest people in the world?

(A) his Twitter traffic

(B) his Tesla stocks

(C) his business collaboration between Space X and NASA

(D) his undergraduate diploma from an Ivy League university

_____ Q4. What can be inferred from this article?

(A) Musk is a Democrat.

(B) Musk is a Republican.

(C) Musk is interested in politics.

(D) Musk wants to run for president.

_____ Q5. Which of the following can be inferred from the article?

(A) Musk is expert in poetry.

(B) Musk knows little about engineering.

(C) Musk has made some contributions to the world.

(D) Musk barely scratched the surface of economics.

▶▶ 解答請見 p.356

4.4

人物傳記 Biography

STEP 5 跟讀 Shadowing

4.4.1_S.mp3

　　請根據母語人士所錄製的音檔，一句一句跟著唸。跟讀時請使用跟讀音檔，每句結束後，請利用句與句之間的空秒時間，複誦前面所聽到的句子。建議第一遍，看著文章跟著唸，第二遍則不看文章，只聽音檔唸。

STEP 6 聽讀 Listening

4.4.1_L.mp3

第一遍

→ 讀者會聽到音檔內母語人士完整且不間斷將本文唸一遍。試著不看文章，聽音檔內的母語人士完整且不間斷地將本文唸一遍，確認自己哪裡聽懂，那裡聽不懂。

第二遍

→ 再聽母語人士不間斷地將本文唸一遍，眼睛注視著正在朗誦的每個句子，針對自己沒聽懂的部分，特別仔細閱讀。

STEP 7 延伸學習

單字 Vocabulary

❶ entrepreneur [ˌɑntrəprəˈnɝ]	n. 企業家 She is a successful entrepreneur. 她是一位成功的企業家。
❷ launch [lɔntʃ]	v. 開啟 He launched a career as an actor last year. 他去年開始了演員的職業生涯。
❸ notable [ˈnotəbl]	adj. 引人注目的 The green color was one of the notable features of his new car. 他的新車最引人注目的特色之一就是綠色。

❹ **soar** [sor]	v. 飆升 Oil prices have been soaring due to high inflation. 因為高通膨的關係，油價持續飆升。
❺ **boom** [bum]	v. 蓬勃發展 Tourism is booming this year. 今年觀光業蓬勃發展。
❻ **surge** [sɝdʒ]	v. 飆升 Egg prices have surged recently. 最近蛋價一直飆高。
❼ **high-profile** [ˈhaɪ ˈprofaɪl]	adj. 高調的 He was a high-profile athlete in high school. 他在高中的時候是一名作風高調的運動員。
❽ **blast** [blæst]	v. 強烈批評，砲轟 The govornment has been blasted for failing to stop inflation. 政府因為抑制通膨不力而被砲轟。
❾ **vocal** [ˈvokl̩]	adj. 口頭的，直言不諱的 She has been vocal in her support of the mayor. 她一直直言不諱地對市長表達支持。
❿ **overhaul** [ovɚˈhɔl]	n. 全面檢修，徹底改革 Lawmakers are calling for a major overhaul of the tax system. 立委要求對於稅制進行徹底改革。

❶ born with a silver spoon (in one's mouth)　含著金（或銀）湯匙出生，生於富裕家庭

She was <u>born with a silver spoon in her mouth</u>.
她出生於富裕家庭。

❷ in the vanguard of　是⋯的先驅

The scholar is <u>in the vanguard of</u> stem cell research.
這位學者是幹細胞研究的先驅。

❸ make one's mark　聲名大噪

He is new to the company but has already <u>made his mark</u> by selling one hundred cars in a week.
他雖然是公司的新人，但他因為在一週內賣掉 100 輛汽車而聲名大噪。

❹ call for　要求，呼籲

They have <u>called for</u> a criminal investigation into the case.
他們已經要求對這個案子進行刑事調查。

A. Fill in the blanks with suitable words or phrases 將適合的字詞填入空格中

ⓐ vocal   **ⓑ** call for   **ⓒ** boom   **ⓓ** blast

1. Many people have _____ for stricter gun control laws.

2. She has been _____ for her dishonesty.

3. He has been _____ in his criticism of the new policy.

4. The gaming industry is _____ this season.

B. Multiple choice questions 選擇題（可利用此題型熟悉多益、英檢考試）

_____ 1. A ------- player in the NBA, Mike is also a vocal critic of game
rules.
(A) new-born (B) low-profile (C) heart-broken (D) high-profile

_____ 2. She loves painting. In fact, she is planning to ------- a career as a
painter next year.
(A) launch (B) twist (C) terminate (D) interrupt

_____ 3. Housing prices are ------- these days. As a result, many people
cannot afford to buy a house.
(A) celebrated (B) soaring (C) dropping (D) generalized

_____ 4. Bright colors are a(n) ------- feature of the work of impressionists
who is preoccupied with the interplay of color and light.
(A) unusual (B) uncommon (C) notable (D) atypical

_____ 5. Airline stock prices have ------- this year due to an increase in
demand.
(A) deteriorated (B) manipulated (C) guaranteed (D) surged

▶▶ 解答請見 p.357

4.4
人物傳記 Biography

Did you know?

[你需要知道的 **10** 件事]

❶ 蒙特梭利博士是一名義大利女性。
❷ 蒙特梭利博士擔任過大學教授、內科醫生、精神病學研究員等。
❸ 蒙特梭利博士出版過許多廣為人知的幼兒教育書籍。
❹ 蒙特梭利博士對於世界各國的幼兒教育有相當大的貢獻。
❺ 蒙特梭利博士相信每個小孩的潛力都是不同的。
❻ 蒙特梭利博士反對一視同仁的傳統填鴨教學法。
❼ 蒙特梭利博士強調孩童的實際體驗、多元發展和探索
❽ 蒙特梭利教學法特色之一為特殊設計的教具。
❾ 所有蒙特梭利幼兒園或學校都是私立的。
❿ 蒙特梭利教師需要接受專業的訓練。

Must-know vocabulary

[你需要知道的 **10** 個單字]

❶ physician *n.* 內科醫生
❷ educationist *n.* 教育家
❸ child-centered *n.* 以孩童為中心的
❹ pre-service teacher *n.* 職前教師
❺ one-size-fits-all approach *n.* 一體適用的方式
❻ revolutionize *v.* 改革，使…出現突破性的改變
❼ intrinsic motivation *n.* 內在動機
❽ hands-on exploration *n.* 手作探索，體驗探索
❾ intellectual potential *n.* 智能潛力
❿ mixed-age grouping *n.* 混齡分組

MARIA
MONTESSO

　　掃讀的目標是在文章中搜尋特定的人名、時間、地點，或相關詞語，就像是在電話簿中搜尋某人的電話號碼一樣，其他內容完全不看。

■ 請於 **30** 秒內在以下文章中找出下列文字並畫線，不要閱讀內容或嘗試理解文章。

❶ physician

❷ educationist

❸ child-centered

❹ pre-service teachers

❺ revolutionized

❻ a one-size-fits-all approach

❼ intrinsic motivation

❽ hands-on exploration

❾ intellectual potential

❿ mixed-age grouping

Maria Montessori

(411 words)　　　　　　　　　　　　　　　　　　　By Yushiang Jou

　　One of the first women in Italy to receive a medical degree and become a physician, Maria Montessori (1870-1952) was also an educationist and author of many seminal books on childhood education. Keenly observant of children's learning dispositions and varying levels of motivation for learning, Montessori developed a child-centered approach to education that highlights hands-on learning and self-directed tasks. Designing learning materials suited to children of different developmental needs, she established Montessori schools and developed programs to train pre-service teachers. The Montessori Method, underpinned by education, anthropology, and philosophy theories, revolutionized early childhood education.

　　Montessori stood in opposition to a one-size-fits-all approach to education practiced in traditional classrooms. She observed that when children were allowed freedom of choice within clear and reasonable boundaries, they learned best, their intrinsic motivation boosted and attention to classroom activities sustained. Therefore, children in a Montessori classroom are given agency to self-select work, a radical departure from traditional classrooms where children are given less

4.4

人物傳記 Biography

freedom and are expected to go with the majority. When Montessori children work individually and in groups to gain knowledge of the world, the teacher serving as a facilitator is neither the focus of children's attention nor the focal center of the classroom. Children's experience of discovering answers for themselves can lead to a deeper understanding of language, art, history, mathematics, and science, among other domains. This hands-on exploration encouraged in Montessori classrooms develops children's problem-solving skills and fosters the development of their intellectual potential.

Another feature of Montessori education is mixed-age grouping. Children of different ages work together in the same classroom where younger children learn from older peers and take on new challenges through observation. Older children can reinforce their learning by demonstrating what they have already mastered, serve as role models in class, and develop leadership skills. Because of this mixed-age grouping, there is more cooperation than competition in the classroom. Since each child's work is individual, children are able to progress in line with the rhythm of their own learning.

While many teachers today carry on Montessori's legacy and empower children in many countries around the world, Montessori education is not without its limitations. Since the acquisition of specially designed Montessori materials can be expensive, it is unlikely for Montessori schools to keep their tuition low. Different from traditional public schools, most Montessori schools are private and therefore cost more than their public counterparts. As a result, Montessori education may not be accessible to children from low-income families.

■ 請選擇正確的意思

_____ ❶ physician   (A) 內科醫生 (B) 外科醫生

_____ ❷ educationist   (A) 學生 (B) 教育家

_____ ❸ child-centered   (A) 以老師為中心的 (B) 以孩童為中心的

_____ ❹ pre-service teacher   (A) 職前教師 (B) 在職教師

_____ ❺ revolutionize   (A) 維持現狀 (B) 改革創新

_____ ❻ one-size-fits-all approach (A) 一體適用的方式 (B) 適性發展的方式

_____ ❼ intrinsic motivation (A) 外在動機 (B) 內在動機

_____ ❽ hands-on exploration (A) 冥想探索 (B) 手作探索

_____ ❾ intellectual potential (A) 智能潛力 (B) 體能潛力

_____ ❿ mixed-age grouping (A) 同齡分組 (B) 混齡分組

▶▶ 解答請見 p.359

STEP 2 略讀 Skimming

針對剛才的文章，用 30 秒鐘瀏覽各段的第一句，粗略了解文章結構與大意即可。

One of the first women in Italy to receive a medical degree and become a physician, Maria Montessori (1870-1952) was also an educationist and author of many seminal books on childhood education. Keenly observant of children's learning dispositions and varying levels of motivation for learning, Montessori developed a child-centered approach to education that highlights hands-on learning and self-directed tasks. Designing learning materials suited to children of different developmental needs, she established Montessori schools and developed programs to train pre-service teachers. The Montessori Method, underpinned by education, anthropology, and philosophy theories, revolutionized early childhood education.

蒙特梭利博士的成就

Montessori stood in opposition to a one-size-fits-all approach to education practiced in traditional classrooms. She observed that when children were allowed freedom of choice within clear and reasonable boundaries, they learned best, their intrinsic motivation boosted and attention to classroom activities sustained. Therefore, children in a Montessori classroom are given agency to self-select work, a radical departure from traditional classrooms where children are given less freedom and are expected to go with the majority. When Montessori

蒙特梭利教學法強調適性發展

4.4

人物傳記 Biography

children work individually and in groups to gain knowledge of the world, the teacher serving as a facilitator is neither the focus of children's attention nor the focal center of the classroom. Children's experience of discovering answers for themselves can lead to a deeper understanding of language, art, history, mathematics, and science, among other domains. This hands-on exploration encouraged in Montessori classrooms develops children's problem-solving skills and fosters the development of their intellectual potential.

Another feature of Montessori education is mixed-age grouping. Children of different ages work together in the same classroom where younger children learn from older peers and take on new challenges through observation. Older children can reinforce their learning by demonstrating what they have already mastered, serve as role models in class, and develop leadership skills. Because of this mixed-age grouping, there is more cooperation than competition in the classroom. Since each child's work is individual, children are able to progress in line with the rhythm of their own learning.

蒙特梭利教學法使用混齡教學

While many teachers today carry on Montessori's legacy and empower children in many countries around the world, Montessori education is not without its limitations. Since the acquisition of specially designed Montessori materials can be expensive, it is unlikely for Montessori schools to keep their tuition low. Different from traditional public schools, most Montessori schools are private and therefore cost more than their public counterparts. As a result, Montessori education may not be accessible to children from low-income families.

蒙特梭利教學的侷限

■ 回答以下問題，確認自己是否正確理解整篇文章的大意：

Q1. _____ Montessori published many books. (T/F)

Q2. _____ Montessori was a doctor. (T/F)

Q3. _____ Many teachers are using the Montessori Method today. (T/F)

Q4. _____ Children are not allowed freedom of choice in a Montessori classroom. (T/F)

Q5. _____ Montessori believed children of different age groups could learn together. (T/F)

▶▶ 解答請見 p.359

STEP 3 細讀 Close reading

請用 60 秒的時間仔細閱讀以下內容，並回答問題。

Montessori stood in opposition to a one-size-fits-all approach to education practiced in traditional classrooms. She observed that when children were allowed freedom of choice within clear and reasonable boundaries, they learned best, their intrinsic motivation boosted and attention to classroom activities sustained. Therefore, children in a Montessori classroom are given agency to self-select work, a radical departure from traditional classrooms where children are given less freedom and are expected to go with the majority.

_____ Q1. According to this passage, which of the following is correct?

(A) Montessori classrooms adopt a standardized approach.

(B) Children's learning motivation cannot be boosted.

(C) Children are required to do the same thing in traditional classrooms.

(D) Children learn best in traditional classrooms.

_____ Q2. According to this passage, children in a Montessori classroom _____.

(A) are given less freedom

(B) are allowed more freedom

(C) are supposed to go with the majority

(D) are required to score high on standardized tests

▶▶ 解答請見 p.359

4.4

人物傳記 Biography

請用 90 秒的時間，看完整篇文章。然後跟著每一個有意義的色塊，提升理解的速度。（請盡量試著不查自己不認識的字，利用前後文去推測意思。）

One of the first women in Italy to receive a medical degree and become a physician, Maria Montessori (1870-1952) was also an educationist and author of many seminal books on childhood education. Keenly observant of children's learning dispositions and varying levels of motivation for learning, Montessori developed a child-centered approach to education that highlights hands-on learning and self-directed tasks . Designing learning materials suited to children of different developmental needs, she established Montessori schools and developed programs to train pre-service teachers. The Montessori Method, underpinned by education, anthropology, and philosophy theories, revolutionized early childhood education.

蒙特梭利博士的成就

Montessori stood in opposition to a one-size-fits-all approach to education practiced in traditional classrooms. She observed that when children were allowed freedom of choice within clear and reasonable boundaries, they learned best, their intrinsic motivation boosted and attention to classroom activities sustained. Therefore, children in a Montessori classroom are given agency to self-select work, a radical departure from traditional classrooms where children are given less freedom and are expected to go with the majority. When Montessori children work individually and in groups to gain knowledge of the world, the teacher serving as a facilitator is neither the focus of children's attention nor the focal center of the classroom. Children's experience of discovering answers for themselves can lead to a deeper understanding of language, art, history, mathematics, and science, among other domains. This hands-on exploration encouraged in Montessori classrooms develops children's problem-solving skills and fosters the development of their intellectual potential.

蒙特梭利教學法強調適性發展

Another feature of Montessori education is mixed-age grouping. Children of mixed ages work together in the same clasroom where younger children learn from older peers and take on new challenges through observation. Older children can reinforce their learning by demonstrating what they have already mastered, serve as role models in class, and develop leadership skills. Because of this mixed-age grouping, there is more cooperation than competition in the classroom. Since each child's work is individual, children are able to progress in line with the rhythm of their own learning.

蒙特梭
利教學
法使用
混齡教
學

While many teachers today carry on Montessori's legacy and empower children in many countries around the world, Montessori education is not without its limitations. Since the acquisition of specially designed Montessori materials can be expensive, it is unlikely for Montessori schools to keep their tuition low. Different from traditional public schools, most Montessori schools are private and therefore cost more than their public counterparts. As a result, Montessori education may not be accessible to children from low-income families.

蒙特梭
利教學
的侷限

■ 請回答以下問題：

_____ Q1. Montessori is NOT _____.

    (A) an author

    (B) a doctor

    (C) a teacher

    (D) an entrepreneur

_____ Q2. Montessori did NOT _____.

    (A) treat patients

    (B) observe how children learned

    (C) publish books on philosophy theories

    (D) develop programs to train teachers

_____ Q3. When children are allowed freedom of choice, which of the following is most likely to happen?

(A) Children do well on standardized exams.

(B) Children discover answers for themselves.

(C) Children lose their motivation for learning.

(D) Their attention to classroom activities begins to wander.

_____ Q4. What can happen in a mixed-age classroom?

(A) Children progress at their own pace.

(B) Older children learn from younger peers.

(C) Younger children serve as role models in class.

(D) Younger children reinforce their knowledge by demonstrating what has been learned.

_____ Q5. Most Montessori schools _____.

(A) are private

(B) expect children to go with the majority

(C) expect children to learn only from their teacher

(D) expect children to do well on standardized exams

▶▶ 解答請見 p.360

4.4.2_S.mp3

STEP 5 跟讀 Shadowing

　　請根據母語人士所錄製的音檔，一句一句跟著唸。跟讀時請使用跟讀音檔，每句結束後，請利用句與句之間的空秒時間，複誦前面所聽到的句子。建議第一遍，看著文章跟著唸，第二遍則不看文章，只聽音檔唸。

第一遍

→ 讀者會聽到音檔內母語人士完整且不間斷將本文唸一遍。試著不看文章，聽音檔內的母語人士完整且不間斷地將本文唸一遍，確認自己哪裡聽懂，那裡聽不懂。

第二遍

→ 再聽母語人士不間斷地將本文唸一遍，眼睛注視著正在朗誦的每個句子，針對自己沒聽懂的部分，特別仔細閱讀。

STEP 7 延伸學習

單字 Vocabulary

❶ **keen** [kin]	adj. 熱衷的，敏銳的 He is a keen student of physics. 他是個對物理相當熱衷的學生。
❷ **disposition** [ˌdɪspəˈzɪʃən]	n. 個人特質 Many people like to work with her because she has a sunny disposition. 因為她很陽光的個人特質，很多人喜歡跟她一起工作。
❸ **varying** [ˈvɛrɪŋ]	adj. 不同的 They joined our team with varying levels of experience. 他們帶著不同階段的經歷加入我們的團隊。
❹ **intrinsic** [ɪnˈtrɪnsɪk]	adj. 本身的，本質上的 The intrinsic value of this stone is low. 這顆寶石本身並不值錢。
❺ **underpin** [ˌʌndɚˈpɪn]	v. 作為⋯的基礎 These are the theories that underpin this teaching method. 這些是作為這種教學法的理論基礎。

❻ **agency** [ˈedʒənsɪ]	n. 動力，作用 In this class, students are given agency to select their own research topic. 在這堂課中，學生們獲得選擇自己研究主題的動力。
❼ **reinforce** [riɪnˈfɔrs]	v. 強化，深化 Many people say that the story reinforces the stereotype of Asian students. 很多人認為這個故事深化了對於亞洲學生的刻板印象。
❽ **rhythm** [ˈrɪðm̩]	n. 節奏，步調 She likes the rhythm of New York City. 她喜歡紐約市的生活步調。
❾ **legacy** [ˈlɛgəsɪ]	n. 遺產，遺留給後人的東西 The war left a legacy of pain. 那場戰爭留下了無盡的傷痛。
❿ **empower** [ɪmˈpaʊɚ]	v. 幫助…（某人）掌控自己，賦予權力 The new laws will empower minorities in the country. 新的法令幫助國內的弱勢族群穩定生活。

❶ one-size-fits-all　一體適用的，通用的

As a student, he prefers a one-size-fits-all approach to education.
身為一位學生，他比較喜歡統一課綱。

❷ a departure from　…的背離／變更

The new surgery is a departure from traditional practices.
新的手術與傳統的做法有所不同。

❸ in line with　與…一致

The inflation rate is in line with expectations.
通膨率符合預期。

❹ not without its limitations　並非無所限制，有侷限

Quantitative easing is not without its limitations.
量化寬鬆政策並非沒有它的限制。

4.4

人物傳記 Biography

A. Fill in the blanks with suitable words or phrases 將適合的字詞填入空格中

> **ⓐ** legacy   **ⓑ** underpin   **ⓒ** in line with   **ⓓ** agency

1. This artwork is the _____ of the artist.

2. Members of this community do not have the _____ to select the color of their house.

3. His behavior was not _____ his promise.

4. Einstein's theories have been used to _____ many cosmological studies.

B. Multiple choice questions 選擇題（可利用此題型熟悉多益、英檢考試）

_____ 1. She loves biking and is a ------- cyclist.
     (A) limited   (B) unmotivated   (C) keen   (D) implicit

_____ 2. This book is helpful and aims to ------- teachers of English in Taiwan.
     (A) discourage   (B) weaken   (C) empower   (D) depress

_____ 3. These students are different in many ways, including ------- levels of motivation for learning.
     (A) varying   (B) identical   (C) skeptical   (D) equivalent

_____ 4. Believing in the importance of inclusion, he does not seek to ------- the stereotypes about ethnic minorities.
     (A) minimize   (B) oppress   (C) slack   (D) reinforce

_____ 5. Not forced by others, she has some ------- interest in mathematics.
     (A) unavoidable   (B) intrinsic   (C) extrinsic   (D) obligatory

▶▶ 解答請見 p.361

NOTE

Did you know?

[你需要知道的 10 件事]

❶「共同基金」的股票名單由專業的基金經理人挑選出來。

❷ 為了分散風險，基金經理人通常管理投資組合，而非單一股票。

❸「指數型基金」的股票名單是依照指數成分股及績效所挑選出來的。

❹「共同基金」是主動的，而「指數型基金」是被動的。

❺ 90 年代之後，「共同基金」的績效鮮少贏過「指數型基金」。

❻ 彼得林奇和巴菲特一樣，都是屬於「價值投資」的投資者。

❼ 巴菲特是極少數以投資股票致富的人之一。

❽ 價值投資著眼公司的商業模式和盈利能力。

❾ 股價越高，公司的市值越高。

❿ 除了長期持有的價值投資之外，擇時交易賺取價差也是常見的股票投資方式。

Must-know vocabulary

[你需要知道的 10 個單字]

❶ best-selling *adj.* 暢銷的

❷ mutual fund *n.* 共同基金

❸ multinational *adj.* 跨國的

❹ annualized return *n.* 年化收益率

❺ hard-and-fast rule n. 硬性規定

❻ aptitude *n.* 天賦

❼ calculated risk *n.* 經過計算的風險

❽ retail investor *n.* 散戶投資人

❾ veteran investor *n.* 資深投資人

❿ diversified portfolio *n.* 多元化的投資組合

掃讀的目標是在文章中搜尋特定的人名、時間、地點，或相關詞語，就像是在電話簿中搜尋某人的電話號碼一樣，其他內容完全不看。

■ 請於 **30** 秒內在以下文章中找出下列文字並畫線，不要閱讀內容或嘗試理解文章。

❶ best-selling
❷ mutual fund
❸ multinational
❹ annualized return
❺ hard-and-fast rule
❻ aptitude
❼ calculated risk
❽ retail investor
❾ veteran investor
❿ diversified portfolio

Peter Lynch

(422 words)   By Yushiang Jou

Peter Lynch is one of the most well-known investors of all time and author of several best-selling books on investing. He earned a Master of Business Administration from the Wharton School, the business school of the University of Pennsylvania. Lynch made his mark as a mutual fund manager, showing a remarkable aptitude for picking stocks. At age 33, he took over the Magellan Fund, a mutual fund of a multinational financial corporation headquartered in Boston, Massachusetts. He ran it from 1977 to 1990. For these 13 years, the fund earned an annualized return of 29.2% under his management, more than twice what the S&P 500 earned during the same period of time. The fund became the world's best-performing mutual fund during his tenure as manager. His success allowed him to retire in 1990 at age 46.

Lynch's investment strategies can be boiled down to a few guiding principles. For starters, his initial evaluation of a stock entailed a thorough understanding of the company, its business model, its competitive edge, and its prospects. Since company revenue formed the building blocks of stock prices, he would also review the historical record of earnings. Just like Warren Buffett, Lynch was a value

4.4

人物傳記 Biography

investor. He took calculated risks and leaned toward investing in small, fast-growing companies whose stocks could be purchased at a reasonable price. In his efforts to mitigate the downside risk of the market, Lynch diversified by investing in a wide range of stocks.

While there are no hard-and-fast rules about investing, Lynch, in his books, offers practical advice to retail investors. When it comes to shopping for stocks, he believes that beginners and veteran investors alike are better off selecting companies or industries with which they are familiar. He suggests that investors do their homework and get the lay of the land before making any investment decisions. They should not be speculative and need to stay away from hot stocks in hot industries. Investors would be ill-advised to jump on the bandwagon. After all, investing is not like betting on red or black in a casino. At the emotional level, he argues that mental toughness is crucial in the face of the volatility of the market. While Lynch has been an advocate of investing for the long term, he does not recommend simply buying and holding a diversified portfolio. He thinks investors are responsible for reviewing their holdings every few months and rechecking the company's business to see if anything has changed. He would sell the stocks when the company's business goes south.

■ 請選擇正確的意思

_____ ❶ best-selling (A) 暢銷的 (B) 滯銷的

_____ ❷ mutual fund (A) 共同基金 (B) 指數基金

_____ ❸ multinational (A) 國內的 (B) 跨國的

_____ ❹ annualized return (A) 月化收益率 (B) 年化收益率

_____ ❺ hard-and-fast rule (A) 硬性規定 (B) 參考建議

_____ ❻ aptitude (A) 後天努力 (B) 天賦

_____ ❼ calculated risk (A) 未知風險 (B) 經過計算的風險

_____ ❽ retail investor (A) 散戶投資人 (B) 機構投資人

_____ ❾ veteran investor (A) 資深投資人 (B) 新手投資人

_____ ❿ diversified portfolio (A) 單一標的的投資 (B) 多元化的投資組合

▶▶ 解答請見 p.363

針對剛才的文章，用 30 秒鐘瀏覽各段的第一句，粗略了解文章結構與大意即可。

Peter Lynch is one of the most well-known investors of all time and author of several best-selling books on investing. He earned a Master of Business Administration from the Wharton School, the business school of the University of Pennsylvania. Lynch made his mark as a mutual fund manager, showing a remarkable aptitude for picking stocks. At age 33, he took over the Magellan Fund, a mutual fund of a multinational financial corporation headquartered in Boston, Massachusetts. He ran it from 1977 to 1990. For these 13 years, the fund earned an annualized return of 29.2% under his management, more than twice what the S&P 500 earned during the same period of time. The fund became the world's best-performing mutual fund during his tenure as manager. His success allowed him to retire in 1990 at age 46.

Lynch
生平
簡介

Lynch's investment strategies can be boiled down to a few guiding principles. For starters, his initial evaluation of a stock entailed a thorough understanding of the company, its business model, its competitive edge, and its prospects. Since company revenue formed the building blocks of stock prices, he would also review the historical record of earnings. Just like Warren Buffett, Lynch was a value investor. He took calculated risks and leaned toward investing in small, fast-growing companies whose stocks could be purchased at a reasonable price. In his efforts to mitigate the downside risk of the market, Lynch diversified by investing in a wide range of stocks.

Lynch
投資
方法

While there are no hard-and-fast rules about investing, Lynch, in his books, offers practical advice to retail investors. When it comes to shopping for stocks, he believes that beginners and veteran investors alike are better off selecting companies or industries with which they

Lynch
投資
建議

4.4

人物傳記 Biography

are familiar. He suggests that investors do their homework and get the lay of the land before making any investment decisions. They should not be speculative and need to stay away from hot stocks in hot industries. Investors would be ill-advised to jump on the bandwagon. After all, investing is not like betting on red or black in a casino. At the emotional level, he argues that mental toughness is crucial in the face of the volatility of the market. While Lynch has been an advocate of investing for the long term, he does not recommend simply buying and holding a diversified portfolio. He thinks investors are responsible for reviewing their holdings every few months and rechecking the company's business to see if anything has changed. He would sell the stocks when the company's business goes south.

■ 回答以下問題，確認自己是否正確理解整篇文章的大意：

Q1. _____ Lynch is a successful investor. (T/F)

Q2. _____ Lynch is an author of best-selling books. (T/F)

Q3. _____ Lynch did not take risks in investing. (T/F)

Q4. _____ Lynch's books offer advice to other investors. (T/F)

Q5. _____ There are hard-and-fast rules about investing. (T/F)

▶▶▶ 解答請見 p.363

STEP 3　細讀 Close reading

請用 60 秒的時間仔細閱讀以下內容，並回答問題。

When it comes to shopping for stocks, he believes that beginners and veteran investors alike are better off selecting companies or industries with which they are familiar. He suggests that investors do their homework and get the lay of the land before making any investment decisions.

_____ Q1. According to this passage, Lynch believes _____.

    (A) investors should know well the stock in which they invest

    (B) investors should do homework at school

    (C) investors should do homework at home

    (D) investors should go shopping before making investment decisions

_____ Q2. According to this passage, what is the key difference between
    beginners and veteran investors?

    (A) age

    (B) education

    (C) intelligence

    (D) not mentioned in this passage

STEP 4 高理解速讀 Speed Reading with Greater Comprehension

請用 90 秒的時間，看完整篇文章。然後跟著每一個有意義的色塊，提升理解的速度。（請盡量試著不查自己不認識的字，利用前後文去推測意思。）

Peter Lynch is one of the most well-known investors of all time and author of several best-selling books on investing. He earned a Master of Business Administration from the Wharton School, the business school of the University of Pennsylvania. Lynch made his mark as a mutual fund manager, showing a remarkable aptitude for picking stocks. At age 33, he took over the Magellan Fund, a mutual fund of a multinational financial corporation headquartered in Boston, Massachusetts. He ran it from 1977 to 1990. For these 13 years, the fund earned an annualized return of 29.2% under his management, more than twice what the S&P 500 earned during the same period of time. The fund became the world's best-performing mutual fund during his tenure as manager. His success allowed him to retire in 1990 at age 46.

Lynch
生平
簡介

4.4

人物傳記 Biography

Lynch's investment strategies can be boiled down to a few guiding principles. For starters, his initial evaluation of a stock entailed a thorough understanding of the company, its business model, its competitive edge, and its prospects. Since company revenue formed the building blocks of stock prices, he would also review the historical record of earnings. Just like Warren Buffett, Lynch was a value investor. He took calculated risks and leaned toward investing in small, fast-growing companies whose stocks could be purchased at a reasonable price. In his efforts to mitigate the downside risk of the market, Lynch diversified by investing in a wide range of stocks.

Lynch
投資
方法

While there are no hard-and-fast rules about investing, Lynch, in his books, offers practical advice to retail investors. When it comes to shopping for stocks, he believes that beginners and veteran investors alike are better off selecting companies or industries with which they are familiar. He suggests that investors do their homework and get the lay of the land before making any investment decisions. They should not be speculative and need to stay away from hot stocks in hot industries. Investors would be ill-advised to jump on the bandwagon. After all, investing is not like betting on red or black in a casino. At the emotional level, he argues that mental toughness is crucial in the face of the volatility of the market. While Lynch has been an advocate of investing for the long term, he does not recommend simply buying and holding a diversified portfolio. He thinks investors are responsible for reviewing their holdings every few months and rechecking the company's business to see if anything has changed. He would sell the stocks when the company's business goes south.

Lynch
投資
建議

■ 請回答以下問題：

_____ Q1. Peter Lynch is known as _____.
      (A) an author   (B) a value investor
      (C) a mutual fund manager   (D) all of the above

_____ Q2. As an investor, Lynch did NOT

(A) invest in hot stocks in hot industries.

(B) review the historical record of earnings.

(C) diversify by investing in a range of stocks.

(D) have a good understanding of a company's business model.

_____ Q3. Which of the following is NOT a piece of advice Lynch offers?

(A) selecting companies with which we are familiar

(B) reviewing our holdings every few months

(C) being speculative

(D) investing for the long term

_____ Q4. Why did Lynch diversify?

(A) to purchase stocks at a reasonable price

(B) to understand companies' prospects

(C) to mitigate risks

(D) to shop for stocks

_____ Q5. At what age did Lynch take over the Magellan Fund?

(A) 46   (B) 33   (C) 29   (D) not mentioned

4.4.3_S.mp3

STEP 5 跟讀 Shadowing

請根據母語人士所錄製的音檔，一句一句跟著唸。跟讀時請使用跟讀音檔，每句結束後，請利用句與句之間的空秒時間，複誦前面所聽到的句子。建議第一遍，看著文章跟著唸，第二遍則不看文章，只聽音檔唸。

4.4
人物傳記 Biography

171

STEP 6 聽讀 Listening

第一遍
→ 讀者會聽到音檔內母語人士完整且不間斷將本文唸一遍。試著不看文章,聽音檔內的母語人士完整且不間斷地將本文唸一遍,確認自己哪裡聽懂,那裡聽不懂。

第二遍
→ 再聽母語人士不間斷地將本文唸一遍,眼睛注視著正在朗誦的每個句子,針對自己沒聽懂的部分,特別仔細閱讀。

STEP 7 延伸學習

單字 Vocabulary

❶ **aptitude** [`æptə͵tjud]	n. 天賦 She has an aptitude for sports. 她有運動天賦。
❷ **tenure** [`tɛnjʊr]	n. 任職期間,任期 His tenure as president will end in November. 他的總統任期到 11 月結束。
❸ **calculated** [`kælkjə͵letɪd]	adj. 計算過的,經審慎評估的 She took calculated risks before buying stocks in a bear market. 她對於風險做過審慎評估後才在熊市買入股票。
❹ **entail** [ɪn`tel]	v. 伴隨著,包含 Investments entail certain risks. 投資會有一定的風險。
❺ **edge** [ɛdʒ]	n. 優勢 What is your competitive edge? 你的競爭優勢是什麼?

❻ prospect [`prɑspɛkt]	n. 前景 She is pessimistic about the prospects of her company. 她對她公司的前景感到悲觀。
❼ mitigate [`mɪtəˌget]	v. 減輕，減少（風險等） The drug can mitigate the pain. 這個藥物可以減輕疼痛。
❽ hard-and-fast [`hɑrd ænd`fæst]	adj. 硬性的（規定等），明文的 There is one hard-and-fast rule about doing research. 做研究有一條明文規定。
❾ ill-advised [`ɪləd`vaɪzd]	adj. 不明智的 She made an ill-advised decision. 她做了一個不明智的決定。
❿ bandwagon [`bændˌwægən]	n. 跟風，潮流 Many politicians have jumped on the bandwagon in support of same-sex marriage. 眾多政治人物跟上支持同性婚姻的潮流。

慣用語和片語 Expressions and Phrases

❶ make one's mark　成名，嶄露頭角

Michael Jordan made his mark in the NBA in the 1990s.
麥可喬丹於 90 年代在美國職籃嶄露頭角。

❷ boil down to sth　可歸結為…（＝be boiled down to...）

These problems can boil down to one thing, a lack of consensus.
這些問題都可以歸結為一件事情 —— 缺乏共識。

❸ get the lay of the land　搞清楚狀況，摸清底細

Since he is new to the company, he is trying to get the lay of the land.
因為他剛來到這家公司，他正試著了解這裡的狀況。

❹ go south　往南，走下坡，越來越差

Their friendship has gone south.
他們的友誼越來越差了。

4.4

人物傳記 Biography

A. Fill in the blanks with suitable words or phrases 將適合的字詞填入空格中

> ⓐ entail　ⓑ boil down to　ⓒ make his mark　ⓓ aptitude

1. These items can _____ just three categories.

2. She is a linguist and has an _____ for languages.

3. Her job _____ international travel.

4. Albert Einstein _____ in the field of theoretical physics.

B. Multiple choice questions 選擇題（可利用此題型熟悉多益、英檢考試）

_____ 1. The stock market went ------- and stock prices fell sharply.
(A) south　(B) north　(C) east　(D) west

_____ 2. He is a very careful person and does not make ------- decisions.
(A) good-looking　(B) never-ending
(C) well-rounded　(D) ill-advised

_____ 3. Students at this school are not allowed to dress freely. There are some ------- rules about dress.
(A) good-for-nothing　(B) hard-and-fast
(C) record-breaking　(D) state-of-the-art

_____ 4. The new medicine is effective and can ------- patients' suffering.
(A) guarantee　(B) mitigate　(C) radiate　(D) wrestle

_____ 5. The car company's unique self-driving technology is its ------- over competitors.
(A) edge　(B) pledge　(C) wedge　(D) fledge

▸▸ 解答請見 p.365

NOTE

4.5 經濟與財經
Economy & Finance

Did you know?
[你需要知道的 10 件事]

❶ 日裔美國人 Robert Kiyosaki（羅伯特・清崎）是美國知名富豪之一。

❷ Robert Kiyosaki 常常對於世界經濟的走向提出自己的見解。

❸ Robert Kiyosaki 是美國前總統川普的好友，曾多次一起受訪。

❹ Robert Kiyosaki 是《窮爸爸、富爸爸》的作者。

❺ Robert Kiyosaki 出版許多理財書籍，在世界各國辦講座教學。

❻ Robert Kiyosaki 認為學校教的理財觀念大部份都是錯誤的。

❼ 大部分的人都很害怕負債，富豪卻很少沒有負債的。

❽ 美國前總統川普很有錢，他不但負債很多，甚至多次破產過。

❾ 正向現金流就是錢流入自己的戶頭。

❿ 負向現金流就是錢從自己的戶頭流出去。

Must-know vocabulary
[你需要知道的 10 個單字]

❶ financial freedom *n.* 財務自由

❷ currency depreciation *n.* 貨幣貶值

❸ inflation *n.* 通貨膨脹

❹ positive cash flow *n.* 正向現金流

❺ negative cash flow *n.* 負向現金流

❻ financial knowledge *n.* 財經知識

❼ rental properties *n.* 出租用的不動產

❽ assets and liabilities *n.* 資產與負債

❾ average people *n.* 一般人

❿ financial literacy *n.* 財經素養

掃讀的目標是在文章中搜尋特定的人名、時間、地點，或相關詞語，就像是在電話簿中搜尋某人的電話號碼一樣，其他內容完全不看。

■ 請於 **30** 秒內在以下文章中找出下列文字並畫線，不要閱讀內容或嘗試理解文章。

❶ financial freedom
❷ currency depreciation
❸ inflation
❹ positive cash flow
❺ negative cash flow
❻ financial knowledge
❼ rental properties
❽ assets and liabilities
❾ average people
❿ financial literacy

Financial Literacy

(402 words)   By Yushiang Jou

Since so many people struggle on their path to financial freedom, investment books are selling like hotcakes these days. Most of these books zero in on such key topics as trading strategies and risk management. The conventional wisdom, however, has been challenged by *Rich Dad Poor Dad*, a groundbreaking book written by Robert Kiyosaki.

Kiyosaki is a renowned investor and educational entrepreneur. He has been invited to hold seminars to help people understand how money works. While many people invest in the stock market, he believes that due to market uncertainty and volatility, they can only be temporarily rich by investing in stocks. He contends that people can never become rich by just banking their money since governments from around the world are always printing money, thereby causing inflation and currency depreciation.

In his book, Kiyosaki seeks to unravel the secret of the rich. He points out that average people tend to believe assets are things they possess such as cars and condos, while the rich define assets and liabilities through the lens of cash flow. For

4.5

經濟與財經 Economy & Finance

example, when a condo is used as a personal residence, it becomes a liability in the sense that maintenance costs take money out of our pocket. Conversely, when a condo is used as a rental property, it becomes an asset that keeps bringing in money. This is why Kiyosaki owns 7000 rental properties, which keep putting money into his pocket. Highlighting the fundamental difference between assets and liabilities, he argues that rich people acquire assets to create a positive cash flow, while the poor (or the middle class) usually acquire liabilities that generate a negative cash flow.

What distinguishes the rich from the poor, Kiyosaki believes, is financial knowledge (or lack thereof). Since financial education is not part of school curriculum, a highly educated person can be financially illiterate. He argues that the main reason why people are financially illiterate is their limited knowledge of debt. Average people have been told to get out of debt, thinking debt will only make them poorer. On the contrary, most rich people see debt as an opportunity to make them richer. They oftentimes borrow money and use borrowed money to buy assets (e.g., rental properties) that can be monetized. By doing so, they are able to turn otherwise non-revenue-generating assets into revenues. Kiyosaki's book concludes that it is people's financial literacy that matters as they make investment decisions.

■ 請選擇正確的意思

_____ ❶ financial freedom　(A) 財經知識 (B) 財務自由

_____ ❷ currency depreciation　(A) 貨幣貶值 (B) 貨幣升值

_____ ❸ inflation　(A) 通貨緊縮 (B) 通貨膨脹

_____ ❹ positive cash flow　(A) 正向現金流 (B) 負向現金流

_____ ❺ negative cash flow　(A) 正向現金流 (B) 負向現金流

_____ ❻ financial knowledge　(A) 財經知識 (B) 財務自由

_____ ❼ rental properties　(A) 銷售物業 (B) 出租用的不動產

_____ ❽ assets and liabilities　(A) 義務與責任 (B) 資產與負債

_____ ❾ average people　(A) 一般人 (B) 有錢人

_____ ❿ financial literacy　(A) 財經素養 (B) 金融管理

針對剛才的文章，用 30 秒鐘瀏覽各段的第一句，粗略了解文章結構與大意即可。

Since so many people struggle on their path to financial freedom, investment books are selling like hotcakes these days. Most of these books zero in on such key topics as trading strategies and risk management. The conventional wisdom, however, has been challenged by *Rich Dad Poor Dad*, a groundbreaking book written by Robert Kiyosaki.

理財書籍很受歡迎

Kiyosaki is a renowned investor and educational entrepreneur. He has been invited to hold seminars to help people understand how money works. While many people invest in the stock market, he believes that due to market uncertainty and volatility, they can only be temporarily rich by investing in stocks. He contends that people can never become rich by just banking their money since governments from around the world are always printing money, thereby causing inflation and currency depreciation.

Kiyosaki 簡介

In his book, Kiyosaki seeks to unravel the secret of the rich. He points out that average people tend to believe assets are things they possess such as cars and condos, while the rich define assets and liabilities through the lens of cash flow. For example, when a condo is used as a personal residence, it becomes a liability in the sense that maintenance costs take money out of our pocket. Conversely, when a condo is used as a rental property, it becomes an asset that keeps bringing in money. This is why Kiyosaki owns 7000 rental properties, which keep putting money into his pocket. Highlighting the fundamental difference between assets and liabilities, he argues that rich people acquire assets to create a positive cash flow, while the poor (or the middle class) usually acquire liabilities that generate a negative cash flow.

Kiyosaki 的書揭露致富的秘密

4.5

經濟與財經 Economy & Finance

What distinguishes the rich from the poor, Kiyosaki believes, is financial knowledge (or lack thereof). Since financial education is not part of school curriculum, a highly educated person can be financially illiterate. He argues that the main reason why people are financially illiterate is their limited knowledge of debt. Average people have been told to get out of debt, thinking debt will only make them poorer. On the contrary, most rich people see debt as an opportunity to make them richer. They oftentimes borrow money and use borrowed money to buy assets (e.g., rental properties) that can be monetized. By doing so, they are able to turn otherwise non-revenue-generating assets into revenues. Kiyosaki's book concludes that it is people's financial literacy that matters as they make investment decisions.

Kiyosaki 的書指出貧富的差別

■ 回答以下問題，確認自己是否正確理解整篇文章的大意：

Q1. _____ People read investment books for no reason. (T/F)

Q2. _____ Investment books are not popular. (T/F)

Q3. _____ Kiyosaki is famous. (T/F)

Q4. _____ Kiyosaki is an author. (T/F)

Q5. _____ Kiyosaki believes financial knowledge is important. (T/F)

▶▶ 解答請見 p.366

STEP 3 細讀 Close reading

請用 60 秒的時間仔細閱讀以下內容，並回答問題。

Since so many people struggle on their path to financial freedom, investment books are selling like hotcakes these days. Most of these books zero in on such key topics as trading strategies and risk management. The conventional wisdom, however, has been challenged by *Rich Dad Poor Dad*, a groundbreaking book written by Robert Kiyosaki.

_____ Q1. According to this passage, which of the following is correct?

  (A) Trading strategies are not important.

  (B) Kiyosaki's book differs from most investment books.

  (C) Mental toughness has nothing to do with investment success.

  (D) Kiyosaki struggles on his path to financial freedom.

_____ Q2. According to this passage, most investment books do not discuss

  _____.

  (A) financial freedom.　　(B) assets and liabilities.

  (C) risk management.　　(D) trading strategies.

▶▶ 解答請見 p.366

STEP 4 高理解速讀 Speed Reading with Greater Comprehension

> 請用 90 秒的時間，看完整篇文章。然後跟著每一個有意義的色塊，提升理解的速度。（請盡量試著不查自己不認識的字，利用前後文去推測意思。）

Since so many people struggle on their path to financial freedom, investment books are selling like hotcakes these days. Most of these books zero in on such key topics as trading strategies and risk management. The conventional wisdom, however, has been challenged by *Rich Dad Poor Dad*, a groundbreaking book written by Robert Kiyosaki.

理財書籍很受歡迎

4.5

經濟與財經 Economy & Finance

Kiyosaki is a renowned investor and educational entrepreneur. He has been invited to hold seminars to help people understand how money works. While many people invest in the stock market, he believes that due to market uncertainty and volatility, they can only be temporarily rich by investing in stocks. He contends that people can never become rich by just banking their money since governments from around the world are always printing money, thereby causing inflation and currency depreciation.

Kiyosaki 簡介

In his book, Kiyosaki seeks to unravel the secret of the rich. He points out that average people tend to believe assets are things they possess such as cars and condos, while the rich define assets and liabilities through the lens of cash flow. For example, when a condo is used as a personal residence, it becomes a liability in the sense that maintenance costs take money out of our pocket. Conversely, when a condo is used as a rental property, it becomes an asset that keeps bringing in money. This is why Kiyosaki owns 7000 rental properties, which keep putting money into his pocket. Highlighting the fundamental difference between assets and liabilities, he argues that rich people acquire assets to create a positive cash flow, while the poor (or the middle class) usually acquire liabilities that generate a negative cash flow.

What distinguishes the rich from the poor, Kiyosaki believes, is financial knowledge (or lack thereof). Since financial education is not part of school curriculum, a highly educated person can be financially illiterate. He argues that the main reason why people are financially illiterate is their limited knowledge of debt. Average people have been told to get out of debt, thinking debt will only make them poorer. On the contrary, most rich people see debt as an opportunity to make them richer. They oftentimes borrow money and use borrowed money to buy assets (e.g., rental properties) that can be monetized. By doing so, they are able to turn otherwise non-revenue-generating assets into revenues. Kiyosaki's book concludes that it is people's financial literacy that matters as they make investment decisions.

■ 請回答以下問題：

_____ Q1. Robert Kiyosaki is NOT _____.

      (A) a university professor

      (B) an entrepreneur

      (C) an investor

      (D) an author

Q2. Which of the following is NOT a typical reason why people read
investment books?

(A) to learn about trading strategies

(B) to learn about risk management

(C) to learn about ways to achieve financial freedom

(D) to learn how to use borrowed money to buy revenue-generating assets

Q3. Which of the following is NOT a result of governments' printing
money?

(A) savings in the bank adversely affected

(B) fewer people reading investment books

(C) currency depreciation

(D) inflation

Q4. What would Kiyosaki say in his seminars?

(A) We should go after profits in the stock market.

(B) We should mitigate risks in the stock market.

(C) We should acquire asserts that create positive cash flow.

(D) We should bank more money.

Q5. According to Kiyosaki, why do many people struggle on their path to
financial freedom?

(A) They do not read enough investment books.

(B) They do not do well in the stock market.

(C) They are financially illiterate.

(D) They do not bank enough money.

▶▶ 解答請見 p.367

STEP 5 跟讀 Shadowing

　　請根據母語人士所錄製的音檔，一句一句跟著唸。跟讀時請使用跟讀音檔，每句結束後，請利用句與句之間的空秒時間，複誦前面所聽到的句子。建議第一遍，看著文章跟著唸，第二遍則不看文章，只聽音檔唸。

4.5.1_L.mp3

STEP 6 聽讀 Listening

第一遍
→ 讀者會聽到音檔內母語人士完整且不間斷將本文唸一遍。試著不看文章，聽音檔內的母語人士完整且不間斷地將本文唸一遍，確認自己哪裡聽懂，那裡聽不懂。

第二遍
→ 再聽母語人士不間斷地將本文唸一遍，眼睛注視著正在朗誦的每個句子，針對自己沒聽懂的部分，特別仔細閱讀。

STEP 7 延伸學習

單字 Vocabulary

❶ **struggle** [ˈstrʌgl]	v. 費力地進行，掙扎 She struggled to do well on the test. 她努力想要考高分。
❷ **groundbreaking** [ˈgraʊn(d)brekɪŋ]	adj. 開創性的，破土的 She did groundbreaking research on immunology. 她在免疫學上做了創新的研究。
❸ **renowned** [rɪˈnaʊnd]	adj. 知名的 Brian Greene is a renowned physicist. 布萊恩格林是一位知名的物理學家。

❹ **volatility** [vɑləˈtɪlətɪ]	n. 反覆無常，不穩定性；（價格等的）波動率 The government is monitoring the volatility of Bitcoin. 政府正密切關注比特幣的波動率。
❺ **unravel** [ʌnˈrævəl]	v. 揭露（秘密），解開（謎團） Many scientists are trying to unravel the secrets of the new variant. 許多科學家正試圖解開新變種病毒的謎團。
❻ **liabilities** [ˌlaɪəˈbɪlətɪz]	n. 負債，債務 The company went bankrupt last year because of heavy liabilities. 這家公司去年因為沉重的負債而破產了。
❼ **illiterate** [ɪˈlɪtərət]	adj. 文盲的，知識淺陋的 She seems to be computer-illiterate. 她似乎對電腦一竅不通。
❽ **literacy** [ˈlɪtərəsɪ]	n. 識字，讀寫能力；（在某領域的）知能 Computer literacy is important these days. 如今，會用電腦是很重要的。
❾ **monetize** [ˈmʌnətaɪz]	v. 從⋯賺錢 The YouTuber is trying to monetize his YouTube channel. 這名網紅正試圖透過他的 YouTube 頻道來賺錢。
❿ **revenue** [ˈrɛvənju]	n. 收入，營收 His YouTube channel is another source of his revenue. 他的 YouTube 頻道是他另一個收入來源。

4.5

經濟與財經 Economy & Finance

❶ sell like hotcakes 很暢銷

The new video game is <u>selling like hotcakes</u>.
這款新推出的電玩遊戲很暢銷。

❷ conventional wisdom 主流想法，傳統觀點

The <u>conventional wisdom</u> about herd immunity has been challenged.
傳統群體免疫的觀點已受到質疑。

❸ zero in on 鎖定，針對

They are <u>zeroing in on</u> the problem of inflation in this meeting.
他們在會議上針對通膨的問題加以討論。

❹ it is... that matters 重要的是，⋯

<u>It is</u> not money <u>that matters</u>, but it is your sincerity I was moved with.
重點不是錢，而是你的誠意打動了我。

A. Fill in the blanks with suitable words or phrases 將適合的字詞填入空格中

ⓐ struggle　**ⓑ** literacy　**ⓒ** illiterate　**ⓓ** volatility

1. He attempts to promote financial _____ in his book.

2. A hallmark of the stock market is its _____ .

3. He _____ to find employment and paid his bills.

4. Many people in undeveloped countries are _____ .

B. Multiple choice questions 選擇題（可利用此題型熟悉多益、英檢考試）

_____ 1. Scientists are trying to ------- the mystery of the universe.
(A) conceal　(B) unravel　(C) haunt　(D) perish

_____ 2. Facebook can ------- its users by means of advertising.
(A) monetize　(B) permeate　(C) salvage　(D) baffle

_____ 3. His ------- work in virology has attracted much attention.
(A) unsuccessful　(B) bastard　(C) void　(D) groundbreaking

_____ 4. Einstein was a ------- scientist famous for his theory of relativity.
(A) genetic　(B) renowned　(C) irrelevant　(D) finite

_____ 5. Can investment in the stock market ------ higher incomes for you?
(A) generate　(B) blockade　(C) fluctuate　(D) radiate

▶▶ 解答請見 p.369

4.5

經濟與財經 Economy & Finance

Did you know?

[你需要知道的 **10** 件事]

❶ 金融市場（包含股票市場和債券市場）具有週期性。

❷ 金融市場一片欣欣向榮稱為牛市（或多頭市場）。

❸ 牛市通常發生在低利率的環境下。

❹ 金融市場慘澹無光稱為熊市（或空頭市場）。

❺ 許多原因可能導致熊市，例如央行升息、戰爭、經濟衰退等。

❻ 牛市持續的時間通常比熊市更長。

❼ 2020 年由新冠疫情引起的熊市為史上最短的熊市，只維持了 33 天。

❽ 藍籌股（blue-chip stocks，或稱「績優股」）泛指財務穩定的大公司股票，例如台積電的股票。

❾ 在金融市場，散戶投資者（retail investor）泛指一般個人投資人。

❿ 在金融市場，機構投資者（institutional investors）泛指各種類型的基金、保險公司、各大企業等。

Must-know vocabulary

[你需要知道的 **10** 個單字]

❶ bull market *n.* 牛市

❷ bear market *n.* 熊市

❸ analogy *n.* 比喻

❹ bond *n.* 債券

❺ cryptocurrency *n.* 加密貨幣

❻ economy *n.* 經濟

❼ optimism *n.* 樂觀情緒

❽ trajectory *n.* 趨勢

❾ blue-chip stock *n.* 藍籌股，績優股

❿ pessimistic *adj.* 悲觀的

掃讀的目標是在文章中搜尋特定的人名、時間、地點，或相關詞語，就像是在電話簿中搜尋某人的電話號碼一樣，其他內容完全不看。

■ 請於 **30** 秒內在以下文章中找出下列文字並畫線，不要閱讀內容或嘗試理解文章。

❶ bull market ❷ bear market

❸ analogy ❹ bond

❺ cryptocurrency ❻ economy

❼ optimism ❽ trajectory

❾ blue-chip stock ❿ pessimistic

Bull and Bear Markets

(403 words)

By Yushiang Jou

Cyclical by nature, financial markets keep oscillating between good times and bad times, also known as bull markets and bear markets. In a bull market, prices continue to go up. This upward trend is called "a bull market" by analogy with the way a bull attacks by lifting its horns upward. Conversely, prices go down in a bear market. This downward trend is called "a bear market" by analogy with the way a bear attacks by swiping its paws downward. While many people try to outsmart the market, investors who can actually beat the bear market are few and far between. While bull and bear markets are often used to refer to the stock market, they can also be applied to anything tradable, such as bonds, foreign currencies, and cryptocurrencies.

The commonly accepted definition of a bull market is a rising market where the majority of investors are buying and stocks rise by 20% or more from their recent lows. Historically speaking, the average length of a bull market is around 3.8 years. A bull market and a strong economy often exist side-by-side. Bull markets are fueled by low interest rates, a rise in corporate profits, and a drop in

4.5

經濟與財經 Economy & Finance

unemployment. As a result, bull markets can breed optimism. Investors who believe that prices will continue to rise are known as "the bulls." Once bull markets run out of steam, investor confidence quickly evaporates and stock prices plummet, a sign of the onset of a bear market.

In sharp contrast to the upward trajectory of a bull market, stocks can easily tumble anywhere from 20% or more in a bear market. Not even blue-chip stocks are a safe haven. Bear markets often go hand in hand with rising interest rates, rising unemployment, declining corporate profits, banking crises, and recessions, among many other factors. The average length of a bear market is a little under 10 months. Even though bear markets tend to be shorter than bull markets, they can be incredibly painful, bad news all over the place. Pessimistic investors who believe that things can only get worse are referred to as "the bears." When the market is out of the woods, the negative market sentiment starts to fade as the economic data is stronger. When a bear market comes to an end, retail and institutional investors alike will be able to breathe easy again and welcome the birth of the next bull market.

■ 請選擇正確的意思

_____ ❶ bull market　(A) 牛市 (B) 熊市

_____ ❷ bear market　(A) 牛市 (B) 熊市

_____ ❸ analogy　(A) 比喻 (B) 誇飾

_____ ❹ bond　(A) 債券 (B) 加密貨幣

_____ ❺ cryptocurrency　(A) 債券 (B) 加密貨幣

_____ ❻ economy　(A) 經濟 (B) 投資

_____ ❼ optimism　(A) 悲觀情緒 (B) 樂觀情緒

_____ ❽ trajectory　(A) 現狀 (B) 趨勢

_____ ❾ blue-chip stock　(A) 藍籌股 (B) 垃圾股

_____ ❿ pessimistic　(A) 悲觀的 (B) 樂觀的

▶▶ 解答請見 p.370

針對剛才的文章，用 30 秒鐘瀏覽各段的第一句，粗略了解文章結構與大意即可。

Cyclical by nature, financial markets keep oscillating between good times and bad times, also known as bull markets and bear markets. In a bull market, prices continue to go up. This upward trend is called "a bull market" by analogy with the way a bull attacks by lifting its horns upward. Conversely, prices go down in a bear market. This downward trend is called "a bear market" by analogy with the way a bear attacks by swiping its paws downward. While many people try to outsmart the market, investors who can actually beat the bear market are few and far between. While bull and bear markets are often used to refer to the stock market, they can also be applied to anything tradable, such as bonds, foreign currencies, and cryptocurrencies.

牛市
與熊市
的簡介

The commonly accepted definition of a bull market is a rising market where the majority of investors are buying and stocks rise by 20% or more from their recent lows. Historically speaking, the average length of a bull market is around 3.8 years. A bull market and a strong economy often exist side-by-side. Bull markets are fueled by low interest rates, a rise in corporate profits, and a drop in unemployment. As a result, bull markets can breed optimism. Investors who believe that prices will continue to rise are known as "the bulls." Once bull markets run out of steam, investor confidence quickly evaporates and stock prices plummet, a sign of the onset of a bear market.

牛市
盛況

In sharp contrast to the upward trajectory of a bull market, stocks can easily tumble anywhere from 20% or more in a bear market. Not even blue-chip stocks are a safe haven. Bear markets often go hand in hand with rising interest rates, rising unemployment, declining corporate profits, banking crises, and recessions, among many other factors. The average length of a bear market is a little under 10 months.

熊市
慘狀

4.5

經濟與財經 Economy & Finance

Even though bear markets tend to be shorter than bull markets, they can be incredibly painful, bad news all over the place. Pessimistic investors who believe that things can only get worse are referred to as "the bears." When the market is out of the woods, the negative market sentiment starts to fade as the economic data is stronger. When a bear market comes to an end, retail and institutional investors alike will be able to breathe easy again and welcome the birth of the next bull market.

■ 回答以下問題，確認自己是否正確理解整篇文章的大意：

Q1. _____ Some financial markets can be bullish forever. (T/F)

Q2. _____ Some financial markets can be bearish forever. (T/F)

Q3. _____ A bull market is a rising market. (T/F)

Q4. _____ A bear market is a rising market. (T/F)

Q5. _____ Bull markets are sometimes similar to bear markets. (T/F)

▶▶ 解答請見 p.370

STEP 3 細讀 Close reading

請用 60 秒的時間仔細閱讀以下內容，並回答問題。

In sharp contrast to the upward trajectory of a bull market, stocks can easily tumble anywhere from 20% or more in a bear market. Not even blue-chip stocks are a safe haven. Bear markets often go hand in hand with rising interest rates, rising unemployment, declining corporate profits, banking crises, and recessions, among many other factors. The average length of a bear market is a little under 10 months.

_____ Q1. According to this passage, which of the following is correct?

  (A) Stocks can rise by 20% or more in bear markets.

  (B) Interest rates usually go down in bear markets.

  (C) Blue-chip stocks are negatively affected by bear markets.

  (D) Corporate profits usually grow in bear markets.

_____ Q2. According to this passage, which of the following can contribute to a bear market?

  (A) a weak economy

  (B) a drop in unemployment

  (C) a rise in corporate profits

  (D) low interest rates

▶▶ 解答請見 p.370

STEP 4 高理解速讀 Speed Reading with Greater Comprehension

　　請用 90 秒的時間，看完整篇文章。然後跟著每一個有意義的色塊，提升理解的速度。（請盡量試著不查自己不認識的字，利用前後文去推測意思。）

Cyclical by nature, financial markets keep oscillating between good times and bad times, also known as bull markets and bear markets. In a bull market, prices continue to go up. This upward trend is called "a bull market" by analogy with the way a bull attacks by lifting its horns upward. Conversely, prices go down in a bear market. This downward trend is called "a bear market" by analogy with the way a bear attacks by swiping its paws downward. While many people try to outsmart the market, investors who can actually beat the bear market are few and far between. While bull and bear markets are often used to refer to the stock market, they can also be applied to anything tradable, such as bonds, foreign currencies, and cryptocurrencies.

牛市
與熊市
的簡介

4.5

經濟與財經 Economy & Finance

The commonly accepted definition of a bull market is a rising market where the majority of investors are buying and stocks rise by 20% or more from their recent lows. Historically speaking, the average length of a bull market is around 3.8 years. A bull market and a strong economy often exist side-by-side. Bull markets are fueled by low interest rates, a rise in corporate profits, and a drop in unemployment. As a result, bull markets can breed optimism. Investors who believe that prices will continue to rise are known as "the bulls." Once bull markets run out of steam, investor confidence quickly evaporates and stock prices plummet, a sign of the onset of a bear market.

牛市盛況

In sharp contrast to the upward trajectory of a bull market, stocks can easily tumble anywhere from 20% or more in a bear market. Not even blue-chip stocks are a safe haven. Bear markets often go hand in hand with rising interest rates, rising unemployment, declining corporate profits, banking crises, and recessions, among many other factors. The average length of a bear market is a little under 10 months. Even though bear markets tend to be shorter than bull markets, they can be incredibly painful, bad news all over the place. Pessimistic investors who believe that things can only get worse are referred to as "the bears." When the market is out of the woods, the negative market sentiment starts to fade as the economic data is stronger. When a bear market comes to an end, retail and institutional investors alike will be able to breathe easy again and welcome the birth of the next bull market.

熊市慘狀

■ 請回答以下問題：

_____ Q1. Bull and bear markets can be applied to _____.
(A) stocks　(B) bonds　(C) cryptocurrencies　(D) all of the above

_____ Q2. What is the average length of a bull market?
(A) a little under 10 months　(B) around 3.8 years
(C) around 2.8 years　　　　(D) none of the above

_____ Q3. What is the average length of a bear market?

  (A) a little under 10 months   (B) around 3.8 years

  (C) around 2.8 years   (D) none of the above

_____ Q4. What happens when a bull market runs out of steam?

  (A) Stock prices can plummet.

  (B) Investor confidence can evaporate.

  (C) A bear market can start.

  (D) all of the above

_____ Q5. A bull market is NOT fueled by _____.

  (A) low interest rates.   (B) a rise in corporate profits.

  (C) a rise in unemployment.   (D) a strong economy.

▶▶ 解答請見 p.371

4.5.2_S.mp3

STEP 5 跟讀 Shadowing

　　請根據母語人士所錄製的音檔，一句一句跟著唸。跟讀時請使用跟讀音檔，每句結束後，請利用句與句之間的空秒時間，複誦前面所聽到的句子。建議第一遍，看著文章跟著唸，第二遍則不看文章，只聽音檔唸。

4.5.2_L.mp3

STEP 6 聽讀 Listening

第一遍

→ 讀者會聽到音檔內母語人士完整且不間斷將本文唸一遍。試著不看文章，聽音檔內的母語人士完整且不間斷地將本文唸一遍，確認自己哪裡聽懂，那裡聽不懂。

第二遍

→ 再聽母語人士不間斷地將本文唸一遍，眼睛注視著正在朗誦的每個句子，針對自己沒聽懂的部分，特別仔細閱讀。

單字 Vocabulary

❶ cyclical [ˈsaɪklɪkl̩]	adj. 循環的 The four seasons are cyclical in many countries. 四季在許多國家中是不斷循環的。
❷ oscillate [ˈɑsl̩et]	v. 來回擺動 The mood of investors oscillates between optimism and pessimism. 投資人的情緒在樂觀與悲觀氣氛之中來回擺盪。
❸ conversely [kənˈvɝslɪ]	adv. 相反地 Investors tend to be optimistic in a bull market. Conversely, they tend to be pessimistic in a bear market. 在牛市，投資人容易感到樂觀。相反地，他們在熊市容易悲觀。
❹ outsmart [ˈaʊtˈsmɑrt]	v. 比…更聰明 This animal outsmarts its prey. 這種動物比牠的獵物更聰明。
❺ side-by-side [ˈsaɪd baɪ ˈsaɪd]	adv. 同時地 She is using two operating systems side-by-side. 她同時使用兩個作業系統。
❻ evaporate [ɪˈvæpəˌret]	v. 蒸發，消散，消失 Her anger evaporated after two hours. 兩個小時之後，她的氣消了。
❼ plummet [ˈplʌmɪt]	v. 暴跌 The stock price of the company plummeted 20 percent yesterday. 這間公司的股價昨天暴跌了 20%。

❽ **onset** [`ɑn͵sɛt]	n. 開始，到來 They are excited about the onset of summer. 他們對於夏天的到來感到興奮。
❾ **sentiment** [`sɛntəmənt]	n. 情緒 Anti-war sentiment is growing in many countries. 許多國家的反戰情緒高漲。
❿ **fade** [fed]	v. 逐漸消失 Her smile faded from her face. 她臉上的笑容漸漸消失了。

慣用語和片語 Expressions and Phrases

❶ by analogy with　與⋯相類比

She attempted to explain this abstract idea by analogy with something concrete.
她試圖用具體的東西來比喻這個抽象的概念。

❷ few and far between　數量很少

Talented basketball players like Michael Jordan are few and far between.
像麥可喬丹那樣有天賦的籃球員少之又少。

❸ run out of steam　失去動力

This bull market ran out of steam in the end of 2021.
牛市在 2021 年底失去了上漲的動力。

❹ breathe easy　鬆一口氣

She could finally breathe easy after the exam.
考試結束之後她終於鬆了一口氣。

4.5

經濟與財經 Economy & Finance

A. Fill in the blanks with suitable words or phrases 將適合的字詞填入空格中

> **ⓐ** breathe easy　**ⓑ** onset　**ⓒ** outsmart　**ⓓ** run out of steam

1. He is trying to _____ his enemy.

2. The market _____ and stock prices went down.

3. The sudden _____ of fever is worrying.

4. The crisis is over now. They will be able to _____ again.

B. Multiple choice questions 選擇題（可利用此題型熟悉多益、英檢考試）

_____ 1. Some politicians expressed anti-immigrant ------- in the election.
      (A) assumptions　(B) sentiments
      (C) attachments　(D) imaginations

_____ 2. NBA players willing to come to Taiwan to play professional
      basketball are -------.
      (A) few and far between　(B) at any expense
      (C) by hook or by crook　(D) down to earth

_____ 3. He suffered a serious setback and his confidence -------.
      (A) fabricated　(B) deliberated　(C) evaporated　(D) reconciliated

_____ 4. Winter is coming and temperatures are expected to ------- next week.
      (A) implicate　(B) plummet　(C) muddle　(D) soar

_____ 5. Antarctica is at the bottom of the globe. -------, the North Pole is at
      the top of the globe.
      (A) Conversely　(B) Fundamentally
      (C) Biologically　(D) Likewise

▶▶ 解答請見 p.372

NOTE

Did you know?

[你需要知道的 10 件事]

❶ 資本市場的價格由供需兩端決定，越多人要的商品，價格就會越貴。

❷ 在全世界每個國家，通貨膨脹每年都會發生。

❸ 當儲蓄的利息低於通膨時，存款的價值就會持續減少。

❹ 當通貨膨脹發生時，手裡的錢就會變薄，能買的東西就會變少。

❺ 房屋、汽車、機票、學費、水電瓦斯費等都會受到通貨膨脹的影響。

❻ 雖然薪資也會每年調高一些，其幅度常常落後於通膨率。

❼ 各國的中央銀行持續監控通貨膨脹率，並調整貨幣政策。

❽ 中央銀行降息可以刺激並活絡經濟。

❾ 中央銀行升息可以抑制消費，冷卻經濟。

❿ 當急劇通膨發生時，國家的貨幣可能會變成像壁紙一樣沒有價值。

Must-know vocabulary

[你需要知道的 10 個單字]

❶ persistent *adj.* 持續的

❷ need-based expense *n.* 生活必要開銷

❸ purchasing power *n.* 購買力

❹ notorious reputation *n.* 惡名昭彰

❺ higher wage *n.* 更高的薪資

❻ consumer sentiment *n.* 消費情緒

❼ out of the blue *adv.* 出乎意料地

❽ upside *n.* 好處

❾ curb *v.* 抑制

❿ interest rate *n.* 利率

掃讀的目標是在文章中搜尋特定的人名、時間、地點，或相關詞語，就像是在電話簿中搜尋某人的電話號碼一樣，其他內容完全不看。

■ 請於 **30** 秒內在以下文章中找出下列文字並畫線，不要閱讀內容或嘗試理解文章。

❶ persistent
❷ need-based expense
❸ purchasing power
❹ notorious reputation
❺ higher wage
❻ consumer sentiment
❼ out of the blue
❽ upside
❾ curb
❿ interest rate

The Upsides & Downsides of Inflation

(444 words)   By Yushiang Jou

Inflation is a persistent and widespread rise in prices, with a resulting loss of purchasing power. When prices are climbing, money cannot buy as much as it used to. For example, if we leave $100 under the mattress for ten years, we would not be able to buy as much as we could today due to inflation. Inflation therefore can lead to higher costs of living, including food and utilities, among other need-based expenses.

Inflation does not just happen out of the blue. When governments want to stimulate the economy, they print money and inject it into the economy. In consequence, people have more money to spend and prices would go up. Another major driver of inflation is an increase in demand for goods and services. That consumers are willing to pay more can also jack up prices.

Despite its notorious reputation, inflation is a necessary evil and has its upsides. Moderate rates of inflation serve as oil for the gears of the economy, making wages more flexible. Stable inflation can increase consumer demand. Some

4.5

經濟與財經 Economy & Finance

companies can even reap the benefits of inflation because, with increased demand and less supply, they are able to charge more for their goods. For example, when housing demand is high, home-building companies may charge higher prices for homes.

However, a high rate of inflation may act as sand in the gears of the economy. As prices take off, employees would ask for higher wages, which in turn would push up costs for businesses. Companies are likely to pass on higher costs to their consumers, thereby driving up prices further and leading to an upward spiral of wages and prices. Elevated levels of inflation can also contribute to a sharp downturn in consumer confidence, causing stock prices to fall and sending ripples across the economy.

When governments print too much money to pay for spending, inflation can quickly get out of hand. That the value of currency tumbles rapidly (e.g., 50% or more each month) can tip the economy into recession, a nightmare for all too many people. Though rare, outrageous levels of inflation recently happened in Zimbabwe in 2008 and in Venezuela in 2016, rendering their currencies effectively worthless.

When inflation is not kept in check, central banks, such as the Federal Reserve or the European Central Bank, would raise interest rates in a bid to curb inflation and prevent widespread economic pain. Interest rates are an inflation-fighting tool that can depress economic activity. With higher interest rates, average consumers are likely to tighten the purse strings, businesses reluctant to raise prices. In other words, lower spending would translate into lower prices, allowing central banks to tame inflation.

■ 請選擇正確的意思

_____ ❶ persistent　(A) 短暫的 (B) 持續的

_____ ❷ need-based expense　(A) 生活必要開銷 (B) 奢侈品消費

_____ ❸ purchasing power　(A) 銷售力 (B) 購買力

_____ ❹ notorious reputation　(A) 惡名昭彰 (B) 名揚四海

_____ ❺ higher wages　(A) 更低的薪資 (B) 更高的薪資

_____ ❻ consumer sentiment　(A) 消費情緒 (B) 儲蓄習慣

_____ ❼ out of the blue　(A) 可預期地 (B) 出乎意料地

_____ ❽ upside　(A) 壞處 (B) 好處

_____ ❾ curb　(A) 放任 (B) 抑制

_____ ❿ interest rate　(A) 利率 (B) 利益

▶▶ 解答請見 p.374

STEP 2　略讀 Skimming

針對剛才的文章，用 30 秒鐘瀏覽各段的第一句，粗略了解文章結構與大意即可。

Inflation is a persistent and widespread rise in prices, with a resulting loss of purchasing power. When prices are climbing, money cannot buy as much as it used to. For example, if we leave $100 under the mattress for ten years, we would not be able to buy as much as we could today due to inflation. Inflation therefore can lead to higher costs of living, including food and utilities, among other need-based expenses.

通膨的
定義

Inflation does not just happen out of the blue. When governments want to stimulate the economy, they print money and inject it into the economy. In consequence, people have more money to spend and prices would go up. Another major driver of inflation is an increase in demand for goods and services. That consumers are willing to pay more can also jack up prices.

通膨
發生的
原因

4.5

經濟與財經 Economy & Finance

Despite its notorious reputation, inflation is a necessary evil and has its upsides. Moderate rates of inflation serve as oil for the gears of the economy, making wages more flexible. Stable inflation can increase consumer demand. Some companies can even reap the benefits of inflation because, with increased demand and less supply, they are able to charge more for their goods. For example, when housing demand is high, home-building companies may charge higher prices for homes.

通膨的
好處

However, a high rate of inflation may act as sand in the gears of the economy. As prices take off, employees would ask for higher wages, which in turn would push up costs for businesses. Companies are likely to pass on higher costs to their consumers, thereby driving up prices further and leading to an upward spiral of wages and prices. Elevated levels of inflation can also contribute to a sharp downturn in consumer confidence, causing stock prices to fall and sending ripples across the economy.

高通膨
的壞處

When governments print too much money to pay for spending, inflation can quickly get out of hand. That the value of currency tumbles rapidly (e.g., 50% or more each month) can tip the economy into recession, a nightmare for all too many people. Though rare, outrageous levels of inflation recently happened in Zimbabwe in 2008 and in Venezuela in 2016, rendering their currencies effectively worthless.

通膨
失控的
後果

When inflation is not kept in check, central banks, such as the Federal Reserve or the European Central Bank, would raise interest rates in a bid to curb inflation and prevent widespread economic pain. Interest rates are an inflation-fighting tool that can depress economic activity. With higher interest rates, average consumers are likely to tighten the purse strings, businesses reluctant to raise prices. In other words, lower spending would translate into lower prices, allowing central banks to tame inflation.

中央銀
行壓制
通膨的
方式

■ 回答以下問題，確認自己是否正確理解整篇文章的大意：

Q1. _____ Inflation leads to a loss of purchasing power. (T/F)

Q2. _____ Inflation happens for a reason. (T/F)

Q3. _____ Inflation has no advantages. (T/F)

Q4. _____ Central banks will respond to a high rate of inflation. (T/F)

Q5. _____ Interest rates are an inflation-fighting tool. (T/F)

▶▶ 解答請見 p.374

STEP 3 細讀 Close reading

請用 60 秒的時間仔細閱讀以下內容，並回答問題。

Inflation does not just happen out of the blue. When governments want to stimulate the economy and create more jobs, they print money and inject it into the economy. In consequence, people have more money to spend and prices would go up. Another major driver of inflation is an increase in demand for goods and services, which can also jack up prices since consumers are willing to pay more.

_____ Q1. According to this passage, which of the following is correct?
   (A) At least two reasons can cause inflation.
   (B) Governments print money to prevent inflation.
   (C) Consumers do not want to pay more for the same thing.
   (D) Governments inject money into the economy to prevent inflation.

_____ Q2. According to this passage, inflation can _____.
   (A) make things cheaper
   (B) help people save more money
   (C) stimulate the economy
   (D) happen for no reason

▶▶ 解答請見 p.374

4.5

經濟與財經 Economy & Finance

請用 90 秒的時間，看完整篇文章。然後跟著每一個有意義的色塊，提升理解的速度。（請盡量試著不查自己不認識的字，利用前後文去推測意思。）

Inflation is a persistent and widespread rise in prices, with a resulting loss of purchasing power. When prices are climbing, money cannot buy as much as it used to. For example, if we leave $100 under the mattress for ten years, we would not be able to buy as much as we could today due to inflation. Inflation therefore can lead to higher costs of living, including food and utilities, among other need-based expenses.

通膨的定義

Inflation does not just happen out of the blue. When governments want to stimulate the economy, they print money and inject it into the economy. In consequence, people have more money to spend and prices would go up. Another major driver of inflation is an increase in demand for goods and services. That consumers are willing to pay more can also jack up prices.

通膨發生的原因

Despite its notorious reputation, inflation is a necessary evil and has its upsides. Moderate rates of inflation serve as oil for the gears of the economy, making wages more flexible. Stable inflation can increase consumer demand. Some companies can even reap the benefits of inflation because, with increased demand and less supply, they are able to charge more for their goods. For example, when housing demand is high, home-building companies may charge higher prices for homes.

通膨的好處

However, a high rate of inflation may act as sand in the gears of the economy. As prices take off, employees would ask for higher wages, which in turn would push up costs for businesses. Companies are likely to pass on higher costs to their consumers, thereby driving up prices further and leading to an upward spiral of wages and prices. Elevated levels of inflation can also contribute to a sharp downturn in consumer confidence, causing stock prices to fall and sending ripples across the economy.

When governments print too much money to pay for spending, inflation can quickly get out of hand. That the value of currency tumbles rapidly (e.g., 50% or more each month) can tip the economy into recession, a nightmare for all too many people. Though rare, outrageous levels of inflation recently happened in Zimbabwe in 2008 and in Venezuela in 2016, rendering their currencies effectively worthless.

When inflation is not kept in check, central banks, such as the Federal Reserve or the European Central Bank, would raise interest rates in a bid to curb inflation and prevent widespread economic pain. Interest rates are an inflation-fighting tool that can depress economic activity. With higher interest rates, average consumers are likely to tighten the purse strings, businesses reluctant to raise prices. In other words, lower spending would translate into lower prices, allowing central banks to tame inflation.

■ 請回答以下問題：

_____ Q1. Which of the following is NOT a sign of inflation?
(A) prices climbing for several months in a row
(B) people buying less with their money
(C) economic activity being depressed
(D) increased demand and less supply

Q2. Which of the following is NOT one of the upsides of inflation?

    (A) flexible wages

    (B) lower housing prices

    (C) increased consumer consumption

    (D) increased business profits

Q3. Which of the following is NOT one of the downsides of inflation?

    (A) companies often passing on higher costs to consumers

    (B) economic activity being stimulated

    (C) downturn in consumer confidence

    (D) falling stock prices

Q4. Why do central banks combat high inflation?

    (A) to keep the economy moving at a sensible speed

    (B) to stimulate the economy

    (C) to increase demand

    (D) to print more money

Q5. Which of the following can be inferred from the article?

    (A) Inflation is a not double-edged sword.

    (B) Inflation is good for savings in the bank.

    (C) High inflation falls back on its own.

    (D) Moderate inflation is a sign of a healthy economy.

▶▶ 解答請見 p.375

4.5.3_S.mp3

STEP 5 跟讀 Shadowing

請根據母語人士所錄製的音檔，一句一句跟著唸。跟讀時請使用跟讀音檔，每句結束後，請利用句與句之間的空秒時間，複誦前面所聽到的句子。建議第一遍，看著文章跟著唸，第二遍則不看文章，只聽音檔唸。

STEP 6 聽讀 Listening

第一遍
→ 讀者會聽到音檔內母語人士完整且不間斷將本文唸一遍。試著不看文章，聽音檔內的母語人士完整且不間斷地將本文唸一遍，確認自己哪裡聽懂，那裡聽不懂。

第二遍
→ 再聽母語人士不間斷地將本文唸一遍，眼睛注視著正在朗誦的每個句子，針對自己沒聽懂的部分，特別仔細閱讀。

STEP 7 延伸學習

單字 Vocabulary

❶ **persistent** [pɚˈsɪstənt]	adj. 持續的 He has had a persistent cough since Monday. 他從週一開始持續咳嗽。
❷ **upside** [ˈʌpˌsaɪd]	n. 好處，優點 One of the upsides of our new house is having great views of the mountains. 我們新家的優點之一就是有超棒的山景。
❸ **curb** [kɝb]	v. 抑制；控制 The government is trying to curb the spread of the new virus variants. 政府正試圖控制新變種病毒的擴散。
❹ **utility** [juˈtɪlɪtɪ]	n. 水電瓦斯的供給 I can't believe your rent does not include utilities. 我不敢相信你的房租竟然沒有包含水電瓦斯。
❺ **inject** [ɪnˈdʒɛkt]	v. 注入，注射 The vaccine is injected into the muscle of the upper arm. 疫苗從上手臂的肌肉處注射。

4.5

經濟與財經 Economy & Finance

❻ driver [ˈdraɪvɚ]	n. 原因，驅使 High inflation is a driver of climbing prices. 高通膨是物價飆漲的原因之一。
❼ reap [rip]	v. 獲取（利潤、好處等） She took calculated risks and reaped profits from her investments in the stock market. 她做好風險管理並從股市投資中獲利。
❽ ripple [ˈrɪpl̩]	n. 波瀾，連鎖反應 Surprisingly, the scandal hardly caused a ripple. 令人驚訝地，這件醜聞幾乎沒有產生任何連鎖反應。
❾ tumble [ˈtʌmbl̩]	v. 暴跌 Oil prices tumbled on Friday. 週五油價暴跌。
❿ tame [tem]	v. 控制住 You have to tame your temper in the meeting. 在會議上你必須控制好你的脾氣。

慣用語和片語 Expressions and Phrases

❶ out of the blue　出乎意料地，晴天霹靂地

He told us, out of the blue, that he was moving to Japan.
他突然跟我們說他要搬到日本了。

❷ jack up　提高（價格等）

The airline has jacked up its ticket prices this year.
航空公司今年已提高票價了。

❸ tighten the purse strings　縮緊開支，縮衣節食

Since she is between jobs now, she has to tighten the purse strings.
她目前因為還在找工作，所以她必須縮衣節食。

❹ a necessary evil　必要之惡

He believes wars are a necessary evil.
他認為戰爭是一種必要之惡。

A. Fill in the blanks with suitable words or phrases 將適合的字詞填入空格中

> ⓐ driver　ⓑ utilities　ⓒ persistent　ⓓ tighten the purse strings

1. _____ are not readily available in some underdeveloped countries.

2. Luck was not a _____ of her success.

3. They do not have enough money and therefore need to _____.

4. A lack of electricity is a _____ problem in this country.

B. Multiple choice questions 選擇題（可利用此題型熟悉多益、英檢考試）

_____ 1. Tigers are wild animals. It is difficult to ------- a tiger.
(A) gobble　(B) tame　(C) provoke　(D) oblige

_____ 2. Current laws fail to effectively ------- carbon emissions.
(A) curb　(B) elevate　(C) obsess　(D) jeopardize

_____ 3. Novelty is one of the ------- of this new product.
(A) emissions　(B) disadvantages　(C) downsides　(D) upsides

_____ 4. In an attempt to increase revenue, the company decided to -------
the prices of its products the following year.
(A) cast away　(B) jack up　(C) put forth　(D) lower down

_____ 5. Due to the outbreak of the war, stock prices ------- yesterday.
(A) tumbled　(B) spiked　(C) hampered　(D) surged

▶▶ 解答請見 p.376

4.5

經濟與財經 Economy & Finance

4.6 資訊與科技
Information & Technology

Did you know?
[你需要知道的 10 件事]

❶ 臉書（Facebook）執行長馬克・祖克柏（Mark Zuckerberg）認為元宇宙（Metaverse）是下一個世代的網路。

❷ 祖克柏相信元宇宙是未來社交互動的方式。

❸ 虛擬實境（virtual reality, VR）是利用電腦模擬三度空間的一個虛擬世界。

❹ 擴增實境（augmented reality, AR）將圖像、影音等資訊，以虛擬的方式疊加在現實環境中。

❺ 混合實境（mixed reality, MR）結合 VR 與 AR 的元素，混合現實與虛擬世界而產生的視覺感受和體驗。

❻ 元宇宙需要使用到 VR、AR 和 MR 的技術。

❼ 阿凡達電影裡面所呈現的就是元宇宙的概念。

❽ 臉書、微軟、亞馬遜等多家科技巨擘都積極投入元宇宙的技術研發。

❾ 已經有許多款知名遊戲使用元宇宙的概念。

❿ 雖然元宇宙一詞已經廣為人知，其應用的技術尚未成熟。

Must-know vocabulary
[你需要知道的 10 個單字]

❶ the metaverse business *n.* 元宇宙業務

❷ avatar *n.*（電腦術語）虛擬替身，下凡化身為人形

❸ physical counterpart *n.* 虛擬替身對應的實體

❹ virtual reality *n.* 虛擬實境（VR）

❺ augmented reality *n.* 擴增實境（AR）

❻ digital transformation *n.* 數位革新

❼ virtual storefront *n.* 虛擬店面

❽ pre-service surgeon *n.* 外科實習醫生

❾ surgical procedure *n.* 外科手術

❿ practicing surgeon 執業的外科醫生

STEP 1 掃讀 Scanning

　　掃讀的目標是在文章中搜尋特定的人名、時間、地點，或相關詞語，就像是在電話簿中搜尋某人的電話號碼一樣，其他內容完全不看。

■ 請於 **30** 秒內在以下文章中找出下列文字並畫線，不要閱讀內容或嘗試理解文章。

❶ the metaverse business   ❷ avatar

❸ physical counterpart   ❹ virtual reality

❺ augmented reality   ❻ digital transformation

❼ virtual storefront   ❽ pre-service surgeon

❾ surgical procedure   ❿ practicing surgeon

....

The Future of the Metaverse

(403 words)   By Yushiang Jou

　　In the end of 2021, Mark Zuckerberg announced that Facebook was changing its name to Meta in an attempt to reflect its increased focus on developing the metaverse business. New to many people, the idea of the metaverse is essentially an immersive virtual environment where people interact as avatars, or digital twins that resemble their physical counterparts. As a buzzword, the metaverse is made possible by virtual reality (VR), augmented reality (AR), and mixed reality (MR) technology, along with other connection devices. After Zuckerberg put the term on the map, the metaverse is poised to change the way we connect and interact with each other. While the metaverse is still under development, metaverse technologies are building up momentum for digital transformation in a range of sectors well beyond the realm of entertainment. Here are some of the potential applications of the metaverse.

4.6

資訊與科技 Information & Technology

213

The possibilities of a virtual world can open up new revenue streams for businesses that venture into the metaverse. In particular, the virtualization of goods and services may streamline customer experience and strengthen after-sales support, thereby boosting sales and attracting repeat customers. Businesses can have virtual storefronts and create an immersive and interactive experience for their customers. For example, store owners can project their holograms for a true-to-life feel in a physical store or interact with prospective customers with their avatars in a virtual space that transcends the limits of time and space. Simply put, as many companies have ventured into the metaverse, it is set to help businesses of all sizes to stay competitive in retail.

The metaverse can also empower medical practitioners and be an invaluable surgical assistance tool. Metaverse technologies would allow surgeons to look inside a patient's body as they perform an operation on the patient. For example, AR and MR headsets can help monitor a patient's data in real time such as temperature, heart rate, respiration rate, and blood pressure, likely improving the precision and speed of surgery. Because of the highly immersive nature of the metaverse, metaverse technologies can equip pre-service surgeons with knowledge and skills necessary for a successful surgery. For example, a practicing surgeon can actively interact with apprentice surgeons and walk them through surgical procedures so that they are well prepared before they perform an operation on a patient. The bottom line is that although we have come a long way, more work is needed as we bring the metaverse to life.

■ 請選擇正確的意思

_____ ❶ the metaverse business (A) 元宇宙業務 (B) 臉書廣告業務

_____ ❷ avatar (A) 虛擬替身 (B) 真人替身

_____ ❸ physical counterpart (A) 虛擬替身對應的實體 (B) 虛擬替身

_____ ❹ virtual reality (A) 擴增實境 (B) 虛擬實境

_____ ❺ augmented reality (A) 擴增實境 (B) 虛擬實境

_____ ❻ digital transformation (A) 數位科技 (B) 數位革新

_____ ❼ virtual storefronts (A) 虛擬店面 (B) 虛擬商品

_____ **8** pre-service surgeon (A) 執業的外科醫生 (B) 外科實習醫生

_____ **9** surgical procedure (A) 手術 (B) 處方藥

_____ **10** practicing surgeon (A) 執業的外科醫生 (B) 外科實習生

▶▶ 解答請見 p.378

STEP 2 略讀 Skimming

針對剛才的文章，用 30 秒鐘瀏覽各段的第一句，粗略了解文章結構與大意即可。

In the end of 2021, Mark Zuckerberg announced that Facebook was changing its name to Meta in an attempt to reflect its increased focus on developing the metaverse business. New to many people, the idea of the metaverse is essentially an immersive virtual environment where people interact as avatars, or digital twins that resemble their physical counterparts. As a buzzword, the metaverse is made possible by virtual reality (VR), augmented reality (AR), and mixed reality (MR) technology, along with other connection devices. After Zuckerberg put the term on the map, the metaverse is poised to change the way we connect and interact with each other. While the metaverse is still under development, metaverse technologies are building up momentum for digital transformation in a range of sectors well beyond the realm of entertainment. Here are some of the potential applications of the metaverse.

臉書轉戰元宇宙

4.6
資訊與科技 Information & Technology

The possibilities of a virtual world can open up new revenue streams for businesses that venture into the metaverse. In particular, the virtualization of goods and services may streamline customer experience and strengthen after-sales support, thereby boosting sales and attracting repeat customers. Businesses can have virtual storefronts and create an immersive and interactive experience for their customers. For example, store owners can project their holograms for a true-to-life

元宇宙可替企業增加收入

feel in a physical store or interact with prospective customers with their avatars in a virtual space that transcends the limits of time and space. Simply put, as many companies have ventured into the metaverse, it is set to help businesses of all sizes to stay competitive in retail.

The metaverse can also empower medical practitioners and be an invaluable surgical assistance tool. Metaverse technologies would allow surgeons to look inside a patient's body as they perform an operation on the patient. For example, AR and MR headsets can help monitor a patient's data in real time such as temperature, heart rate, respiration rate, and blood pressure, likely improving the precision and speed of surgery. Because of the highly immersive nature of the metaverse, metaverse technologies can equip pre-service surgeons with knowledge and skills necessary for a successful surgery. For example, a practicing surgeon can actively interact with apprentice surgeons and walk them through surgical procedures so that they are well prepared before they perform an operation on a patient. The bottom line is that although we have come a long way, more work is needed as we bring the metaverse to life.

元宇宙
可協助
醫療
手術

■ 回答以下問題，確認自己是否正確理解整篇文章的大意：

Q1. _____ Mark Zuckerberg is not interested in the metaverse. (T/F)

Q2. _____ The metaverse can help businesses make more money. (T/F)

Q3. _____ The metaverse can replace medical professionals. (T/F)

Q4. _____ The metaverse has no value to surgery. (T/F)

Q5. _____ The metaverse is virtual. (T/F)

▶▶ 解答請見 p.378

請用 60 秒的時間仔細閱讀以下內容，並回答問題。

Because of the highly immersive nature of the metaverse, metaverse technologies can equip pre-service surgeons with knowledge and skills necessary for a successful surgery. For example, a practicing surgeon can actively interact with apprentice surgeons and walk them through surgical procedures so that they are well prepared before they perform an operation on a patient.

_____ Q1. According to this passage, which of the following is correct?
(A) The metaverse looks very different from reality.
(B) Surgeons need to take a walk before surgery.
(C) The metaverse can be used to train new surgeons.
(D) Surgical procedures do not involve special knowledge and skills.

_____ Q2. According to this passage, pre-service surgeons need to _____.
(A) do exercise regularly
(B) perform surgery on patients after training
(C) train practicing surgeons
(D) not mentioned in this passage

▶▶ 解答請見 p.378

STEP 4 高理解速讀 Speed Reading with Greater Comprehension

請用 90 秒的時間，看完整篇文章。然後跟著每一個有意義的色塊，提升理解的速度。（請盡量試著不查自己不認識的字，利用前後文去推測意思。）

4.6

資訊與科技 Information & Technology

217

In the end of 2021, Mark Zuckerberg announced that Facebook was changing its name to Meta in an attempt to reflect its increased focus on developing the metaverse business. New to many people, the idea of the metaverse is essentially an immersive virtual environment where people interact as avatars, or digital twins that resemble their physical counterparts. As a buzzword, the metaverse is made possible by virtual reality (VR), augmented reality (AR), and mixed reality (MR) technology, along with other connection devices. After Zuckerberg put the term on the map, the metaverse is poised to change the way we connect and interact with each other. While the metaverse is still under development, metaverse technologies are building up momentum for digital transformation in a range of sectors well beyond the realm of entertainment. Here are some of the potential applications of the metaverse.

臉書
轉戰
元宇宙

The possibilities of a virtual world can open up new revenue streams for businesses that venture into the metaverse. In particular, the virtualization of goods and services may streamline customer experience and strengthen after-sales support, thereby boosting sales and attracting repeat customers. Businesses can have virtual storefronts and create an immersive and interactive experience for their customers. For example, store owners can project their holograms for a true-to-life feel in a physical store or interact with prospective customers with their avatars in a virtual space that transcends the limits of time and space. Simply put, as many companies have ventured into the metaverse, it is set to help businesses of all sizes to stay competitive in retail.

元宇宙
可替企
業增加
收入

The metaverse can also empower medical practitioners and be an invaluable surgical assistance tool. Metaverse technologies would allow surgeons to look inside a patient's body as they perform an operation on the patient. For example, AR and MR headsets can help monitor a patient's data in real time such as temperature, heart rate, respiration rate, and blood pressure, likely improving the precision and speed of surgery. Because of the highly immersive nature of the

元宇宙
可協助
醫療
手術

metaverse, metaverse technologies can equip pre-service surgeons with knowledge and skills necessary for a successful surgery. For example, a practicing surgeon can actively interact with apprentice surgeons and walk them through surgical procedures so that they are well prepared before they perform an operation on a patient. The bottom line is that although we have come a long way, more work is needed as we bring the metaverse to life.

■ 請回答以下問題：

_____ Q1. What is possible in a virtual storefront?
   (A) Businesses can provide an interactive experience that goes beyond the limits of time and distance.
   (B) Customer experience can be improved
   (C) After-sales support can be improved.
   (D) All of the above are possible.

_____ Q2. Metaverse technology would NOT enable a surgeon to
   (A) look inside patients' bodies as they treat patients.
   (B) perform surgery without AR and MR technology.
   (C) improve the precision of surgical procedures.
   (D) monitor real-time patient data such as heart rate and blood pressure.

_____ Q3. What is Mark Zuckerberg's attitude toward the metaverse?
   (A) uncertain   (B) doubtful   (C) excited   (D) fearful

_____ Q4. Which metaverse application is NOT mentioned in the article?
   (A) military training
   (B) entertainment
   (C) surgery
   (D) gaming

_____ Q5. Which of the following can be inferred from the article?

    (A) The metaverse has been well known for years.

    (B) Only small businesses can benefit from the metaverse.

    (C) VR and AR technologies are all you need to enter the metaverse.

    (D) The metaverse has wide-ranging implications.

▶▶ 解答請見 p.379

4.6.1_S.mp3

STEP 5 跟讀 Shadowing

    請根據母語人士所錄製的音檔，一句一句跟著唸。跟讀時請使用跟讀音檔，每句結束後，請利用句與句之間的空秒時間，複誦前面所聽到的句子。建議第一遍，看著文章跟著唸，第二遍則不看文章，只聽音檔唸。

4.6.1_L.mp3

STEP 6 聽讀 Listening

第一遍

→ 讀者會聽到音檔內母語人士完整且不間斷將本文唸一遍。試著不看文章，聽音檔內的母語人士完整且不間斷地將本文唸一遍，確認自己哪裡聽懂，那裡聽不懂。

第二遍

→ 再聽母語人士不間斷地將本文唸一遍，眼睛注視著正在朗誦的每個句子，針對自己沒聽懂的部分，特別仔細閱讀。

單字 Vocabulary

❶ immersive [ɪˈmɝ·sɪv]	adj. 身歷其境的 This immersive video game is popular. 這款身歷其境的電玩遊戲很受歡迎。
❷ avatar [ˈɑvətɑr]	n. 虛擬替身 His avatar in the chat room is a polar bear. 他在聊天室裡的虛擬替身是一隻北極熊。
❸ counterpart [ˈkaʊntə·pɑrt]	n. 相對應職位的人，相對應的事物 The U.S. President is meeting his Asian counterparts this Sunday. 美國總統將於本週日會見亞洲國家的領袖。
❹ buzzword [ˈbʌzwɝd]	n. 時下流行的詞語 The metaverse has been a buzzword in Wall Street. 元宇宙已成為華爾街流行的名詞。
❺ momentum [moˈmɛntəm]	n. 向前進的能量，勢頭 The team wants to maintain its momentum in the next season. 球隊希望在下一季維持本季的勢頭。
❻ sector [ˈsɛktə·]	n. 行業，部門 The banking sector has lost much money this year. 銀行業今年損失了很多錢。
❼ prospective [prəˈspɛktɪv]	adj. 潛在的（客人、學生等） They are looking for prospective buyers for their house. 他們在找想要買他們房子的人。
❽ streamline [ˈstrimlaɪn]	v. 提高⋯的效率 The company is trying to streamline operations and increase productivity. 公司想要提高營運的效率並增加產能。

❾ **invaluable** [ɪnˈvæljʊəbəl]	adj. 實用的，寶貴的 Her advice has been invaluable to me. 她的建議對我而言相當寶貴。
❿ **apprentice** [əˈprɛntɪs]	n. 實習生，學徒 He is working as an apprentice chef in a restaurant. 他在餐廳擔任實習廚師。

慣用語和片語 Expressions and Phrases

❶ in an attempt to...　為了⋯

Central banks raise interest rates in an attempt to control inflation.
央行升息的目的是為了抑制通膨。

❷ beyond the realm of　在⋯的領域之外

The benefits of artificial intelligence extend beyond the realm of computer science.
人工智慧的好處延伸至電腦科學的領域之外。

❸ a range of...　各式各樣的⋯

Students are required to participate in a range of classroom activities.
學生要參加各式各樣的課堂活動。

❹ the bottom line　底線，最重要的事

The bottom line is that we need to stop gun violence.
最重要的是，我們必須阻止槍枝暴力。

A. Fill in the blanks with suitable words or phrases 將適合的字詞填入空格中

ⓐ buzzword **ⓑ** momentum **ⓒ** sector **ⓓ** the bottom line

1. The President says _____ is that we need to control inflation.

2. The tourism _____ has been adversely affected by the pandemic.

3. The internet was a _____ 20 years ago.

4. Her team lost _____ in the last 10 minutes of the game.

B. Multiple choice questions 選擇題（可利用此題型熟悉多益、英檢考試）

_____ 1. The military is sometimes using ------- video games for training.
(A) immersive   (B) problematic
(C) irrelevant   (D) unsuccessful

_____ 2. She has a job in sales and therefore needs to call ------- clients.
(A) barbarian   (B) hardline   (C) negligible   (D) prospective

_____ 3. This article was written by a famous statistics teacher. Many
students found her article ------- for their learning statistics.
(A) mischievous   (B) irrelevant   (C) invaluable   (D) valueless

_____ 4. The Prime Minister spoke with her Canadian ------- at the Leaders
Summit on Friday.
(A) oppressor   (B) counterpart   (C) monopoly   (D) subordinate

_____ 5. He wants to use a Pikachu ------- in this game.
(A) knuckle   (B) entrance   (C) originator   (D) avatar

▶▶ 解答請見 p.380

4.6

資訊與科技 Information & Technology

Part 2

Opportunities and Challenges of Self-driving Cars（自駕車的商機與挑戰）

Did you know?

[你需要知道的 10 件事]

❶ 自動駕駛車（自駕車）分成不同等級的自動駕駛能力。

❷ 電動車與自駕車是兩個不同的東西。

❸ 電動車與燃油車都可以成為自駕車。

❹ 美國加州已經有合法的自駕計程車載送一般乘客。

❺ Uber Eats 也在美國加州推出自駕車的送餐服務。

❻ 有礙於交通事故肇責歸屬等問題，自駕車目前尚未全面合法化。

❼ AI 人工智慧為自駕車的核心技術之一。

❽ 特斯拉是電動車，同時也是半自動駕駛車。

❾ 除了特斯拉之外，蘋果等大型科技公司也在積極研發自駕車。

❿ 許多人誤以為特斯拉是全自動駕駛車，而造成應注意而未注意的交通事故。

Must-know vocabulary

[你需要知道的 10 個單字]

❶ state-of-the-art *adj.* 尖端的

❷ automobile industry *n.* 汽車產業

❸ autopilot *n.* 自動駕駛

❹ concentration *n.* 專注力

❺ attentive *adj.* 專心的

❻ autonomous vehicle *n.* 自動駕駛車（自駕車）

❼ fatigue *n.* 疲勞

❽ human error *n.* 人為疏失

❾ pedestrian *n.* 行人

❿ ethical dilemma *n.* 道德困境

掃讀的目標是在文章中搜尋特定的人名、時間、地點，或相關詞語，就像是在電話簿中搜尋某人的電話號碼一樣，其他內容完全不看。

■ 請於 **30** 秒內在以下文章中找出下列文字並畫線，不要閱讀內容或嘗試理解文章。

❶ state-of-the-art ❷ automobile industry

❸ autonomous ❹ concentration

❺ attentive ❻ autopilot

❼ fatigue ❽ human error

❾ pedestrian ❿ ethical dilemma

Opportunities and Challenges of Self-driving Cars

(465 words) By Yushiang Jou

Self-driving cars, also known as autonomous cars, are vehicles that can drive by themselves, with or without a human driver behind the wheel. These cars are fitted with a GPS system and use a combination of sensors, cameras, and state-of-the-art AI technology. Self-driving cars are gaining traction in the automobile industry, with big companies like Tesla and Google racing to develop fully autonomous vehicles. However, these cars are not yet ready for prime time.

The Society of Automotive Engineers defines six levels of vehicle automation, ranging from level 0 (fully manual) to level 5 (fully autonomous). Most vehicles on the roadway today are level 0 and level 1 vehicles. The driver is entirely in charge of steering, accelerating, braking, and parking. Therefore, a high level of concentration is necessary. At level 1, the driver remains responsible for controlling the vehicle, which has automatic features such as adaptive cruise control. Level 2 vehicles, such as Tesla and Waymo cars, are the most autonomous on the market today. They sometimes allow drivers to take their hands off the wheel. However, the driver needs to be attentive at all times. A level 3 vehicle can drive on its own

4.6

資訊與科技 Information & Technology

under certain conditions, the driver ready to take control of the vehicle if need be. While level 4 vehicles can drive by themselves most of the time, the driver still has the option to override the autopilot in case of an emergency. Lastly, a level 5 vehicle does not have a steering wheel or brake pedal as no one is behind the wheel. The driver does not have the option to take control of the vehicle in an emergency.

One of the potential benefits of self-driving cars would be fewer traffic accidents. According to the W.H.O., millions of people die from traffic accidents worldwide each year, the majority of these accidents caused by human error. Since self-driving cars do not drive drunk or suffer from fatigue, they are expected to reduce traffic injuries and deaths. These cars promise to improve road safety by removing human error from the equation.

However, the development of self-driving cars raises an ethical question of whose safety would be prioritized in the event of an unavoidable accident. For example, when a self-driving car needs to stop at a red light and the brakes fail, the AI system would have to choose between two evils. It can opt to swerve and crash into a lamppost to avoid hitting other road users like pedestrians and motorcyclists, or alternatively to keep driving forward and save the driver at all costs. Since fully autonomous vehicles are not yet legal on the road today, this ethical dilemma may still be a way off. With all these challenges, however, what do the next 20 years have in store for us?

■ 請選擇正確的意思

_____ ❶ state-of-the-art　(A) 落伍的 (B) 尖端的

_____ ❷ automobile industry　(A) 汽車產業 (B) 電子產業

_____ ❸ autopilot　(A) 手動駕駛 (B) 自動駕駛

_____ ❹ concentration　(A) 分心 (B) 專注

_____ ❺ attentive　(A) 分心的 (B) 專心的

_____ ❻ autonomous vehicle　(A) 自動駕駛 (B) 人工駕駛汽車

_____ ❼ fatigue　(A) 亢奮 (B) 疲勞

_____ ❽ human error　(A) 人為疏失 (B) 機械故障

_____ **9** pedestrian　(A) 駕駛 (B) 行人

_____ **10** ethical dilemma　(A) 道德困境 (B) 道德瑕疵

▶▶ 解答請見 p.382

STEP 2 略讀 Skimming

針對剛才的文章，用 30 秒鐘瀏覽各段的第一句，粗略了解文章結構與大意即可。

　　Self-driving cars, also known as autonomous cars, are vehicles that can drive by themselves, with or without a human driver behind the wheel. These cars are fitted with a GPS system and use a combination of sensors, cameras, and state-of-the-art AI technology. Self-driving cars are gaining traction in the automobile industry, with big companies like Tesla and Google racing to develop fully autonomous vehicles. However, these cars are not yet ready for prime time.

自駕車簡介

　　The Society of Automotive Engineers defines six levels of vehicle automation, ranging from level 0 (fully manual) to level 5 (fully autonomous). Most vehicles on the roadway today are level 0 and level 1 vehicles. The driver is entirely in charge of steering, accelerating, braking, and parking. Therefore, a high level of concentration is necessary. At level 1, the driver remains responsible for controlling the vehicle, which has automatic features such as adaptive cruise control. Level 2 vehicles, such as Tesla and Waymo cars, are the most autonomous on the market today. They sometimes allow drivers to take their hands off the wheel. However, the driver needs to be attentive at all times. A level 3 vehicle can drive on its own under certain conditions, the driver ready to take control of the vehicle if need be. While level 4 vehicles can drive by themselves most of the time, the driver still has the option to override the autopilot in case of an

自動駕駛等級

4.6

資訊與科技 Information & Technology

emergency. Lastly, a level 5 vehicle does not have a steering wheel or brake pedal as no one is behind the wheel. The driver does not have the option to take control of the vehicle in an emergency.

One of the potential benefits of self-driving cars would be fewer traffic accidents. According to the W.H.O., millions of people die from traffic accidents worldwide each year, the majority of these accidents caused by human error. Since self-driving cars do not drive drunk or suffer from fatigue, they are expected to reduce traffic injuries and deaths. These cars promise to improve road safety by removing human error from the equation.

自駕車優點：預期將減少車禍

However, the development of self-driving cars raises an ethical question of whose safety would be prioritized in the event of an unavoidable accident. For example, when a self-driving car needs to stop at a red light and the brakes fail, the AI system would have to choose between two evils. It can opt to swerve and crash into a lamppost to avoid hitting other road users like pedestrians and motorcyclists, or alternatively to keep driving forward and save the driver at all costs. Since fully autonomous vehicles are not yet legal on the road today, this ethical dilemma may still be a way off. With all these challenges, however, what do the next 20 years have in store for us?

自駕車的道德困境

■ 回答以下問題，確認自己是否正確理解整篇文章的大意：

Q1. _____ Self-driving cars are known as autonomous cars. (T/F)

Q2. _____ Self-driving cars require a human driver behind the wheel. (T/F)

Q3. _____ There are five levels of vehicle automation. (T/F)

Q4. _____ Self-driving cars are expected to reduce traffic accidents. (T/F)

Q5. _____ There are ethical questions about self-driving cars. (T/F)

▸▸ 解答請見 p.382

請用 60 秒的時間仔細閱讀以下內容，並回答問題。

For example, when a self-driving car needs to stop at a red light and the brakes fail, the AI system would have to choose between two evils. It can opt to swerve and crash into a lamppost to avoid hitting other road users like pedestrians and motorcyclists, or alternatively to keep driving forward and save the driver at all costs.

_____ Q1. According to this passage, which of the following is correct?
        (A) Self-driving cars can prevent all from being hurt.
        (B) It is possible that the brakes of Self-driving cars suddenly fail.
        (C) The AI system installed on the self-driving cars needs maintaining once a year.
        (D) Self-driving cars will save other road users at all costs.

_____ Q2. According to this passage, what can cause brakes to fail?
        (A) pedestrians
        (B) lampposts
        (C) traffic lights
        (D) not mentioned in this passage

▶▶ 解答請見 p.382

4.6

資訊與科技 Information & Technology

STEP 4 高理解速讀 Speed Reading with Greater Comprehension

請用 90 秒的時間，看完整篇文章。然後跟著每一個有意義的色塊，提升理解的速度。（請盡量試著不查自己不認識的字，利用前後文去推測意思。）

Self-driving cars, also known as autonomous cars, are vehicles that can drive by themselves, with or without a human driver behind the wheel. These cars are fitted with a GPS system and use a combination of sensors, cameras, and state-of-the-art AI technology. Self-driving cars are gaining traction in the automobile industry, with big companies like Tesla and Google racing to develop fully autonomous vehicles. However, these cars are not yet ready for prime time.

自駕車
簡介

The Society of Automotive Engineers defines six levels of vehicle automation, ranging from level 0 (fully manual) to level 5 (fully autonomous). Most vehicles on the roadway today are level 0 and level 1 vehicles. The driver is entirely in charge of steering, accelerating, braking, and parking. Therefore, a high level of concentration is necessary. At level 1, the driver remains responsible for controlling the vehicle, which has automatic features such as adaptive cruise control. Level 2 vehicles, such as Tesla and Waymo cars, are the most autonomous on the market today. They sometimes allow drivers to take their hands off the wheel. However, the driver needs to be attentive at all times. A level 3 vehicle can drive on its own under certain conditions, the driver ready to take control of the vehicle if need be. While level 4 vehicles can drive by themselves most of the time, the driver still has the option to override the autopilot in case of an emergency. Lastly, a level 5 vehicle does not have a steering wheel or brake pedal as no one is behind the wheel. The driver does not have the option to take control of the vehicle in an emergency.

自動駕
駛等級

One of the potential benefits of self-driving cars would be fewer traffic accidents. According to the W.H.O., millions of people die from traffic accidents worldwide each year, the majority of these accidents caused by human error. Since self-driving cars do not drive drunk or suffer from fatigue, they are expected to reduce traffic injuries and deaths. These cars promise to improve road safety by removing human error from the equation.

自駕車
優點：
預期將
減少
車禍

However, the development of self-driving cars raises an ethical question of whose safety would be prioritized in the event of an unavoidable accident. For example, when a self-driving car needs to stop at a red light and the brakes fail, the AI system would have to choose between two evils. It can opt to swerve and crash into a lamppost to avoid hitting other road users like pedestrians and motorcyclists, or alternatively to keep driving forward and save the driver at all costs. Since fully autonomous vehicles are not yet legal on the road today, this ethical dilemma may still be a way off. With all these challenges, however, what do the next 20 years have in store for us?

自駕車
的道德
困境

■ 請回答以下問題：

_____ Q1. How many levels of vehicle automation are defined by the Society of Automotive Engineers?

(A) six   (B) five   (C) four   (D) three

_____ Q2. At what level of automation is a Tesla?

(A) level 1   (B) level 2   (C) level 3   (D) level 4

_____ Q3. Self-driving cars are equipped with _____.

(A) sensors   (B) cameras   (C) a GPS system   (D) all of the above

_____ Q4. Most car accidents are caused by _____.

(A) bad weather conditions
(B) mechanical failure
(C) human error
(D) none of the above

_____ Q5. Why would the development of self-driving cars raise ethical
questions?

(A) because human error is responsible for car accidents

(B) because fully autonomous vehicles are not legal today

(C) because some accidents are unavoidable

(D) because the W.H.O is concerned about drunk driving

▶▶ 解答請見 p.383

4.6.2_S.mp3

STEP 5 跟讀 Shadowing

　　請根據母語人士所錄製的音檔，一句一句跟著唸。跟讀時請使用跟讀音檔，每句結束後，請利用句與句之間的空秒時間，複誦前面所聽到的句子。建議第一遍，看著文章跟著唸，第二遍則不看文章，只聽音檔唸。

4.6.2_L.mp3

STEP 6 聽讀 Listening

第一遍

→ 讀者會聽到音檔內母語人士完整且不間斷將本文唸一遍。試著不看文章，聽音檔內的母語人士完整且不間斷地將本文唸一遍，確認自己哪裡聽懂，那裡聽不懂。

第二遍

→ 再聽母語人士不間斷地將本文唸一遍，眼睛注視著正在朗誦的每個句子，針對自己沒聽懂的部分，特別仔細閱讀。

單字 Vocabulary

❶ traction [`trækʃən]	n. 牽引（力），拖拉；受歡迎程度 The idea of self-learning is gaining traction in recent years. 近年來自學的概念越來越受歡迎。
❷ industry [`ɪndəstrɪ]	n. 產業 He wants to make some changes to the manufacturing industry. 他想要對製造業做些改變。
❸ concentration [ˌkɑnsɛn`treʃən]	n. 專注（力） He lost his concentration easily. 他很容易分心。
❹ attentive [ə`tɛntɪv]	adj. 注意的 He asked that his audience be attentive at all times. 他要求他的觀眾們全程專注聆聽。
❺ manual [`mænjʊəl]	adj. 手動的 He wants to buy a car that has a manual transmission. 他想要買一輛有手排功能的車。
❻ autopilot [ɔtə`paɪlət]	n. 自動駕駛 The plane was flying on autopilot after takeoff. 飛機起飛之後進入了自動駕駛的模式。
❼ fatigue [fə`tig]	n. 疲倦 Fatigue is one of the drug's side effects. 疲倦是這種藥的副作用之一。
❽ state-of-the-art [`stet əf ði `ɑrt]	adj. 尖端的，最先進的 His new computer is state-of-the-art. 他的新電腦是最先進的。

4.6

資訊與科技 Information & Technology

❾ promise [ˋprɑmɪs]	v. 承諾，預期會… The metaverse promises to change the way people connect with each other. 元宇宙預期將會改變人們相互聯繫的方式。
❿ opt [ɑpt]	v. 選擇 Most people opt to be vaccinated. 大部分人選擇接種疫苗。

慣用語和片語 Expressions and Phrases

❶ ready for prime time　準備迎接黃金時段，準備大發利市

The app is almost ready for prime time.

這款應用程式幾乎準備好要大發利市了。

❷ remove... from the equation　把…拿掉（就可解決問題了）

She wanted to remove money from the equation.

她想要把金錢這個因素拿掉。

❸ a way off　還要很久，還有一段漫長的路

Being a man of wealth is still a way off for him.

對他來說，成為富翁還要很久。

❹ in store (for someone)　會發生（在某人身上）

A recession may be in store.

經濟衰退可能會發生。

A. Fill in the blanks with suitable words or phrases 將適合的字詞填入空格中

> **ⓐ** autopilot **ⓑ** traction **ⓒ** ready for prime time **ⓓ** promise

1. Fully autonomous vehicles are not _____.

2. The metaverse is gaining _____ along with the development of VR technology.

3. In the movie, the self-driving car was on _____.

4. The metaverse _____ to redefine how people connect with each other.

B. Multiple choice questions 選擇題（可利用此題型熟悉多益、英檢考試）

_____ 1. The stock market has been speculative. In consequence, a stock market bubble may be -------.
(A) to date   (B) in store   (C) on board   (D) for good

_____ 2. She did not go to school because she ------- to be educated at home.
(A) caressed   (B) vomited   (C) opted   (D) deceased

_____ 3. The new smart phone uses ------- technology.
(A) state-of-the-art   (B) traditional
(C) outdated   (D) manufacturing

_____ 4. A feeling of ------- is one of the drug's side effects.
(A) coherence   (B) salvation   (C) pastime   (D) fatigue

_____ 5. It is January now. Thanksgiving is -------.
(A) coming soon   (B) a way off
(C) on the run   (D) around the corner

▶▶ 解答請見 p.384

4.6
資訊與科技 Information & Technology

Did you know?

[你需要知道的 10 件事]

❶ 許多士兵在戰場上受傷需要截肢，裝上義肢後才能活動。
❷ 美國隊長的哥哥是冬日戰士，他的左手即為仿生機械義肢。
❸ 全球有上千萬的截肢者。
❹ 有些孩童天生肢體不全，需要安裝義肢。
❺ 有些人意外受傷截肢，也需要安裝義肢。
❻ 有些糖尿病患者足部潰瘍，需要截肢並安裝義肢。
❼ 除了義肢之外，常見的義體包含手掌、手指、眼球、耳朵等。
❽ 傳統義肢的價格並不高。
❾ 傳統義肢通常並無實際的功能。
❿ 仿生機械義肢通常要價不菲。

Must-know vocabulary

[你需要知道的 10 個單字]

❶ limb *n.* 肢體
❷ amputee *n.* 截肢者
❸ prosthesis *n.* 義肢，義體
❹ mobility *n.* 行動能力
❺ artificial *adj.* 人造的
❻ mimic *v.* 模仿
❼ conventional *adj.* 傳統的
❽ gait *n.* 步態
❾ sensory feedback *n.* 知覺回饋
❿ bionic *adj.* 仿生機械的

掃讀的目標是在文章中搜尋特定的人名、時間、地點，或相關詞語，就像是在電話簿中搜尋某人的電話號碼一樣，其他內容完全不看。

■ 請於 **30** 秒內在以下文章中找出下列文字並畫線，不要閱讀內容或嘗試理解文章。

❶ limb
❷ amputee
❸ prosthesis
❹ mobility
❺ artificial
❻ mimic
❼ conventional
❽ gait
❾ sensory feedback
❿ bionic

....

Bionic Technology

(427 words)   By Yushiang Jou

Many are living with limb loss in the world. According to the Amputee Coalition of America, a nonprofit organization based in Washington, D.C., about 1.9 million people are living with limb loss in the U.S. alone, and this number is expected to double by 2050. These amputees rely on prostheses of some kind to restore mobility. A prosthesis is an artificial device that replaces such a missing body part as a hand, arm, leg, knee, and ankle. For millions of people who are amputees, the need for prostheses is real.

Traditionally, prostheses are designed to mimic the appearance of the human body. However, traditional plastic and metal prostheses do not have functions that go beyond aesthetics. Since traditional prostheses are passive devices, the quality of their lives can be reduced. For example, people fitted with a prosthetic leg usually walk with an unnatural gait, which can lead to limited mobility and higher risks of falls. People who use these artificial limbs tend to overuse the side of their body without an amputation, which can cause back and shoulder problems that ultimately require extra medical care.

4.6

資訊與科技 Information & Technology

In an effort to restore the body function that is lost, some amputees turn to bionic technology to cope with disabilities. Many universities, including the University of Michigan and the Massachusetts Institute of Technology, are researching how machine can be merged with humans to replicate the function of body parts. Bionic prostheses are battery-powered and mind-controlled. The users control bionic body parts by translating their thoughts into movements. They are capable of controlling each finger independently, walking with a natural gait, and even doing such sports as motorcycling, skiing, and surfing. While traditional prostheses lack the sensation of touch, bionic ones can replicate the sense of touch through built-in sensors. These sensors relay sensory feedback to the brain in real time, allowing amputees to feel like the bionic prosthesis is part of their own body. Therefore, they would be able to tell the difference between hot and cold objects with their bionic hands.

While bionic technology promises to give amputees a new lease on life, affordable bionic prostheses remain out of reach. Most bionic prostheses cost tens of thousands of dollars. As a result, many amputees are intimidated by their high costs and have no choice but to settle for traditional ones. Thanks to recent innovations in 3D printing, the use of low-cost 3D printed materials helps bring down the cost of bionic prostheses. 3D-printed prostheses are poised to make bionic technology affordable for all amputees, especially those of low economic status.

■ 請選擇正確的意思

_____ ❶ limb   (A) 肢體 (B) 軀幹

_____ ❷ amputee   (A) 義肢 (B) 被截肢者

_____ ❸ prosthesis   (A) 義肢 (B) 肢體

_____ ❹ mobility   (A) 思考能力 (B) 行動能力

_____ ❺ artificial   (A) 天然的 (B) 人造的

_____ ❻ mimic   (A) 模仿 (B) 原創

_____ ❼ conventional   (A) 創新的 (B) 傳統的

_____ ❽ gait   (A) 手勢 (B) 步態

_____ **❾** sensory feedback　(A) 知覺回饋 (B) 無知覺

_____ **❿** bionic　(A) 仿生機械的 (B) 仿生塑膠的

STEP 2　略讀 Skimming

針對剛才的文章，用 30 秒鐘瀏覽各段的第一句，粗略了解文章結構與大意即可。

Bionic Technology

Many are living with limb loss in the world. According to the Amputee Coalition of America, a nonprofit organization based in Washington, D.C., about 1.9 million people are living with limb loss in the U.S. alone, and this number is expected to double by 2050. These amputees rely on prostheses of some kind to restore mobility. A prosthesis is an artificial device that replaces such a missing body part as a hand, arm, leg, knee, and ankle. For millions of people who are amputees, the need for prostheses is real.

義肢的
需求
很大

Traditionally, prostheses are designed to mimic the appearance of the human body. However, traditional plastic and metal prostheses do not have functions that go beyond aesthetics. Since traditional prostheses are passive devices, the quality of their lives can be reduced. For example, people fitted with a prosthetic leg usually walk with an unnatural gait, which can lead to limited mobility and higher risks of falls. People who use these artificial limbs tend to overuse the side of their body without an amputation, which can cause back and shoulder problems that ultimately require extra medical care.

傳統
義肢

4.6

資訊與科技 Information & Technology

In an effort to restore the body function that is lost, some amputees turn to bionic technology to cope with disabilities. Many universities, including the University of Michigan and the Massachusetts Institute of Technology, are researching how machine can be merged with humans to replicate the function of body parts. Bionic prostheses are battery-powered and mind-controlled. The users control bionic body parts by translating their thoughts into movements. They are capable of controlling each finger independently, walking with a natural gait, and even doing such sports as motorcycling, skiing, and surfing. While traditional prostheses lack the sensation of touch, bionic ones can replicate the sense of touch through built-in sensors. These sensors relay sensory feedback to the brain in real time, allowing amputees to feel like the bionic prosthesis is part of their own body. Therefore, they would be able to tell the difference between hot and cold objects with their bionic hands.

仿生機械義肢

While bionic technology promises to give amputees a new lease on life, affordable bionic prostheses remain out of reach. Most bionic prostheses cost tens of thousands of dollars. As a result, many amputees are intimidated by their high costs and have no choice but to settle for traditional ones. Thanks to recent innovations in 3D printing, the use of low-cost 3D printed materials helps bring down the cost of bionic prostheses. 3D-printed prostheses are poised to make bionic technology affordable for all amputees, especially those of low economic status.

3D 列印的仿生機械義肢

■ 回答以下問題，確認自己是否正確理解整篇文章的大意：

Q1. _____ The number of people who live with limb loss is expected to drop. (T/F)

Q2. _____ Prostheses usually look like their parts of human body. (T/F)

Q3. _____ Bionic technology can help people who live with disabilities. (T/F)

Q4. _____ Bionic prostheses can be functional. (T/F)

Q5. _____ Most bionic prostheses are not expensive. (T/F)

▶▶ 解答請見 p.386

請用 60 秒的時間仔細閱讀以下內容，並回答問題。

    Bionic prostheses are battery-powered and mind-controlled. The users control bionic body parts by translating their thoughts into movements. They are capable of controlling each finger independently, walking with a natural gait, and even doing such sports as motorcycling, skiing, and surfing.

_____ Q1. According to this passage, which of the following is correct?

    (A) Bionic prostheses involve VR technology.

    (B) There are several bottoms on bionic prostheses.

    (C) Bionic prostheses enable amputees to move more naturally.

    (D) Bionic prostheses are manually powered.

_____ Q2. With bionic prostheses, amputees can _____.

    (A) go surfing

    (B) take a walk

    (C) ride a motorcycle

    (D) all of the above

▶▶ 解答請見 p.386

STEP 4 高理解速讀 Speed Reading with Greater Comprehension

    請用 90 秒的時間，看完整篇文章。然後跟著每一個有意義的色塊，提升理解的速度。（*請盡量試著不查自己不認識的字，利用前後文去推測意思。*）

4.6
資訊與科技 Information & Technology

Many are living with limb loss in the world. According to the Amputee Coalition of America, a nonprofit organization based in Washington, D.C., about 1.9 million people are living with limb loss in the U.S. alone, and this number is expected to double by 2050. These amputees rely on prostheses of some kind to restore mobility. A prosthesis is an artificial device that replaces such a missing body part as a hand, arm, leg, knee, and ankle. For millions of people who are amputees, the need for prostheses is real.

義肢的
需求
很大

Traditionally, prostheses are designed to mimic the appearance of the human body. However, traditional plastic and metal prostheses do not have functions that go beyond aesthetics. Since traditional prostheses are passive devices, the quality of their lives can be reduced. For example, people fitted with a prosthetic leg usually walk with an unnatural gait, which can lead to limited mobility and higher risks of falls. People who use these artificial limbs tend to overuse the side of their body without an amputation, which can cause back and shoulder problems that ultimately require extra medical care.

傳統
義肢

In an effort to restore the body function that is lost, some amputees turn to bionic technology to cope with disabilities. Many universities, including the University of Michigan and the Massachusetts Institute of Technology, are researching how machine can be merged with humans to replicate the function of body parts. Bionic prostheses are battery-powered and mind-controlled. The users control bionic body parts by translating their thoughts into movements. They are capable of controlling each finger independently, walking with a natural gait, and even doing such sports as motorcycling, skiing, and surfing. While traditional prostheses lack the sensation of touch, bionic ones can replicate the sense of touch through built-in sensors. These sensors relay sensory feedback to the brain in real time, allowing amputees to feel like the bionic prosthesis is part of their own body. Therefore, they would be able to tell the difference between hot and cold objects with their bionic hands.

仿生機
械義肢

While bionic technology promises to give amputees a new lease on life, affordable bionic prostheses remain out of reach. Most bionic prostheses cost tens of thousands of dollars. As a result, many amputees are intimidated by their high costs and have no choice but to settle for traditional ones. Thanks to recent innovations in 3D printing, the use of low-cost 3D printed materials helps bring down the cost of bionic prostheses. 3D-printed prostheses are poised to make bionic technology affordable for all amputees, especially those of low economic status.

3D 列印的仿生機械義肢

■ 請回答以下問題：

_____ Q1. What is true about conventional prostheses?
(A) They do not have functions beyond aesthetics.
(B) They can replicate human sensation of touch.
(C) They can control each finger independently.
(D) They are mind-controlled.

_____ Q2. What is one of the primary reasons why some people's legs are amputated?
(A) intense sports
(B) car accidents
(C) unknown diseases
(D) not mentioned in this article

_____ Q3. What can happen to amputees wearing a conventional prosthesis?
(A) They may walk with a leg-dragging gait.
(B) They may not fall down easily.
(C) They may experience an enhanced quality of life.
(D) They may not overuse the side of their body without an amputation.

4.6

資訊與科技 Information & Technology

_____ Q4. Why would some amputees turn to 3D-printed bionic prostheses?

(A) because they are battery-powered

(B) because they are more affordable

(C) because they are more powerful

(D) because they mimic the appearance of human body

_____ Q5. How many people are expected to live with limb loss in the U.S. by 2050?

(A) around 1.9 million   (B) around 2.9 million

(C) around 3.8 million   (D) around 4.8 million

▶▶ 解答請見 p.387

4.6.3_S.mp3

STEP 5 跟讀 Shadowing

　　請根據母語人士所錄製的音檔，一句一句跟著唸。跟讀時請使用跟讀音檔，每句結束後，請利用句與句之間的空秒時間，複誦前面所聽到的句子。建議第一遍，看著文章跟著唸，第二遍則不看文章，只聽音檔唸。

4.6.3_L.mp3

STEP 6 聽讀 Listening

第一遍

→ 讀者會聽到音檔內母語人士完整且不間斷將本文唸一遍。試著不看文章，聽音檔內的母語人士完整且不間斷地將本文唸一遍，確認自己哪裡聽懂，那裡聽不懂。

第二遍

→ 再聽母語人士不間斷地將本文唸一遍，眼睛注視著正在朗誦的每個句子，針對自己沒聽懂的部分，特別仔細閱讀。

單字 Vocabulary

❶ **amputate** [`æmpjə͵tet]	v. 截肢 His left leg needs to be amputated. 他的左腿需要截肢。
❷ **disability** [dɪsə`bɪlətɪ]	n. 殘疾 His disability did not prevent him from climbing the highest mountain in the world. 他的殘疾未能阻止他登上世界之巔。
❸ **prosthesis** [`prɑsθɪsɪs]	n. 義肢，義體 His prosthesis cost him $10,000. 他的義肢花了他一萬元。
❹ **mimic** [`mɪmɪk]	v. 模仿 She tried to mimic her teacher's Irish accent. 她試著模仿她老師的愛爾蘭腔。
❺ **aesthetics** [ɛs`θɛtɪks]	n. 美觀 The value of art goes beyond aesthetics. 藝術的價值不只是美觀而已。
❻ **gait** [get]	n. 步態 She walked with an awkward gait. 她的步態不自然。
❼ **replicate** [`rɛplɪ͵ket]	v. 複製 We know how DNA replicates itself. 我們知道 DNA 如何自我複製。
❽ **affordable** [ə`fɔrdəbl]	adj. 可負擔的，平價的 She likes to buy clothes at affordable prices. 她喜歡買比較平價的衣服。

4.6

資訊與科技 Information & Technology

❾ intimidate [ɪn`tɪmə,det]	v. 嚇到 She was intimidated by the height of the building. 她被這大樓的高度嚇到。
❿ settle [`sɛtl̩]	v. 安頓／平靜下來（settle for... 妥協接受） She is a perfectionist and will not settle for less. 她是一位完美主義者，不願意退而求其次。

慣用語和片語 Expressions and Phrases

❶ cope with　應對

He has been learning to <u>cope with</u> stress.
他一直在學習應對壓力。

❷ in real time　即時，立即

They are chatting on Facebook <u>in real time</u>.
他們正在用臉書的即時通訊聊天。

❸ a new lease on life　重獲新生，重新燃起希望

The new drug gave him <u>a new lease on life</u>.
新藥讓他重新燃起希望。

❹ out of reach　做不到的，得不到的

Her goals are <u>out of reach</u>.
她達不到她的目標。

A. Fill in the blanks with suitable words or phrases 將適合的字詞填入空格中

> **ⓐ** intimidate **ⓑ** in real time **ⓒ** replicate **ⓓ** settle for less

1. They are having a video conference _____.

2. He is not ambitious and tends to _____.

3. Children are usually _____ on their first day in preschool.

4. RNA viruses can _____ themselves in the human body.

B. Multiple choice questions 選擇題（可利用此題型熟悉多益、英檢考試）

_____ 1. His plan is not realistic and is -------.
(A) in real time   (B) out of reach
(C) by no means   (D) on the whole

_____ 2. Although the problem was serious, he managed to ------- it.
(A) cope with   (B) face off   (C) carry out   (D) take over

_____ 3. Health insurance in Taiwan is fairly -------.
(A) wretched   (B) passionate   (C) expansive   (D) affordable

_____ 4. Artificial intelligence is able to ------- human intelligence.
(A) wedge   (B) embark   (C) mimic   (D) ratify

_____ 5. ------- is a disability.
(A) Paradox   (B) Volatility   (C) Blindness   (D) Sleepiness

▶▶ 解答請見 p.388

4.6

資訊與科技 Information & Technology

4.7 社會議題
Social Issues

Did you know?

[你需要知道的 10 件事]

❶ 全世界有許多國家可以合法使用大麻。

❷ 大麻可以作為醫療用途。

❸ 美國大部分的州可以合法使用醫療用大麻。

❹ 娛樂用途的大麻備受爭議。

❺ 美國近半數的州已經可以合法使用娛樂用大麻。

❻ 大麻多以吸入的方式使用。

❼ 大麻也可以以食用方式使用。

❽ 食用類大麻被人體吸收的比例小於吸入性大麻。

❾ 美國許多年輕人都曾經吸食過大麻。

❿ 大麻和酒精一樣都可能會成癮。

Must-know vocabulary

[你需要知道的 10 個單字]

❶ cannabis legalization *n.* 大麻合法化

❷ criminalization of cannabis *n.* 大麻非法化

❸ psychoactive *adj.* 影響情緒和精神狀態的

❹ controversial *adj.* 有爭議的

❺ chronic pain *adj.* 慢性疼痛

❻ medical marijuana *n.* 醫療用大麻

❼ recreational marijuana *n.* 娛樂用大麻

❽ tax revenue 稅收

❾ psychosis *n.* 思覺失調

❿ abnormality *n.* 異常

掃讀的目標是在文章中搜尋特定的人名、時間、地點，或相關詞語，就像是在電話簿中搜尋某人的電話號碼一樣，其他內容完全不看。

■ 請於 **30** 秒內在以下文章中找出下列文字並畫線，不要閱讀內容或嘗試理解文章。

❶ cannabis legalization   ❷ criminalization of cannabis

❸ psychoactive   ❹ controversial

❺ chronic pain   ❻ medical marijuana

❼ recreational marijuana   ❽ tax revenue

❾ psychosis   ❿ abnormality

......

Conflicting Views on Marijuana Legalization in the U.S.

(421 words)   By Yushiang Jou

Cannabis, the scientific name for marijuana, is a plant containing a psychoactive ingredient that makes people high. While marijuana legalization has been a controversial issue in the U.S. for so many years, public opinion seems to be tipping away from the criminalization of marijuana. Most people in the U.S. have warmed to the idea of legalizing marijuana use over the last few decades. Public support for legalizing marijuana went from 12% in 1969 to 68% in 2021, according to Gallup polling data. A Pew Research Center poll also found that 91% of U.S. adults think marijuana should be legal, either medically, recreationally or both.

Marijuana is legal in an increasing number of states. California was the first state to legalize medical marijuana in 1996 to treat chronic pain in adults. Many other states took a leaf out of California's book and have legalized marijuana consumption for not only medical but also recreational use. Recreational marijuana, also known as adult-use marijuana, was first legalized in Colorado and Washington in 2012. According to the National Conference of State Legislatures, 39 states and the Washington, D.C. have legalized the medical use of marijuana, with 19 states and the Washington, D.C. allowing recreational marijuana. The U.S. House of

4.7

社會議題 Social Issues

Representatives just passed a bill in 2022 to decriminalize marijuana at the federal level. Legalizing marijuana nationwide could mean a big push for the economy, likely creating hundreds of thousands of jobs and increasing tax revenues. While this is not set in stone, the U.S. Senate is expected to follow suit.

However, there has been pushback on legalizing marijuana, particularly recreational marijuana. People who are against legalizing marijuana, including the American Society of Addiction Medicine and the American Academy of Child and Adolescent Psychiatry, warn of risks from a public health standpoint. Critics of legalizing marijuana believe policy makers are oblivious to brain health risks. For example, Harvard researchers found that recreational marijuana smokers showed abnormalities in certain areas of their brains. Since the forebrain does not fully mature until around age 25, children and adolescents are particularly vulnerable to harmful effects of marijuana. Researchers at McGill University and Yale University suggest that marijuana use during adolescence may affect brain functions like attention and memory. Other research indicates that marijuana consumption may be linked to mental illnesses such as psychosis and schizophrenia. Chronic use of marijuana can also lead to addiction in much the same way people become addicted to alcohol and other drugs. While laws that legalize marijuana are now on the books, much remains uncharted territory.

■ 請選擇正確的意思

_____ ❶ cannabis legalization　(A) 大麻合法化 (B) 大麻非法化

_____ ❷ criminalization of cannabis　(A) 大麻合法化 (B) 大麻非法化

_____ ❸ psychoactive　(A) 影響情緒和精神狀態的 (B) 精神狀態正常的

_____ ❹ controversial　(A) 取得共識的 (B) 有爭議的

_____ ❺ chronic pain　(A) 急性疼痛 (B) 慢性疼痛

_____ ❻ medical marijuana　(A) 醫療用大麻 (B) 娛樂用大麻

_____ ❼ recreational marijuana　(A) 醫療用大麻 (B) 娛樂用大麻

_____ ❽ tax revenue　(A) 稅收 (B) 營業額

_____ ❾ psychosis　(A) 焦慮症狀 (B) 思覺失調

_____ ❿ abnormality (A) 異常 (B) 正常

▶▶ 解答請見 p.390

STEP 2 略讀 Skimming

針對剛才的文章，用 30 秒鐘瀏覽各段的第一句，粗略了解文章結構與大意即可。

Cannabis, the scientific name for marijuana, is a plant containing a psychoactive ingredient that makes people high. While marijuana legalization has been a controversial issue in the U.S. for so many years, public opinion seems to be tipping away from the criminalization of marijuana. Most people in the U.S. have warmed to the idea of legalizing marijuana use over the last few decades. Public support for legalizing marijuana went from 12% in 1969 to 68% in 2021, according to Gallup polling data. A Pew Research Center poll also found that 91% of U.S. adults think marijuana should be legal, either medically, recreationally or both.

大麻
合法化
備受爭
議

Marijuana is legal in an increasing number of states. California was the first state to legalize medical marijuana in 1996 to treat chronic pain in adults. Many other states took a leaf out of California's book and have legalized marijuana consumption for not only medical but also recreational use. Recreational marijuana, also known as adult-use marijuana, was first legalized in Colorado and Washington in 2012. According to the National Conference of State Legislatures, 39 states and the Washington, D.C. have legalized the medical use of marijuana, with 19 states and the Washington, D.C. allowing recreational marijuana. The U.S. House of Representatives just passed a bill in 2022 to decriminalize marijuana at the federal level. Legalizing marijuana nationwide could mean a big push for the economy, likely creating hundreds of thousands of jobs and increasing tax revenues. While this is not set in stone, the U.S. Senate is expected to follow suit.

州政府
和聯邦
政府的
立法進
度

4.7

社會議題 Social Issues

However, there has been pushback on legalizing marijuana, particularly recreational marijuana. People who are against legalizing marijuana, including the American Society of Addiction Medicine and the American Academy of Child and Adolescent Psychiatry, warn of risks from a public health standpoint. Critics of legalizing marijuana believe policy makers are oblivious to brain health risks. For example, Harvard researchers found that recreational marijuana smokers showed abnormalities in certain areas of their brains. Since the forebrain does not fully mature until around age 25, children and adolescents are particularly vulnerable to harmful effects of marijuana. Researchers at McGill University and Yale University suggest that marijuana use during adolescence may affect brain functions like attention and memory. Other research indicates that marijuana consumption may be linked to mental illnesses such as psychosis and schizophrenia. Chronic use of marijuana can also lead to addiction in much the same way people become addicted to alcohol and other drugs. While laws that legalize marijuana are now on the books, much remains uncharted territory.

反對
娛樂用
大麻
的立場

■ 回答以下問題，確認自己是否正確理解整篇文章的大意：

Q1. _____ Cannabis legalization has been a controversial issue in the U.S. (T/F)

Q2. _____ Public opinion is against the legalization of cannabis. (T/F)

Q3. _____ Marijuana is legal in many states in the U.S. (T/F)

Q4. _____ Many states have legalized medical marijuana. (T/F)

Q5. _____ Some people do not support legalizing recreational marijuana. (T/F)

▶▶ 解答請見 p.390

請用 60 秒的時間仔細閱讀以下內容,並回答問題。

Other research indicates that marijuana consumption may be linked to mental illnesses such as psychosis and schizophrenia. Chronic use of marijuana can also lead to addiction in much the same way people become addicted to alcohol and other drugs. While laws that legalize marijuana are now on the books, much remains uncharted territory.

_____ Q1. According to this passage, which of the following is correct?

(A) There are no risks associated with marijuana use.

(B) Marijuana users may suffer from psychosis or schizophrenia.

(C) People addicted to marijuana will be addicted to alcohol.

(D) People addicted to marijuana will be addicted to other drugs.

_____ Q2. According to this passage, how likely is it for medical marijuana users to suffer from mental illnesses?

(A) possible

(B) highly likely

(C) impossible

(D) not mentioned here

▶▶▶ 解答請見 p.390

STEP 4 高理解速讀 Speed Reading with Greater Comprehension

請用 90 秒的時間,看完整篇文章。然後跟著每一個有意義的色塊,提升理解的速度。(*請盡量試著不查自己不認識的字,利用前後文去推測意思。*)

Cannabis, the scientific name for marijuana, is a plant containing a psychoactive ingredient that makes people high. While marijuana legalization has been a controversial issue in the U.S. for so many years, public opinion seems to be tipping away from the criminalization of marijuana. Most people in the U.S. have warmed to the idea of legalizing marijuana use over the last few decades. Public support for legalizing marijuana went from 12% in 1969 to 68% in 2021, according to Gallup polling data. A Pew Research Center poll also found that 91% of U.S. adults think marijuana should be legal, either medically, recreationally or both.

Marijuana is legal in an increasing number of states. California was the first state to legalize medical marijuana in 1996 to treat chronic pain in adults. Many other states took a leaf out of California's book and have legalized marijuana consumption for not only medical but also recreational use. Recreational marijuana, also known as adult-use marijuana, was first legalized in Colorado and Washington in 2012. According to the National Conference of State Legislatures, 39 states and the Washington, D.C. have legalized the medical use of marijuana, with 19 states and the Washington, D.C. allowing recreational marijuana. The U.S. House of Representatives just passed a bill in 2022 to decriminalize marijuana at the federal level. Legalizing marijuana nationwide could mean a big push for the economy, likely creating hundreds of thousands of jobs and increasing tax revenues. While this is not set in stone, the U.S. Senate is expected to follow suit.

However, there has been pushback on legalizing marijuana, particularly recreational marijuana. People who are against legalizing marijuana, including the American Society of Addiction Medicine and the American Academy of Child and Adolescent Psychiatry, warn of risks from a public health standpoint. Critics of legalizing marijuana believe policy makers are oblivious to brain health risks. For example, Harvard researchers found that recreational marijuana smokers showed abnormalities in certain areas of their brains. Since the forebrain does not fully mature until around age 25, children and adolescents are particularly vulnerable to harmful effects of marijuana. Researchers at McGill University and Yale University suggest that marijuana use during adolescence may affect brain functions like attention and memory. Other research indicates that marijuana consumption may be linked to mental illnesses such as psychosis and schizophrenia. Chronic use of marijuana can also lead to addiction in much the same way people become addicted to alcohol and other drugs. While laws that legalize marijuana are now on the books, much remains uncharted territory.

■ 請回答以下問題：

_____ Q1. Which state was the first to legalize medical marijuana?
　　　　 (A) Florida　(B) California　(C) Colorado　(D) New York

_____ Q2. When was recreational marijuana first legalized?
　　　　 (A) in 2022　(B) in 2021　(C) in 1996　(D) in 2012

_____ Q3. How many states have legalized the medical use of marijuana?
　　　　 (A) 19　(B) 25　(C) 39　(D) 40

_____ Q4. How many states have legalized recreational marijuana?
　　　　 (A) 19　(B) 20　(C) 39　(D) 40

_____ Q5. Why are adolescents particularly vulnerable to adverse effects of marijuana?
　　　　 (A) because marijuana use may be linked to mental illnesses
　　　　 (B) because repeated marijuana use can lead to addiction
　　　　 (C) because the forebrain does not mature until around age 25
　　　　 (D) none of the above

▶▶ 解答請見 p.391

4.7

社會議題 Social Issues

STEP 5　跟讀 Shadowing

　　請根據母語人士所錄製的音檔，一句一句跟著唸。跟讀時請使用跟讀音檔，每句結束後，請利用句與句之間的空秒時間，複誦前面所聽到的句子。建議第一遍，看著文章跟著唸，第二遍則不看文章，只聽音檔唸。

4.7.1_L.mp3

STEP 6　聽讀 Listening

第一遍
→ 讀者會聽到音檔內母語人士完整且不間斷將本文唸一遍。試著不看文章，聽音檔內的母語人士完整且不間斷地將本文唸一遍，確認自己哪裡聽懂，那裡聽不懂。

第二遍
→ 再聽母語人士不間斷地將本文唸一遍，眼睛注視著正在朗誦的每個句子，針對自己沒聽懂的部分，特別仔細閱讀。

STEP 7　延伸學習

單字 Vocabulary

❶ **criminalization** [ˌkrɪmɪnəlarˈzeʃən]	n. 罪犯化，非法化 She supported the criminalization of adultery. 她支持通姦罪犯化。
❷ **chronic** [ˈkrɑnɪk]	adj.（疾病等）慢性的 She has suffered from a chronic disease for many years. 她多年來一直承受著慢性病之苦。
❸ **consume** [kənˈsjum]	v. 食用，飲用 She consumed a lot of alcohol last night. 她昨晚喝了很多酒。

❹ **economy** [ɪˋkɑnəmɪ]	n. 經濟（情況） She believes the U.S. economy is strong. 她認為美國經濟表現強勁。
❺ **pushback** [ˋpʊʃˌbæk]	n. 反對 There is pushback from public health experts. 有來自公衛專家的反對意見。
❻ **oblivious** [əˋblɪvɪəs]	adj. 未注意到的，遺忘的 He was seemingly oblivious to the loud noise. 他似乎沒有注意到那很大聲的噪音。
❼ **abnormality** [ˌæbnɔrˋmælətɪ]	n. 異常 Dyslexia may be caused by brain abnormalities. 讀寫障礙可能肇因於腦部異常。
❽ **vulnerable** [ˋvʌlnərəbl]	adj. 易受傷害的，脆弱的 Patients are vulnerable to infection after surgery. 手術過後的病人容易受到感染。
❾ **adolescent** [ˌædlˋɛsnt]	n. 青少年 Her children have become adolescents. 她的小孩都已經成為青少年了。
❿ **addicted** [əˋdɪkt]	adj. 成癮的 He is addicted to heroin. 他吸食海洛因成癮。

慣用語和片語 Expressions and Phrases

❶ take a leaf out of sb's book　效仿某人，以某人為借鏡

She took a leaf out of John's book and started to go to sleep early.
她開始學約翰一樣早睡。

❷ set in stone　已成定局的

Our schedule is not set in stone and can be changed.
我們的行程尚未定案，仍可修改。

❸ follow suit　也跟著做

Her mother was a physician and she followed suit.
她追隨母親的腳步，也成為了一位內科醫生。

❹ uncharted territory　未知的領域

Long COVID remains uncharted territory.
人們對長新冠所知甚少。

A. Fill in the blanks with suitable words or phrases 將適合的字詞填入空格中

> **ⓐ** uncharted territory **ⓑ** pushback **ⓒ** vulnerable to **ⓓ** follow suit

1. Elderly people are particularly _____ the COVID-19 virus.

2. He had no _____ because everyone agreed with him.

3. Colonizing Mars is _____.

4. John's brother was an actor. John _____ and also became an actor.

B. Multiple choice questions 選擇題（可利用此題型熟悉多益、英檢考試）

_____ 1. She is healthy and her medical report shows no evidence of any
-------.
(A) productivity   (B) infidelity   (C) regularity   (D) abnormality

_____ 2. Teenage rebellion is also known as ------- rebellion.
(A) deficient   (B) lieutenant   (C) adolescent   (D) marginal

_____ 3. Since there has been a ------- shortage of food in this country,
children have been frequeutly hungry for many years.
(A) chronic   (B) grammatical   (C) tactical   (D) medieval

_____ 4. Smoking is legal because most people do not support the ------- of
smoking.
(A) normalization   (B) standardization
(C) legalization   (D) criminalization

_____ 5. The decision is set -------. Nothing can be changed now.
(A) to date   (B) in stone   (C) at large   (D) on the spot

▶▶ 解答請見 p.392

4.7
社會議題 Social Issues

Did you know?

[你需要知道的 **10** 件事]

❶ 多元性別（LGBTQI+）包含女同性戀者（lesbian）、男同性戀者（gay）、雙性戀者（bisexual）、跨性別者（transgender）、非異性戀者（queer）、雙性人（intersex）…等。

❷ 有些宗教（例如伊斯蘭教）反對同性婚姻。

❸ 2015 年，美國最高法院判決同性婚姻受到憲法保障。

❹ 在美國，民主黨比較傾向支持多元性別的平權法案。

❺ 截至目前為止，全球共有 34 個國家已將同性婚姻合法化。

❻ 在亞洲，大部份的國家未將同性婚姻合法化。

❼ 2019 年，台灣成為亞洲第一個同性婚姻合法的國家。

❽ 除了台灣之外，越南和泰國也對於多元性別族群有較高的包容性。

❾ 即便是在同性婚姻合法的國家，歧視仍不罕見。

❿ 在同性婚姻合法的國家，許多同婚者仍面臨來自原生家庭的反對。

Must-know vocabulary

[你需要知道的 **10** 個單字]

❶ LGBTQI+ *n.* 多元性別

❷ same-sex marriage *n.* 同性婚姻

❸ injustice *n.* 不公義

❹ discrimination *n.* 歧視

❺ sexual orientation *n.* 性向

❻ gender identity *n.* 性別認同

❼ prejudice *n.* 偏見

❽ harassment *n.* 騷擾

❾ tension *n.* 緊張關係

❿ legislation *n.* 立法

掃讀的目標是在文章中搜尋特定的人名、時間、地點，或相關詞語，就像是在電話簿中搜尋某人的電話號碼一樣，其他內容完全不看。

■ 請於 **30** 秒內在以下文章中找出下列文字並畫線，不要閱讀內容或嘗試理解文章。

❶ LGBTQI+   ❷ same-sex marriage
❸ injustice   ❹ discrimination
❺ sexual orientation   ❻ gender identity
❼ prejudice   ❽ harassment
❾ tension   ❿ legislation

LGBTQI+ Rights

(402 words)   By Yushiang Jou

　　While lesbian, gay, bisexual, transgender, queer, and intersex (LGBTQI+) people have been trying to break away from binary gender identities, they are usually discouraged by cultural norms and religious beliefs. In some countries, the authorities routinely deny their equal rights, thus resulting in a low level of acceptance of LGBTQI+ people. For example, the United Arab Emirates, Saudi Arabia, and Iran are set against legalizing same-sex marriage and even treat LGBTQI+ people as criminals. Since religion is one of the most commonly cited reasons, they constantly suffer religion-based discrimination. This social injustice fuels the simmering discontent within the LGBTQI+ community.

　　In many corners of the world, members of the LGBTQI+ community face discrimination on the basis of sexual orientation or gender identity. It is not uncommon that LGBTQI+ people are treated unfairly at work and school, among other activities. They encounter rampant prejudice in their attempts to find employment. Some LGBTQI+ people are less likely to be employed compared with non-LGBTQI+ individuals. At school, they usually experience bullying and

4.7

社會議題 Social Issues

harassment, which are not always unlawful. All the while, discrimination against the LGBTQI+ community has fanned the flames of tension.

But the picture is not all bleak. Many countries in the world have attempted to advance the rights of LGBTQI+ people by fulfilling their unmet needs. For example, same-sex marriage has been legalized in several countries, including the U.S., the U.K., Australia, and Brazil, with more countries down the path to same-sex marriage legalization. LGBTQI+ people in these countries make no bones about their sexual orientation in much the same way people openly talk about their religious beliefs or political views.

In the U.S., same-sex marriage was declared a constitutional right by the Supreme Court in 2015. A growing number of people are of the view that the LGBTQI+ community's rights are a passport to collective happiness. According to the nonpartisan Public Religion Research Institute, the majority of Americans believe they should promote equality for LGBTQI+ people in areas such as employment, housing, and education. Despite the increasing acceptance of LGBTQI+ communities, state laws are inconsistent and discrimination alive. Many states have not explicitly prohibited discrimination against gender identity. According to the Equality Federation, nearly 400 anti-LGBTQI+ bills were considered by state legislatures in 2021. The introduction of these bills endangered the rights and well-being of LGBTQI+ communities. In the absence of federal legislation, the struggle for LGBTQI+ rights remains an uphill battle.

■ 請選擇正確的意思

_____ ❶ LGBTQI+　(A) 單一性別 (B) 多元性別

_____ ❷ same-sex marriage　(A) 異性婚姻 (B) 同性婚姻

_____ ❸ injustice　(A) 不公義 (B) 正義

_____ ❹ discrimination　(A) 公平 (B) 歧視

_____ ❺ sexual orientation　(A) 性向 (B) 生理性別

_____ ❻ gender identity　(A) 性別認同 (B) 身分認同

_____ ❼ prejudice　(A) 偏見 (B) 公平

_____ ❽ harassment　(A) 協助 (B) 騷擾

_____ ❾ tension　(A) 緊張關係 (B) 融洽氣氛

_____ ❿ legislation　(A) 輿論 (B) 立法

▶▶ 解答請見 p.394

STEP 2　略讀 Skimming

針對剛才的文章，用 30 秒鐘瀏覽各段的第一句，粗略了解文章結構與大意即可。

LGBTQI+ Rights

While lesbian, gay, bisexual, transgender, queer, and intersex (LGBTQI+) people have been trying to break away from binary gender identities, they are usually discouraged by cultural norms and religious beliefs. In some countries, the authorities routinely deny their equal rights, thus resulting in a low level of acceptance of LGBTQI+ people. For example, the United Arab Emirates, Saudi Arabia, and Iran are set against legalizing same-sex marriage and even treat LGBTQI+ people as criminals. Since religion is one of the most commonly cited reasons, they constantly suffer religion-based discrimination. This social injustice fuels the simmering discontent within the LGBTQI+ community.

多元性別族群常受到歧視

In many corners of the world, members of the LGBTQI+ community face discrimination on the basis of sexual orientation or gender identity. It is not uncommon that LGBTQI+ people are treated unfairly at work and school, among other activities. They encounter rampant prejudice in their attempts to find employment. Some LGBTQI+ people are less likely to be employed compared with non-LGBTQI+ individuals. At school, they usually experience bullying and harassment, which are not always unlawful. All the while, discrimination against the LGBTQI+ community has fanned the flames of tension.

針對多元性別族群的不公待遇

4.7

社會議題 Social Issues

263

But the picture is not all bleak. Many countries in the world have attempted to advance the rights of LGBTQI+ people by fulfilling their unmet needs. For example, same-sex marriage has been legalized in several countries, including the U.S., the U.K., Australia, and Brazil, with more countries down the path to same-sex marriage legalization. LGBTQI+ people in these countries make no bones about their sexual orientation in much the same way people openly talk about their religious beliefs or political views.

In the U.S., same-sex marriage was declared a constitutional right by the Supreme Court in 2015. A growing number of people are of the view that the LGBTQI+ community's rights are a passport to collective happiness. According to the nonpartisan Public Religion Research Institute, the majority of Americans believe they should promote equality for LGBTQI+ people in areas such as employment, housing, and education. Despite the increasing acceptance of LGBTQI+ communities, state laws are inconsistent and discrimination alive. Many states have not explicitly prohibited discrimination against gender identity. According to the Equality Federation, nearly 400 anti-LGBTQI+ bills were considered by state legislatures in 2021. The introduction of these bills endangered the rights and well-being of LGBTQI+ communities. In the absence of federal legislation, the struggle for LGBTQI+ rights remains an uphill battle.

美國的輿論和法律規範

■ 回答以下問題，確認自己是否正確理解整篇文章的大意：

Q1. _____ LGBTQI+ people are welcomed by most cultures. (T/F)

Q2. _____ LGBTQI+ people are welcomed by most religions. (T/F)

Q3. _____ People can face discrimination because of their sexual orientation. (T/F)

Q4. _____ People can face discrimination because of their gender identity. (T/F)

Q5. _____ Same-sex marriage has been legal in the U.S. for more than seven years. (T/F)

請用 60 秒的時間仔細閱讀以下內容，並回答問題。

But the picture is not all bleak. Many countries in the world have attempted to advance the rights of LGBTQI+ people by fulfilling their unmet needs. For example, same-sex marriage has been legalized in several countries, including the U.S., the U.K., Australia, and Brazil, with more countries down the path to same-sex marriage legalization. LGBTQI+ people in these countries make no bones about their sexual orientation in much the same way people openly talk about their religious beliefs or political views.

_____ Q1. According to this passage, which of the following is true?
  (A) Many countries have provided support for LGBTQI+ people.
  (B) In Brazil, people are not allowed to talk about their political views.
  (C) In Brazil, people are not allowed to talk about their religious beliefs.
  (D) In Brazil, people are not allowed to talk about their sexual orientation.

_____ Q2. According to this passage, how many countries have legalized same-sex marriage?
  (A) five
  (B) six
  (C) seven
  (D) not mentioned in this passage

▶▶ 解答請見 p.394

4.7

社會議題 Social Issues

請用 90 秒的時間，看完整篇文章。然後跟著每一個有意義的色塊，提升理解的速度。（*請盡量試著不查自己不認識的字，利用前後文去推測意思。*）

LGBTQI+ Rights

While lesbian, gay, bisexual, transgender, queer, and intersex (LGBTQI+) people have been trying to break away from binary gender identities, they are usually discouraged by cultural norms and religious beliefs. In some countries, the authorities routinely deny their equal rights, thus resulting in a low level of acceptance of LGBTQI+ people. For example, the United Arab Emirates, Saudi Arabia, and Iran are set against legalizing same-sex marriage and even treat LGBTQI+ people as criminals. Since religion is one of the most commonly cited reasons, they constantly suffer religion-based discrimination. This social injustice fuels the simmering discontent within the LGBTQI+ community.

多元性別族群常受到歧視

In many corners of the world, members of the LGBTQI+ community face discrimination on the basis of sexual orientation or gender identity. It is not uncommon that LGBTQI+ people are treated unfairly at work and school, among other activities. They encounter rampant prejudice in their attempts to find employment. Some LGBTQI+ people are less likely to be employed compared with non-LGBTQI+ individuals. At school, they usually experience bullying and harassment, which are not always unlawful. All the while, discrimination against the LGBTQI+ community has fanned the flames of tension.

針對多元性別族群的不公待遇

But the picture is not all bleak. Many countries in the world have attempted to advance the rights of LGBTQI+ people by fulfilling their unmet needs. For example, same-sex marriage has been legalized in several countries, including the U.S., the U.K., Australia, and Brazil,

許多國家推動多元性別平等

with more countries down the path to same-sex marriage legalization. LGBTQI+ people in these countries make no bones about their sexual orientation in much the same way people openly talk about their religious beliefs or political views.

In the U.S., same-sex marriage was declared a constitutional right by the Supreme Court in 2015. A growing number of people are of the view that the LGBTQI+ community's rights are a passport to collective happiness. According to the nonpartisan Public Religion Research Institute, the majority of Americans believe they should promote equality for LGBTQI+ people in areas such as employment, housing, and education. Despite the increasing acceptance of LGBTQI+ communities, state laws are inconsistent and discrimination alive. Many states have not explicitly prohibited discrimination against gender identity. According to the Equality Federation, nearly 400 anti-LGBTQI+ bills were considered by state legislatures in 2021. The introduction of these bills endangered the rights and well-being of LGBTQI+ communities. In the absence of federal legislation, the struggle for LGBTQI+ rights remains an uphill battle.

美國的
輿論和
法律規
範

■ 請回答以下問題：

_____ Q1. Which of the following country is set against legalizing same-sex marriage?
　　(A) Iran　　　　　　　　　(B) Saudi Arabia
　　(C) the United Arab Emirates　(D) all of the above

_____ Q2. Same-sex marriage has been legalized in _____.
　　(A) Australia　(B) the U.K.　(C) Brazil　(D) all of the above

_____ Q3. What results in a low level of acceptance of LGBTQI+ people?
　　(A) The governments deny their equal rights.
　　(B) The governments try to advance their rights.
　　(C) Most people believe LGBTQI+ people's rights are important.
　　(D) Same-sex marriage is legalized.

_____ Q4. Most Americans believe equality for LGBTQI+ should be promoted in

_____.

(A) education (B) housing (C) employment (D) all of the above

_____ Q5. How many anti-LGBTQI+ bills were considered by U.S. state

legislatures in 2021?

(A) nearly 200 anti-LGBTQI+ bills

(B) nearly 300 anti-LGBTQI+ bills

(C) nearly 400 anti-LGBTQI+ bills

(D) nearly 500 anti-LGBTQI+ bills

▶▶ 解答請見 p.395

4.7.2_S.mp3

STEP 5 跟讀 **Shadowing**

請根據母語人士所錄製的音檔,一句一句跟著唸。跟讀時請使用跟讀音檔,每句結束後,請利用句與句之間的空秒時間,複誦前面所聽到的句子。建議第一遍,看著文章跟著唸,第二遍則不看文章,只聽音檔唸。

4.7.2_L.mp3

STEP 6 聽讀 **Listening**

第一遍

→ 讀者會聽到音檔內母語人士完整且不間斷將本文唸一遍。試著不看文章,聽音檔內的母語人士完整且不間斷地將本文唸一遍,確認自己哪裡聽懂,那裡聽不懂。

第二遍

→ 再聽母語人士不間斷地將本文唸一遍,眼睛注視著正在朗誦的每個句子,針對自己沒聽懂的部分,特別仔細閱讀。

單字 Vocabulary

❶ **binary** [`baɪnərɪ]	adj. 雙類別的 She is an astronomer who studies binary star systems. 她是研究聯星系統的天文學家。
❷ **identity** [aɪ`dɛntətɪ]	n. 身份 We do not know the identity of the heart donor. 我們不知道這位心臟捐贈者的身份。
❸ **routinely** [ru`tinlɪ]	adv. 經常地，固定地，依照慣例地 The company routinely ignored customer complaints. 這間公司經常不理會顧客的抱怨。
❹ **constantly** [`kɑnstəntlɪ]	adv. 不斷地，經常地 She is constantly changing her mind. In fact, she does not know what she really wants. 她不斷改變其心意。事實上，她根本不知道自己想要的究竟是什麼。
❺ **discrimination** [dɪˏskrɪmə`neʃən]	n. 歧視 Many people still fight racial discrimination. 許多人仍在對抗種族歧視。
❻ **fuel** [`fjʊəl]	v. 引起，激起 Their criticism fueled her anger. 他們的批評引起她的憤怒。
❼ **simmering** [`sɪmərɪŋ]	adj. 積壓已久的，一觸即發的 There is simmering discontent over this policy. 對這個政策有股積壓已久的不滿情緒。
❽ **rampant** [`ræmpənt]	adj. 猖獗的 Corruption has been rampant in this country. 這個國家貪汙十分猖獗。

4.7

社會議題 Social Issues

❾ harassment [ˈhærəsmənt]	n. 騷擾 Sexual harassment is not uncommon in the workplace. 職場上的性騷擾並非罕見。
❿ explicit [ɪkˈsplɪsɪt]	adj. 明確的 Classroom instruction has to be explicit so that students can understand better. 課堂教學要解說清楚，學生才能更加理解。

慣用語和片語 Expressions and Phrases

❶ fan the flames　煽風點火

They attempt to fan the flames of racial tension.
他們企圖煽動種族間的緊張關係。

❷ all bleak　完全沒有希望的，慘澹的

The future is not all bleak.
未來並不是了無希望。

❸ make no bones about　直言不諱地說出……

She made no bones about her dissatisfaction with the food.
她直言不諱地說她對食物不滿意。

❹ an uphill battle　一場硬仗

Many economists believe controlling high inflation would be an uphill battle.
許多經濟學家認為將高通膨控制下來會是一場硬仗。

A. Fill in the blanks with suitable words or phrases 將適合的字詞填入空格中

> **ⓐ** an uphill battle　**ⓑ** rampant　**ⓒ** routinely　**ⓓ** fan the flames

1. The teacher _____ encouraged her students to think critically.

2. The airline faced _____ due to pandemic-related travel restrictions.

3. His speech _____ of racism yesterday.

4. The disease is _____ in the city and many people are hospitalized.

B. Multiple choice questions 選擇題（可利用此題型熟悉多益、英檢考試）

_____ 1. It is important to acquire ------- knowledge of grammar.
　　(A) superficial　(B) modish　(C) lethal　(D) explicit

_____ 2. Her baseless accusations of fraud ------- rumors.
　　(A) saluted　(B) narrated　(C) fueled　(D) lessened

_____ 3. As the mayor of the city, he has made a number of poor decisions.
　　As a result, there is ------- discontent about his leadership.
　　(A) simmering　　(B) glamorous
　　(C) controversial　(D) problematic

_____ 4. She is optimistic and believes that the future is not all -------.
　　(A) acute　(B) bleak　(C) blunt　(D) hoarse

_____ 5. He is a workaholic. He ------- talks about his work.
　　(A) partially　(B) occasionally　(C) tentatively　(D) constantly

▶▶ 解答請見 p.396

Did you know?

[你需要知道的 10 件事]

❶ 每年全球有數十萬人死於槍枝暴力。

❷ 在大多數國家中，持有槍械是非法的。

❸ 有些國家的憲法保障人民合法購買並持有槍械，供自我防衛使用。

❹ 即便是可以合法持有槍械的國家（例如美國），非法或走私槍械依舊十分氾濫。

❺ 美國不時發生大規模槍擊案件，通常在學校或公共場所。

❻ 美國人民對於合法槍枝的控管沒有共識。

❼ 美國民主黨的支持者傾向更嚴格地管控合法槍枝。

❽ 美國合法槍枝的數量多於美國總人口。

❾ 在美國購買槍枝並不昂貴而且很方便。

❿ 美國有些州禁止在公共場所攜帶合法取得的槍械，但此禁令被美國最高法院推翻並判決違憲。

Must-know vocabulary

[你需要知道的 10 個單字]

❶ homicide *n.* 兇殺案，殺人罪

❷ politcal spectrum *n.* 政治光譜

❸ high-profile *adj.* 高調的

❹ political hot potato *n.* 政治上的燙手山芋

❺ developed country *n.* 已開發國家

❻ gunshot *n.* 槍擊

❼ advocate *n.* 支持者

❽ gun-related death *n.* 槍擊相關的死亡

❾ self-defense *n.* 自我防衛

❿ law-abiding citizen *n.* 守法公民

掃讀的目標是在文章中搜尋特定的人名、時間、地點，或相關詞語，就像是在電話簿中搜尋某人的電話號碼一樣，其他內容完全不看。

■ 請於 **30** 秒內在以下文章中找出下列文字並畫線，不要閱讀內容或嘗試理解文章。

❶ homicide
❷ gunshots
❸ developed countries
❹ high-profile
❺ politcal spectrum
❻ a political hot potato
❼ advocates
❽ gun-related deaths
❾ self-defense
❿ law-abiding citizens

The Politics of Gun Control

(443 words)

By Yushiang Jou

Arguably a global issue and a tragedy affecting countless lives around the world, gun violence is frequently the lead story on the evening news and receives extensive media coverage. According to the 2018 Switzerland-based Small Arms Survey, 44% of homicides globally involved gunshots. In particular, the United States has the highest firearm homicide rate among developed countries, about eight times greater than that of Canada . For example, a gunman killed 49 people in Orlando in 2016. 58 people died in mass shootings in Las Vegas in 2017, the deadliest mass shooting ever in the United States. High-profile mass shootings have plagued the United States for far too long.

Despite an outpouring of grief and sympathy, the debate over gun laws has been a political hot potato in the United States. Lawmakers across the political spectrum have rarely agreed on gun control. People are split along ideological lines over whether gun laws should be further tightened, Democrats more likely than Republicans to see firearm violence as a dire problem, according to the Pew Research Center's survey in 2021.

4.7

社會議題 Social Issues

Gun control advocates are convinced that loose gun-control laws are the primary source of gun violence, particularly given that there are guns all over the place in some communities. They believe more gun control laws like background checks that include criminal records would reduce gunshot-related deaths. Moreover, they point out that countries doing so, such as Switzerland and Finland, have lower gun-related homicide rates. Many proponents therefore argue that limiting access to guns would curb gun violence and save lives. Proponents of increased gun control acknowledge the fact that the U.S. Constitution protects an individual's right to own a gun. However, they argue that guns are rarely used in self-defense within the home or in public places, and instead often threaten the right to life on the street.

Opponents of gun control, sitting on the other side of the desk, push back hard against more restrictions. They argue that gun control laws infringe the constitutional right of law-abiding citizens to defend themselves. Believing gun-control proponents are barking up the wrong tree, the opponents suggest that stricter gun control is not a solution since states with some of the most stringent gun laws, like New York and Illinois, suffer from high rates of gun violence. Seeing that the vast majority of criminals obtain their firearms through illegal means, gun control laws are unlikely to prevent criminals from obtaining guns. In consequence, gun-control measures, such as background checks, may be a futile effort. Everyone seems to agree that people's safety is second to none, and yet the problem of gun violence is approached from different angles.

■ 請選擇正確的意思

_____ ❶ homicide (A) 搶案 (B) 兇殺案

_____ ❷ gunshot (A) 刀械 (B) 槍擊

_____ ❸ developed country (A) 開發中國家 (B) 已開發國家

_____ ❹ high-profile (A) 低調的 (B) 高調的

_____ ❺ political spectrum (A) 政治光譜 (B) 政治素人

_____ ❻ a political hot potato (A) 政治上的馬鈴薯 (B) 政治上的燙手山芋

_____ ❼ advocate (A) 支持者 (B) 反對者

_____ ❽ gun-related death　(A) 槍擊相關的死亡 (B) 刀械相關的死亡

_____ ❾ self-defense　(A) 自我傷害 (B) 自我防衛

_____ ❿ law-abiding citizen　(A) 守法公民 (B) 不守法公民

▶▶ 解答請見 p.398

STEP 2　略讀 Skimming

針對剛才的文章，用 30 秒鐘瀏覽各段的第一句，粗略了解文章結構與大意即可。

　　Arguably a global issue and a tragedy affecting countless lives around the world, gun violence is frequently the lead story on the evening news and receives extensive media coverage. According to the 2018 Switzerland-based Small Arms Survey, 44% of homicides globally involved gunshots. In particular, the United States has the highest firearm homicide rate among developed countries, about eight times greater than that of Canada. For example, a gunman killed 49 people in Orlando in 2016. 58 people died in mass shootings in Las Vegas in 2017, the deadliest mass shooting ever in the United States. High-profile mass shootings have plagued the United States for far too long.

槍枝暴力是全球的重大議題

　　Despite an outpouring of grief and sympathy, the debate over gun laws has been a political hot potato in the United States. Lawmakers across the political spectrum have rarely agreed on gun control. People are split along ideological lines over whether gun laws should be further tightened, Democrats more likely than Republicans to see firearm violence as a dire problem, according to the Pew Research Center's survey in 2021.

槍枝議題在美國是燙手山芋

4.7

社會議題 Social Issues

Gun control advocates are convinced that loose gun-control laws are the primary source of gun violence, particularly given that there are guns all over the place in some communities. They believe more gun control laws like background checks that include criminal records would reduce gunshot-related deaths. Moreover, they point out that countries doing so, such as Switzerland and Finland, have lower gun-related homicide rates. Many proponents therefore argue that limiting access to guns would curb gun violence and save lives. Proponents of increased gun control acknowledge the fact that the U.S. Constitution protects an individual's right to own a gun. However, they argue that guns are rarely used in self-defense within the home or in public places, and instead often threaten the right to life on the street.

反槍陣營主張嚴格管控

Opponents of gun control, sitting on the other side of the desk, push back hard against more restrictions. They argue that gun control laws infringe the constitutional right of law-abiding citizens to defend themselves. Believing gun-control proponents are barking up the wrong tree, the opponents suggest that stricter gun control is not a solution since states with some of the most stringent gun laws, like New York and Illinois, suffer from high rates of gun violence. Seeing that the vast majority of criminals obtain their firearms through illegal means, gun control laws are unlikely to prevent criminals from obtaining guns. In consequence, gun-control measures, such as background checks, may be a futile effort. Everyone seems to agree that people's safety is second to none, and yet the problem of gun violence is approached from different angles.

擁槍陣營反對嚴格管控

■ 回答以下問題，確認自己是否正確理解整篇文章的大意：

Q1. _____ Gun violence is common but rarely reported on news outlets. (T/F)

Q2. _____ Gun violence happens in the U.S only. (T/F)

Q3. _____ Gun violence is a political issue in the U.S. (T/F)

Q4. _____ Gun control advocates are against gun-control laws. (T/F)

Q5. _____ Gun control opponents support gun-control laws. (T/F)

▶▶ 解答請見 p.398

STEP 3 細讀 Close reading

請用 60 秒的時間仔細閱讀以下內容，並回答問題。

Despite an outpouring of grief and sympathy, the debate over gun laws has been a political hot potato in the United States. Lawmakers across the political spectrum have rarely agreed on gun control. People are split along ideological lines over whether gun laws should be further tightened, Democrats more likely than Republicans to see firearm violence as a dire problem, according to the Pew Research Center's survey in 2021.

_____ Q1. According to this passage, which of the following is true?
  (A) Most lawmakers have agreed on stricter gun laws.
  (B) Most people believe gun laws should be tightened.
  (C) Political ideologies are more important than gun laws.
  (D) It is more common to see a Democrat calling for stricter gun laws.

_____ Q2. According to this passage, how is the issue of gun-control laws perceived in the U.S.?
  (A) peacefully
  (B) indifferently
  (C) controversially
  (D) none of the above

▶▶ 解答請見 p.398

4.7

社會議題 Social Issues

請用 90 秒的時間，看完整篇文章。然後跟著每一個有意義的色塊，提升理解的速度。（請盡量試著不查自己不認識的字，利用前後文去推測意思。）

Arguably a global issue and a tragedy affecting countless lives around the world, gun violence is frequently the lead story on the evening news and receives extensive media coverage. According to the 2018 Switzerland-based Small Arms Survey, 44% of homicides globally involved gunshots. In particular, the United States has the highest firearm homicide rate among developed countries, about eight times greater than that of Canada. For example, a gunman killed 49 people in Orlando in 2016. 58 people died in mass shootings in Las Vegas in 2017, the deadliest mass shooting ever in the United States. High-profile mass shootings have plagued the United States for far too long.

槍枝暴力是全球的重大議題

Despite an outpouring of grief and sympathy, the debate over gun laws has been a political hot potato in the United States. Lawmakers across the political spectrum have rarely agreed on gun control. People are split along ideological lines over whether gun laws should be further tightened, Democrats more likely than Republicans to see firearm violence as a dire problem, according to the Pew Research Center's survey in 2021.

槍枝議題在美國是燙手山芋

Gun control advocates are convinced that loose gun-control laws are the primary source of gun violence, particularly given that there are guns all over the place in some communities. They believe more gun control laws like background checks that include criminal records would reduce gunshot-related deaths. Moreover, they point out that countries doing so, such as Switzerland and Finland, have lower gun-related homicide rates. Many proponents therefore argue that limiting access to guns would curb gun violence and save lives. Proponents of

反槍陣營主張嚴格管控

increased gun control acknowledge the fact that the U.S. Constitution protects an individual's right to own a gun. However, they argue that guns are rarely used in self-defense within the home or in public places, and instead often threaten the right to life on the street.

Opponents of gun control, sitting on the other side of the desk, push back hard against more restrictions. They argue that gun control laws infringe the constitutional right of law-abiding citizens to defend themselves. Believing gun-control proponents are barking up the wrong tree, the opponents suggest that stricter gun control is not a solution since states with some of the most stringent gun laws, like New York and Illinois, suffer from high rates of gun violence. Seeing that the vast majority of criminals obtain their firearms through illegal means, gun control laws are unlikely to prevent criminals from obtaining guns. In consequence, gun-control measures, such as background checks, may be a futile effort. Everyone seems to agree that people's safety is second to none, and yet the problem of gun violence is approached from different angles.

擁槍陣
營反對
嚴格
管控

■ 請回答以下問題：

_____ Q1. How many people die of gunshots each year in the US?
(A) 49   (B) 58   (C) 100   (D) not mentioned in this passage

_____ Q2. Which of the following is NOT one of the gun-control proponents' claims?
(A) Gun ownership can cause more crime.
(B) Gun control laws do not prevent criminals from obtaining guns.
(C) Guns can easily turn a murder into a mass murder.
(D) Countries with restrictive gun control laws have lower gun homicide.

_____ Q3. Which of the following is NOT one of the opponents' clams?

    (A) Gun ownership is a fundamental right of law-abiding citizens.

    (B) Gun ownership is probably not the root cause of gun violence.

    (C) Strict regulations of firearms are an effective way of reducing gun violence.

    (D) Advocates' expectation that more gun control laws will deter crime may be based on shaky assumptions.

_____ Q4. Which of the following can be inferred from the article?

    (A) Mass shootings do not fuel gun control debates.

    (B) Perceptions of gun control do not differ widely in the U.S.

    (C) Mass shootings normally receive little media coverage.

    (D) Many believe loose gun-control laws should be held accountable for gun violence.

_____ Q5. Which of the following states has some of the most stringent gun laws?

    (A) the state of New York

    (B) the state of Mississippi

    (C) the state of Arizona

    (D) the state of Kentucky

▶▶ 解答請見 p.399

4.7.3_S.mp3

STEP 5 跟讀 Shadowing

請根據母語人士所錄製的音檔，一句一句跟著唸。跟讀時請使用跟讀音檔，每句結束後，請利用句與句之間的空秒時間，複誦前面所聽到的句子。建議第一遍，看著文章跟著唸，第二遍則不看文章，只聽音檔唸。

STEP 6 聽讀 Listening

第一遍
→ 讀者會聽到音檔內母語人士完整且不間斷將本文唸一遍。試著不看文章，聽音檔內的母語人士完整且不間斷地將本文唸一遍，確認自己哪裡聽懂，那裡聽不懂。

第二遍
→ 再聽母語人士不間斷地將本文唸一遍，眼睛注視著正在朗誦的每個句子，針對自己沒聽懂的部分，特別仔細閱讀。

STEP 7 延伸學習

單字 Vocabulary

❶ **homicide** [ˈhɑməsaɪd]	n. 兇殺案，殺人罪 The number of homicides has increased this year. 今年的兇殺案件數有增加。
❷ **plague** [pleg]	v. 折磨；使…受到煎熬 Gun violence has continued to plague the U.S. 槍枝暴力持續使美國民眾受到煎熬。
❸ **grief** [grif]	n. 悲痛 She has recovered from her grief at her dog's death. 她已經從其愛犬往生的悲痛中走出來了。
❹ **ideology** [aɪdɪˈɑlədʒɪ]	n. 意識形態 Ideology plays a role in language learning. 意識形態能夠影響語言學習。
❺ **dire** [daɪr]	adj. 急迫的 Their country is in dire need of water. 他們的國家嚴重缺水。
❻ **law-abiding** [ˈlɔˈbaɪdɪŋ]	adj. 守法的 He wants to be a law-abiding citizen. 他想要做一位守法的好市民。

4.7

社會議題 Social Issues

❼ **infringe** [ɪnˈfrɪndʒ]	v. 侵犯（權益等） Making copies of her book infringes her copyright. 複印她的書侵犯了她的著作權。
❽ **constitutional** [kɑnstɪˈtjuʃənəl]	adj. 憲法的 Freedom of speech is his constitutional right. 言論自由是憲法賦予他的權力。
❾ **stringent** [ˈstrɪndʒənt]	adj. 嚴格的 This country has stringent air quality standards. 這個國家有嚴格的空氣品質標準。
❿ **futile** [ˈfjutl̩]	adj. 徒勞無功的 The government made a futile attempt to control inflation. 政府未能成功地控制通膨。

慣用語和片語 Expressions and Phrases

❶ given that　有鑑於

Given that she was required by her parents to read these books for the exam, she did not read them by choice.

有鑑於她父母要求她為了考試去讀這些書，她並不是自己選擇要讀的。

❷ across the political spectrum　橫跨政治光譜，不分黨派地

Racism has been a serious problem for Americans across the political spectrum.

種族歧視對於各種政治傾向的美國人來說一直是個嚴重的問題。

❸ bark up the wrong tree　用錯方法，搞錯重點（或對象）

He failed because he barked up the wrong tree.

他用錯了方法所以沒有成功。

❹ second to none　首屈一指，最重要的

The President's safety is second to none to the Secret Service.

總統的安危是秘勤局最重要的工作。

A. Fill in the blanks with suitable words or phrases 將適合的字詞填入空格中

> **ⓐ** stringent　　**ⓑ** law-abiding　　**ⓒ** ideology　　**ⓓ** second to none

1. He is extremely greedy. To him, money is _____.

2. Democratic _____ is popular in the world today.

3. According to his background check, he seems to be a _____ citizen.

4. They are supportive of _____ traffic regulations.

B. Multiple choice questions 選擇題（可利用此題型熟悉多益、英檢考試）

_____ 1. ------- that they disliked the candidate, they did not vote for him.
(A) Except　(B) Aside from　(C) Given　(D) Apart from

_____ 2. Unfortunately, it was a(n) ------- rescue attempt.
(A) timely　(B) futile　(C) effective　(D) nutritious

_____ 3. Although she tried to stay strong, she could not hide her deep ------- over the death of her best friend.
(A) tactics　(B) deficiency　(C) grief　(D) novice

_____ 4. The basketball player was ------- with knee injuries last year.
(A) plagued　(B) strengthened　(C) empowered　(D) tangled

_____ 5. Because he is so sick, he is in ------- need of treatment.
(A) tedious　(B) casual　(C) pious　(D) dire

▶▶ 解答請見 p.400

4.7

社會議題 Social Issues

4.8 自然與科學
Nature and Science

Part **1** **Neuroscience in Focus: The Human Nervous System**（聚焦神經科學：人類的神經系統）

Did you know?

[你需要知道的 **10** 件事]

❶ 神經系統佈滿全身各部位。
❷ 因為有神經系統，我們才能夠做出各式各樣的動作。
❸ 因為有神經系統，我們才能夠有知覺和各種感受。
❹ 即使是在睡眠的狀態中，神經系統仍持續地運作。
❺ 人體的行為可分為有意識和無意識兩種。
❻ 反射動作即為無意識的行為。
❼ 反射動作不需經過大腦思考，即可完成。
❽ 神經系統主要分為二個：中樞神經系統和末梢神經系統。
❾ 中樞神經系統包含大腦和脊髓，負責接收各種訊息，並發出指令。
❿ 神經損傷可以自我修復，但是修復的速度相當緩慢。

Must-know vocabulary

[你需要知道的 **10** 個單字]

❶ overstatement *n.* 言過其實
❷ the nervous system *n.* 神經系統
❸ the central nervous system *n.* 中樞神經系統
❹ the peripheral nervous system *n.* 末梢神經系統
❺ command center *n.* 指揮中心
❻ the spinal cord *n.* 脊髓
❼ involuntary *adj.* 無意識的，不自主的
❽ reflex *n.* 反射動作
❾ sensation *n.* 知覺
❿ conscious *adj.* 有意識的

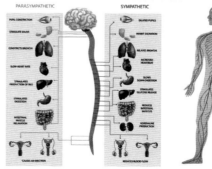

HUMAN NERVOUS SYSTEM

掃讀的目標是在文章中搜尋特定的人名、時間、地點，或相關詞語，就像是在電話簿中搜尋某人的電話號碼一樣，其他內容完全不看。

■ 請於 **30** 秒內在以下文章中找出下列文字並畫線，不要閱讀內容或嘗試理解文章。

❶ overstatement   ❷ the nervous system

❸ the central nervous system   ❹ the peripheral nervous system

❺ command center   ❻ the spinal cord

❼ involuntary   ❽ reflex

❾ sensation   ❿ conscious

Neuroscience in Focus: The Human Nervous System

(451 words)   By Yushiang Jou

It is not an overstatement to say that the nervous system is one of the most complex parts of human body. Controlling what we think and feel as well as what our body can do like walking and running, the nervous system is a network of nerves sending signals throughout the body. Thanks to the nerves all over our body, we are able to feel sensations, such as pain. Specifically, our body has two nervous systems that work in tandem with each other: the central and peripheral nervous system.

The central nervous system is made up of the brain and spinal cord. The brain, in particular, is the command center for our body, controlling body functions by receiving and sending signals through nerves. The largest part of our brain can be divided into left and right halves. The left side is considered logical and rational, in charge of skills such as math and science. The right side is thought to be more creative and artistic, responsible for subjects like art and music. On the other hand, the spinal cord serves as the bridge that connects the brain to the peripheral nervous system. Both the brain and the spinal cord can send signals via motor nerves to the rest of the body, telling the body what actions should be taken.

4.8

自然與科學 Nature and Science

The peripheral nervous system is like two-way traffic. Sensory nerves of the peripheral nervous system constantly receive information from the eyes, ears, mouth, nose, and skin, and relay it back to the central nervous system. Motor nerves then take orders from the brain and spinal cord to perform actions such as eating and swallowing. In addition to these voluntary actions, the peripheral nervous system has another card up its sleeve—involuntary actions that operate independently of conscious awareness. These involuntary actions, such as heartbeat and breathing, continue even when we are asleep.

Another feature of the peripheral nervous system is the reflex response. Reflexes, such as blinking, are quick and involuntary actions that keep us safe from danger. For example, when a tiny stone is flying toward our eye, our eyelid would slam shut way before we are aware of the stone. Reflex responses can also take place when we are holding a hot cup of tea. Sensory nerves in the skin would immediately send a message to the brain that the cup is hot and harmful. The brain then would send a message back telling the muscles in our hand to pull away. Most of the time, however, these messages do not even get to the brain. The spinal cord, when receiving a message in the first place, would send one right back to the muscles to react, without any conscious effort.

■ 請選擇正確的意思

_____ ❶ overstatement   (A) 平鋪直敘 (B) 言過其實

_____ ❷ the nervous system   (A) 神經系統 (B) 神經損傷

_____ ❸ the central nervous system   (A) 末梢神經系統 (B) 中樞神經系統

_____ ❹ the peripheral nervous system   (A) 末梢神經系統 (B) 中樞神經系統

_____ ❺ command center   (A) 指揮中心 (B) 物流中心

_____ ❻ the spinal cord   (A) 四肢 (B) 脊髓

_____ ❼ involuntary   (A) 有意識的 (B) 無意識的

_____ ❽ reflex   (A) 反射動作 (B) 反制行動

_____ ❾ sensation   (A) 知覺 (B) 知識

_____ ❿ conscious   (A) 有意識的 (B) 無意識的

▶▶ 解答請見 p.402

針對剛才的文章，用 30 秒鐘瀏覽各段的第一句，粗略了解文章結構與大意即可。

It is not an overstatement to say that the nervous system is one of the most complex parts of human body. Controlling what we think and feel as well as what our body can do like walking and running, the nervous system is a network of nerves sending signals throughout the body. Thanks to the nerves all over our body, we are able to feel sensations, such as pain. Specifically, our body has two nervous systems that work in tandem with each other: the central and peripheral nervous system.

神經
系統的
功能

The central nervous system is made up of the brain and the spinal cord. The brain, in particular, is the command center for our body, controlling body functions by receiving and sending signals through nerves. The largest part of our brain can be divided into left and right halves. The left side is considered logical and rational, in charge of skills such as math and science. The right side is thought to be more creative and artistic, responsible for subjects like art and music. On the other hand, the spinal cord serves as the bridge that connects the brain to the peripheral nervous system. Both the brain and the spinal cord can send signals via motor nerves to the rest of the body, telling the body what actions should be taken.

中樞神
經系統

The peripheral nervous system is like two-way traffic. Sensory nerves of the peripheral nervous system constantly receive information from the eyes, ears, mouth, nose, and skin, and relay it back to the central nervous system. Motor nerves then take orders from the brain and spinal cord to perform actions such as eating and swallowing. In addition to these voluntary actions, the peripheral nervous system has another card up its sleeve—involuntary actions that operate independently of conscious awareness. These involuntary actions, such as heartbeat and breathing, continue even when we are asleep.

末梢神
經系統

4.8

自然與科學 Nature and Science

Another feature of the peripheral nervous system is the reflex response. Reflexes, such as blinking, are quick and involuntary actions that keep us safe from danger. For example, when a tiny stone is flying toward our eye, our eyelid would slam shut way before we are aware of the stone. Reflex responses can also take place when we are holding a hot cup of tea. Sensory nerves in the skin would immediately send a message to the brain that the cup is hot and harmful. The brain then would send a message back telling the muscles in our hand to pull away. Most of the time, however, these messages do not even get to the brain. The spinal cord, when receiving a message in the first place, would send one right back to the muscles to react, without any conscious effort.

末梢神
經系統
的反射
動作

■ 回答以下問題，確認自己是否正確理解整篇文章的大意：

Q1. _____ The human nervous system is complicated. (T/F)

Q2. _____ The brain is the only part of human nervous system. (T/F)

Q3. _____ The spine is the only part of human nervous system. (T/F)

Q4. _____ The peripheral nervous system controls reflex responses. (T/F)

Q5. _____ The central nervous system controls reflex responses. (T/F)

▶▶ 解答請見 p.403

STEP 3 細讀 Close reading

請用 60 秒的時間仔細閱讀以下內容，並回答問題。

Reflex responses can also take place when we are holding a hot cup of tea. Sensory nerves in the skin would immediately send a message to the brain that the cup is hot and harmful. The brain then would send a message back telling the muscles in our hand to pull away. Most of the time, however, these messages do not even get to the brain. The spinal cord, when receiving a message in the first place, would send one right back to the muscles to react, without any conscious effort.

_____ Q1. According to this passage, which of the following is incorrect?
      (A) Reflex responses can happen when we are holding a hot cup of tea.
      (B) The brain receives all messages from sensory nerves.
      (C) The spinal cord receives messages from sensory nerves.
      (D) Reflex responses are sometimes unconscious.

_____ Q2. According to this passage, what is the function of reflex responses?
      (A) to hold a hot cup of tea
      (B) to send messages to the brain
      (C) to send messages to the spinal cord
      (D) to keep us away from danger

▶▶ 解答請見 p.402

STEP 4 高理解速讀 Speed Reading with Greater Comprehension

請用 90 秒的時間，看完整篇文章。然後跟著每一個有意義的色塊，提升理解的速度。（請盡量試著不查自己不認識的字，利用前後文去推測意思。）

It is not an overstatement to say that the nervous system is one of the most complex parts of human body. Controlling what we think and feel as well as what our body can do like walking and running, the nervous system is a network of nerves sending signals throughout the body. Thanks to the nerves all over our body, we are able to feel sensations, such as pain. Specifically, our body has two nervous systems that work in tandem with each other: the central and peripheral nervous system.

神經
系統的
功能

4.8

自然與科學 Nature and Science

The central nervous system is made up of the brain and the spinal cord. The brain, in particular, is the command center for our body, controlling body functions by receiving and sending signals through nerves. The largest part of our brain can be divided into left and right halves. The left side is considered logical and rational, in charge of skills such as math and science. The right side is thought to be more creative and artistic, responsible for subjects like art and music. On the other hand, the spinal cord serves as the bridge that connects the brain to the peripheral nervous system. Both the brain and the spinal cord can send signals via motor nerves to the rest of the body, telling the body what actions should be taken.

The peripheral nervous system is like two-way traffic. Sensory nerves of the peripheral nervous system constantly receive information from the eyes, ears, mouth, nose, and skin, and relay it back to the central nervous system. Motor nerves then take orders from the brain and spinal cord to perform actions such as eating and swallowing. In addition to these voluntary actions, the peripheral nervous system has another card up its sleeve—involuntary actions that operate independently of conscious awareness. These involuntary actions, such as heartbeat and breathing, continue even when we are asleep.

Another feature of the peripheral nervous system is the reflex response. Reflexes, such as blinking, are quick and involuntary actions that keep us safe from danger. For example, when a tiny stone is flying toward our eye, our eyelid would slam shut way before we are aware of the stone. Reflex responses can also take place when we are holding a hot cup of tea. Sensory nerves in the skin would immediately send a message to the brain that the cup is hot and harmful. The brain then would send a message back telling the muscles in our hand to pull away. Most of the time, however, these messages do not even get to the brain. The spinal cord, when receiving a message in the first place, would send one right back to the muscles to react, without any conscious effort.

■ 請回答以下問題：

_____ Q1. The human nervous system allows us to _____.
　　　　　　(A) think　　(B) feel　　(C) walk　　(D) all of the above

_____ Q2. Where are the nerves located?
　　　　　　(A) all over the body
　　　　　　(B) only in the brain
　　　　　　(C) only in the spine
　　　　　　(D) only on the skin

_____ Q3. Which was likely to be true about Einstein?
　　　　　　(A) His reflex responses were stronger than those of most people.
　　　　　　(B) Both sides of the largest part of his brain were equally strong.
　　　　　　(C) The left side of the largest part of his brain was stronger.
　　　　　　(D) The right side of the largest part of his brain was stronger.

_____ Q4. Which of the following can be inferred from the article?
　　　　　　(A) Involuntary actions are the same as reflex responses.
　　　　　　(B) Nervous systems do not function when we are asleep.
　　　　　　(C) The peripheral nervous system is the command center for our body.
　　　　　　(D) Both the central and peripheral nervous systems are important.

_____ Q5. When would a reflex NOT be triggered?
　　　　　　(A) when we are swimming
　　　　　　(B) when we are stung by a bee
　　　　　　(C) when we are holding a hot cup of coffee
　　　　　　(D) when a tiny stone is flying toward our eye

4.8
自然與科學 Nature and Science

4.8.1_S.mp3

STEP 5 跟讀 Shadowing

　　請根據母語人士所錄製的音檔，一句一句跟著唸。跟讀時請使用跟讀音檔，每句結束後，請利用句與句之間的空秒時間，複誦前面所聽到的句子。建議第一遍，看著文章跟著唸，第二遍則不看文章，只聽音檔唸。

4.8.1_L.mp3

STEP 6 聽讀 Listening

第一遍
→ 讀者會聽到音檔內母語人士完整且不間斷將本文唸一遍。試著不看文章，聽音檔內的母語人士完整且不間斷地將本文唸一遍，確認自己哪裡聽懂，那裡聽不懂。

第二遍
→ 再聽母語人士不間斷地將本文唸一遍，眼睛注視著正在朗誦的每個句子，針對自己沒聽懂的部分，特別仔細閱讀。

STEP 7 延伸學習

單字 Vocabulary

❶ sensation [sɛn`seʃən]	n. 知覺 She said she had no sensation in her right arm. 她說她右手臂沒有知覺。
❷ artistic [ɑr`tɪstɪk]	adj. 藝術的 Her parents are proud of her artistic achievements. 她的父母對於她的藝術成就引以為傲。
❸ constant [`kɑnstənt]	adj. 經常性的，持續的 He has been suffering from constant headaches. 他承受著長期的頭痛之苦。

❹ **relay** [rɪ`le]	v. 傳遞 He wants to relay this message to his colleagues. 他想要將這個消息傳達給他的同事知道。
❺ **involuntary** [ɪn`vɑlən‚tɛrɪ]	adj. 無意識的 Breathing is an involuntary action. 呼吸是一種無意識的行為。
❻ **heartbeat** [`hɑrt‚bit]	n. 心跳 He had irregular heartbeats this morning. 他今天早上心跳不規律。
❼ **reflex** [`riflɛks]	n. 反射動作 The doctor tested his reflexes. 醫生測試了他的反射動作是否正常。
❽ **blink** [blɪŋk]	v. 眨眼睛 Blinking is an involuntary action. 眨眼睛是一種無意識的行為。
❾ **eyelid** [`aɪ‚lɪd]	n. 眼瞼 What is the function of eyelids? 眼瞼的功能是什麼？
❿ **harmful** [`hɑrmfəl]	adj. 有害的 The new drug may have harmful side effects. 這款新藥可能產生有害的副作用。

4.8

自然與科學 Nature and Science

❶ in tandem (with)　與…攜手合作

He wants to run this company in tandem with his best friend.
他想要跟他最好的朋友攜手合作一起經營這公司。

❷ two-way traffic　雙向來往的交通（車輛或道路）

This road is too narrow for trucks to be in two-way traffic.
這條路太窄了，大卡車根本無法雙向通行。

❸ have another card up one's sleeve　還有秘密武器，還留一手

The lawyer is confident of winning the case because he has another card up his sleeve.
這位律師有信心打贏這場官司，因為他還有一張王牌。

❹ in the first place　剛開始的時候

She did not want to study hard in the first place.
她剛開始的時候還不想要用功讀書。

A. Fill in the blanks with suitable words or phrases 將適合的字詞填入空格中

> **ⓐ** reflex   **ⓑ** stomachache   **ⓒ** relay   **ⓓ** first place

1. She suffered from a _____ last night.

2. He did not plan to buy a car in the _____ .

3. _____ are meant to keep us safe from danger.

4. It is imperative that you _____ this information to your co-workers.

B. Multiple choice questions 選擇題（可利用此題型熟悉多益、英檢考試）

_____ 1. Blinking is a(n) ------- action.
     (A) involuntary   (B) voluntary   (C) numerical   (D) obligatory

_____ 2. These viruses are ------- to humans.
     (A) beneficial   (B) irrelevant   (C) nutritious   (D) harmful

_____ 3. Monet, a very famous French painter, is known for his -------
     achievements.
     (A) scientific   (B) literary   (C) artistic   (D) mathematical

_____ 4. She worked ------- several scientists to develop the new vaccine.
     (A) as a consequence of   (B) in tandem with
     (C) on account of   (D) in opposition to

_____ 5. After the car accident, he was badly injured and lost ------- in his
     left leg.
     (A) familiarity   (B) sensation   (C) hormone   (D) temperament

▶▶ 解答請見 p.404

4.8

自然與科學 Nature and Science

Did you know?

[你需要知道的 10 件事]

❶ 大部份的行星都有一顆或多顆天然衛星。

❷ 太陽系有超過 150 顆天然衛星。

❸ 木星是太陽系八大行星中最大的行星。

❹ 木星有 79 顆比木星小很多的天然衛星。

❺ 海王星是太陽系八大行星中排名第四大的行星。

❻ 海王星有 14 顆比海王星小很多的天然衛星。

❼ 火星只有兩顆很小的天然衛星。水星沒有任何衛星。

❽ 地球是太陽系八大行星中排名第五大的行星。

❾ 相對於地球的大小，月球是比例相當大的天然衛星。

❿ 月球是太陽系最大的天然衛星之一。

Must-know vocabulary

[你需要知道的 10 個單字]

❶ habitability *n.* 適居性

❷ gravity *n.* 引力

❸ tide *n.* 潮汐

❹ spin *v.* 旋轉

❺ equator *n.* 赤道

❻ nuclear explosion *n.* 核爆

❼ corroborative *adj.* 可證實的

❽ computer simulation *n.* 電腦模擬

❾ collision *n.* 撞擊

❿ hypothesis *n.* 假說

> 掃讀的目標是在文章中搜尋特定的人名、時間、地點，或相關詞語，就像是在電話簿中搜尋某人的電話號碼一樣，其他內容完全不看。

■ 請於 **30** 秒內在以下文章中找出下列文字並畫線，不要閱讀內容或嘗試理解文章。

❶ habitability   ❷ gravity
❸ tide   ❹ spin
❺ equator   ❻ nuclear explosion
❼ corroborative   ❽ computer simulation
❾ collision   ❿ hypothesis

....

The Origin of the Moon

(441 words)   By Yushiang Jou

Having been circling the Earth for over four billion years, the moon plays an important role in the habitability of the Earth. The moon, to a certain extent, helps stabilize the tilt of the Earth's rotational pole. This tilt is responsible for the four seasons on Earth and a relatively stable climate. The moon's gravity also interacts with the Earth's oceans, controlling the ebb and flow of the tide. Without the moon, life on Earth would have looked different.

But just how did the moon form? This is a million-dollar question. There are at least five plausible hypotheses about how the moon formed. Firstly, the co-formation hypothesis suggests that both the Earth and the moon formed together. However, if both started with the same mass of iron, why does the Earth have an iron core, while the moon does not?

Another one is the capture hypothesis. This hypothesis holds that the moon was already formed elsewhere in the universe and was later captured by Earth's gravity when the moon passed by the Earth. Yet, this hypothesis has been on shaky ground since analyses of rocks collected from the moon showed that both the moon and the Earth formed roughly around the same time.

Some proposed the fission hypothesis, stating that the Earth once spun so fast that part of it split off and formed the moon. If this were the case, however, the moon would have been orbiting the equator. Moreover, while the Pacific Ocean basin is the most likely site from which the moon comes, it is much younger than the moon. Therefore, many astronomers do not support this hypothesis.

Another hypothesis suggests that high concentrations of radioactive elements, such as uranium, triggered a natural nuclear explosion on early Earth. This explosion ejected a moon-size chunk of Earth that eventually formed the moon. Due to a lack of corroborative evidence, however, this hypothesis has been disproved.

What is widely accepted by the scientific community is the giant-impact hypothesis. This hypothesis suggests that the moon was formed from a collision between the Earth and a planet roughly the size of Mars. A large chunk ejected from this collision eventually became the moon. Computer simulations have confirmed the possibility of forming the moon this way. Simulations of this collision also suggest that the moon would have been composed mainly of the material from this planet. However, geological evidence says otherwise. Analyses of lunar rocks indicate that these rocks share similar minerals with Earth rocks, implying the moon and the Earth have a common origin. With many questions left unanswered, more research is needed to yield new insights into our only natural satellite.

■ 請選擇正確的意思

_____ ❶ habitability　(A) 適居性 (B) 居民

_____ ❷ gravity　(A) 引力 (B) 力學

_____ ❸ tide　(A) 海水 (B) 潮汐

_____ ❹ spin　(A) 旋風 (B) 旋轉

_____ ❺ equator　(A) 赤道 (B) 回歸線

_____ ❻ nuclear explosion　(A) 核武 (B) 核爆

_____ ❼ corroborative　(A) 可證實的 (B) 偽造的

_____ ❽ computer simulation　(A) 電腦模擬 (B) 人工繪圖

_____ ❾ collision　(A) 攻擊 (B) 撞擊

_____ ❿ hypothesis　(A) 假說 (B) 證實

▶▶ 解答請見 p.406

STEP 2　略讀 Skimming

針對剛才的文章，用 30 秒鐘瀏覽各段的第一句，粗略了解文章結構與大意即可。

　　Having been circling the Earth for over four billion years, the moon plays an important role in the habitability of the Earth. The moon, to a certain extent, helps stabilize the tilt of the Earth's rotational pole. This tilt is responsible for the four seasons on Earth and a relatively stable climate. The moon's gravity also interacts with the Earth's oceans, controlling the ebb and flow of the tide. Without the moon, life on Earth would have looked different.

月球對於地球的適居性關係密切

　　But just how did the moon form? This is a million-dollar question. There are at least five plausible hypotheses about how the moon formed. Firstly, the co-formation hypothesis suggests that both the Earth and the moon formed together. However, if both started with the same mass of iron, why does the Earth have an iron core, while the moon does not?

月球形成之共構假說

4.8

自然與科學 Nature and Science

　　Another one is the capture hypothesis. This hypothesis holds that the moon was already formed elsewhere in the universe and was later captured by Earth's gravity when the moon passed by the Earth. Yet, this hypothesis has been on shaky ground since analyses of rocks collected from the moon showed that both the moon and the Earth formed roughly around the same time.

月球形成之捕捉假說

Some proposed the fission hypothesis, stating that the Earth once spun so fast that part of it split off and formed the moon. If this were the case, however, the moon would have been orbiting the equator. Moreover, while the Pacific Ocean basin is the most likely site from which the moon comes, it is much younger than the moon. Therefore, many astronomers do not support this hypothesis.

月球形
成之分
裂假說

Another hypothesis suggests that high concentrations of radioactive elements, such as uranium, triggered a natural nuclear explosion on early Earth. This explosion ejected a moon-size chunk of Earth that eventually formed the moon. Due to a lack of corroborative evidence, however, this hypothesis has been disproved.

月球形
成之核
爆假說

What is widely accepted by the scientific community is the giant-impact hypothesis. This hypothesis suggests that the moon was formed from a collision between the Earth and a planet roughly the size of Mars. A large chunk ejected from this collision eventually became the moon. Computer simulations have confirmed the possibility of forming the moon this way. Simulations of this collision also suggest that the moon would have been composed mainly of the material from this planet. However, geological evidence says otherwise. Analyses of lunar rocks indicate that these rocks share similar minerals with Earth rocks, implying the moon and the Earth have a common origin. With many questions left unanswered, more research is needed to yield new insights into our only natural satellite.

月球形
成之大
撞擊
假說

■ 回答以下問題，確認自己是否正確理解整篇文章的大意：

Q1. _____ Humans can survive well on Earth without the moon. (T/F)

Q2. _____ We know how the moon formed for sure. (T/F)

Q3. _____ The capture hypothesis is the most widely accepted by the scientific community. (T/F)

Q4. _____ Many astronomers support the fission hypothesis. (T/F)

Q5. _____ The giant-impact hypothesis is the most widely accepted by the scientific community. (T/F)

STEP 3 細讀 Close reading

請用 60 秒的時間仔細閱讀以下內容，並回答問題。

A large chunk ejected from this collision eventually became the moon. Computer simulations have confirmed the possibility of forming the moon this way. Simulations of this collision also suggest that the moon would have been composed mainly of the material from this planet. However, geological evidence says otherwise. Analyses of lunar rocks indicate that these rocks share similar minerals with Earth rocks, implying the moon and the Earth have a common origin.

_____ Q1. According to this passage, which of the following is correct?
   (A) Computer simulations and geological evidence do not match.
   (B) The planet-sized body became the earth after the collision.
   (C) We now know for sure how the moon formed.
   (D) Computer simulations suggest that the moon and the Earth have a common origin.

_____ Q2. According to this passage, what do we know about the moon?
   (A) The moon could not have formed after a collision.
   (B) Lunar rocks have already been analyzed.
   (C) Lunar rocks do not share similar minerals with Earth rocks.
   (D) Computers are not used to study the origin of the moon.

解答請見 p.406

4.8

自然與科學 Nature and Science

請用 90 秒的時間，看完整篇文章。然後跟著每一個有意義的色塊，提升理解的速度。（*請盡量試著不查自己不認識的字，利用前後文去推測意思。*）

The Origin of the Moon

Having been circling the Earth for over four billion years, the moon plays an important role in the habitability of the Earth. The moon, to a certain extent, helps stabilize the tilt of the Earth's rotational pole. This tilt is responsible for the four seasons on Earth and a relatively stable climate. The moon's gravity also interacts with the Earth's oceans, controlling the ebb and flow of the tide. Without the moon, life on Earth would have looked different.

月球對於地球的適居性關係密切

But just how did the moon form? This is a million-dollar question. There are at least five plausible hypotheses about how the moon formed. Firstly, the co-formation hypothesis suggests that both the Earth and the moon formed together. However, if both started with the same mass of iron, why does the Earth have an iron core, while the moon does not?

月球形成之共構假說

Another one is the capture hypothesis. This hypothesis holds that the moon was already formed elsewhere in the universe and was later captured by Earth's gravity when the moon passed by the Earth. Yet, this hypothesis has been on shaky ground since analyses of rocks collected from the moon showed that both the moon and the Earth formed roughly around the same time.

月球形成之捕捉假說

Some proposed the fission hypothesis, stating that the Earth once spun so fast that part of it split off and formed the moon. If this were the case, however, the moon would have been orbiting the equator. Moreover, while the Pacific Ocean basin is the most likely site from which the moon comes, it is much younger than the moon. Therefore, many astronomers do not support this hypothesis.

月球形成之分裂假說

Another hypothesis suggests that high concentrations of radioactive elements, such as uranium, triggered a natural nuclear explosion on early Earth. This explosion ejected a moon-size chunk of Earth that eventually formed the moon. Due to a lack of corroborative evidence, however, this hypothesis has been disproved.

月球形
成之核
爆假說

What is widely accepted by the scientific community is the giant-impact hypothesis. This hypothesis suggests that the moon was formed from a collision between the Earth and a planet roughly the size of Mars. A large chunk ejected from this collision eventually became the moon. Computer simulations have confirmed the possibility of forming the moon this way. Simulations of this collision also suggest that the moon would have been composed mainly of the material from this planet. However, geological evidence says otherwise. Analyses of lunar rocks indicate that these rocks share similar minerals with Earth rocks, implying the moon and the Earth have a common origin. With many questions left unanswered, more research is needed to yield new insights into our only natural satellite.

月球形
成之大
撞擊
假說

■ 請回答以下問題：

_____ Q1. What is NOT related to the moon?

   (A) the size of the Earth
   (B) Earth's changing seasons
   (C) the tilt of Earth's rotational pole
   (D) the tide on Earth

_____ Q2. Which hypothesis is the most widely accepted by the scientific community?

   (A) the fission hypothesis
   (B) the capture hypothesis
   (C) the giant-impact hypothesis
   (D) the co-formation hypothesis

_____ Q3. According to this passage, what is the purpose of computer simulations?

(A) to study the concentrations of radioactive elements on Earth

(B) to study how the moon formed

(C) to study the Earth's habitability

(D) to study the iron core of the moon

_____ Q4. According to this article, which of the following is incorrect?

(A) The moon's gravity interacts with Earth's oceans.

(B) The moon orbits around the equator.

(C) The Earth has an iron core.

(D) The moon and the Earth formed roughly around the same time.

_____ Q5. How many hypotheses are there about the origin of the moon?

(A) three   (B) four   (C) five   (D) more than five

▶▶ 解答請見 p.407

4.8.2_S.mp3

STEP 5 跟讀 Shadowing

　　請根據母語人士所錄製的音檔，一句一句跟著唸。跟讀時請使用跟讀音檔，每句結束後，請利用句與句之間的空秒時間，複誦前面所聽到的句子。建議第一遍，看著文章跟著唸，第二遍則不看文章，只聽音檔唸。

4.8.2_L.mp3

STEP 6 聽讀 Listening

第一遍

→ 讀者會聽到音檔內母語人士完整且不間斷將本文唸一遍。試著不看文章，聽音檔內的母語人士完整且不間斷地將本文唸一遍，確認自己哪裡聽懂，那裡聽不懂。

第二遍

→ 再聽母語人士不間斷地將本文唸一遍，眼睛注視著正在朗誦的每個句子，針對自己沒聽懂的部分，特別仔細閱讀。

單字 Vocabulary

❶ **hypothesis** [haɪˋpɑθəsɪs]	n. 假說 She needs to do more research to confirm her hypothesis. 她需要做更多的研究來驗證她的假說。
❷ **tilt** [tɪlt]	n. 傾斜 Her dog reacted to a loud noise with a tilt of its head. 她的狗歪著頭回應一個很大的吵雜聲。
❸ **rotational** [roˋteʃənl]	adj. 旋轉的 We have a good understanding of the rotational motion of the Earth. 我們了解地球的自轉運動。
❹ **primary** [ˋpraɪˌmɛrɪ]	adj. 主要的 Their primary goal is to control inflation. 他們的主要目標是抑制通膨。
❺ **state** [stet]	v. 說明，聲明 The rules of the game are clearly stated on this page. 這頁清楚說明了比賽的規則。
❻ **orbit** [ˋɔrbɪt]	v. 繞…的軌道運行 The moon orbits the Earth. 月球繞行地球。
❼ **eject** [ɪˋdʒɛkt]	v. 彈射出去 The fighter pilot ejected before his plane crashed. 在墜機之前，戰鬥機的飛行員將自己彈射出去了。
❽ **simulation** [ˌsɪmjəˋleʃən]	n. 模擬 The military uses a computer simulation to train fighter pilots. 軍方使用電腦模擬訓練戰鬥機的飛行員。

4.8

自然與科學 Nature and Science

❾ **geological** [dʒɪə`ladʒɪkl]	adj. 地質的 She is interested in geological sciences. 她對地質科學有興趣。
❿ **lunar** [`lunɚ]	adj. 月球的 She has never seen a lunar eclipse. 她從未看過月蝕。

慣用語和片語 Expressions and Phrases

❶ ebb and flow （海水的）漲落，起伏

The company is aware of the <u>ebb and flow</u> of consumer demand.
這間公司了解消費者需求的起伏。

❷ million-dollar question 重要卻難以回答的問題

How much money people need to feel happy is a <u>million-dollar question</u>.
人到底需要多少錢才能感到快樂，是一個重要卻難以回答的問題。

❸ on shaky ground 站不住腳的，未必正確的

Her hypothesis was <u>on shaky ground</u> and was rejected in the end.
她的假說站不住腳，後來還被推翻了。

❹ to a certain extent 在某種程度上

<u>To a certain extent</u>, these two opposing views are both right.
在某種程度上來說，這兩個對立的觀點都是對的。

A. Fill in the blanks with suitable words or phrases 將適合的字詞填入空格中

> **ⓐ** eject   **ⓑ** the million-dollar   **ⓒ** orbit   **ⓓ** on shaky ground

1. The pilot did not _____ in time and died when the plane crashed.

2. His argument was _____ and therefore was not convincing.

3. _____ question is whether this pandemic will come to an end next year.

4. Many weather satellites _____ the Earth.

B. Multiple choice questions 選擇題（可利用此題型熟悉多益、英檢考試）

_____ 1. He likes to collect rocks and is interested in ------- sciences.
  (A) mathmetical   (B) medical   (C) geological   (D) political

_____ 2. John ------- clearly that he had nothing to do with the accident.
  (A) required   (B) notified   (C) targeted   (D) stated

_____ 3. She studies the moon and is particularly interested in the ------- surface.
  (A) lunar   (B) hierarchic   (C) universal   (D) solar

_____ 4. This job is important to Jean. To keep the job was her ------- goal.
  (A) unexpected   (B) primary   (C) secondary   (D) irrelevant

_____ 5. This ------- has been rejected due to a lack of evidence.
  (A) questionnaire   (B) geometry
  (C) bibliography   (D) hypothesis

▶▶ 解答請見 p.408

4.8

自然與科學 Nature and Science

Did you know?

[你需要知道的 10 件事]

❶ 當人類的主觀認知與客觀事實不符合的時候，即會產生認知偏誤。

❷ 自我感覺良好即是一種認知偏誤。

❸ 人類的認知與記憶皆是主觀的。

❹ 人類的記憶可能會隨著時間而改變。

❺ 翻譯也可能會產生認知偏誤。

❻ 許多人偏誤地將 critical thinking 翻譯為「批判性思考」。

❼ 批判性思考有負面的含意，彷彿 critical thinking 就是批評與找碴。

❽ critical thinking 指客觀地評估並分析一件事的正反兩面。

❾ critical thinking 較為正確的翻譯為「思辨能力」。

❿ 具有思辨能力（critical thinking）的人較不容易受到認知偏誤的影響。

Must-know vocabulary

[你需要知道的 10 個單字]

❶ cognitive bias *n.* 認知偏誤

❷ false interpretation *n.* 錯誤的詮釋

❸ prejudice *n.* 偏見

❹ favorable evidence *n.* 有利的證據

❺ fact-check *v.* 事實查核

❻ blind spot *n.* 盲點

❼ a know-it-all *n.* 自以為無所不知的人

❽ susceptible *adj.* 易受影響的

❾ constructive criticism *n.* 有建設性的評論

❿ critical thinking *n.* 思辨能力

掃讀的目標是在文章中搜尋特定的人名、時間、地點，或相關詞語，就像是在電話簿中搜尋某人的電話號碼一樣，其他內容完全不看。

■ 請於 30 秒內在以下文章中找出下列文字並畫線，不要閱讀內容或嘗試理解文章。

❶ cognitive bias   ❷ false interpretations

❸ prejudice   ❹ favorable evidence

❺ fact-check   ❻ blind spot

❼ a know-it-all   ❽ susceptible

❾ constructive criticism   ❿ critical thinking

The Science of Mind and Behavior: Cognitive Biases

(427 words)   By Yushiang Jou

Contrary to what common sense might tell us, humans are not always logical and rational. In fact, it is not uncommon to see people make false interpretations and poor decisions. One of the main drivers of this problem is a flaw in reasoning and judgment. This tendency of people to perceive information based on their own prejudice, often unconsciously, is known as a cognitive bias. Such examples abound. For instance, even though many people fact-check on Google, most of them tend to turn a blind eye to information at odds with their beliefs, thus unconsciously only looking for sources that reinforce their beliefs. In other words, they more likely pay attention to things that confirm what they think or what they already know. This tendency to seek favorable evidence but avoid information from alternative viewpoints is known as the confirmation bias. This can happen to any one of us.

Another common cognitive bias is the bandwagon effect, which refers to people's tendency to go along with the majority simply because everyone else is doing it. An example is that a restaurant with more people inside feels like a safe bet. When it comes to politics, most people do not want to be the odd one out and they often lean toward voting for the candidate who is leading in the polls. People's desire to go along with the majority makes them susceptible to the bandwagon effect. This effect can also be observed in finance. When people see that others are pumping money into the stock market, they may be prompted to do the same. Rather than making an independent assessment of investments, people are likely to follow suit for fear of missing out.

People can also have a blind spot when it comes to their own knowledge and competence, which is known as the Dunning-Kruger effect. This cognitive bias suggests that people with less competence in a given area are more likely to be cocksure of themselves, while those with more knowledge and skills are sometimes full of doubt. That is, a tiny bit of knowledge of a subject can often lead people to mistakenly believe that they know all there is to know about it. However, a know-it-all can, in fact, know nothing at all. This unwarranted confidence stems from blind spots that prevent people from seeing where they are going wrong. A way to combat cognitive biases is to be open to constructive criticism and develop critical thinking. Being able to evaluate our options critically would prevent us from falling victim to a cognitive bias.

■ 請選擇正確的意思

_____ ❶ cognitive bias　(A) 認知偏誤 (B) 記憶錯誤

_____ ❷ false interpretation　(A) 正確的詮釋 (B) 錯誤的詮釋

_____ ❸ prejudice　(A) 偏見 (B) 客觀

_____ ❹ favorable evidence　(A) 不利的證據 (B) 有利的證據

_____ ❺ fact-check　(A) 事實查核 (B) 捏造事實

_____ ❻ blind spot　(A) 優點 (B) 盲點

_____ ❼ a know-it-all　(A) 自以為無所不知的人 (B) 博識但謙遜的人

_____ ❽ susceptible　(A) 不受影響的 (B) 易受影響的

_____ ❾ constructive criticism　(A) 偏頗的批評 (B) 有建設性的評論

_____ ❿ critical thinking　(A) 思辨能力 (B) 批評他人的能力

▶▶ 解答請見 p.410

針對剛才的文章，用 30 秒鐘瀏覽各段的第一句，粗略了解文章結構與大意即可。

Contrary to what common sense might tell us, humans are not always logical and rational. In fact, it is not uncommon to see people make false interpretations and poor decisions. One of the main drivers of this problem is a flaw in reasoning and judgment. This tendency of people to perceive information based on their own prejudice, often unconsciously, is known as a cognitive bias. Such examples abound. For instance, even though many people fact-check on Google, most of them tend to turn a blind eye to information at odds with their beliefs, thus unconsciously only looking for sources that reinforce their beliefs. In other words, they more likely pay attention to things that confirm what they think or what they already know. This tendency to seek favorable evidence but avoid information from alternative viewpoints is known as the confirmation bias. This can happen to any one of us.

認知
偏誤的
定義

Another common cognitive bias is the bandwagon effect, which refers to people's tendency to go along with the majority simply because everyone else is doing it. An example is that a restaurant with more people inside feels like a safe bet. When it comes to politics, most people do not want to be the odd one out and they often lean toward voting for the candidate who is leading in the polls. People's desire to be with the majority makes them susceptible to the bandwagon effect. This effect can also be observed in finance. When people see that others are pumping money into the stock market, they may be prompted to do the same. Rather than making an independent assessment of investments, people are likely to follow suit for fear of missing out.

從眾
效應

People can also have a blind spot when it comes to their own knowledge and competence, which is known as the Dunning-Kruger effect. This cognitive bias suggests that people with less competence in

達克
效應

4.8

自然與科學 Nature and Science

a given area are more likely to be cocksure of themselves, while those with more knowledge and skills are sometimes full of doubt. That is, a tiny bit of knowledge of a subject can often lead people to mistakenly believe that they know all there is to know about it. However, a know-it-all can, in fact, know nothing at all. This unwarranted confidence stems from blind spots that prevent people from seeing where they are going wrong. A way to combat cognitive biases is to be open to constructive criticism and develop critical thinking. Being able to evaluate our options critically would prevent us from falling victim to a cognitive bias.

■ 回答以下問題，確認自己是否正確理解整篇文章的大意：

Q1. _____ Humans are always rational. (T/F)

Q2. _____ We tend to go along with the majority. (T/F)

Q3. _____ We always know what we know and what we do not know. (T/F)

Q4. _____ We always know what we are capable of doing. (T/F)

Q5. _____ We become more cautious when everyone else is doing the same thing. (T/F)

▶▶ 解答請見 p.410

STEP 3 細讀 Close reading

請用 60 秒的時間仔細閱讀以下內容，並回答問題。

Another common cognitive bias is the bandwagon effect, which refers to people's tendency to go along with the majority simply because everyone else is doing it. An example is that a restaurant with more people inside feels like a safe bet. When it comes to politics, most people do not want to be the odd one out and they often lean toward voting for the candidate who is leading in the polls.

_____ Q1. According to this passage, which of the following is incorrect?

      (A) The bandwagon effect is a cognitive bias.

      (B) Many people do not go along with the majority.

      (C) People tend to support the candidate leading in the polls.

      (D) People tend to choose a restaurant with more people inside.

_____ Q2. Why do people tend to go along with the majority?

      (A) because they want to feel special

      (B) because they feel lonely

      (C) because they are afraid of making mistakes

      (D) not mentioned in this passage

▶▶▶ 解答請見 p.410

STEP 4 高理解速讀 Speed Reading with Greater Comprehension

請用 90 秒的時間，看完整篇文章。然後跟著每一個有意義的色塊，提升理解的速度。（請盡量試著不查自己不認識的字，利用前後文去推測意思。）

Contrary to what common sense might tell us, humans are not always logical and rational. In fact, it is not uncommon to see people make false interpretations and poor decisions. One of the main drivers of this problem is a flaw in reasoning and judgment. This tendency of people to perceive information based on their own prejudice, often unconsciously, is known as a cognitive bias. Such examples abound. For instance, even though many people fact-check on Google, most of them tend to turn a blind eye to information at odds with their beliefs, thus unconsciously only looking for sources that reinforce their beliefs. In other words, they more likely pay attention to things that confirm what they think or what they already know. This tendency to seek favorable evidence but avoid information from alternative viewpoints is known as the confirmation bias. This can happen to any one of us.

認知偏誤的定義

4.8

自然與科學 Nature and Science

Another common cognitive bias is the bandwagon effect, which refers to people's tendency to go along with the majority simply because everyone else is doing it. An example is that a restaurant with more people inside feels like a safe bet. When it comes to politics, most people do not want to be the odd one out and they often lean toward voting for the candidate who is leading in the polls. People's desire to go along with the majority makes them susceptible to the bandwagon effect. This effect can also be observed in finance. When people see that others are pumping money into the stock market, they may be prompted to do the same. Rather than making an independent assessment of investments, people are likely to follow suit for fear of missing out.

從眾
效應

People can also have a blind spot when it comes to their own knowledge and competence, which is known as the Dunning-Kruger effect. This cognitive bias suggests that people with less competence in a given area are more likely to be cocksure of themselves, while those with more knowledge and skills are sometimes full of doubt. That is, a tiny bit of knowledge of a subject can often lead people to mistakenly believe that they know all there is to know about it. However, a know-it-all can, in fact, know nothing at all. This unwarranted confidence stems from blind spots that prevent people from seeing where they are going wrong. A way to combat cognitive biases is to be open to constructive criticism and develop critical thinking. Being able to evaluate our options critically would prevent us from falling victim to a cognitive bias.

達克
效應

■ 請回答以下問題：

_____ Q1. The tendency to seek favorable evidence is known as

(A) the Dunning-Kruger effect.

(B) the bandwagon effect.

(C) the confirmation bias.

(D) none of the above

_____ Q2. According to the article, what is likely to happen when we see most people are pumping money into the stock market?

(A) We would probably not do anything.

(B) We would probably do the same.

(C) We would be able to see where we are going wrong.

(D) We would stay away from the stock market.

_____ Q3. The Dunning-Kruger effect stems from _____.

(A) a blind spot preventing us from seeing our own weaknesses

(B) an attempt to fact-check on Google

(C) a desire to vote for the candidate leading in the polls

(D) a desire to find a restaurant with more people inside

_____ Q4. Which kind of cognitive biases is more common?

(A) the Dunning-Kruger effect

(B) the bandwagon effect

(C) the confirmation bias

(D) not mentioned in this article

_____ Q5. How can we combat cognitive biases?

(A) to develop critical thinking

(B) to be open to constructive criticism

(C) to evaluate our options critically

(D) all of the above

▶▶ 解答請見 p.411

4.8

自然與科學 Nature and Science

STEP 5 跟讀 Shadowing

　　請根據母語人士所錄製的音檔，一句一句跟著唸。跟讀時請使用跟讀音檔，每句結束後，請利用句與句之間的空秒時間，複誦前面所聽到的句子。建議第一遍，看著文章跟著唸，第二遍則不看文章，只聽音檔唸。

STEP 6 聽讀 Listening

第一遍
→ 讀者會聽到音檔內母語人士完整且不間斷將本文唸一遍。試著不看文章，聽音檔內的母語人士完整且不間斷地將本文唸一遍，確認自己哪裡聽懂，那裡聽不懂。

第二遍
→ 再聽母語人士不間斷地將本文唸一遍，眼睛注視著正在朗誦的每個句子，針對自己沒聽懂的部分，特別仔細閱讀。

STEP 7 延伸學習

單字 Vocabulary

❶ **rational** [ˋræʃənl]	adj. 理性的 He tried to make a rational decision. 他試圖做出一個理性的決定。
❷ **false** [fɔls]	adj. 錯誤的，假的 The news about the car accident was false. 那條車禍的新聞是錯誤的。
❸ **flaw** [flɔ]	n. 缺陷，瑕疵 There is a flaw in his argument. 他的論點有個瑕疵。

❹ tendency [ˈtɛndənsɪ]	n. 傾向 He has a tendency to exaggerate the size of the problem. 他習慣把問題講得很嚴重。
❺ perceive [pəˈsiv]	v. 認為，看待 Jeff Bezos is perceived as one of the richest people in the world. 貝佐斯被認為是全世界最富有的人之一。
❻ prejudice [ˈprɛdʒədɪs]	n. 偏見 She has been a victim of racial prejudice. 她長期遭受種族歧視。
❼ abound [əˈbaʊnd]	v. 大量存在 Saudi Arabia is a country where oil abounds. 沙烏地阿拉伯是一個蘊藏大量石油的國家。
❽ fact-check [fækt tʃɛk]	v. 事實查核 Journalists need to fact-check their sources before reporting the news. 記者報導新聞之前，必須去查核來源是否屬實。
❾ susceptible [səˈsɛptəbḷ]	adj. 易受影響的 Elderly people are susceptible to lung infections. 老年人的肺部容易受到感染。
❿ cocksure [ˈkɑkˈʃʊr]	adj. 自以為是的 She does not like his cocksure attitude. 她不喜歡他那自以為是的態度。

慣用語和片語 Expressions and Phrases

❶ turn a blind eye to　對於…視而不見

The President **turned a blind eye to** the problem of inflation.
總統對於通膨的問題視而不見。

❷ the odd one out　異類

He was **the odd one out** in his family.
他是他們家的異類。

❸ a safe bet　安全牌，勝算很大的選項

A watch is **a safe bet** as a gift for her father.
送她爸爸手錶當作禮物是一個安全的選項。

❹ fall victim to　被…所害，成為…的受害者

The company **has fallen victim to** the economic recession.
這間公司被經濟衰退所拖累。

A. Fill in the blanks with suitable words or phrases 將適合的字詞填入空格中

> **ⓐ** fall victim to   **ⓑ** the odd one out   **ⓒ** cocksure   **ⓓ** turn a blind eye to

1. He is arrogant and nobody likes his _____ attitude.

2. Many countries have _____ the pandemic.

3. She was special and was _____ in her class.

4. The teachers _____ the fact that a few students cheated on the exam.

B. Multiple choice questions 選擇題（可利用此題型熟悉多益、英檢考試）

_____ 1. She was wrong because there was a(n) ------- in her reasoning.
(A) agitation   (B) flaw   (C) boredom   (D) strength

_____ 2. He loves chocolate. Giving him a box of chocolate will be a -------.
(A) last gasp   (B) close call   (C) safe bet   (D) side effect

_____ 3. Since he was emotional, he was unable to make a(n) -------
decision.
(A) awkward   (B) astonishing   (C) irrational   (D) rational

_____ 4. She did not cheat. The news about her cheating on the test was
-------.
(A) authentic   (B) false   (C) noticeable   (D) realistic

_____ 5. She believes in equality and fights against sexual -------.
(A) prejudices   (B) differences
(C) opportunities   (D) relationships

▶▶ 解答請見 p.412

4.8
自然與科學 Nature and Science

NOTE

解答篇

解答、解析與中譯

4.1 Part 1 - New Zealand

Step 1 掃讀 Scanning

■ 選擇正確的意思

B A B A A B A B B A

Step 2 略讀 Skimming

F F T F F

■ 答案解析

Q1. (F) 由首段第一句可知，紐西蘭的土地面積與英國差不多。

Q2. (F) 由首段第一句可知，紐西蘭位於南半球的南太平洋。

Q3. (T) 由首段第一句可知，紐西蘭是有山脈的島國。

Q4. (F) 由第二段第一句可知，在紐西蘭的森林健行並不危險。

Q5. (F) 由第三段第一句可知，kiwi 有許多意思。

Step 3 細讀 Close reading

B C

■ 答案解析

Q1. 依據短文內容，下列哪個敘述為真？

    (A) 奇異果是紐西蘭的土產水果。

    (B) 奇異果可以在中國北部生長。

    (C) 奇異果最早是由一位老師在紐西蘭種植的。

    (D) 1904 年以前沒有奇異果這種水果。

> **解析** 由第一句可知奇異果是中國北部的土產水果，故答案是 (B)。

Q2. 依據短文內容，奇異鳥的顏色為何？

    (A) 黑色   (B) 黃色   (C) 咖啡色   (D) 白色

> **解析** 在指定閱讀的這一小部分內容中，雖然作者沒有直接說出奇異鳥的顏色，但由於作者說奇異果外型貌似奇異鳥，故可以推論奇異鳥應該跟奇異果一樣是咖啡色的，所以正確答案是 (C)。

Step 4 高理解速讀 Reading with greater comprehension and speed

D A D B D

■ 答案解析

Q1. 以下關於紐西蘭的敘述，何者為非？

(A) 全球最早看到日出的國家

(B) 跟英國的面積相仿

(C) 有許多不會飛的鳥

(D) 每年從中國北部進口高品質的奇異果

> 解析 第三段說紐西蘭出口的奇異果很有名，但是並沒有說紐西蘭每年都會從中國進口奇異果，所以正確答案是 (D)。

Q2. 下列哪個不是 kiwi 的意思？

(A) 紐西蘭的大型雞蛋　　(B) 奇異果

(C) 奇異鳥　　　　　　(D) 紐西蘭人

> 解析 第三段說明 kiwi 的三種意思，kiwi 沒有大型雞蛋的意思，所以正確答案是 (A)。

Q3. 在紐西蘭，同一日內可以體驗到何種天氣？

(A) 夏天　　(B) 冬天　　(C) 春天　　(D) 上述所有天氣

> 解析 由第一段 "...one can experience spring, summer, fall and winter within one single day." 可知，同一日內可以體驗到春夏秋冬四種不同的天氣，所以正確答案是 (D)。

Q4. 下列哪一項是奇異鳥的特徵？

(A) 夜間飛行

(B) 有咖啡色羽毛

(C) 對於在森林健行的人造成危險

(D) 任何時間都會出現

> 解析 由第二段 "The kiwi is about the size of a chicken and has soft brown feathers." 可知，只有 (B) 是奇異鳥的正確描述。

Q5. 在紐西蘭可以看見甚麼？

(A) 火山　　(B) 森林　　(C) 丘陵　　(D) 以上皆是

Step 8 模擬測驗

■ 解答

A. 1. exports 2. intra-day 3. nocturnal 4. resembles

B. 1. (D) 2. (A) 3. (C) 4. (D) 5. (B)

文章中譯

　　紐西蘭的土地面積大約是英國那麼大，它位於南太平洋，是一個多山的小島國。奧克蘭是紐西蘭的最大城市，它周圍有兩個港口，座落於五萬年前因火山活動而形成的七座山丘上。由於國際換日線就在該國東部右邊，所以它還是地球上每天早上第一個見到旭日東昇的地方。許多遊客可能對於這特別國度在一天內天氣劇烈變化的事實感到驚訝，且不誇張地說，一天之內就可以感受到春夏秋冬。早上可能是個艷陽高照的日子，但下午可能變冷了。

　　紐西蘭沒有危險的野生動物、蛇或昆蟲，除了一種罕見的有毒蜘蛛之外。這讓紐西蘭成為一個「一天中任何時候，都可以漫步森林」的安全地方。紐西蘭的森林獨到之處就是該國的國鳥 — 奇異鳥。奇異鳥這名字就來自這種鳥發出的聲音：「ki-wi」。牠們經常發出這有趣的聲音。牠們是夜行性動物，經常生活在遠離人群的森林中。奇異鳥大約有一隻雞那麼大，且有柔軟的棕色羽毛。牠們的食物主要是昆蟲和蠕蟲以及漿果和種子。奇異鳥是不尋常的鳥類，因為與紐西蘭的許多其他本土鳥類一樣都不會飛。在人類和陪伴他們的寵物探索紐西蘭之前，奇異鳥沒有躲避敵人的必要。因此，奇異鳥失去了飛行的能力，如今牠們的一雙翅膀幾乎是無用武之地。

　　有趣的是，kiwi（奇異）這個字還有其他含義。kiwi 這個字最早由紐西蘭在海外作戰的士兵所使用。在那之後，紐西蘭人開始稱自己為「奇異人」。也就是說，紐西蘭總理也被稱為「奇異總理」。kiwi 的另一個廣為人知的含義是「kiwifruit（奇異果）」，在許多其他國家簡稱為 kiwi。事實上奇異果原產於中國北方，於 1904 年被一位來訪的學校老師帶回紐西蘭。這種水果在紐西蘭生長良好。當它開始要出口至國外時，因外形酷似奇異鳥而被命名為奇異果。現在有幾個奇異果的品種，但最常見的奇異果，大約就是一個大雞蛋的大小，外皮是棕色的，中心部位柔軟、綠色且有甜味。

4.1 Part 2 - Cruise Vacations

Step 1 掃讀 Scanning

■ 選擇正確的意思

A A B B A　A B A B B

Step 2 略讀 Skimming

T F F T T

■ 答案解析

Q1. (T) 由首段第一句可知，郵輪旅遊受歡迎並令人放鬆。

Q2. (F) 由第二段第一句可知，郵輪提供適合各年齡的娛樂活動。

Q3. (F) 由第三段第一句可知，郵輪通常會造訪數個地點。

Q4. (T) 由第四段第一句可知，有些人擔心會暈船。

Q5. (T) 由第四段第一句可知，有些人不願意搭乘郵輪。

Step 3 細讀 Close reading

D A

■ 答案解析

Q1. 根據這段短文內容，下列何項敘述為真？

(A) 郵輪的乘客必會暈船。

(B) 大多數的乘客會暈船。

(C) 船身平衡器在風浪較大的海域中並不重要。

(D) 一百年前的郵輪無法很輕易地在大海中平穩地航行。

> 解析 由 "Since cruise ships these days are designed to effortlessly sail through the open sea..." 的內容可知，一百年前的郵輪不像今日的先進郵輪，能夠輕易地在大海中平穩地航行，所以正確答案是 (D)。

Q2. 根據這段短文內容，在郵輪上嚴重暈船有多常見？

(A) 不常見　　(B) 常見　　(C) 相當常見　　(D) 極度常見

> 解析 由 "Thanks to ship stabilizers that help steady the ship, seasickness is in fact a rarity." 的內容可知，在郵輪上嚴重暈船並不常見，所以正確答案是 (A)。

解答、解析與中譯

B D D C A

■ 答案解析

Q1. 郵輪上面沒有下列何項設施？

(A) 游泳池　　(B) 棒球場　　(C) 籃球場　　(D) 迷你高爾夫球場

> 解析 由第二段 "Most ships are equipped with..." 可知，只有 a baseball field 不會是郵輪上的設施，故正確答案是 (B)。

Q2. 在郵輪上有什麼夜晚的娛樂活動？

(A) 夜店跳舞　　(B) 看戶外電影　　(C) 賭場賭博　　(D) 上述全部

> 解析 由第二段 "Nightly entertainment often includes..." 可知，(A)、(B)、(C) 皆是郵輪夜晚的娛樂活動，所以正確答案是 (D)。

Q3. 下列哪個是郵輪可能造訪的地點？

(A) 義大利　　(B) 佛羅倫斯　　(C) 伊斯坦堡　　(D) 上述全部

> 解析 由第三段 "...some sail to Alaska, Spain, Italy... visit such historic cities as Barcelona, Rome, Florence, Pompeii, and Istanbul." 可知，(A)、(B)、(C) 皆是郵輪可能造訪的地點，所以正確答案是 (D)。

Q4. 郵輪旅遊的行程通常是幾天？

(A) 超過 12 晚　　(B) 7 至 12 晚　　(C) 2 至 6 晚　　(D) 1 至 3 晚

> 解析 由第一段 "Cruise tours usually range from two to six nights." 可知，郵輪旅遊的行程通常是 2 至 6 晚，所以正確答案是 (C)。

Q5. 每年全世界約有多少人搭乘郵輪？

(A) 約 3 千萬人

(B) 約 4 千萬人

(C) 約 5 千萬人

(D) 約 6 千萬人

> 解析 由第一段 "According to the Cruise Lines International Association, around 30 million people worldwide take a cruise vacation each year." 可知，每年全世界約有 3 千萬人搭乘郵輪，所以正確答案是 (A)。

Step 8 模擬測驗

■ 解答

A. 1. unwind 2. resorts 3. fits 4. prone

B. 1. (B) 2. (D) 3. (C) 4. (A) 5. (D)

文章中譯

　　郵輪假期是放鬆身心的一種很受歡迎的方式。根據「國際郵輪公司協會」的統計，全世界每年約有 3,000 萬人去享受郵輪假期。郵輪旅行通常為二至六晚。在郵輪上，有數千名乘客一起乘坐一艘大船進行國際旅行。郵輪有各種規模和載客量，大型船隻可容納多達 5,000 人。郵輪提供 24 小時客房服務，就像一個漂浮的度假村，提供多種餐飲選擇，包括吃到飽的自助餐、自助沙拉吧和深夜食堂小吃。

　　郵輪為所有年層旅客提供各式各樣的娛樂活動。遊客可能被太多可以為他們假期增添趣味的娛樂選擇搞得眼花繚亂。大多數船隻都配備了游泳池、水療中心、溜冰場、籃球場、迷你高爾夫球場、攀岩牆等。熱衷於跑步的人可以選擇健身房內的跑步機或戶外的慢跑跑道。夜間娛樂活動通常包括喜劇表演、現場音樂表演和藝術品拍賣。乘客還可以唱卡拉 OK、在夜總會跳舞、在賭場賭博、看戶外電影，或者只是在鋼琴酒吧放鬆一下都可以。

　　對於打算在一趟旅程中停留多個景點的人來說，郵輪假期超划算的。有許多郵輪從佛羅里達州和新英格蘭出發，前往世界各地必玩的景點。雖然大多數郵輪會往加勒比海去，但也有一些是往阿拉斯加、西班牙、義大利、南美等地。例如，12 天假期的地中海郵輪將前往巴塞隆納、羅馬、佛羅倫斯、龐貝和伊斯坦堡等歷史名城。在南美洲的旅程中，您可以探索哥斯大黎加的熱帶雨林，並品嚐智利的葡萄酒。

　　然而，暈船的恐懼感，是不願踏上郵輪之旅的最常見原因之一。近來由於郵輪都設計成可於開闊海域中平穩地航行，事實上暈船已非必然。還好有幫助於穩定船舶的船身平衡器，事實上暈船的情況是罕見的。在波濤洶湧的水域中，船身平衡器可以平衡船舶並防止其搖晃。對於容易感覺到腳底下會搖晃的人來說，船上都會有藥物可以讓他們重新穩住腳步。或者，可以選擇住在船中間下層甲板中的客艙，那位置最不容易感受到搖晃。

4.1 Part 3 - Antarctica Tours

Step 1 掃讀 Scanning

■ 選擇正確的意思

A B B A B B A A A B

Step 2 略讀 Skimming

F F F T F

■ 答案解析

Q1. (F) 由首段第一句可知，南極面積約為澳洲的兩倍大。

Q2. (F) 由首段第一句可知，南極的氣候很極端。

Q3. (F) 由第二段第一句可知，即便是這樣的氣候，南極仍有很多動物。

Q4. (T) 由首段第一句可知，南極洲是全球海拔最高的洲。

Q5. (F) 由第三段第一句可知，南極的旅遊季是每年的 11 月到 3 月。

Step 3 細讀 Close reading

A D

■ 答案解析

Q1. 根據短文內容，以下何者是不正確的？

(A) 南極沒有黑夜

(B) 觀光客可以在二月份看到鯨魚

(C) 十一月到三月之間的氣溫比較溫暖

(D) 觀光客可以在一月初看到企鵝

> 解析 由 "...during the Antarctic summer, when there is endless sunlight." 的內容可知，南極的「夏季」沒有黑夜，並非是指整年都沒有黑夜，所以 (A) 是不正確的敘述，故正確答案是 (A)。而從 "February and early March are peak times for whale sightings." 及 "The best time for penguin spotting is late December or early January." 可知，觀光客可以在二月份看到鯨魚、一月初看到企鵝。從 "The Antarctic travel season lasts from November to March, when the icy ocean starts to thaw. Temperatures range from -10°C to 10°C." 可知，十一月到三月之間南極的氣溫比較溫暖（正負十度C上下）。所以 (B)、(C)、(D) 皆為正確的敘述。

Q2. 根據這段短文內容，為何南極的旅遊季從十一月份開始？
   (A) 因為南極在十一月之前比較溫暖
   (B) 因為鯨魚十一月才來南極
   (C) 因為企鵝十一月才來南極
   (D) 因為從十一月開始，船隻才能夠安全地航行

   解析 由 "The Antarctic travel season lasts from November to March, when the icy ocean starts to thaw." 可知，南極洲的旅遊季節從 11 月持續到 3 月，這是當冰冷的海洋開始融化之時，亦即這時候船隻才能夠安全地航行進入南極，所以正確答案是 (D)。

Step 4 高理解速讀 Reading with greater comprehension and speed

B D D C D

■ 答案解析

Q1. 在南極可以看到幾種企鵝？
   (A) 七
   (B) 八
   (C) 九
   (D) 上述皆非

   解析 由第二段 "Eight different species of penguins can be seen here." 可知，正確答案是 (B)。

Q2. 在南極可以看到下列哪一種動物？
   (A) 鯨魚
   (B) 海鳥
   (C) 海豹
   (D) 以上皆是

   解析 由第二段 "Many species thrive here, including a variety of penguins, seals, whales, and seabirds." 可知，在南極可以看到鯨魚、海鳥、海豹，所以正確答案是 (D)。

Q3. 在南極，下列何者是可能發生的？
   (A) 正十度 C 的氣溫
   (B) 持續的黑夜

(C) 持續的日照

(D) 上述全部

> 解析 由第三段 "Temperatures range from -10°C to 10°C." 可知，(A) 是正確的敘述；由第一段 "Antarctica is in darkness for six months of the year and in constant daylight throughout the austral summer." 可知，南極洲一年當中有六個月處於黑暗中，而整個地球南端在夏季時處於白晝恆常的狀態，所以 (B)、(C) 也是正確的敘述，故正確答案是 (D)。

Q4. 南極的旅遊季為 ＿＿＿＿ 。

　　(A) 五月到八月

　　(B) 二月到三月

　　(C) 十一月到三月

　　(D) 十二月到一月

> 解析 由第三段第一句 "The Antarctic travel season lasts from November to March..." 可知，南極的旅遊季為十一月到三月，所以正確答案是 (C)。

Q5. 南極是

　　(A) 一個洲

　　(B) 一個不毛之地

　　(C) 一個沒有固定居民的地方

　　(D) 上述全部

> 解析 由第一段 "Antarctica is the highest, coldest, driest, and windiest continent on Earth." 可知，(A) 是正確的敘述；由 "Antarctica is a large ice-covered desert with no trees or bushes." 可知，(B) 是正確的敘述；由 "It is the only continent on the planet with no permanent residents." 可知，(C) 是正確的敘述。所以正確答案是 (D)。

Step 8 模擬測驗

■ 解答

　A. 1. marine 2. feasted on 3. thrive 4. continent

　B. 1. (C) 2. (A) 3. (D) 4. (B) 5. (B)

　　南極洲的面積幾乎是澳洲的兩倍大，且是地球上海拔最高、最寒冷、最乾燥、風最強的大陸。有記錄以來的最低溫度是 1983 年的 -89.2°C。南極洲內部平均溫度約為 -57°C。南極洲大陸有 99% 冰雪覆蓋的土地。地球上約 70% 的淡水鎖在南極洲的冰蓋內。南極洲一年當中有六個月處於黑暗中，而整個南極的夏季時處於白晝恆常的狀態。南極洲是白雪皚皚的山脈和火山的所在地，也是一片冰天雪地的大沙漠，沒有樹木或灌木叢。它是地球上唯一沒有永久居民的大陸。南極洲的科學研究和商業旅遊受到 1991 年簽署的《南極環境議定書》之管制，確保所有人類活動受到審慎管理。

　　儘管環境看似無人居住，但這塊冰凍的大陸絕非毫無生機。許多物種在這裡繁衍生長，包括各種企鵝、海豹、鯨魚和海鳥。對於想將這個旅遊目的地從他們的人生解鎖清單中勾選出來的人來說，野生動物可能是南極洲之旅的主要原因之一。企鵝是南極洲最常見的、不會飛翔的鳥類。在這裡可以看到八種不同種的企鵝。除了企鵝之外，人們還會在牠們的自然環境中看見海豹和鯨魚等海洋哺乳類動物。南極有六種海豹。遊客可能看到海豹捕獵企鵝。南極之旅的另一個很棒的體驗就是賞鯨。在南極洲可以觀賞到八種以上的鯨魚。人們可能發現鯨魚到這裡來吃磷蝦及享用海豹大餐。南極洲也是個賞鳥天堂，可以近距離觀賞海鳥。

　　南極洲的旅遊季為 11 月到隔年 3 月，這是當結冰的海洋開始融化之時。此時的氣溫是 -10°C 到 10°C。觀賞企鵝的最佳時間是近 12 月底至 1 月初。賞鯨的熱門時間則是二月至三月初。每年約 50,000 名遊客在南極的夏季踏上南極洲，適逢「陽光不斷電」之時。大多數南極洲之旅的郵輪，從距離南極洲 620 英里的阿根廷南端起航。郵輪會經過高聳的冰山。若天氣狀況允許的話，遊客可以下船近距離觀賞野生動物並參與短途的足旅。這個全球第七大陸地提供絕無僅有的與世隔絕冒險之旅。遊客切勿將垃圾留下，才不會對這個生態系統造成影響。

4.2 Part 1 - The Giants of the Renaissance

Step 1 掃讀 Scanning

■ 選擇正確的意思

A B A B B A A B B A

Step 2 略讀 Skimming

F T T F F

■ 答案解析

Q1. (F) 由首段第一句可知,文藝復興是指「一段時期」,不是「一項運動」。

Q2. (T) 由首段第一句可知,文藝復興是指在歐洲的一段時期。

Q3. (T) 由第二段第一句可知,許多藝術家在文藝復興時期成名。

Q4. (F) 由第三段第一句可知,莎士比亞並不是文藝復興時期唯一知名的作家。

Q5. (F) 由第四段第一句可知,文藝復興時期的科學發現也相當重要。

Step 3 細讀 Close reading

C D

■ 答案解析

Q1. 根據短文內容,以下何者是正確的?

(A) 文藝復興時期主要是關於藝術的發展。

(B) 文藝復興時期主要是關於文學的發展。

(C) 文藝復興時期影響了許多不同的領域。

(D) 文藝復興時期始於希臘和羅馬。

> 解析 由最後一句可知,文藝復興時期影響了許多不同的領域,所以正確答案是 (C)。

Q2. 文藝復興時期的文化運動發生在_____。

(A) 義大利　　(B) 法國　　(C) 英國　　(D) 上述全部

> 解析 由這部份的內容可知,文藝復興時期的文化運動發生於義大利以及歐洲其他的地方,所以正確答案是 (D)。

C A D D B

■ 答案解析

Q1.《雅典學院》是誰的畫作？

(A) 達文西　　(B) 但丁　　(C) 拉斐爾　　(D) 米開朗基羅

> 解析 由第二段最後的 "Another famous Italian painter is Raphael. He is best known for *the School of Athens*." 可知，《雅典學院》是拉斐爾（Raphael）的畫作，所以正確答案是 (C)。

Q2. 誰提出太陽是太陽系中心的概念？

(A) 哥白尼　　(B) 克卜勒　　(C) 伽利略　　(D) 密爾頓

> 解析 由第四段 "Copernicus, ...arguing that the Sun, not the Earth, was the center of the solar system." 可知，哥白尼認為太陽是太陽系中心，所以正確答案是 (A)。

Q3.《失樂園》是誰的作品？

(A) 但丁　　(B) 伽利略　　(C) 莎士比亞　　(D) 密爾頓

> 解析 由第三段 "Another well-known English poet is Milton. He is noted for his epic poem *Paradise Lost*." 可知，《失樂園》的作者為密爾頓，所以正確答案是 (D)。

Q4.《大衛》是誰的雕塑作品？

(A) 達文西　　(B) 但丁　　(C) 拉斐爾　　(D) 米開朗基羅

> 解析 由第二段 "Michelangelo was a painter and sculptor who carved *David*, a sculpture depicting..." 可知，《大衛》是米開朗基羅的雕塑作品，所以正確答案是 (D)。

Q5. 誰發現三大行星運動定律？

(A) 哥白尼　　(B) 克卜勒　　(C) 伽利略　　(D) 密爾頓

> 解析 由第四段 "Kepler's discovery of the three principles of planetary motion" 可知，克卜勒發現太陽系的三大行星運動定律，所以正確答案是 (B)。

解答、解析與中譯

■ 解答

A. 1. in existence 2. characterized 3. nothing short of 4. to prominence
B. 1. (C) 2. (A) 3. (B) 4. (A) 5. (C)

文章中譯

　　文藝復興常被視為「中世紀」和「現代」之間的橋樑，它是指在歐洲十四至十七世紀的這段時期。它始於佛羅倫斯的一場文化運動，後來散播至歐洲其他地區。以核心價值來說，文藝復興是關於喚醒古希臘及古羅馬的思想和文化，特別是在藝術、文學和科學等領域。

　　許多藝術家在文藝復興時期聲名大噪，包括達文西、米開朗基羅和拉斐爾。達文西是一位義大利的畫家、建築師及科學家。他特別熱衷於以 3D（立體）效果重新呈現「人類的美」。他的作品《蒙娜麗莎》據說是有史以來最著名的油畫，每年有超過 1000 萬人前往巴黎的羅浮宮觀賞這部作品。米開朗基羅是一位畫家兼雕塑家，他的雕塑品《大衛》栩栩如生地描繪出人類的形態。他的作品《亞當的創造》也頗具名氣，這是一幅掛在梵蒂岡西斯汀教堂的巨大天花板壁畫。另一位著名的義大利畫家是拉斐爾。他最為人知的作品是《雅典學院》。

　　文藝復興時期的文學也以人文主義的主題為特徵，其中一些最著名的作家包括莎士比亞、米爾頓和但丁。英國詩人並莎士比亞可能是史上最著名的劇作家。他擁抱人性，以他的戲劇《哈姆雷特》和《羅密歐與朱麗葉》舉世聞名。另一位著名的英國詩人是米爾頓。他以其史詩作品《失樂園》而聞名。他這部詩作的長度高超過一萬行，講述著亞當和夏娃的創造，以及他們未能抵擋誘惑的故事。但丁是義大利的詩人兼哲學家。他寫了《神曲》這部作品，從中他呈現出基督教對人類永恆命運的觀點。

　　文藝復興時期的科學發現也相當非比尋常。在科學上有著非常大的進展，特別是在天文學和數學方面。例如，波蘭天文學家暨數學家哥白尼提出以太陽為中心的太陽系，他斷然地宣稱太陽，而非地球，是太陽系的中心。同樣具重要性的是，克卜勒發現了行星運動的三定律。他還闡明太陽系的空間組織之重要性。義大利天文學家暨物理學家伽利略強化了折射望遠鏡觀測夜空的能力。

4.2 Part 2 - The Legacy of Impressionism

Step 1 掃讀 Scanning

■ 選擇正確的意思

A A B A B A A A B B

Step 2 略讀 Skimming

T T T F F

■ 答案解析

Q1. (T) 由首段第一句可知，印象派是最早的現代藝術運動。

Q2. (T) 由第二段第一句可知，印象派畫家偏好明亮的色彩。

Q3. (T) 由第三段第一句可知，印象派畫家偏好在戶外作畫。

Q4. (F) 由第三段第一句可知，印象派畫家偏好在戶外作畫。

Q5. (F) 由第四段第一句可知，印象派畫家創作時較前期畫家迅速。

Step 3 細讀 Close reading

A A

■ 答案解析

Q1. 根據短文內容，印象派畫家對何項主題沒有興趣？

(A) 亞當和夏娃　　(B) 街頭的咖啡廳　　(C) 橋樑　　(D) 山脈

> **解析** 由 "the Impressionists were adept at rural scenes such as..." 可知，"Adam and Eve" 不屬於 "rural scenes" 的範圍，所以正確答案是 (A)。

Q2. 根據短文內容，下列何者是正確的？

(A) 印象派畫家是創新的。

(B) 印象派畫家是保守的。

(C) 沙龍畫展對於現代化的主題感興趣。

(D) 印象派畫家對於歷史的主題感興趣。

> **解析** 由 "the Impressionists were adept at... They also embraced modernity..." 的敘述可知，印象派畫家是 innovative（創新的），所以正確答案是 (A)。

CDCDA

■ 答案解析

Q1. 哪一種顏色是 19 世紀末期大部分畫家常使用的？

(A) 橘色　　(B) 綠色　　(C) 灰色　　(D) 黃色

解析 從第二段的 "Most of their (Impressionists') contemporaries, by contrast, tended to prime their canvases with a dark background and use such drab colors as black, gray, and dark brown." 可知，本題正確答案是 (C)。

Q2. 下列何項主題不受沙龍畫展青睞？

(A) 神話的主題　　(B) 歷史的主題
(C) 聖經的主題　　(D) 鄉村風景的主題

解析 由第三段 "the Salon favored such traditional subject matter as historical, biblical and mythological themes" 可知，鄉村風景的主題不受沙龍畫展所青睞，所以正確答案是 (D)。

Q3. 沙龍畫展是什麼？

(A) 第一個現代藝術運動　　(B) 印象派畫家贊助的畫展
(C) 政府贊助的畫展　　　　(D) 一間巴黎有名的理髮廳

解析 由第一段 "... by the Salon, the state-sponsored exhibition" 可知，沙龍畫展是由政府舉辦的畫展，所以正確答案是 (C)。

Q4. 印象派畫家擅長繪畫_____。

(A) 河岸　　(B) 花園　　(C) 鄉村　　(D) 以上皆是

解析 由第三段 "they usually opted to paint outdoors" 以及 "Impressionists were adept at rural scenes such as landscapes, gardens, and riverbanks" 可知，(A)、(B)、(C) 皆是印象派畫家所擅長繪畫的內容，所以正確答案是 (D)。

Q5. 沙龍畫展如何評價印象派畫家的作品？

(A) 負面地　　(B) 正面地　　(C) 中性地　　(D) 文中未提及

由第一段 "Most of their paintings came into conflict with mainstream artistic expectations and thus were rejected by the Salon" 可知，當時主流的沙龍畫展並不青睞印象派畫家的作品，所以正確答案是 (A)。

Step 8 模擬測驗

■ 解答

A. 1. preoccupied with 2. rural 3. leaned 4. a flavor of
B. 1. (B) 2. (A) 3. (D) 4. (B) 5. (C)

文章中譯

　　印象主義是第一個現代化的藝術運動，始於近十九世紀末的法國。主要人物包括克勞德・莫內（Claude Monet）和愛德加・竇加（Edgar Degas），以及其他志同道合的油畫家。他們大部分的畫作都與主流藝術家的期望相牴觸，因此也不被由國家贊助的「沙龍畫展」所接受。於是這些印象派畫家尋求獨立自主並發起自己的展覽會，而他們第一場自行發起的展覽於 1874 年在巴黎舉行。他們的畫作特點是，極度著重顏色與亮度的表現、非傳統性題材以及厚重的筆觸。

　　相較於其過去藝術活動中使用的顏色，印象派偏好的顏色更加鮮明。他們通常使用明亮的顏色，像是紅、綠、黃和橘色。而相比之下，其當代大部分藝術家傾向於在畫布上塗上深色背景，並使用黑色、灰色和深棕色等單調的顏色。由於印象派畫家注重色彩和光線的交互作用，他們通常選擇在戶外作畫。例如，莫內曾在一天中的不同時間一遍又一遍地畫同一個地方，就是為了在光線消失之前捕捉那轉瞬即逝的效果。

　　他們以戶外為導向的題材讓我們了解其生活的品味。沙龍派偏好歷史、聖經和神話的主題等傳統題材，而印象派畫家則擅長風景、花園和河岸等鄉村場景。他們也擁抱現代化的特性並描繪著城市景觀，像是巴黎繁忙的街道，及其周圍越來越工業化的情況。因此，印象派畫家傾向於使用可以隨身攜帶到戶外的較小畫布，而不是在工作室中根據草圖來完成繪畫作品，這是沙龍派所重視的一種普遍方式。

　　印象主義者的作品以粗獷及素描般的筆觸為特色，就因為在光線改變之前，他們還沒有足夠的時間來完成。不同於其當代大多數藝術品清晰描繪的人物，他們並不重視精密的細節，且刻意避免其畫布上的清晰度。批評家貶抑印象派作品缺乏細節。實際上，「印象派」一詞源於藝術評論家路易斯・勒羅伊（Louis Leroy）撰寫的諷刺評論，他稱莫內的一幅畫作是一種「印象」。令勒羅伊詫異的是，印象派藝術家對藝術不尋常的品味被認為在當時具有革命性的影響。如今他們的畫作在世界各地的博物館展出，並在拍賣會上的銷售額已達數百萬美元。毫不誇張地說，印象主義在一定程度上造就了現代藝術的演進。

4.2 Part 3 - A Cross-Cultural Perspective on Altruism

Step 1 掃讀 Scanning

■ 選擇正確的意思

B B A A B B A A A B

Step 2 略讀 Skimming

F T F T F

■ 答案解析

Q1. (F) 由首段第一句可知,利他行為並不以利己為出發點。

Q2. (T) 由首段第一句可知,利他行為是自願性的。

Q3. (F) 由第二段第一句可知,利他行為的發生有許多不同的解釋。

Q4. (T) 由第四段第一句可知,在東方文化中也能觀察到具有文化色彩的
利他行為。

Q5. (F) 由首段第一句可知,利他並不是只有物質的捐贈而已。

Step 3 細讀 Close reading

D A

■ 答案解析

Q1. 根據短文內容,以下何者是正確的?

(A) 利他是一張彩色圖片。

(B) 利他行為在不同文化裡都以相同方式呈現。

(C) 只有某些人才會有利他行為。

(D) 從文化的視角可以了解利他行為。

> **解析** 由第一句可知,文化的視角可以讓我們了解利他行為的全貌,所
> 以正確答案是 (D)。

Q2. 根據短文內容,利他行為如何影響我們的社會?

(A) 正面地　　(B) 中性地　　(C) 負面地　　(D) 無意識地

> **解析** 這段最後一句說利他行為對我們的社會有正面的影響,所以正確
> 答案是 (A)。

B D C D A

■ 答案解析

Q1. 以下何者不是利他行為？

(A) 捐贈健康的腎臟給陌生人　　(B) 去圖書館借書
(C) 加入義工活動　　　　　　　(D) 參與慈善事業

> 解析 由第一段「利他的定義」可知，去圖書館借書並不是利他的行為，所以正確答案是 (B)。

Q2. 何者是發生利他行為可能的解釋？

(A) 軍中命令　　(B) 政府強制令
(C) 學校規定　　(D) 能夠感知他人需求和痛苦的大腦

> 解析 由第二段 "Many explanations have been offered to explain altruistic acts. Psychologists argue that the answer emerges from a brain sensitive to other people's emotions." 可知，心理學家認為有利他行為的人能夠感受到別人的需求和痛楚，所以正確答案是 (D)。

Q3. 下列何項不是西方文化的利他動機？

(A) 平等　　(B) 多元　　(C) 謙遜　　(D) 共融

> 解析 由第三段 "equity, diversity, and inclusion are key drivers of their helping behavior" 可知，謙遜並不是西方文化裡的利他動機，所以正確答案是 (C)。

Q4. 一個人是否值得擁有平等的機會是取決於

(A) 種族背景。　　(B) 社經地位。　　(C) 性別傾向。　　(D) 以上皆非

> 解析 由第三段 "no one should be denied an equal opportunity to thrive due to their ethnicity, nationality, socioeconomic status, sexual orientation, and disability" 可知，(A)、(B)、(C) 皆不應該剝奪一個人的平等機會，所以正確答案是 (D)。

Q5. 下列何者是本文的結論？

(A) 人的憐憫與同理心在東方與西方文化中都是存在的。
(B) 在東方文化裡利他行為必然是宗教性的。
(C) 在東方文化裡人們不會捐贈健康的腎臟。

(D) 心理學家與社會科學家對於利他行為的看法是一致的。

> **解析** 由第四段最後一句 "Yet, despite these differences, altruism is arguably a positive force within our community and is surely within everyone's reach." 可知正確答案是 (A)。

Step 8 模擬測驗

■ 解答

A. 1. integral 2. Sustainable 3. ingrained 4. far-reaching

B. 1. (D) 2. (B) 3. (A) 4. (D) 5. (B)

文章中譯

利他主義，以最通俗的說法是，自願為他人的最大利益而行事，而不是為了自己的利益，包括在時間、金錢或其他資源方面的自我犧牲，且不期望獲得回報。很多人似乎與生俱來就有同情心，這不只是對於他們認識或有關係的人，還有對於陌生人也是。例如，有些人會捐一大筆錢給慈善機構或是「和平工作團」中海外執行任務的志工。也有人自願接受摘除自己一顆健康腎臟的大手術，並將其移植到一個病入膏肓且完全陌生的人身上。

有許多說法用來解釋利他的行為。心理學家聲稱，答案來自對於他人情緒反應具有敏感度的大腦。這個論點暗指著，我們對於別人的困苦都能夠產生同理心。另一方面，據社會科學家們的觀察，對於文化的理解有助於利他主義出現時，展現珍貴的見解，因為利他主義的信念與行為的動機可能來自不同文化的價值觀與規範。

在西方文化中，人們天生就有根深蒂固的利他行為傾向。特別是，公平性、多樣性和包容性是他們助人行為的關鍵驅動因素。基於普世道德準則，所有人都同樣是值得幫助的，任何人都不應因種族、國籍、社經地位、性取向和殘疾，而被剝奪平等的成功機會。由於西方人的利他行為動機來自社會群體價值觀和道德感，所以能夠包容多樣性，且這群體裡每個人都能感覺受歡迎和重視。這種群體的精神特質將打造出一種持續性的包容氛圍 — 人們會關心他人的福利。因此，當看到別人痛苦或需要幫助時，他們會以同情心做出回應，且不會讓自己置身事外。

在東方文化中也可以觀察到文化衍生的利他主義。道教與佛教 — 堪稱文化遺產中不可或缺的部分 — 皆強調慈悲、同理心與謙卑的重要性。道教與佛教的教義已實踐數百年之久，對於東方人的利他行為有著深遠的影響。引導他們善行的另一個世界觀是，世人皆平等且具有價值。因此，我們不僅要尊重人類，還要尊重所有生物。雖然以文化為導向的觀點有助於繪出一幅豐富的利他主義圖案，但喚起我們本性中更好的天使的方式，隨不同文化而異。然而，儘管存在這些差異，利他主義可以說是我們人類社群中一股積極的力量，而且當然，那是每個人都可以做得到的。

4.3 Part 1 - The Mental Health Impacts of COVID-19

Step 1 掃讀 Scanning

■ 選擇正確的意思

A A B A A B B A B B

Step 2 略讀 Skimming

F F F F T

■ 答案解析

Q1. (F) 由首段第一句可知，新冠病毒可能會引起某些未知的病痛。

Q2. (F) 由第三段第一句可知，新冠疫情尤其影響兒童與青少年的生活。

Q3. (F) 由第三段第一句可知，孩童與青少年是最受影響的族群。

Q4. (F) 由第四段第一句可知，許多方式可以幫助保持身心的健康。

Q5. (T) 由第二段第一句可知，在新冠疫情期間，許多人生活並不開心。

Step 3 細讀 Close reading

B A

■ 答案解析

Q1. 根據這段短文內容，以下何者是正確的？

(A) 新冠病毒的影響只有在身體的層面。

(B) 新冠病毒只傷害到一個器官。

(C) 人們不夠重視由新冠疫情所造成的心理健康問題。

(D) 新冠疫情所造成的心理健康影響是暫時性的。

> 解析 由 "For the most part, discussions surrounding COVID-19 … the toll of COVID-19 is not entirely physical." 可知，人們不常討論（不太重視）新冠疫情所造成的心理健康問題，所以正確答案是 (C)。

Q2. 根據這段短文內容，以下何者是不正確的？

(A) 疫情已造成社交上的衝擊。

(B) 疫情已造成經濟上的衝擊。

(C) 許多人因為這場疫情而失去了工作。

(D) 疫情僅對於失去工作的人造成壓力

由 "the pandemic has been stressful and continues to harm the mental health and well-being of people around the world." 當中的 "people around the world" 可知，新冠疫情不只是對失去工作的人造成了壓力，所以正確答案是 (D)。

Step 4 高理解速讀 Reading with greater comprehension and speed

D D D C C

■ 答案解析

Q1. 新冠病毒可能會影響_____。

(A) 心臟

(B) 上呼吸道系統

(C) 下呼吸道系統

(D) 以上皆是

解析 由第一段 "...discussions surrounding COVID-19 have focused on its impact on the respiratory system and other major organs across the body." 可知，整個身體的主要器官都可能受到新冠病毒影響，故正確答案是 (D)。

Q2. 根據本文，新冠疫情可能會造成

(A) 沮喪

(B) 焦慮

(C) 壓力

(D) 以上皆是

解析 由第二段 "Most people feel frustrated or stressed at this time of uncertainty." 以及 "a significant increase in prevalence of anxiety and depression" 可知，新冠疫情可能會使人沮喪焦慮並帶來壓力，所以正確答案是 (D)。

Q3. 阻斷病毒傳播鏈的措施包含

(A) 封城

(B) 檢疫隔離

(C) 自我隔離

(D) 上述全部

解析 由第二段 "The measures to break the chain of transmission, such as lockdowns and quarantines..." 以及 " People can also experience loneliness and suffer from..." 可知，阻斷病毒傳播鏈的措施包含 (A)、(B)、(C) 三項，所以正確答案是 (D)。

Q4. 什麼原因使孩童和青少年的心理狀態受到了負面的影響？
(A) 回去學校實體上課
(B) 與同儕互動
(C) 停止課外活動
(D) 上述全部

解析 由第三段 "...the mental state of children and adolescents has been adversely affected as a result of school closures, suspension from extracurricular activities, and a lack of interaction with their peers." 可知，停止課外活動負面地影響了孩童和青少年的心理狀態，所以正確答案是 (C)。

Q5. 如果夜晚難以入眠，下列何項建議可能會有幫助？
(A) 睡覺前滑手機
(B) 三餐定時定量
(C) 冥想
(D) 上述全部

解析 由第四段 "Taking deep breaths or meditating can be helpful as well." 可知，如果夜晚難以入眠，深呼吸或冥想也會有幫助，所以正確答案是 (C)。

Step 8 模擬測驗

■ 解答
A. 1. unprecedented 2. exacerbated 3. evoked 4. in one piece
B. 1. (A) 2. (D) 3. (B) 4. (A) 5. (C)

文章中譯

　　COVID-19 可導致一系列已知和未知的疾病。以最常見的狀況來說，圍繞於 COVID-19 的討論焦點主要是對於呼吸系統以及整個身體內其他主要器官的影響。然而，COVID-19 敲響的喪鐘，不完全是物理層面的。COVID-19 的大流行，以前所未有的形式帶來社會與經濟層面的後果。有無數的人們失去了工作且經濟呈現蕭條狀態。因此，這場全球性的瘟疫持續帶給人們壓力，且對於世界各地人們造成心理健康和幸福的傷害。

大多數人在這個不確定的年代都會感到沮喪或壓力。根據世界衛生組織所述，COVID-19 的疫情導致全球人民的焦慮及憂鬱症罹患率明顯增加。許多人一直擔心自己以及可能接觸過病毒的摯愛家人的健康。再者，阻斷病毒傳播鏈的措施，例如封城和隔離，已經引起了揮之不去的憂心。人們也會感受到孤獨，以及社交上的孤立所導致的憂鬱症。對於本來就有心理健康問題的人，其症狀可能因延後或疏漏就醫而變得更嚴重。

正當我們所有人都承受著 COVID-19 的衝擊，兒童和青少年對於這場全球疫情所帶來的騷亂顯得更加脆弱。由於學校停課，有些人的學習落後了。在這波疫情的不同階段中，許多人必須時而在線上上課，時而在實體教室上課。據「聯合國國際兒童緊急基金」所述，由於學校停課、課外活動暫停以及缺少與同儕的互動，兒童和青少年的精神狀態都受到不利的影響。

為因應疫情帶來的壓力，人們可以嘗試不同的方法來促進心理健康。首先，無法與家人和朋友團聚將增加內心的孤立感。在虛擬空間中與他們保持聯繫有助於克服孤獨感。雖然了解最新的消息很重要，但過度接觸媒體對疫情的報導可能令人不安，並可能導致情緒上的壓力。對於夜晚難以入睡的人來說，保持規律的睡眠時程，且睡前一小時避免使用電子設備，也有助於緩解壓力並獲得更佳的睡眠。深呼吸或沉思也會有幫助。藉由這些建議，或許我們可以從艱困時期中全身而退。

4.3 Part 2 - Controversies over COVID-19 Vaccine Mandates

Step 1 掃讀 Scanning

■ 選擇正確的意思

B A B A A B B A B A

Step 2 略讀 Skimming

T T F T T

■ 答案解析

Q1. (T) 由首段第一句可知，人類從 1796 年就開始研究疫苗了。

Q2. (T) 由首段第一句可知，天花病毒已絕跡。

Q3. (F) 由第二段第一句可知，新冠病毒所使用的疫苗是 2020 年開始研發的新疫苗。

Q4. (T) 由第四段第一句可知，未施打新冠疫苗的人受到網路霸凌。

Q5. (T) 由第四段第一句可知，施打任何疫苗都是一種基本人權，需要徵求個人的同意。

Step 3 細讀 Close reading

B A

■ 答案解析

Q1. 根據這段短文內容，以下何者是正確的？

(A) 新冠疫苗的風險是眾所皆知的。

(B) 美國食品藥物管理局（FDA）已授權新冠疫苗的使用。

(C) 加速完成的疫苗是最好的疫苗。

(D) 新冠疫苗沒有風險。

> 解析 由第三句可知，美國食品藥物管理局已給予新冠疫苗緊急許可證，並聲稱新冠疫苗利大於弊，所以正確答案是 (B)。

Q2. 根據這段短文內容，為何新冠疫苗獲得緊急許可證？

(A) 沒有足夠的時間開發這些疫苗。

(B) 緊急許可的疫苗與正式許可的疫苗是相同的。

(C) 這些疫苗已經完美地研發出來了。

(D) 這些疫苗已經研發很久了。

Step 4 高理解速讀 Reading with greater comprehension and speed

C B A A B

■ **答案解析**

Q1. 下列何者不是打疫苗的常見副作用？

    (A) 腫脹　　　(B) 疲倦　　　(C) 死亡　　　(D) 發燒

> 解析 由第一段最後一句可知，施打疫苗後死亡是罕見的副作用，所以正確答案是 (C)。

Q2. 哪一項關於疫苗的描述是不正確的？

    (A) 疫苗每年拯救了許多生命。

    (B) 疫苗對每個人來說都是絕對安全的。

    (C) 疫苗要經過很費時的臨床試驗。

    (D) 疫苗可以預防住院。

> 解析 由第一段 "vaccines are not perfectly safe for everyone..." 可知，疫苗對每個人並非是相同的，因為每個人的免疫反應不同，對某些人來說疫苗並不是絕對安全的，所以正確答案是 (B)。

Q3. 有什麼是研究專家們的發現？

    (A) 已施打疫苗者仍可傳播病毒。

    (B) 已施打疫苗者不太可能被感染

    (C) 已施打疫苗者不太可能因染疫而住院。

    (D) 已施打疫苗者不太可能死於新冠病毒。

> 解析 由第四段 "Their studies found no significant differences in the likelihood of being infected" 可知，在染疫之後，已經施打疫苗的人與未施打疫苗的人同樣可以傳播病毒，所以正確答案是 (A)。

Q4. 關於強制施打疫苗，以下何者正確？

    (A) 有些人不同意疫苗強制令。

    (B) 美國所有的大學都實施疫苗強制令。

    (C) 英國的大學實施疫苗強制令。

(D) 加拿大的大學實施疫苗強制令。

> 解析 由第三段 "some people are set against the idea of being mandatorily vaccinated..." 可知，有些人並不同意強制施打疫苗，所以正確答案是 (A)。

Q5. 愛德華加納 _____ 。
(A) 是一位美國內科醫生
(B) 做了重要的研究
(C) 幫助人類根除新冠病毒
(D) 死於天花病毒

> 解析 由第一段第一句可知，愛德華加納是一位英國的內科醫生，他做了很重要的疫苗研究，所以正確答案是 (B)。

Step 8 模擬測驗

■ 解答
A. 1. in the wake of 2. turned a blind eye to 3. pharmaceutical 4. at odds with
B. 1. (B) 2. (A) 3. (C) 4. (A) 5. (D)

文章中譯

　　世界上第一支疫苗是在 1796 年由英國的醫師愛德華‧詹納（Edward Jenner）所開發，他這項創舉促成了天花疫苗的開發，並幫助天花從這世上絕跡。如今，其他各種疫苗不斷被開發，且每年拯救了無數生命。在每一款疫苗獲准量產之前，都要經過嚴格且耗時的臨床試驗。儘管做出了這些努力，疫苗並不是絕對安全的，因為人們對疫苗會有不同的反應。常見的副作用包括，例如，腫脹、肌肉疼痛、疲倦和發燒。在一些極少數案例中，可能會有嚴重的不良反應，甚至導致死亡。

　　2020 年，隨著 SARS-CoV-2（又名 COVID-19）爆發，人們再次將希望寄託在疫苗上。根據世界衛生組織的數據，截至 2022 年底，COVID-19 已在全球造成超過 650 萬人死亡，超過 6.5 億人受到感染。為努力降低死亡人數，製藥公司在不到一年的時間內推出 COVID-19 疫苗。當 COVID-19 疫苗從加速開發到部署完成，迄今已成為開發速度最快的疫苗。這些疫苗已獲得美國食藥署（FDA）的緊急使用授權（EUA），且 FDA 聲稱，疫苗利大於弊。

在全球對抗這個共同敵人的時候，學界對於推出 COVID-19 疫苗來因應疫情蔓延是如何看待呢？為防止人們住院和死亡，美國大多數大學都要求教職員工和學生完整接種疫苗。另一方面，有些人基於醫療、宗教或政治等因素對於強制接種疫苗抱持反對態度。因此，關於是否應該取消疫苗強制令一直存在著激烈的爭論。事實上，在英國和加拿大等國家的大學中，新冠疫苗的接種並不是強制性的。

　　儘管全球多所大學都認為自願同意接種疫苗，如同所有醫療中的程序一樣，屬於一種基本人權，但未接種疫苗者因未施打疫苗而受到霸凌的情況並非少見。例如，網路上煽動仇恨者或網路霸凌者經常責罵他們，且認為未接種疫苗者，該為病毒的蔓延以及導致他人的死亡負責。然而，他們的指控並未得到科學證據的支持。科羅拉多大學、加州大學舊金山分校和牛津大學的研究人員，對於已接種疫苗者和未接種疫苗者如何免於 COVID-19 變種病毒侵害做過研究調查。他們的研究並未發現這兩者的染疫機率有明顯的差異，這暗示著，無論接種疫苗與否都可能染疫，且一旦感染都能夠傳播病毒。儘管有這些發現，有些人卻對於與其根深蒂固之信念相牴觸的資訊視而不見。

4.3 Part 3 - A Close-up of Human Immunity

Step 1 掃讀 Scanning

■ 選擇正確的意思
B A B B A A B B A B

Step 2 略讀 Skimming

T T T F F

■ 答案解析
Q1. (T) 由首段第一句可知，在我們生活周遭有許多細菌病毒等病原體。
Q2. (T) 由第二段第一句可知，先天免疫系統對於來犯的病毒會立即啟動防護機制。
Q3. (T) 由第四段第一句可知，後天免疫系統能夠記住同一種病毒。
Q4. (F) 由第三段第一句可知，後天免疫系統可以產生抗體。
Q5. (F) 由第五段第一句可知，人類的免疫系統需要特定的養分以維持其正常運作。

Step 3 細讀 Close reading

D B

■ 答案解析
Q1. 根據這段短文內容，下列何項敘述是正確的？
    (A) 後天免疫系統能夠記憶來犯的病毒。
    (B) 先天免疫系統無法記憶來犯的病毒。
    (C) 後天免疫系統無法記憶新冠病毒的變種。
    (D) 只是輕微感染的新冠病患也許無法保有免疫記憶。

    解析 由第一句 "its capacity for memory, which can be protective as our body encounters the same intruder a second time" 可知，後天免疫系統可以記憶來犯的病毒，所以正確答案是(A)。

Q2. 根據這段短文內容，先天免疫系統的天然殺手細胞能夠 ——。
    (A) 產生抗體
    (B) 記憶相同的病毒
    (C) 收集入侵病毒的證據
    (D) 造成嚴重感染

Step 4 高理解速讀 Reading with greater comprehension and speed

C B A D B

■ 答案解析

Q1. 下列何者可由本文推論出？
(A) 先天免疫系統沒有任何免疫記憶。
(B) 後天免疫系統遺傳自父母。
(C) 到處都有細菌和病毒。
(D) 後天免疫系統對於來犯的病毒會有立即的反應

解析 第四段第一句 "New evidence suggests that... with their capacity for memory-like responses..." 可知，(A) 是錯誤的；由第三段 "This adaptive immunity is built up as we are exposed to diseases or are vaccinated." 可知，當我們生了病或接種疫苗時，這種後天免疫就會被建立起來，因此 (B) 是錯誤的；第三段提到 "However, the adaptive immune system is slower in response and can take a few days or even weeks..."，所以 (D) 也是錯誤的；故正確答案是 (C) Bacteria and viruses are all over the place.。

Q2. 先天免疫系統能夠＿＿＿＿。
(A) 區分不同類型的病毒
(B) 立即反應以阻止感染
(C) 產生抗體對抗入侵者
(D) 由接種疫苗來啟動

解析 由第二段 "Present from birth, innate immunity... reacting almost instantly to prevent pathogens from making their ways to our body." 可知，當感染剛發生時，先天免疫系統就會立即啟動，預防進一步的感染發生，所以正確答案是 (B)。

Q3. 後天免疫系統能夠＿＿＿＿。
(A) 讓人終其一生藉由受到病毒感染或施打疫苗而產生
(B) 作為人體免疫的第一道防線

(C) 立即反應以防止感染

(D) 對於皮膚上的割傷立即反應

> 解析 由第三段 "This adaptive immunity is built up as we are exposed to diseases or are vaccinated." 可知，後天免疫系統終生都可以產生，產生的方式為自然感染或是施打疫苗，所以正確答案是 (A)。

Q4. 下列何者可以增強人體免疫力？

(A) 鋅　　(B) 維他命 C　　(C) 維他命 D　　(D) 上述全部

> 解析 由第五段 "we need to give our immune cells the kind of nutrients they need, the most important of which are zinc, vitamin C, and vitamin D" 可知，鋅、維他命 C、和維他命 D 都是免疫細胞所需養分，所以正確答案是 (D)。

Q5. 以下關於天然殺手細胞，何者為真？

(A) 天然殺手細胞無法受到先天免疫系統的差遣。

(B) 天然殺手細胞具有先天和後天免疫系統的特徵。

(C) 天然殺手細胞能夠殺死所有入侵的細菌和病毒。

(D) 天然殺手細胞不是遺傳自父母的基因。

> 解析 由第四段 "New evidence suggests that natural killer cells of the innate immune system are capable of memory-like responses, something previously thought to be..." 可知，隸屬於先天免疫系統的天然殺手細胞具有後天免疫系統的免疫記憶能力，所以正確答案是 (B)。

Step 8 模擬測驗

■ 解答

A. 1. clinical　2. foothold　3. kicked in　4. breach

B. 1. (C)　2. (A)　3. (D)　4. (B)　5. (C)

文章中譯

　　我們的身體一直受到我們所呼吸的空氣和吃進去食物中的病原體（例如細菌、病毒和其他致病生物）的攻擊。對於阻止這些病原體侵入體內，人體的免疫力相當重要，因為侵入的病原體在病程的確認上扮演關鍵角色。具體來說，人體免疫力有兩條基本防線：先天免疫和後天免疫。

　　從出生開始，先天免疫力就作為抵禦任何入侵者的第一道防線，且幾乎是立即作出反應，以防止病原體進入我們的身體。例如，皮膚上的一道傷口或鼻子、喉嚨或腸道的粘膜表面破裂導致發紅和腫脹時，許多免疫細胞就會立即被徵召到感染的部位。在大多數情況下，單憑先天免疫力就能夠將感染排除掉。但要是讓入侵者溜走了，先天免疫系統就會呼叫後天免疫系統以尋求協助。這就是後天免疫力發揮作用的時候。

　　後天免疫系統是第二道防線，能夠區分不同類型的病原體，並產生數百萬抗體來抵禦敵人。然而，後天免疫系統的反應速度較慢，可能需要幾天甚至幾週才能啟動。當我們生了病或接種疫苗時，後天免疫力才會被建立起來。因此也被稱為「獲得性免疫」。

　　後天免疫的一個特點就是它的記憶能力，當我們的身體第二次遇到同一個入侵者時，它可以產生保護作用。不過，這種「免疫記憶」的產生並不是絕對的。例如，針對 COVID-19 患者的研究指出，只有重症感染的患者能夠保有免疫記憶力。傳統上科學家們認為，先天免疫系統的記憶力是無法實現的，亦即，若再次受到感染，無法記憶相同的病原體。有新的證據指出，先天免疫系統中的天然殺手細胞具有類似記憶的反應能力 — 過去被認為只有在後天免疫系統中才可能存在。

　　為確保我們的先天和後天免疫系統產生有效用和效率的作用，我們還得為我們的免疫細胞提供其所需的營養，其中最重要的是鋅、維生素 C，以及維生素 D。其他日常營養補充品，如蜂膠和紫錐花，也可以增強我們的免疫力。然而，增強人體免疫力絕不只是服用增強免疫力的補品。增強免疫力的最佳方法是遵循健康的生活型態，要有均衡的飲食、規律的運動和充足的睡眠。

4.4 Part 1 - Elon Musk

Step 1 掃讀 Scanning

■ 選擇正確的意思

A B B A B B B B A A

Step 2 略讀 Skimming

F T F T T

■ 答案解析

Q1. (F) 由首段第一句可知，馬斯克出生於富裕家庭。

Q2. (T) 由第二段第一句可知，馬斯克因為特斯拉而聲名大噪。

Q3. (F) 由第三段第一句可知，馬斯克對於太空探索很有興趣。

Q4. (T) 由第四段第一句可知，馬斯克在社群媒體的聲量很大。

Q5. (T) 由第四段第一句可知，非常多人在社群媒體上關注馬斯克。

Step 3 細讀 Close reading

A C

■ 答案解析

Q1. 依據這段短文內容，以下何者是正確的？

(A) 馬斯克擁有兩個學士學位。

(B) 馬斯克取得史丹佛大學的博士學位。

(C) 馬斯克因害怕失敗而無法拓展他的事業。

(D) 馬斯克在高中之前住在美國。

> 解析 由第一句可知，馬斯克從美國賓州大學取得經濟學和物理學兩個學士學位（he earned a bachelor's degree in physics and another in economics），所以正確答案是 (A)。

Q2. 根據這段短文內容，我們知道關於馬斯克的什麼？

(A) 他在賓州大學攻讀博士學位。

(B) 他完成了博士學位。

(C) 他修過經濟學的課程。

(D) 他是個連續創業家，每一家公司都非常成功。

> 解析 由第一句可知，馬斯克有一個經濟學的學士學位，可知他修過經濟學的課程，所以正確答案是 (C)。

D A B C C

■ 答案解析

Q1. 「為九位在世小孩的父親」是什麼意思？

　　(A) 馬斯克目前有九個小孩。

　　(B) 馬斯克已經領養了九個小孩。

　　(C) 馬斯克有幾個小孩他不認得。

　　(D) 馬斯克至少有一個小孩已去世。

> 解析 living 是「活著的」、「仍在世的」意思，所以可推知馬斯克至少有一個小孩已早么，故正確答案是 (D)。

Q2. 為何馬斯克在史丹佛大學時輟學？

　　(A) 他想要創業。

　　(B) 他不夠用功。

　　(C) 他考試的成績不好。

　　(D) 他沒有足夠的錢付學費。

> 解析 從第一段中間部分提到的 "Musk dropped out of his doctoral program and launched a business career." 可知，馬斯克因為想要創業，所以中斷了在史丹佛大學的學位，故正確答案是 (A)。

Q3. 是什麼讓馬斯克成為世界上最富有的人之一？

　　(A) 他在推特上的社群流量

　　(B) 他的特斯拉股票

　　(C) 他的太空探索技術公司與美國太空總署的商業合作

　　(D) 他的常春藤名校學士文憑

> 解析 從第二段最後提到的 "Tesla's stock has surged... one of the world's richest people " 可知，馬斯克因為特斯拉股票的飆升，而成為世界上最富有的人之一，所以正確答案是 (B)。

Q4. 從文章中我們可以推論出什麼？

　　(A) 馬斯克是一名民主黨員。

　　(B) 馬斯克是一名共和黨員。

　　(C) 馬斯克對政治有興趣。

　　(D) 馬斯克想要競選總統。

解析 從第四段的 "He is vocal about politics, education, and space exploration, ..." 可知，馬斯克會在推特上發表自己對政治議題的看法，因此可以推論他對政治是有興趣的，所以正確答案是 (C)。

Q5. 下列何者可由本文推論出？
(A) 馬斯克是詩詞方面的專家。
(B) 馬斯克對工程領域的了解甚少。
(C) 馬斯克對世界做出了貢獻。
(D) 馬斯克只知經濟學的皮毛而已。

解析 從第三段的 "...his contributions have been recognized. In 2022, Musk was elected to the National Academy of Engineering..." 可知，馬斯克因為在工程領域方面對世界做出了貢獻，故獲選為美國國家工程院院士，所以正確答案是 (C)。

Step 8 模擬測驗

■ 解答
A. 1. called for 2. blasted 3. vocal 4. booming
B. 1. (D) 2. (A) 3. (B) 4. (C) 5. (D)

文章中譯

　　在南非長大的埃隆・馬斯克，是含著金湯匙出生的。馬斯克高中畢業後移居美國，並進入賓夕法尼亞大學就讀，且獲得物理學和經濟學的學士學位。在那不久之後，他進入史丹佛大學攻讀物理系的博士學位。然而，馬斯克後來在唸博士時輟學了，並且開啟了經商的生涯。他成為一名創辦數家企業的連續創業者，其中有幾家非常成功。儘管他有所成就了，但他的生活充滿了挑戰，且隨時都有失敗的可能性。除了是九個在世孩子的父親之外，他一直是身兼數職的，其中最著名的可能是企業家、火箭科學家和意見領袖（KOL）。

　　馬斯克最為人道的，或許就是特斯拉了，那是他在 2003 年創辦的一家電動汽車（EV）公司。由於人們越來越擔憂碳廢氣的排放，使得電動車業蓬勃發展。即使面臨日益激烈的市場競爭，他也不會活在失敗或困難的恐懼中。特斯拉現在是一家擁有約 10 萬名員工的公司，也是全球第一家獲利的電動車製造商。另外相關的是，特斯拉的股票自 2010 年上市以來，已飆漲超過 20,000%，使得馬斯克成為全球最富有的人之一。

馬斯克身為一名訓練有素的物理學家，長期以來一直是火星殖民的支持者。他在火箭科學上投入不少資金，並創立一家領導商業太空探索領域的火箭公司 SpaceX。在成功將兩名 NASA 太空人送進太空中後，SpaceX 正積極推動可再利用火箭技術的開發計畫。當馬斯克以自己的用詞來定義太空旅行時，他的貢獻獲得了認可。2022 年馬斯克憑藉其成就當選了美國國家工程院的院士。

　　在社交媒體中有其一席之地的馬斯克，是一位高調並具影響力的人物，他的「推特（Twitter）」擁有超過 1.2 億追蹤者。他在政治、教育和太空探索…等領域中，有相當的聲量。每次他發推文時，他無數的推特追蹤者都會給予「按讚」並分享他的推文。他針對特斯拉股票所發的推文可輕易引發股票的暴漲或拋售。他對於比特幣和狗狗幣等加密貨幣也有極大的影響。在社交媒體上相當活躍的馬斯克，曾抨擊推特的言論審查制度，並呼籲其言論政策應進行重大改革。令人大感意外的是，馬斯克於 2022 年收購了推特。

4.4 Part 2 - Maria Montessori

Step 1 掃讀 Scanning

■ 選擇正確的意思
 A B B A B A B B A B

Step 2 略讀 Skimming

 T T T F T

■ 答案解析
 Q1. (T) 由首段第一句可知，蒙特梭利博士出版過許多書籍。
 Q2. (T) 由首段第一句可知，蒙特梭利博士也是一位醫生。
 Q3. (T) 由第四段第一句可知，今日仍有許多老師使用蒙特梭利教學法。
 Q4. (F) 由第二段第一句可知，蒙特梭利教學法給予孩童一定程度的選擇
      自由。
 Q5. (T) 由第三段第一句可知，蒙特梭利教學法採取混齡教學。

Step 3 細讀 Close reading

 C B

■ 答案解析
 Q1. 根據這段短文內容，下列何項敘述是正確的？
    (A) 蒙特梭利教室採取標準化的教學方式。
    (B) 孩童的學習動機無法被提升。
    (C) 在傳統的教室裡，孩童們被要求做相同的事。
    (D) 孩童們在傳統教室裡的學習成效最好。

    > 解析 由 "... traditional classrooms where children are given less
    > freedom and are expected to go with the majority." 可知，傳統的教室
    > 採取標準化的統一教學方式，孩童們被要求做相同的事，所以正確答
    > 案是 (C)。

 Q2. 根據這段短文內容，可知蒙特梭利教室裡的學童_____。
    (A) 比較不自由
    (B) 擁有更多自由
    (C) 應該要和大部分同學一起行事
    (D) 被要求在標準化的考試中取得高分

解答、解析與中譯

由 "... children in a Montessori classroom are given agency to self-select work, a radical departure from conventional classrooms where children are given less freedom..." 可知，蒙特梭利教學法給予孩童更多的學習和探索新知的自由，所以正確答案是 (B)。

Step 4 高理解速讀 Reading with greater comprehension and speed

D C B A A

■ 答案解析

Q1. 蒙特梭利博士不是＿＿＿＿。

(A) 一位作者　　　(B) 一位醫生

(C) 一位老師　　　(D) 一位企業家

> 解析 由第一段 "...become a physician, Maria Montessori (1870-1952) was also an educationist and author of many seminal books on childhood education." 中可知，蒙特梭利博士不是一位企業家，所以正確答案是 (D)。

Q2. 蒙特梭利博士沒有＿＿＿＿。

(A) 治療病人

(B) 觀察孩童如何學習

(C) 出版哲學理論的書籍

(D) 提供師資培訓課程

> 解析 承第一題的解析內容即可判斷，(A)、(B)、(D) 都是蒙特梭利博士會做的事；雖然她也是一位作者，但本文未提到蒙特梭利博士出版過關於哲學理論的書籍，所以正確答案是 (C)。

Q3. 當孩子們擁有選擇的自由時，以下何事最有可能發生？

(A) 孩童在標準化的考試中表現良好。

(B) 孩童自己探索問題的答案。

(C) 孩童失去學習動機。

(D) 孩童無法專注於課堂活動。

Q4. 在混齡的教室裡可能會發生什麼事？
(A) 孩童能夠按照自己的節奏進步。
(B) 較年長的孩童向年幼的孩童學習。
(C) 較年幼的孩童作為課堂上的模範。
(D) 較年幼的孩童藉由示範已學會的內容來強化自己的素養。

Q5. 大部分的蒙特梭利學校_____。
(A) 是私立的
(B) 期待孩童跟大部分的同儕相同
(C) 期待孩童只向他們的老師學習
(D) 期待孩童在標準化的考試中表現良好

Step 8 模擬測驗

■ 解答
A. 1. legacy 2. agency 3. in line with 4. underpin
B. 1. (C) 2. (C) 3. (A) 4. (D) 5. (B)

文章中譯

　　瑪麗亞・蒙特梭利（Maria Montessori, 1870-1952）是義大利最先取得醫學學位且擔任醫生的女性之一，她也是一位教育家以及許多關於兒童教育的開創性書籍的作者。蒙特梭利敏銳地觀察兒童的學習傾向及各種不同程度的學習動機，並開發一種以兒童為中心的教育方法，強調的是體驗探索及自我引導的任務。她設計出的學習材料適合不同發展需求的兒童，並建立多所蒙特梭利學校，且製定出職前教師的培訓計畫。「蒙特梭利教育法」以教育、人類學和哲學理論為基礎，對於早期幼兒教育有著革命性的影響。

蒙特梭利反對傳統課堂上一體適用的教育法，她觀察到，當孩子們被允許在明確且合理的範圍內有選擇自由時，他們展現最佳學習力、激發出他們內在的動力，並對於課堂活動的注意力更加持久。因此，蒙特梭利教室裡的孩子們獲得了自主選擇作業的動力，這與傳統教室裡的孩子們 — 被賦予較少的自由且被期望跟著多數人一起作業 — 截然不同。當蒙特梭利的兒童們以獨立自主及團體分組的方式探索這個世界的知識時，作為引導者的教師既不是兒童們的關注對象，也不是課堂上要注意的焦點。孩子們自己發現答案的經歷可以讓他們更深入了解語言、藝術、歷史、數學和科學……等領域。在蒙特梭利課上鼓勵孩子手動探索的方式，養成他們解決問題的能力，以及培養他們的智力潛能。

蒙特梭利教育的另一個特點是混齡分組。不同年齡的孩子們在同一個教室中上課；在這裡，較年幼的孩子可以向較年長的同學學習，並透過觀察來接受新的挑戰。較年長的孩子可藉由展現其已熟悉的東西、擔任課堂上學習的榜樣，以及培養領導技能，來強化他們的學習。由於進行混齡分組，課堂上的同學合作多過於競爭。因為每個孩子的作業都是個人化的，孩子們能夠按照自己的學習節奏持續進步。

如今雖然許多老師傳承蒙特梭利的遺產，並讓全球許多國家的兒童強化了他們的能力，但蒙特梭利教育並非不會遇到瓶頸。由於要取得特別設計的蒙特梭利教材可能要花大筆錢，蒙特梭利學校的學費不太可能維持低價位。不同於傳統公立學校，多數蒙特梭利學校都是私立的，因此學費高於公立的。因此，低收入家庭的孩子可能無法接受蒙特梭利教育。

4.4 Part 3 – Peter Lynch

Step 1 掃讀 Scanning

■ 選擇正確的意思

A A B B A B B A A B

Step 2 略讀 Skimming

T T F T F

■ 答案解析

Q1. (T) 由首段第一句可知，Lynch 是一位成功的投資者。

Q2. (T) 由首段第一句可知，Lynch 撰寫過數本暢銷書籍。

Q3. (F) 由第二段第一句可知，Lynch 會承擔經過計算的風險。

Q4. (T) 由第三段第一句可知，Lynch 的書籍提供投資的建議。

Q5. (F) 由第三段第一句可知，投資沒有硬性規定。

Step 3 細讀 Close reading

A D

■ 答案解析

Q1. 根據這段短文內容，Lynch 認為 _____ 。

(A) 投資者應該要很了解自己投資的股票

(B) 投資者應該要在學校做功課

(C) 投資者應該要在家裡做功課

(D) 投資者應該要在做投資決策之前先去購物

> 解析 由 "...beginners and veteran investors alike are better off selecting companies or industries with which they are familiar." 的內容可知，Lynch 認為投資者必須很了解自己所投資的股票，所以正確答案是 (A)。

Q2. 根據這段短文內容，投資菜鳥與投資老手的關鍵差異為何？

(A) 年齡　　(B) 教育背景　　(C) 智商　　(D) 文中未提及

> 解析 這段短文內容未提及投資菜鳥與投資老手的關鍵差異，所以正確答案是 (D)。

D A C C B

■ 答案解析

Q1. Lynch 是一位_____。

　　(A) 作者　(B) 價值投資者　(C) 共同基金經理人　(D) 上述全部

> **解析** 由第一段 "one of the most well-known investors of all time and author of several best-selling books " 以及 "The fund became the world's best-performing mutual fund during his tenure as manager." 可知，正確答案是 (D)。

Q2. 身為投資人的 Lynch 不會_____。

　　(A) 投資熱門產業的熱門股

　　(B) 評估歷年的營收紀錄

　　(C) 分散投資多種股票

　　(D) 充分了解公司的經營模式

> **解析** 由第三段 "...and need to stay away from hot stocks in hot industries" 可知，Lynch 不會投資熱門產業的熱門股，所以正確答案是 (A)。

Q3. 下列何項敘述不是 Lynch 的建議？

　　(A) 選擇投資我們熟悉的公司

　　(B) 每數月重新評估手上的持股

　　(C) 投機

　　(D) 長期投資

> **解析** 由第三段 "They should't be speculative and need to stay away from hot stocks..." 可知，Lynch 並不建議投機，所以正確答案是 (C)。

Q4. 為何 Lynch 要分散投資？

　　(A) 因為想要以合理的價格購買股票

　　(B) 因為想要了解公司的前景

　　(C) 因為想要降低風險

　　(D) 因為想要購買股票

> **解析** 由第二段最後一句 "In his efforts... stocks." 可知，Lynch 分散投資的原因是想要降低風險，所以正確答案是 (C)。

Q5. Lynch 從幾歲開始管理麥哲倫基金？
   (A) 46 歲　　(B) 33 歲　　(C) 29 歲　　(D) 本文未提及

> **解析** 由第一段 "At age 33, he took over the Magellan Fund" 可知，
> Lynch 從 33 歲開始管理麥哲倫基金，所以正確答案是 (B)。

Step 8 模擬測驗

■ 解答
A. 1. boil / be boiled down to　2. aptitude　3. entails/entailed　4. made his mark
B. 1. (A)　2. (D)　3. (B)　4. (B)　5. (A)

文章中譯

　　彼得‧林奇是史上最有名的投資大師之一，同時也是一些投資類暢銷書籍的作者。他取得沃頓商學院（賓州大學的商學院）的商業管理碩士學位。林奇在某共同基金擔任經理人時嶄露頭角，他表現出非凡的選股能力。他在 33 歲時接管了麥哲倫基金 ─ 一家跨國金融企業的共同基金，總部位於麻州的波士頓。他在 1977 ~ 1990 年間管理該基金。在 13 年的管理期間，該基金的年報率為 29.2%，超過同期標普 500 指數獲利的兩倍。在他擔任經理期間，該基金成為全球績效最好的共同基金。他的成功讓他能夠在 1990 年 46 歲時退休。

　　林奇的投資策略可以歸結出一些指導原則。首先，他對於一家公司股票的初步評估包含對於公司本身、其商業模式、競爭優勢和前景的透徹了解。由於公司營收是股價的構件，他也會檢視公司獲利的歷史紀錄。就像華倫‧巴菲特一樣，林奇是一位價值投資者。他會估算風險且傾向於投資小型、成長快速，且能夠以合理股價買進的公司。為了在股市趨勢向下時減輕風險，林奇會藉由投資一系列的股票來進行多元投資。

　　關於投資，雖然沒有鐵律，但林奇在他的書中提供散戶投資人實用的建議。提到買股票，他認為無論是菜鳥投資客或是投資老手最好選擇自己熟悉的公司或產業。他建議投資人在做出任何投資的決定之前，先做好功課並實際掌握狀況。他也建議投資人不應有投機的心態，且要遠離熱門產業裡的熱門股。投資人往往會受到誤導而跟進一股潮流。畢竟，投資不像在賭場押大或押小。就情感層面而言，他認為心理的韌性在面對市場的波動時相當重要。雖然林奇一直是「做長期投資」的倡議者，但他不建議只是買進並一直持有一個多元化的投資組合。他認為投

資人有責任每隔數月檢視一次其持股情況，並再次檢視公司的營運，看是否有任何變化。當公司營運下滑時，他會賣出股票。

4.5 Part 1 - Financial Literacy

Step 1 掃讀 Scanning

■ 選擇正確的意思

　B A B A B　A B B A A

Step 2 略讀 Skimming

　F F T T T

■ 答案解析

Q1. (F) 由首段第一句可知人們閱讀投資理財相關書籍的原因。

Q2. (F) 由首段第一句可知，投資理財相關的書籍銷售量很好。

Q3. (T) 由第二段第一句可知，Kiyosaki 很有名氣。

Q4. (T) 由第三段第一句可知，Kiyosaki 也是一名作者。

Q5. (T) 由第四段第一句可知，Kiyosaki 認為財經知識很重要。

Step 3 細讀 Close reading

　B B

■ 答案解析

Q1. 根據這段短文內容，以下何者是正確的？

(A) 交易策略不重要。

(B) Kiyosaki 的書與大部分的投資理財書籍不同。

(C) 心理素質與投資成功與否不相關。

(D) Kiyosaki 一直努力於爭取財務自由。

> 解析 由 "The conventional wisdom, however, has been challenged... by Robert Kiyosaki" 可知，Kiyosaki 的書與大部分的投資理財書籍截然不同，所以正確答案是 (B)。

Q2. 根據這段短文內容，大部分的投資理財書籍並不探討_____。

(A) 財務自由　(B) 資產與負債　(C) 風險管理　(D) 交易策略

> **解析** 由 "... On their path to finanial freedom..." 以及 "Most of these books zero in on such key topics as trading strategies and risk management." 可知，大部分的投資理財書籍並不會探討資產與負債在投資上的意義，所以正確答案是 **(B)**。

Step 4 高理解速讀 Reading with greater comprehension and speed

A D B C C

■ 答案解析

Q1. Robert Kiyosaki 不是_____。

(A) 一位大學教授

(B) 一位企業家

(C) 一位投資者

(D) 一位作者

> **解析** 由第一、二段的 *Rich Dad Poor Dad*, a groundbreaking book written by Robert Kiyosaki 以及 "Kiyosaki is a renowned investor and educational entrepreneur." 可知，Robert Kiyosaki 不是一位大學教授，所以正確答案是 **(A)**。

Q2. 下列何者不是一般人閱讀投資理財書籍的原因？

(A) 學習交易策略

(B) 學習風險管理

(C) 學習達到財務自由的方法

(D) 學習如何利用借來的資金購買可帶來營收的資產

> **解析** 由第一段 "... on their path to financial freedom..." 以及 "Most of these books zero in on such key topics as trading strategies and risk management." 可知，(A)、(B)、(C) 都是一般人閱讀投資理財書籍的原因，「借錢來投資」不會是理財書籍鼓勵的，故正確答案是 **(D)**。

Q3. 下列何項不是政府印鈔票的後果？

(A) 銀行的存款縮水

(B) 看投資書籍的人會減少

(C) 貨幣貶值

(D) 通貨膨脹

由第二段 "He contends that people can never become rich by just banking their money since governments from around the world are always printing money, thereby causing inflation and currency depreciation." 可知，政府印鈔票將導致通貨膨脹、貨幣貶值以及銀行存款縮水，與看投資書籍的人減少無關，故正確答案是 (B)。

Q4. Kiyosaki 在他的研討會上會說什麼？
(A) 我們應該在股市追求獲利。
(B) 投資股票應該要減少風險。
(C) 我們應該購買能夠帶來正向現金流的資產。
(D) 我們應該存更多的錢。

文章中提到 Kiyosaki 的研討會只有在第二段，但並未提及他在研討會上説了什麼，所以我們可以從他的理念或是他出版的書籍當中去判斷。第三段提到 "the rich define assets and liabilities through the lens of cash flow"，這表示他認為富人透過資金流來定義資產與負債，故正確答案應為 (C)。從第二段 "While many invest in the stock market, he believes that..., they can only be temporarily rich by investing in stocks" 以及 "... people can never become rich by just banking their money..." 可知，(A)、(B)、(D) 都是錯誤的。

Q5. 根據 Kiyosaki 所述，為何這麼多人在追求財務自由的路上如此艱辛？
(A) 他們投資書籍讀得不夠。
(B) 他們在股市裡沒有獲利。
(C) 他們的財經素養不足。
(D) 他們沒有在銀行存足夠的錢。

由於首段第一句就提到 "Since so many people struggle on their path to financial freedom, investment books are selling like hotcakes..."，表示「為何這麼多人在追求財務自由的路上如此艱辛」就是整篇文章的主旨，我們便可以直接從文章標題 Financial Literacy（財經素養），或是文章最後一句 "Kiyosaki's book concludes that it is people's financial literacy that matters..." 來確認正確答案是 (C)。

■ 解答

A. 1. literacy 2. volatility 3. struggled 4. illiterate

B. 1. (B) 2. (A) 3. (D) 4. (B) 5. (A)

文章中譯

由於相當多的人在追求財務自由的路上跌跌撞撞，因此投資類書籍最近相當暢銷。大部分這類書籍都將焦點擺在像是交易策略與風險管理等關鍵主題。然而，這些傳統智慧卻受到羅伯特・清崎（Robert Kiyosaki）的開創性著作《富爸爸・窮爸爸》的挑戰。

Kiyosaki 是一位著名的投資人及教育企業家。一直有單位邀請他舉辦研討會，以幫助人們了解金錢的運作方式。雖然很多人投資股市，但他認為，由於股市的不確定性和波動性，一般投資股市的致富都是暫時性的。而他堅稱，只是把錢存在銀行裡也不可能致富，因為世界各國政府總是一直在印鈔票，進而導致通貨膨脹與貨幣貶值。

在 Kiyosaki 的書中，他試圖揭開富人的秘密。他指出，一般人傾向於認為資產就是他們所擁有的東西，像是汽車和房產，但富人是透過現金流來定義資產與負債。例如，當房子作為個人住宅用，那麼它就成為一種債務，因為我們得從口袋掏錢出來做裝修。相反地，若房子作為出租用不動產，它就變成一種持續帶來收益的資產。這就是為什麼 Kiyosaki 擁有 7000 件出租物業，讓金錢不斷流入他的口袋。他要強調的是資產與負債間的根本區別，並認為富人獲得的資產會產生正向的現金流，而窮人（或中產階級）通常取得的是會產生負向現金流的負債。

Kiyosaki 認為，富人和窮人的區別在於理財知識（或缺乏此類知識）。因為理財教育並非學校課程的一部分，即使受過高等教育的人也可能是理財痴。他聲稱，一般成為理財痴的主要原因來自他們對於債務的知識有限。一般人都被教導要擺脫債務，認為債務只會讓他們變得更窮。相反地，大多數富人將債務視為讓自己變得更富有的機會。他們經常借錢，且用借來的錢購買「可以賺錢之資產」（例如出租用房地產）。如此一來，他們反而能夠將不產生收益的資產轉化為資金的收入。在 Kiyosaki 的著作中得出一個結論：當人們在做投資時，最重要的就是他們的財經素養。

4.5 Part 2 - Bull and Bear Markets

Step 1 掃讀 Scanning

■ 選擇正確的意思

A B A A B A B B A A

Step 2 略讀 Skimming

F F T F F

■ 答案解析

Q1. (F) 由首段第一句可知，金融市場在牛市與熊市間不斷地循環。

Q2. (F) 由首段第一句可知，金融市場在牛市與熊市間不斷地循環。

Q3. (T) 由第二段第一句可知，牛市是一個正在上漲的市場。

Q4. (F) 由第三段第一句可知，熊市是一個正在下跌的市場。

Q5. (F) 由第三段第一句可知，牛市與熊市截然不同。

Step 3 細讀 Close reading

C A

■ 答案解析

Q1. 根據短文內容，以下何者是正確的？

　　(A) 在熊市，股票可能上漲超過 20%。

　　(B) 在熊市，利率通常會下降。

　　(C) 藍籌股會被熊市所拖累。

　　(D) 在熊市，公司獲利通常會增長。

> **解析** 由 "...stocks can easily tumble anywhere from 20% or more in a bear market. Not even blue-chip stocks are a safe haven." 的內容可知，藍籌股也會被熊市所拖累，所以正確答案是 (C)。

Q2. 根據這段短文內容，以下何者可能導致熊市？

　　(A) 疲軟的經濟

　　(B) 失業率下降

　　(C) 公司獲利增長

　　(D) 低利率

解析 由 "Bear markets often go hand in hand with rising interest rates, rising unemployment, declining corporate profits, banking crises, and recessions, among many other factors." 的內容可知，疲軟的經濟是造成熊市的原因之一，所以正確答案是(A)。

Step 4 高理解速讀 Reading with greater comprehension and speed

D B A D C

■ 答案解析

Q1. 牛市和熊市可以運用於

(A) 股票。

(B) 債券。

(C) 加密貨幣。

(D) 以上皆可

解析 由第一段最後 "While bull and bear markets are usually used to refer to the stock market, they can also be applied to anything tradable, such as bonds, foreign currencies, and cryptocurrencies." 可知，牛市和熊市可以用在股票、債券、加密貨幣等，所以正確答案是 (D)。

Q2. 牛市平均歷時多久？

(A) 略少於 10 個月

(B) 約 3.8 年

(C) 約 2.8 年

(D) 上述皆非

解析 由第二段 "Historically speaking, the average length of a bull market is around 3.8 years. " 可知，牛市平均歷時約 3.8 年，所以正確答案是 (B)。

Q3. 熊市平均歷時多久？

(A) 略少於 10 個月

(B) 約 3.8 年

(C) 約 2.8 年

(D) 上述皆非

Q4. 當牛市失去動力時，會發生什麼事?
　　(A) 股價可能會暴跌。
　　(B) 投資人可能會失去信心。
　　(C) 熊市可能會到來。
　　(D) 上述皆是

Q5. 牛市不會因為_____而發生。
　　(A) 低利率
　　(B) 公司獲利增長
　　(C) 失業率上升
　　(D) 經濟榮景

Step 8 模擬測驗

■ 解答

A. 1. outsmart　2. ran out of steam　3. onset　4. breathe easy
B. 1. (B)　2. (A)　3. (C)　4. (B)　5. (A)

文章中譯

　　金融市場本質上是週期性的，在大環境的好壞之間維持上下波動，也被稱為「多頭市場」和「空頭市場」。在多頭市場中，價格持續上漲。這種上升趨勢被稱為「牛市」，就好像一頭公牛要進行攻擊時，將牛角往上抬起的樣子。相反地，在空頭市場中，價格會往下走。這種下降趨勢被稱為「熊市」，如同一隻熊進行攻擊時，會用牠的爪子往下刷動。儘管許多人試圖在金融市場中成為佼佼者，但真正能夠戰勝熊市的投資人寥寥無幾。雖然牛市和熊市通常用來指稱股市，但也可以運用於任何可交易的事物，例如債券、外幣和加密貨幣。

　　一般認定牛市的定義是一個趨勢向上的市場，其中多數投資人做出買進動作，而股價從他們最近的低點上漲兩成以上。就歷史觀點來看，牛市的平均時間長度大約是 3.8 年。牛市與強勁的經濟往往是並存的。低利率、企業獲利上升及失業率下降都是推動牛市的因素。因此，牛市可以孕育出樂觀氣氛。認定股市將繼續上漲的投資人被稱為「多頭」。一旦多頭市場失去動力，投資人信心會迅速蒸發，然後股價暴跌，這是空頭市場開始的跡象。

　　與多頭市場的上升軌跡形成鮮明對比的是，股市在空頭市場中很容易暴跌超過兩成。即使是績優股（藍籌股）也不會是資金避風港。空頭市場通常伴隨著利率上升、失業率上升、企業獲利減少、銀行危機、經濟衰退以及許多其他因素。空頭市場的平均時間長度略低於 10 個月。儘管熊市往往比牛市的時間短，但可能帶來巨大的痛苦。四處瀰漫著壞消息，而認為情況只會變更糟的悲觀投資人被稱為「空頭」。當市場走出困境時，隨著經濟數據走強，負面的市場情緒開始消退。當一個空頭市場走到盡頭時，散戶和法人投資者將能夠再次鬆口氣，並迎接下一個多頭市場的誕生。

4.5 Part 3 - The Upsides & Downsides of Inflation

Step 1 掃讀 Scanning

■ 選擇正確的意思

B A B A B A B B B A

Step 2 略讀 Skimming

T T F T T

■ 答案解析

Q1. (T) 由首段第一句可知，通膨造成消費力下降。

Q2. (T) 由第二段第一句可知，通膨的發生其來有自。

Q3. (F) 由第三段第一句可知，通膨有其好處。

Q4. (T) 由第六段第一句可知，央行會出手壓制過高的通膨。

Q5. (T) 由第六段第一句可知，利率是一種抗通膨的工具。

Step 3 細讀 Close reading

A C

■ 答案解析

Q1. 根據短文內容，以下何者是正確的？

(A) 至少有兩個原因可以導致通膨。

(B) 政府印鈔票預防通膨。

(C) 消費者不想要付更多的錢購買同樣的商品。

(D) 政府注入更多的錢來預防通膨。

> 解析 由 "Another major driver of inflation is..." 可知，至少有兩個主要原因可以導致通膨，所以正確答案是 (A)。

Q2. 根據這段短文內容，通膨能夠＿＿＿＿。

(A) 使東西變便宜

(B) 幫助人們存更多的錢

(C) 刺激經濟

(D) 沒有任何理由就發生

> 解析 由 "When governments want to stimulate the economy and create more jobs, they print money and inject it into the economy." 可知，通膨能夠刺激並活絡經濟，所以正確答案是 (C)。

CBBAD

■ 答案解析

Q1. 下列何項不是通膨的現象？
(A) 物價連續數月攀高
(B) 人們以相同的錢可以購買的東西變少
(C) 經濟活動被抑制
(D) 需求增加，供給減少

> **解析** 由第一段 "Inflation is a persistent and widespread rise in price..." 可知，通貨膨脹是指物價持續且普遍性的上漲，故物價連續數個月攀高是通膨的現象之一，(B)、(D) 也能從其它段內容中看到：第一段的 "money cannot buy as much as it used to" 以及第三段的 "Some companies can even reap the benefits of inflation because, with increased demand and less supply..."。由第六段的 "Interest rates are an inflation-fighting tool that can depress economic activity." 可知，當央行升息壓制通膨時，經濟活動會被抑制，所以正確答案是 (C)。

Q2. 下列何項不是通膨的好處之一？
(A) 有彈性的薪資
(B) 房價下跌
(C) 增加的消費
(D) 增加的企業獲利

> **解析** 由第三段可知，通膨的好處包括 "making wages more flexible"、" increase consumer demand"、"Some companies can even reap the benefits of inflation"，因此 (A)、(C)、(D) 皆為適度通膨的好處。而從最後一句的 "home-building companies may charge higher prices for homes" 可知，房價下跌並非通膨的現象，所以也不可能是通膨的好處，故正確答案是 (B)。

Q3. 下列何項不是通膨的壞處之一？
(A) 企業通常將更高的成本轉嫁給消費者
(B) 經濟活動被刺激活絡
(C) 消費者信心指數下調
(D) 股價下跌

解答、解析與中譯

Q4. 為何中央銀行要壓制高通膨？
    (A) 為了讓經濟維持健康的成長率
    (B) 為了刺激經濟
    (C) 為了增加需求
    (D) 為了印更多的錢

Q5. 下列何項敘述可以從本文推斷出？
    (A) 通膨不是雙刃劍。
    (B) 通膨對於銀行存款有利。
    (C) 高通膨能夠自然回落。
    (D) 溫和的通膨是健康經濟的現象。

Step 8 模擬測驗

■ 解答
A. 1. Utilities 2. driver 3. tighten the purse strings 4. persistent
B. 1. (B) 2. (A) 3. (D) 4. (B) 5. (A)

　　通貨膨脹是指物價持續且普遍性的上漲，它伴隨著購買力逐漸喪失的結果。當物價攀升時，金錢無法維持像過去一樣的購買力。舉例來說，十年前的 100 美元，由於通貨膨脹的因素，在今日恐無法購買像以前一樣多的東西。因此，通貨膨脹可能導致生活成本增加，包括食品和公用事業，以及其他生活必要開銷。

　　通貨膨脹不會突如其來地發生。當政府想要刺激經濟時，他們會印鈔票並將其注入經濟活動中。結果是，人們有更多的錢可以花，那麼物價就會上漲。還有一項會導致通貨膨脹的因素，就是對於商品與服務的需求增加。當消費者願意以更高的價格購物，也會將物價推升上去。

　　儘管通膨似乎是惡名昭彰的，但它仍是一種必要之惡，並且也有其優點。適度的通膨率可作為經濟齒輪的潤滑油，讓工資更靈活地變化。穩定的通貨膨脹可以增加消費者需求。有些公司甚至可以從通貨膨脹中獲得利益，因為，需求增加而供應減少了，他們可將其商品訂出更高的價格。例如，當房產需求高時，房屋建商可能提高房子的售價。

　　然而，高通膨率可能成為經濟齒輪中的沙子。當物價上漲時，員工會要求公司給更高的薪資，進而推升企業的營運成本。此時公司可能將提高的營運成本轉嫁給其消費者，然後又導致物價被推得更高些，同時也讓薪資與物價呈螺旋式上升趨勢。通膨的等級升高也可能導致消費者信心和情緒急劇下滑，並造成股市下跌，在整體經濟中產生一些連鎖效應。

　　當政府為了應付支出而過度印鈔時，很快會造成通膨的失控。幣值迅速崩跌（例如，每月下跌 50% 以上）可能讓經濟陷入衰退，這對許多人來說都是一場噩夢。發生在 2008 年辛巴威以及 2016 年委內瑞拉令人崩潰的通膨，儘管是罕見的，事實上卻造成其貨幣一文不值。

　　當通貨膨脹無法被控制住時，中央銀行 — 像是美國聯準會或是歐洲央行 — 會為了抑制通膨與避免大規模經濟困頓而做出升息的動作。利率是一種對抗通膨的工具，可以用來冷卻經濟活動。由於升息的關係，一般消費者可能勒緊荷包，同時業者比較不會讓其商品漲價。亦即，降低支出等同降低物價，讓央行可以抑制通貨膨脹。

4.6 Part 1 - The Future of the Metaverse

Step 1 掃讀 Scanning

■ 選擇正確的意思

A A A B A B A B A A

Step 2 略讀 Skimming

F T F F T

■ 答案解析

Q1. (F) 由首段第一句可知，馬克祖克柏很重視元宇宙。

Q2. (T) 由第二段第一句可知，元宇宙可帶來更多的營收。

Q3. (F) 由第三段第一句可知，元宇宙可提供醫療協助，並非取代醫療人員。

Q4. (F) 由第三段第一句可知，元宇宙可以是很重要的手術輔助工具。

Q5. (T) 由第二段第一句可知，元宇宙是虛擬的。

Step 3 細讀 Close reading

C B

■ 答案解析

Q1. 根據短文內容，下列何項為真？

(A) 元宇宙看起來與真實世界差異很大。

(B) 外科醫生在手術前需要散步。

(C) 元宇宙可以被用來訓練新進的外科醫生。

(D) 外科手術不涉及特殊的知識和技能。

> **解析** 由 "the metaverse technologies can equip pre-service surgeons..." 可知，元宇宙的科技可以被用來訓練新進外科醫生，所以正確答案是 (C)。

Q2. 根據短文內容，實習外科醫生需要_____。

(A) 規律運動

(B) 在受過專業訓練之後對病人施行手術

(C) 訓練已經在執業的外科醫師

(D) 此部分未提及

解析 由 "a practicing surgeon can actively interact with apprentice surgeons... before they perform an operation on a patient" 可知，實習外科醫生需要在受過專業訓練之後，對病人施行手術，所以正確答案是 (B)。

Step 4 高理解速讀 Reading with greater comprehension and speed

D B C A D

■ 答案解析

Q1. 何者是虛擬商店可能做得到的事？

(A) 商家可以提供不受時間和距離限制的互動體驗。

(B) 可以提升顧客的體驗。

(C) 可以改善售後服務。

(D) 以上皆是。

解析 由第二段 "...in a virtual space that transcends the limits of time and space" 以及 "In particular, the virtualization of goods and services may streamline customer experience and strengthen after-sales support..." 可知，(A)、(B)、(C) 都是虛擬店面可以做到的事，所以正確答案是 (D)。

Q2. 元宇宙科技無法讓外科醫生

(A) 在治療病人的同時查看病人的身體內部狀況

(B) 在不使用 AR 和 MR 科技的情況下施行手術

(C) 改善手術精準度

(D) 監測病人的同步數據，例如心跳和血壓

解析 由第三段 "Metaverse technologies would allow surgeons to look inside a patient's body..., and blood pressure, likely improving the precision and speed of surgery." 可知，元宇宙的技術可以讓外科醫生做到 (A)、(C)、(D)，且必須使用 AR 和 MR 科技，所以正確答案是 (B)。

Q3. 馬克・祖克柏對於元宇宙的態度為何？

(A) 不確定性的　　(B) 懷疑的　　(C) 興奮的　　(D) 恐懼的

解析 由第一段可知，馬克祖克柏非常重視元宇宙的發展並投入相當多的心血，所以正確答案是 (C)。

Q4. 哪一項元宇宙的應用是本文中未提及的？
(A) 軍事訓練　　(B) 娛樂　　(C) 外科手術　　(D) 電玩

解析 從第一段的 "...in a range of sectors well beyond the realm of entertainment" 以及第三段的外科手術應用，可知本文並未提及軍事訓練的部分，故正確答案是 (A)。

Q5. 以下何者可由本文推論出？
(A) 元宇宙已經眾所周知很多年了。
(B) 只有小型企業能夠從元宇宙獲利。
(C) 進入元宇宙只需要 VR 和 AR 科技而已。
(D) 元宇宙的應用相當廣泛。

解析 由第一段 "New to many people..." 可知，(A) 是錯誤的；從第二段 "...can open up new revenue streams for businesses that venture into the metaverse" 可知，(B) 是錯誤的；從第一段 "...the metaverse is made possible by virtual reality (VR), augmented reality (AR), and mixed reality (MR) technology" 可知，(C) 是錯誤的；故正確答案應為 (D) 元宇宙的應用相當廣泛。

Step 8 模擬測驗

■ 解答
A. 1. the bottom line 2. sector 3. buzzword 4. momentum
B. 1. (A) 2. (D) 3. (C) 4. (B) 5. (D)

文章中譯

　　2021 年底時，馬克・祖克伯宣布 Facebook 將更名為 Meta，試圖反映出其越來越關注元宇宙業務的發展。元宇宙對許多人來說是個新概念，本質上它是一個身歷其境的虛擬環境，人們在這環境中以化身，或是與其本人（實體）相似的「數位雙胞胎」來進行互動。目前仍是個流行語的元宇宙，將透過虛擬實境（VR）、擴充實境（AR）以及混合實境（MR）再搭配其他連接設備的技術來實現。在祖克伯將這個詞彙公諸於世之後，元宇宙將改變我們相互聯繫和互動的方式。雖然元宇宙仍在發展階段，但元宇宙技術正為遊戲與娛樂領域以外的多種產業面建立起數位化轉型的動力。以下是宇宙的一些潛在應用。

　　虛擬世界的可能性可以為投入這項新事業的公司開闢新的營收來源。特別是，商品和服務的虛擬化可讓顧客體驗及取得更強的售後支援，進而促進銷售並吸引回流顧客。企業可擁有虛擬店面，並為顧客們打造身歷其境的互動體驗，而不是片面及被動的體驗。例如，店家可以將他們仿真的全像投影到實體辦公室內，以進行逼真的展演，或者在超越時空限制的共享虛擬空間中與潛在顧客進行互動。簡言之，隨著許多公司已開始涉足元宇宙，它將幫助各種規模的公司保持零售競爭力。

　　元宇宙還能夠增強醫療從業人員的能力，並成為一種寶貴的手術輔助工具。元宇宙技術將允許外科醫生在為患者進行手術時，深入患者身體內部進行查看。例如，AR 和 MR 耳機可以幫助監測患者的實時數據，像是體溫、心率、呼吸頻率及血壓，可能提升手術過程的精密度與速度。由於元宇宙的高度身歷其境之特性，元宇宙科技還可以為職前外科醫生提供成功的外科手術所需之知識與技術。比方說，執業的外科醫生可以主動與實習外科醫生進行互動，並引導他們完成手術程序，進而在他們為患者動手術前，讓手術的準備工作做得更好。但目前結論是，雖然我們已走了很長一段路，但要將元宇宙帶進生活還有很多的工作要做。

4.6 Part 2 - Opportunities and Challenges of Self-driving Cars

Step 1 掃讀 Scanning

■ 選擇正確的意思

B A B B B A B A B A

Step 2 略讀 Skimming

T F F T T

■ 答案解析

Q1. (T) 由首段第一句可知，自駕車又稱為自動車。

Q2. (F) 由首段第一句可知，自駕車不一定需要一位駕駛員。

Q3. (F) 由第二段第一句可知，自動駕駛共有 6 個等級。

Q4. (T) 由第三段第一句可知，自駕車可望減少交通事故。

Q5. (T) 由第四段第一句可知，自駕車會產生道德爭議。

Step 3 細讀 Close reading

B D

■ 答案解析

Q1. 根據短文內容，以下何者是正確的？

(A) 自駕車可以防止所有人受到傷害。

(B) 自駕車煞車突然失靈是可能會發生的意外事故。

(C) 安裝在自駕車上的人工智慧系統需每年進行一次維護。

(D) 自駕車會不計一切代價拯救其他用路人。

> 解析 由 "...when a self-driving car needs to stop at a red light and the brakes suddenly fail, the AI system would have to choose between two evils." 的內容可知，煞車失靈是可能會發生的意外事故，所以正確答案是 (B)。

Q2. 根據短文內容，可能造成自駕車煞車失靈者為何？

(A) 行人　　(B) 路燈　　(C) 紅綠燈　　(D) 文中未提及

> 解析 這部分的內容並未提及什麼原因造成煞車失靈，所以正確答案是 (D)。

A B D C C

■ 答案解析

Q1. 汽車工程學會將自動駕駛分為幾個等級？
  (A) 6 個等級　　(B) 5 個等級　　(C) 4 個等級　　(D) 3 個等級

  > 解析 由第二段 "The Society of Automotive Engineers defines six levels of vehicle automation, ranging from..." 可知，汽車工程學會將自動駕駛分為 6 個等級，所以正確答案是 (A)。

Q2. 特斯拉的自動駕駛等級為何？
  (A) 等級 1　　(B) 等級 2　　(C) 等級 3　　(D) 等級 4

  > 解析 由第二段 "Level 2 vehicles, such as Tesla and Waymo cars, are the most autonomous ones on the market today." 可知，特斯拉的自動駕駛屬於第二等級，所以正確答案是 (B)。

Q3. 自駕車配備有＿＿＿＿＿。
  (A) 感應器　　　　　　(B) 攝像機
  (C) 全球定位系統　　　(D) 以上皆是

  > 解析 由第一段 "These cars are fitted with a GPS system and use a combination of sensors, cameras, and state-of-the-art AI technology." 可知，自駕車配備有 (A)、(B)、(C)，所以正確答案是 (D)。

Q4. 大部份汽車交通事故的肇因為何？
  (A) 惡劣的天氣狀況　　(B) 機械故障
  (C) 人為疏失　　　　　(D) 上述皆非

  > 解析 由第三段 "...the majority of these accidents caused by human error" 可知，大部份汽車交通事故的肇因是人為疏失，所以正確答案是 (C)。

Q5. 為何自駕車的發展會產生道德爭議？
  (A) 因為人為疏失是汽車交通事故的肇因
  (B) 因為全自駕車尚未合法
  (C) 因為有些交通意外是無法避免的
  (D) 因為世界衛生組織擔憂酒後駕車

解答、解析與中譯

Step 8 模擬測驗

■ 解答

A. 1. ready for prime time 2. traction 3. autopilot 4. promises

B. 1. (B) 2. (C) 3. (A) 4. (D) 5. (B)

文章中譯

　　自駕車，也稱為自動車，是車子本身可以自行駕駛的車輛，無論是否有人類駕駛員在車上。這些車輛配備 GPS 系統，並結合感測器、攝影鏡頭以及尖端科技的人工智慧（AI）技術。自駕車在汽車市場中越來越受歡迎，特斯拉和 Google 等大企業正競相研發全自動車輛。然而，目前還不是這些車輛的蓬勃發展階段。

　　「汽車工程師協會」將「車輛自動化」定義出 0 級（完全手動）至 5 級（完全自動）等六個級別。目前道路上大多數車輛都是 0 級與 1 級車輛。駕駛人完全負責轉向、加速、煞車及停車時。因此，需要的是高度的專注力。以等級 1 而言，駕駛人仍負責控制車輛，但該車擁有像是「主動式定速巡航控制」等自動化功能。就等級 2 的車輛來說，像是 Tesla 和 Waymo 的車，是當今車市中「最自動」的品牌。這些車子允許駕駛人有時可將手從方向盤上移開。但駕駛人仍必須隨時保持專注。就等級 3 而言，可以讓車子在一定條件下自動行駛，但駕駛人得於必要時準備控制車輛。雖然等級 4 的車子大部分時候可自行駕駛，但在緊急情況下，駕駛人仍可選擇取代自動駕駛。最後，等級 5 的車子沒有方向盤或煞車踏板，因為車子是沒有人在駕駛的。駕駛員甚至在緊急情況下沒有掌控車輛的選擇。

　　自駕車的潛在優勢之一就是讓交通事故減少了。根據世界衛生組織（WHO）的數據，全世界每年有數百萬人死於交通事故，其中大多數事故都是人為疏失造成的。由於自駕車不會有酒駕或疲勞駕駛的問題，因此預期交通事故受傷與死亡數將減少。這些車輛可望免除人為疏失，以確保道路安全的提升。

　　然而，自駕車的發展引發了一個道德上的問題，即：若發生了無法避免的事故，誰的安全應被優先考慮？比方說，當一輛自駕車必須在紅綠燈前停下來但卻突然剎車失靈，此時人工智慧系統就必須在兩害中做選擇了。它可以選擇轉向然後撞上燈柱，以避免撞上其他行人和機車騎士等用路人，亦或保持向前行駛，無論如何都要保護駕駛人。今日由於完全自駕車尚未能合法上路，這樣的道德困境可能還得存在很長一段時間。然而，伴隨著這些挑戰，未來 20 年還有什麼等著我們呢？

4.6 Part 3 - Bionic Technology

Step 1 掃讀 Scanning

■ 選擇正確的意思

A B A B B　A B B A A

Step 2 略讀 Skimming

F T T T F

■ 答案解析

Q1. (F) 由第一段可知，這個數字不會減少，預計到 2050 年會再增加一倍。

Q2. (T) 由第二段第一句可知，義肢通常與人體的外表相仿。

Q3. (T) 由第三段第一句可知，仿生機械義肢能夠幫助有殘疾的人。

Q4. (T) 由第三段第一句可知，仿生機械義肢能夠有實際功能。

Q5. (F) 由第四段第一句可知，仿生機械義肢並不便宜。

Step 3 細讀 Close reading

C D

■ 答案解析

Q1. 根據短文內容，以下何者是正確的？

(A) 仿生機械義肢與虛擬實境技術有關。

(B) 仿生機械義肢上面有許多按鈕。

(C) 仿生機械義肢能夠讓截肢者更自然地活動。

(D) 仿生機械義肢以手動方式驅動。

> 解析 由 "They are capable of controlling each finger independently, walking with a natural gait..." 的內容可知，仿生機械義肢能夠讓截肢者更自然地活動，所以正確答案是 (C)。

Q2. 仿生機械義肢能夠讓截肢者_____。

(A) 衝浪　　(B) 散步　　(C) 騎摩托車　　(D) 以上皆可

> 解析 由 "...doing such sports as motorcycling, skiing, and surfing." 的內容可知，仿生機械義肢能夠讓截肢者進行衝浪、散步、騎摩托車等運動，所以正確答案是 (D)。

A D A B C

■ 答案解析

Q1. 關於傳統義肢，何者為真？

(A) 它們除了美觀沒有任何功能。

(B) 它們能夠複製人類的知覺。

(C) 它們能夠控制每一隻手指頭。

(D) 它們可以能夠由思想控制。

> **解析** 由第二段 "...traditional plastic or mental prostheses do not have functions that go beyond aesthetics" 可知，只有 (A) 是正確的敘述。

Q2. 腿部截肢的主要原因之一為何？

(A) 激烈運動　　(B) 車禍　　(C) 不明疾病　　(D) 本文未提及

> **解析** 本文並未提及腿部截肢的主要原因，所以正確答案是 (D)。

Q3. 穿戴傳統型義肢的人可能發生什麼事？

(A) 他們可能會有拖行的步態。

(B) 他們可能不容易跌倒。

(C) 他們的生活品質可能會因此提升。

(D) 他們可能不會過度使用未被截肢的肢體。

> **解析** 由第二段 "...people fitted with a prosthetic leg usually walk with an unnatural gait..." 可知，穿戴傳統型義肢的人可能會有拖行的步態，所以正確答案是 (A)。

Q4. 為何有些人選擇 3D 列印的仿生機械義肢？

(A) 因為它們是由電池驅動的

(B) 因為它們的造價較便宜

(C) 因為它們更有力量

(D) 因為它們與人體的外表相仿

> **解析** 由第四段最後一句 "3D-printed prostheses are poised to make bionic technology affordable for all amputees, especially those of low economic status." 可知，選擇 3D 列印的仿生機械義肢的原因是因為它們的造價較便宜，所以正確答案是 (B)。

Q5. 到了 2050 年的時候，美國預估共會有多少人截肢？
    (A) 約 190 萬人   (B) 約 290 萬人
    (C) 約 380 萬人   (D) 約 480 萬人

> **解析** 由第一段 "...about 1.9 million people are living with limb loss in the U.S. alone, and this number is expected to double by 2050." 可知，到了 2050 年的時候，美國預估共會有約 380 萬人截肢，所以正確答案是 (C)。

Step 8 模擬測驗

■ 解答
A. 1. in real time 2. settle for less 3. intimidated 4. replicate
B. 1. (B) 2. (A) 3. (D) 4. (C) 5. (C)

文章中譯

　　世界上有許多人喪失了肢體。根據總部位於華盛頓特區的非營利組織「美國截肢者聯盟」所述，光是在美國就有約 190 萬人肢體喪失，且這個數字預計到 2050 年會再增加一倍。這些截肢者依靠某種義肢來恢復活動能力。義肢是一種人工裝置，用來替代手、手臂、腿、膝蓋及腳踝等缺失的身體部位。對於數百萬的截肢者來說，確實對於義肢是有需求的。

　　傳統上，義肢是以模仿人體外觀為設計。然而，傳統塑料及精神上的義肢不具備美觀以外的功能。由於傳統義肢是被動型的裝置，他們的生活品質會下降。例如，裝上義腿的人通常會以不自然的步態行走，從而導致行動受限且摔倒的風險性更高。使用這些人工肢體的人往往會過度使用身體沒有截肢那一側，因此導致背部及肩部問題，最終需要額外的醫療照護。

　　為了努力找回身體失去的功能，有些截肢者尋求仿生技術來因應殘障的問題。許多大學，包括密西根大學和麻省理工學院，都在研究如何將機器與人體結合在一起，以重現人體的功能。仿生機械義肢透過電池供電並以大腦控制。這些使用者將他們的想法轉化為動作，以控制仿生機械的身體部位。他們能夠獨立控制每一根手指、以自然的步態行走，甚至可以做運動，像是騎摩托車、滑雪及衝浪等。雖然傳統義肢缺乏觸覺上的感知，但仿生機械義肢可藉由嵌入的感測器來重現觸覺。這些感測器將「知覺回饋」即時傳遞給大腦，讓截肢者可以感覺到仿生義肢是他們自己身體的一部分。因此，他們可以用仿生機械手來分辨冷或熱的物體。

　　雖然仿生技術可望讓截肢者重獲新生，但一般人可負擔得起的仿生義肢仍是遙不可及的。大多數仿生義肢動輒數萬美元。因此，許多截肢者對於這高昂的費用望之怯步，他們還是不得不接受傳統的義肢。所幸有最新的 3D 列印技術的創新，使用低成本的 3D 列印材料有助於降低機械義肢的費用。3D 列印的義肢可望提供所有截肢者可負擔的仿生技術，特別是經濟地位較低的截肢者。

4.7 Part 1 - Conflicting Views on Marijuana Legalization in the U.S.

Step 1 掃讀 Scanning

■ 選擇正確的意思

A B A B B A B A B A

Step 2 略讀 Skimming

T F T T T

■ 答案解析

Q1. (T) 由首段第一句可知，大麻合法化在美國是一個備受爭議的議題。

Q2. (F) 由首段第一句可知，輿論支持大麻合法化。

Q3. (T) 由第二段第一句可知，大麻在美國很多州都是合法的。

Q4. (T) 由第二段第一句可知，醫療用大麻在許多州已經合法化。

Q5. (T) 由第三段第一句可知，有些人並不支持娛樂用大麻合法化。

Step 3 細讀 Close reading

B A

■ 答案解析

Q1. 根據短文內容，下列何項敘述是正確的？

(A) 使用大麻沒有有風險。

(B) 吸食大麻者可能會思覺失調或罹患精神分裂症。

(C) 大麻成癮者也會酒精成癮。

(D) 大麻成癮者也會對其他藥物成癮。

> 解析 由 "marijuana consumption may be linked to mental illnesses such as..." 的內容可知，使用大麻可導致精神疾病，所以正確答案是 (B)。

Q2. 根據短文內容，吸食醫用大麻者罹患精神疾病的可能性為何？

(A) 有可能　　(B) 極有可能　　(C) 不可能　　(D) 沒有提到

> 解析 短文僅針對大麻的使用後果，並未提及醫用大麻，所以正確答案是 (D)。

ＢＤＣＡＣ

■ 答案解析

Q1. 哪一個州首度將醫療用大麻合法化？

　　(A) 佛羅里達州　　　(B) 加州　　　(C) 科羅拉多州　　　(D) 紐約州

> 解析 由第二段 "California was the first state to legalize medical marijuana in 1996 to treat chronic pain in adults." 可知，加州是第一個醫療用大麻合法的州，所以正確答案是 (B)。

Q2. 娛樂用大麻首度被合法化是在什麼時候？

　　(A) 在 2022 年　(B) 在 2021 年　(C) 在 1996 年　(D) 在 2012 年

> 解析 由第二段 "Recreational marijuana, ...was first legalized ... in 2012." 可知，娛樂用大麻首次合法化是在 2012 年時，所以正確答案是 (D)。

Q3. 有幾個州已將醫療用大麻合法化？

　　(A) 19　　　(B) 25　　　(C) 39　　　(D) 40

> 解析 由第二段 "According to the National Conference of State Legislatures, 39 states and the Washington D.C. have legalized the medical use of marijuana..." 可知，共有 39 個州已經合法化醫療用大麻，所以正確答案是 (C)。

Q4. 有幾個州已將娛樂用大麻合法化？

　　(A) 19　　　(B) 20　　　(C) 39　　　(D) 40

> 解析 由第二段 "...with 19 states and the Washington D.C. allowing recreational marijuana" 可知，共有 19 個州已經合法化醫療用大麻，所以正確答案是 (A)。

Q5. 為何青少年特別容易受到大麻的危害？

　　(A) 因為大麻的使用與精神疾病有關

　　(B) 因為反覆使用大麻可能會成癮

　　(C) 因為前腦要到 25 歲左右才發育完成

　　(D) 以上皆非

解析 由第三段 "Since the forebrain does not fully mature until around age 25, adolescents are particularly vulnerable to harmful effects of marijuana." 可知，因為前腦要到 25 歲左右才發育完成，故青少年特別容易受到大麻的傷害，所以正確答案是 (C)。

Step 8 模擬測驗

■ 解答

A. 1. vulnerable to 2. pushback 3. uncharted territory 4. followed suit

B. 1. (D) 2. (C) 3. (A) 4. (D) 5. (B)

文章中譯

　　大麻（Cannabis）是 marijuana 的學名，它是一種植物，含有某種使人興奮、影響情緒及精神狀態的成分。雖然大麻合法化多年來在美國一直是個爭議性議題，但民意似乎與「大麻非法化」背道而馳。過去數十年以來，美國多數人民皆傾向於支持大麻使用的合法化。根據蓋洛普（Gallup）民調數據，民眾對大麻合法化的支持度從 1969 年的 12% 上升到 2021 年的 68%。皮尤研究中心一項民調也發現，91% 的美國成年人認為大麻應是合法的，無論是在醫學上、娛樂上，或兩者皆是。

　　越來越多的州肯定大麻是合法的。加州於 1996 年成為第一個讓醫療用大麻合法化的州，用來治療成人的慢性疼痛。許多其他州都以加州為借鏡，並將吸食大麻合法化，不僅於醫療用途，還用於娛樂方面。娛樂用大麻，也稱為「成人用大麻」，於 2012 年在科羅拉多州和華盛頓州首次被合法化。根據「全美州議會聯合會」的統計，有 39 個州及華府特區已將大麻醫療用途合法化，其中 19 個州和華府特區允許娛樂用大麻。美國眾議院於 2022 年時才剛以聯邦政府的層級通過一項大麻合法化的法案。讓全國的大麻合法化可能意味著，給經濟打了一劑強心針，也可能帶來數十萬就業機會以及稅收的增加。儘管尚未成定局，但美國參議院預計將會跟進。

　　然而，大麻的合法化一直有反對聲浪，尤其是娛樂性大麻。對大麻持反對意見者，包括「美國成癮藥物協會」以及「美國兒童與青少年精神醫學會」，以公衛的立場提出風險警告。批評大麻合法化的人認為，決策者忽略了對於人類腦部的健康風險。例如，哈佛大學的研究人員發現，吸食娛樂性大麻者的大腦部分區域出現異常現象。由於前腦部位要到 25 歲左右才完全發育成熟，因此青少年特別容易受到吸食大麻的危害。麥吉爾大學和耶魯大學的研究人員指出，在青春期吸食大麻可能會影響專注力及記憶力等大腦功能。其他研究指出，思覺失調和精神分裂症等精神疾病可能與吸食大麻有關。長期吸食大麻也會導致上癮，就像人們對酒精和其他藥物成癮一樣。雖然使大麻合法化的法律現已定案，但仍存在許多待探討的未知領域。

4.7 Part 2 - LGBTQI+ Rights

Step 1 掃讀 Scanning

■ 選擇正確的意思

B B A B A A A B A B

Step 2 略讀 Skimming

F F T T T

■ 答案解析

Q1. (F) 由首段第一句可知，許多文化排斥多元性別的族群。

Q2. (F) 由首段第一句可知，許多宗教排斥多元性別的族群。

Q3. (T) 由第二段第一句可知，人們可能會因為本身的性取向而受到歧視。

Q4. (T) 由第二段第一句可知，人們可能會因為本身性別認同問題而受到歧視。

Q5. (T) 由第四段第一句可知，同性婚姻在美國已經合法超過七年了。

Step 3 細讀 Close reading

A D

■ 答案解析

Q1. 根據短文內容，以下何者為真？

(A) 許多國家支持多元性別認同者。

(B) 在巴西，人們不被允許談論他們的政治見解。

(C) 在巴西，人們不被允許談論他們的宗教信仰。

(D) 在巴西，人們不被允許談論他們的性向。

> 解析 由 "Many countries in the world have attempted to advance the rights of LGBTQI+ people..." 的內容可知，許多國家支持多元性別認同者，所以正確答案是 (A)。由最後一句 "LGBTQI+ people in these countries make no bones about their sexual orientation in much the same way people openly talk about their religious beliefs or political views." 可知，(B)、(C)、(D) 都是錯誤的。

Q2. 根據短文內容，共有多少國家已經將同性婚姻合法化？

(A) 五個國家

(B) 六個國家

(C) 七個國家

(D) 文中未提及

解析 由 "...same-sex marriage has been legalized in several counties, including..." 的內容可知，同性婚姻在一些國家已經合法化，但並未提及共有多少國家已將同性婚姻合法化，所以正確答案是 (D)。

Step 4 高理解速讀 Reading with greater comprehension and speed

D D A D C

■ 答案解析

Q1. 下列哪個國家反對同性婚姻合法化？

(A) 伊朗

(B) 沙烏地阿拉伯

(C) 阿拉伯聯合大公國

(D) 以上皆是

解析 由第一段 "For example, the United Arab Emirates, Saudi Arabia, and Iran are set against legalizing same-sex marriage..." 可知，上述三個國家皆反對同性婚姻合法化，所以正確答案是 (D)。

Q2. 同性婚姻在以下哪個地方已合法化？

(A) 澳洲

(B) 英國

(C) 巴西

(D) 以上皆是

解析 由第三段 "For example, same-sex marriage has been legalized in several countries, including the U.S., the U.K., Australia, and Brazil..." 可知，上述三個國家皆已經將同性婚姻合法化，所以正確答案是(D)。

Q3. 什麼原因導致社會上對於多元性別族群的接受度較低？

(A) 政府剝奪他們的平等權。

(B) 政府嘗試提升他們的權利。

(C) 多數人相信賦予多元性別族群的平等權利是重要的事。

(D) 同性婚姻合法化。

解析 由第一段 "...the authorities routinely deny their equal rights, thus resulting in a low level of acceptance of LGBTQI+ people..." 可知，當政府剝奪他們平等的權利時，社會上對於多元性別族群的接受度會比較低，所以正確答案是 (A)。

Q4. 大部份美國人相信多元性別族群在哪些方面應獲得公平的待遇？
　　(A) 教育
　　(B) 居住
　　(C) 工作
　　(D) 以上皆是

解析 由第四段 "...the majority of Americans believe they should promote equality for LGBTQI+ people in areas such as employment, housing, and education." 可知，大部份美國人相信多元性別族群在教育、居住、工作等方面都應獲得公平的待遇，所以正確答案是 (D)。

Q5. 在 2021 年，美國各州的議會共有多少反對多元性別族群的法案被審查？
　　(A) 近 200 個反對多元性別族群的法案
　　(B) 近 300 個反對多元性別族群的法案
　　(C) 近 400 個反對多元性別族群的法案
　　(D) 近 500 個反對多元性別族群的法案

解析 由第四段 "According to the Equality Federation, nearly 400 anti-LGBTQI+ bills were considered by state legislatures in 2021." 可知，在 2021 年，美國各州的議會共有近 400 個反對多元性別族群的法案被審查討論，所以正確答案是 (C)。

Step 8 模擬測驗

■ 解答

A. 1. routinely 2. an uphill battle 3. fanned the flames 4. rampant

B. 1. (D) 2. (C) 3. (A) 4. (B) 5. (D)

文章中譯

　　雖然女同性戀、男同性戀、雙性戀、跨性別、酷兒（非異性戀者）和雙性等的人士（LGBTQI+），一直試圖擺脫二元化的性別認同，但他們通常因文化規範與宗教信仰而感到挫敗。在一些國家中，當局經常否定他們的平等權，進而導致一般對於「LGBTQI+ 人士」的接受度低。例如，阿拉伯聯合大公國、沙烏地阿拉伯及伊朗反對同性婚姻合法化，甚至將其視為罪犯。由於宗教是最常被歸咎的因素之一，他們必須經常對抗以宗教為由的歧視。在社會中這樣不公不義的事，點燃了 LGBTQI+ 社群中積壓已久的憤怒。

　　在世界許多個角落裡，LGBTQI+ 的族群因性取向或性別認同等因素而必須面對歧視。LGBTQI+ 人士在工作、學校和其他活動中受到不公平對待的情況並不少見。他們在求職過程中也會遇到人們肆無忌憚的偏見。相較於非 LGBTQI+ 者，有些 LGBTQI+ 人士獲得雇用的機會較低。在學校，他們通常會經歷受到霸凌與騷擾的窘境，而這些行為不一定是違法的。一直以來，對於 LGBTQI+ 族群的歧視一直煽動著緊張的火焰。

　　但情況並非全然悲觀的。世界上有許多國家一直試圖協助 LGBTQI+ 者獲得不被滿足的需求，以提昇他們的權利。例如，同性婚姻在一些國家已經合法化，包括美國、英國、澳大利亞以及巴西，且越來越多國家正走上同性婚姻合法化一途。這些國家的 LGBTQI+ 人士毫無掩飾地高談闊論他們的性取向，這就像人們公開談論他們的宗教信仰或政治觀點一樣。

　　在美國，同性婚姻於 2015 年被最高法院宣佈為憲法權利。越來越多人認為，LGBTQI+ 族群的權利是通往集體幸福的通行證。根據無黨派的「公共宗教研究所（PRRI）」所述，大多數美國人認為他們應該在就業、住房及教育等領域推動 LGBTQI+ 人士的平等權。儘管越來越多人願意接受 LGBTQI+ 族群，但州法律仍未跟上，歧視的情況依然存在。許多州沒有明確禁止對於性別認同的歧視。根據「人權平等聯合會」的數據，2021 年有近 400 個反 LGBTQI+ 法案於州立法機構進行審議。這些法案的引進威脅著 LGBTQI+ 族群的權利與福祉。在聯邦政府沒有立法的情況下，爭取 LGBTQI+ 權利仍是一場硬戰。

4.7 Part 3 - The Politics of Gun Control

Step 1 掃讀 Scanning

■ 選擇正確的意思

B B B B A B A A B A

Step 2 略讀 Skimming

F F T F F

■ 答案解析

Q1. (F) 由首段第一句可知，新聞媒體常常報導世界各地的槍枝暴力。

Q2. (F) 由首段第一句可知，槍枝暴力不只有發生在美國而已。

Q3. (T) 由第二段第一句可知，槍枝暴力在美國是一個政治議題。

Q4. (F) 由第三段第一句可知，反槍人士認為槍枝管控法律應更嚴格。

Q5. (F) 由第四段第一句可知，擁槍人士並不支持槍枝管控法律。

Step 3 細讀 Close reading

D C

■ 答案解析

Q1. 根據短文內容，以下何者為真？

    (A) 大多數國會議員在嚴格控管槍枝上有共識。

    (B) 大多數人認為槍枝控管應該要更嚴格。

    (C) 政治上的意識形態比槍枝控管的法律更重要。

    (D) 人們較常見到民主黨員呼籲加強槍枝控管。

> 解析 由最後一句 "... Democrats are more likely than Republicans to see firearm violence as a dire problem..." 可知，我們會較常見到民主黨人呼籲更嚴格的槍枝管控，所以正確答案是 (D)。

Q2. 根據短文內容，美國人民如何看待槍枝控管的法律？

    (A) 和平地　　(B) 冷漠地　　(C) 爭議地　　(D) 以上皆非

> 解析 從 "People are split along ideological lines over whether gun laws should be further tightened..." 這句話可知，此議題在美國長期沒有共識，社會上充滿爭議性的看法，所以正確答案是 (C)。

D B C D A

■ 答案解析

Q1. 每年美國有多少人死於槍下？

(A) 49 人　　(B) 58 人　　(C) 100 人　　(D) 本文未提及

> 解析 本文提到美國「槍擊死亡」的數字部分只有在第一段，但並未提及每年有多少人死於槍下的數據，所以正確答案是 (D)。

Q2. 下列何者不是支持槍枝管控者的論點？

(A) 槍枝擁有權可能會造成更多的犯罪。

(B) 槍枝管控的法律無法避免罪犯取得槍枝。

(C) 槍枝可以輕易讓單一謀殺案變成大規模謀殺事件。

(D) 在槍枝管控嚴格的國家中，持槍謀殺案件較少。

> 解析 由第三段 "loose gun-control laws are the primary source of gun violence" 可知，(A) 是反槍陣營（支持槍枝管制者）的論點；(B) 明顯不是反槍陣營，而是擁槍陣營的論點，故正確答案是 (B)；第一段最後提到 "High-profile mass shootings have plagued the United States for far too long"，故 (C) 也是反槍陣營的論點；第三段提到 "... countries doing so such as Switzerland and Finland, have lower gun-related homicide rates"，所以 (D) 也是反槍陣營的論點。

Q3. 下列何者不是擁槍陣營的論點？

(A) 槍枝擁有權是守法公民的基本人權。

(B) 槍枝擁有權很可能不是槍枝暴力的元凶。

(C) 嚴格的槍枝管控是減少槍枝暴力的有效方法。

(D) 反槍陣營聲稱更嚴格的槍枝控管便能夠嚇阻槍枝暴力的論點站不住腳。

解析 由第四段 "They argue that gun control laws infringe the constitutional right of law-abiding citizens to defend themselves. " 可知，(A) 是擁槍陣營的論點；從 "gun control laws are unlikely to prevent criminals from obtaining guns" 可知，(B) 是擁槍陣營的論點；(C) 顯然是反槍陣營的論點，擁槍陣營並不認為嚴格的槍枝管控是減少槍枝暴力的有效方法，所以正確答案是 (C)；從 "the vast majority of criminals obtain their firearms through illegal means, gun control laws are unlikely to prevent criminals from obtaining guns" 可知，(D) 也是擁槍陣營的論點。

Q4. 下列何項敘述可由本文推論出？
(A) 大規模槍擊事件沒有引起關於槍枝控管議題的激辯。
(B) 在美國對於槍枝控管的看法分歧很小。
(C) 大規模槍擊事件通常不會受到媒體太多的關注。
(D) 許多人認為槍枝暴力的原因是鬆散的槍枝控管法律。

解析 本文探討槍枝管控（gun control）的支持與反對論點，且從一開始的 "gun violence is frequently the lead story on the evening news and receives extensive media coverage" 可知，(A)、(C) 是錯誤的；而從最後一句 "Everyone seems to agree that... from different angles" 可知，美國對於槍枝控管的看法有很大的分歧，故 (B) 也是錯的；從第三段 "loose gun-control laws are the primary source of gun violence" 可知，反槍陣營認為槍枝暴力的原因是鬆散的槍枝控管法律，所以正確答案是 (D)。

Q5. 下列何州有較嚴格的槍枝控管規範？
(A) 紐約州　　(B) 密西西比州　　(C) 亞利桑那州　　(D) 肯塔基州

解析 由第四段 "states with some of the most stringent gun laws, like New York and Illinois..." 可知，紐約州有較嚴格的槍枝控管規範，所以正確答案是 (A)。

Step 8 模擬測驗

■ 解答
A. 1. second to none 2. ideology 3. law-abiding 4. stringent
B. 1. (C) 2. (B) 3. (C) 4. (A) 5. (D)

　　槍枝暴力可說是全球性的問題，也是世界各地無數生命受到影響的悲劇，它經常躍上晚間新聞的頭條，並受到廣泛媒體的報導。根據 2018 年瑞士《小型武器調查》的數據，全球 44% 的兇殺案與槍擊事件有關。特別是美國，在已開發國家中擁有最高的槍械兇殺率，大約是加拿大的 8 倍多。舉例來說，2016 年在奧蘭多一名槍手殺死了 49 人。2017 年在拉斯維加斯的大規模槍擊事件造成 58 人死亡，是美國有史以來死亡數最多的大規模槍擊事件。備受矚目的大規模槍擊屠殺事件困擾美國太久了。

　　儘管湧入了悲傷與同情的氣氛，但關於槍枝法律的辯論，在美國一直是個政界的燙手山芋。朝野各政黨國會議員鮮少在槍枝管制的議題上有共識。根據 2021 年皮尤（Pew）研究中心的調查，人們對於是否應進一步強化槍枝管控法，存在意識形態的分歧，而民主黨則比共和黨更可能視槍枝暴力為迫切性的問題。

　　槍枝管控的支持者堅信，槍枝暴力的主要源頭就是槍枝管制法過於寬鬆，尤其反應在某些社區槍枝氾濫的問題。他們認為，增加更多槍枝管制法，例如納入犯罪紀錄的背景調查，將可減少槍擊相關的死亡人數此外，他們指出瑞士和芬蘭等國家的持槍殺人案件數較低。所以許多支持者認為，限制槍枝的取得可遏止槍枝暴力及挽救生命。加強槍枝管制的支持者承認，美國憲法保護個人擁有槍枝的權利。然而，他們仍認為槍枝很少用於家庭或公共場所的自衛，反而經常用於在街道上性命受到威脅時。

　　槍枝管制反對者 — 持反對意見的一方 — 強力反對採取更多限制。他們聲稱，槍枝管制法侵犯了守法公民自我防衛的憲法權利。反方認為，槍枝管制的支持者搞錯對象了，他們認為，槍枝管制不是解決辦法，因為擁有一些最嚴格槍管法律的城市，如紐約和芝加哥，以及紐約州和伊利諾伊州，其槍枝暴力犯罪的比率很高。有鑑於絕大多數罪犯都是透過非法手段取得槍枝，槍枝管制法不太可能阻擋罪犯的槍枝取得。因此，諸如背景調查等槍管措施可能徒勞無功。似乎大家都認同沒有什麼比人身安全更重要了，但處理槍枝暴力的問題卻有不同的觀點。

4.8 Part 1 - Neuroscience in Focus: The Human Nervous System

Step 1 掃讀 Scanning

■ 選擇正確的意思

B A B A A B B A A A

Step 2 略讀 Skimming

T F F T F

■ 答案解析

Q1. (T) 由首段第一句可知，神經系統是人體最複雜的系統之一。

Q2. (F) 由第二段第一句可知，中樞神經系統包含大腦和脊髓。

Q3. (F) 由第二段第一句可知，中樞神經系統包含大腦和脊髓。

Q4. (T) 由第四段第一句可知，末梢神經系統支配反射反應。

Q5. (F) 由第四段第一句可知，末梢神經系統支配反射反應。

Step 3 細讀 Close reading

B D

■ 答案解析

Q1. 根據短文內容，以下何者是錯誤的？

(A) 當我們手握一杯熱茶的時候，反射的反應會發生。

(B) 大腦會接收到所有來自知覺神經的訊息。

(C) 脊椎神經會接收知覺神經的訊息。

(D) 反射的反應有時候是無意識的。

> 解析 由 "Most of the time, however, these messages do not even get to the brain." 可知，大腦有時候並不會接收到來自知覺神經的訊息，所以正確答案是 (B)。

Q2. 根據短文內容，反射的反應功能為何？

(A) 讓我們能夠用手去拿一杯熱茶

(B) 傳送訊息到大腦

(C) 傳送訊息到脊椎神經

(D) 避免發生危險

由 "The brain then would send a message back telling the muscles in our hand to pull away." 可知，當我們拿著一杯熱茶時，皮膚內的知覺神經會立即向大腦發出「這杯子是熱的且會傷人」的訊息，然後大腦會告訴我們的手要做出離開的動作，以避免發生危險。所以正確答案是(D)。

Step 4 高理解速讀 Reading with greater comprehension and speed

D A C D A

■ 答案解析

Q1. 人體的神經系統讓我們能夠_____。

(A) 思考　　　(B) 有知覺　　　(C) 行走　　　(D) 以上皆是

解析 由第一段 "Controlling what we think and feel as well as what our body can do like walking and running, the nervous system is..." 可知，思考、知覺、行走皆由神經系統掌控，故正確答案是 (D)。

Q2. 神經分布在哪個部位？

(A) 全身各處　　　　　(B) 只有在大腦裡

(C) 只有在脊椎裡　　　(D) 只有在皮膚上

解析 由第一段 "...the nervous system is a network of nerves sending signals throughout the body" 可知，神經分布在全身各處，所以正確答案是 (A)。

Q3. 何項關於愛因斯坦的敘述可能為真？

(A) 他的反射動作比大部分人更強烈。

(B) 他大腦最大區塊的左右兩側一樣強大。

(C) 他大腦最大區塊的左側較強大。

(D) 他大腦最大區塊的右側較強大。

解析 本篇文章雖未提到愛因斯坦，但可由第二段 "The left side is considered logical and rational, in charge of skills such as math and science." 推斷，發明相對論的物理學家愛因斯坦，其大腦最大區塊的左側應該較右側強大，所以正確答案是 (C)。

Q4. 以下何者可從本文推論出來？
   (A) 非自主行為與反射動作是一樣的。
   (B) 神經系統不會在我們睡覺的時候運作。
   (C) 末梢神經系統是人體的指揮中心。
   (D) 中樞神經系統和末梢神經系統都很重要。

> **解析** 由第三、四段的 " In addition to these voluntary actions, the peripheral nervous system has another card up its sleeve — involuntary actions..." 以及 "Another feature of the peripheral nervous system is the reflex response." 可知非自主行為與反射動作都是末梢神經系統的特徵之一，但兩者並非是一樣的，故 (A) 是錯誤的；從第三段的 "These involuntary actions, such as heartbeat and breathing, continue even when we are asleep." 可知，神經系統會在我們睡覺的時候運作，故 (B) 是錯誤的；由第二段 "The central nervous system is made up of the brain and the spinal cord. The brain, in particular, is the command center for our body..." 可知，屬於中樞神經系統的大腦是我們身體的指揮中心，故 (C) 是錯誤的；中樞神經系統和末梢神經系統對人體都很重要，所以正確答案是 (D)。

Q5. 什麼時候的動作與反射行為無關？
   (A) 當我們在游泳的時候
   (B) 當我們被蜜蜂螫到的時候
   (C) 當我們用手去拿一杯熱茶的時候
   (D) 當一顆小石子飛向我們眼睛的時候

> **解析** 反射動作在第四段被提及，它屬於「無意識的」反應作為，特別是人體遇到危險狀況時，因此只有游泳的行為與反射動作無關，故正確答案是(A)。

Step 8 模擬測驗

■ 解答
A. 1. stomachache 2. first place 3. Reflexes 4. relay
B. 1. (A) 2. (D) 3. (C) 4. (B) 5. (B)

文章中譯

　　若說神經系統是人體最複雜的部分之一，並不為過。神經系統控制我們的思想和感覺，以及我們身體可以做的事，像是走路及跑步，它是個發送訊號至全身的網絡。幸虧我們有遍及全身的神經，我們才能產生知覺，比如說疼痛。具體來說，我們的身體有兩個互相協調合作的神經系統：中樞神經系統和末梢神經系統。

　　中樞神經系統由大腦和脊髓組成。尤其是大腦，是我們身體的指揮中心，它藉由神經接收及發送訊號，以掌控身體的功能。我們大腦最大的那個區域可分為左右兩半。左半邊被認為傾向於邏輯與理性思考，像是數學和科學等技能。右半邊被認為傾向於創意及藝術思維，負責像是藝術與音樂之類的主題。另一方面，脊髓作為連接大腦和末梢神經系統的橋樑。大腦和脊髓都可以透過運動神經，將訊號傳送至身體其他部位，即告訴身體應該採取什麼行動。

　　末梢神經系統就像是一條雙向的交通路線。末梢神經系統的感知神經會不斷接收來自眼、耳、嘴、鼻及皮膚的訊息，並將訊息傳回中樞神經系統。接著運動神經接收來自大腦和脊髓的命令，執行像是進食和吞嚥等動作。除了這些自主性的行為之外，末梢神經系統還有另一個功能 — 非自主性的行為，它獨立於人的有意識行為之外。這些非自主的動作，即使在我們入睡時也會持續進行，例如心跳和呼吸。

　　末梢神經系統的另一個特徵是反射動作。諸如眨眼之類的反射動作是快速且非自主的行為，可以使我們免於陷入危險中。舉例來說，當一顆小石子飛向我們的眼睛時，我們的眼瞼會在我們意識到那顆石頭之前猛地閉上。而當我們拿著一杯熱茶時，也會發生反射的動作。皮膚內的知覺神經會立即向大腦發出「這杯子是熱的且會傷人」的訊息。然後大腦會送回一道訊息，告訴我們手上的肌肉要做出離開的動作。不過，大多數時候，這些訊息也不一定會傳送至大腦。若是脊髓先收到訊息，就會立即送回給肌肉作出反應，不需要任何有意識的作為。

解答、解析與中譯

4.8 Part 2 - The Origin of the Moon

Step 1 掃讀 Scanning

■ 選擇正確的意思

A A B B A B A A B A

Step 2 略讀 Skimming

F F F F T

■ 答案解析

Q1. (F) 由首段第一句可知，月球對地球的生態影響巨大。

Q2. (F) 由第二段第一句可知，我們並無法確定月球是如何形成的。

Q3. (F) 由第三段可知，這項假說一直是站不住腳的，因為從月球蒐集到的岩石分析顯示，月球和地球大致在同一時間形成。。

Q4. (F) 由第四段最後一句可知，大多數天文學家不支持這項假說。

Q5. (T) 由第六段第一句可知，大撞擊假說是目前最受科學家普遍接受的假說。

Step 3 細讀 Close reading

A B

■ 答案解析

Q1. 根據短文內容，以下何者是正確的？

(A) 電腦模擬的結果與地質證據並不吻合。

(B) 在撞擊之後，這個行星大小的天體最終形成了月球。

(C) 我們現在已經明確知道月球是如何形成的。

(D) 電腦模擬的結果表示月球和地球應該有共同的起源。

> 解析 由 "However, geological evidence says otherwise." 的內容可知，電腦模擬的結果與地質證據並不吻合，所以正確答案是 (A)。由 "Computer simulations have confirmed the possibility of forming the moon this way." 可知，"A large chunk ejected from this collision eventually became the moon." 只是個可能性，故 (B) 是錯誤的；目前對於月球的形成有五大假說，既然是「假說」，顯然 (C) 就是錯誤的；由 "Analyses of lunar rocks indicate that these rocks share similar minerals with Earth rocks" 可知，是「月球岩石的分析結果」表示月球和地球應該有共同的起源，而非「電腦模擬結果」，故 (D) 是錯誤的。

Q2. 根據短文內容，我們可以了解關於月亮的什麼事？

(A) 月球無法在撞擊之後形成。

(B) 月球的岩石已經被分析過。

(C) 月球和地球的岩石沒有類似的礦物質。

(D) 電腦沒有被用來研究月球的起源。

> 解析 由 " A large chunk ejected from this collision eventually became the moon." 可知，(A) 是錯誤的；由 "Analyses of lunar rocks indicate that..." 可知，科學家已經分析過月球的岩石，所以正確答案是 (B)。由 "these rocks share similar minerals with Earth rocks" 可知，(C) 是錯誤的；由 "Computer simulations have confirmed the possibility of forming the moon this way." 可知，(D) 是錯誤的。

Step 4 高理解速讀 Reading with greater comprehension and speed

A C B B D

■ 答案解析

Q1. 何者與月球無關？

(A) 地球的大小　　　　　　(B) 地球上季節的變化

(C) 地球自轉軸的傾斜角度　(D) 地球的潮汐

> 解析 由第一段 "The moon, to a certain extent, helps stabilize the tilt of the Earth's rotational pole. This tilt is responsible for the four seasons on Earth and a relatively stable climate. The moon's gravity also interacts with the Earth's oceans, controlling the ebb and flow of the tide." 可知，(B)、(C)、(D) 皆與月球有關，只有 (A) 是無關的，故 (A) 是正確答案。

Q2. 哪一項假說是目前最受科學家普遍接受的？

(A) 分裂假說　　(B) 捕捉假說　　(C) 大撞擊假說　　(D) 共構假說

> 解析 由第六段第一句 "What is widely accepted by the scientific community is the giant-impact hypothesis." 可知，大撞擊假說是目前最受科學家普遍接受的，所以正確答案是 (C)。

Q3. 依據本文，電腦模擬的目的為何？

(A) 為了研究地球上放射性物質的濃度

(B) 為了研究月球是如何形成的

(C) 為了研究地球的適居性

(D) 為了研究月球的鐵質核心

解析 由第六段 "Computer simulations have confirmed the possibility of forming the moon this way." 可知，電腦模擬用來研究月球是如何形成的，所以正確答案是 (B)。

Q4. 依據本文內容，以下何者是不正確的？

(A) 月球的引力與地球的海洋產生交互作用。

(B) 月球沿著地球的赤道運行。

(C) 地球有鐵質的核心。

(D) 月球和地球大約在同一個時期形成。

解析 由第一段 "The moon's gravity also interacts with the Earth's oceans..." 可知，(A) 是正確的敘述；由第四段 "If this were the case, however, the moon would have been orbiting around the equator." 可知，事實上月球並非沿著地球的赤道運行，為錯誤的敘述，故正確答案是 (B)。由第二段最後的 "...why does the Earth have an iron core, while the moon does not?" 可知，(C) 是正確的敘述；根據第二段 "...the co-formation hypothesis suggests that both the Earth and the moon formed together." 可知，(D) 是正確的敘述。

Q5. 關於月球的起源，有幾種假說？

(A) 三　　(B) 四　　(C) 五　　(D) 多於五種

解析 由第二段 "There are at least five plausible hypotheses about how the moon formed." 可知，月球的起源「至少」有五種假說，表示還有非主流的假說，所以正確答案是 (D)。

Step 8 模擬測驗

■ 解答

A. 1. eject 2. on shaky ground 3. The million-dollar 4. orbit

B. 1. (C) 2. (D) 3. (A) 4. (B) 5. (D)

　　繞著地球運行超過 40 億年的月球，對於地球的宜居性扮演著重要角色。月球，就某種程度來說，對於地球自轉極的傾斜具有穩定作用。這樣的傾斜造就了地球上的四季變化，及其相對穩定的氣候。月球的引力也與地球的海洋產生交互作用，控制著潮汐的起落。如果沒有月球，地球上的生活早就和現在不一樣了。

　　但是月球是怎麼形成的呢？這是一個重要卻難以回答的問題。關於月球的形成，至少有五種被認同的假設。首先，「共構」假說指出，地球和月球是同時形成的。然而，若兩者以同一個鐵芯圓塊開始成形，為何地球有鐵芯，而月球沒有？

　　再來是「捕捉」假說。該假說認為，月球老早就在宇宙的某個位置形成，後來在它經過地球時受到其引力的捕獲。然而，這項假說一直是站不住腳的，因為從月球蒐集到的岩石分析顯示，月球和地球大致在同一時間形成。

　　一些人提出了「分裂」假說，指出地球曾經非常快速地旋轉，以致於其某部分分裂而形成月球。然而，果真如此，月球應該繞著赤道運行。此外，雖然太平洋盆地是月球最有可能的發源地，但太平洋卻比月球年輕得多。因此，多數天文學家不支持這項假說。

　　另有一種假說指出，高濃度的放射性元素，如鈾，在早期的地球上引發了自然「核爆」。這次爆炸噴射出一塊月球大小的地球，最終形成了月球。然而，由於缺乏確鑿的證據，這項假設已被推翻。

　　受到科學界廣泛接受的是「大撞擊」假說。這項假說指出，月球的形成來自地球與一顆大約火星大小的行星發生碰撞。從這次碰撞中噴出的一大塊物體最終變成了月球。電腦模擬已經證實月球如此形成的可能性。對這次碰撞的模擬也指出，月球主要由來自這個行星的物質所組成。然而，地質上的證據卻有不同的看法。對於月球上的岩石進行的分析指出，這些岩石與地球上的岩石具有相似的礦物，這意味著月球和地球有共同的起源。由於許多問題沒有得到解答，還需要更多的研究來對我們這唯一的天然衛星產生新的見解。

4.8 Part 3 - The Science of Mind and Behavior: Cognitive Biases

Step 1 掃讀 Scanning

■ 選擇正確的意思

A B A B A B A B B A

Step 2 略讀 Skimming

F T F F F

■ 答案解析

Q1. (F) 由首段第一句可知，人類並非總是理性的。

Q2. (T) 由第二段第一句可知，我們常常受到多數人的影響。

Q3. (F) 由第三段第一句可知，我們有時對於自身的認知有盲點。

Q4. (F) 由第三段第一句可知，我們有時對於自身的能力有盲點。

Q5. (F) 由第二段第一句可知，當我們看見大家都在做同一件事情的時候，我們並不會變得更加小心謹慎。

Step 3 細讀 Close reading

B D

■ 答案解析

Q1. 根據短文內容，以下何者是不正確的？

(A) 從眾效應是一種認知偏誤。

(B) 許多人不會去跟隨大多數人。

(C) 人們傾向支持在民調中領先的候選人。

(D) 人們傾向選擇一間裡面有較多人的餐廳。

> 解析 由 "...people's tendency to go along with the majority simply because everyone else is doing it." 的內容可知，從眾效應指的是「因為大多數人都這麼做，所以跟著做」的傾向，因此人們通常會去跟隨大多數人的做法，所以正確答案是 (B)。

Q2. 為何人們通常會去跟隨大多數人的做法？

(A) 因為他們想要感覺與眾不同　　(B) 因為他們感到孤單

(C) 因為他們害怕犯錯　　(D) 這部分的內容並未說明原因

> 解析 這部分的內容並未說明為何人們通常會受到多數人影響的原因，所以正確答案是 (D)。

C B A D D

■ 答案解析

Q1. 找尋對於自己有利證據的傾向稱為
(A) 達克效應。　　　(B) 從眾效應。
(C) 驗證性偏見。　　(D) 上述皆非

> 解析 由第一段 "This tendency to seek favorable evidence but avoid information from alternative viewpoints is known as the confirmation bias." 可知，(C) 是正確答案。

Q2. 根據本文，當我們看見多數人在投資股市時，可能發生什麼事？
(A) 我們可能不會做任何事。
(B) 我們可能也會做同樣的事。
(C) 我們可能能夠知道我們哪裡做錯了。
(D) 我們可能會遠離股市。

> 解析 由第二段 "When people see that many others are pumping money into the stock market, they may be prompted to do the same." 可知，當看見多數人都在投資股市時，我們可能也會做同樣的事，所以正確答案是 (B)。

Q3. 達克效應來自＿＿＿＿。
(A) 讓我們自己無法看見自身弱點的盲點
(B) 透過 Google 進行事實查核的意圖
(C) 想要投票給民調領先的候選人
(D) 想要找一間裡面有更多客人的餐廳

> 解析 由第三段第一句 "People can also have a blind spot when it comes to their own knowledge and competence, which is known as the Dunning-Kruger effect." 可知，達克效應是指人們看不清自己本身的知識與能力（有盲點），所以正確答案是 (A)。

Q4. 哪一種認知偏誤是比較常見的？
(A) 達克效應　　　(B) 從眾效應
(C) 驗證性偏見　　(D) 本文並未提及

> 解析 本文並未提及何項認知偏誤更常見，所以正確答案是 (D)。

Q5. 我們如何可以矯正認知偏誤？

　　(A) 培養思辨能力

　　(B) 接受建設性的評論

　　(C) 以思辨的態度評估我們的選項

　　(D) 以上皆是

解析 由第三段 "A way to combat cognitive biases is to be open to constructive criticism and develop critical thinking. Being able to evaluate our options critically..." 可知，(A)、(B)、(C) 皆可以幫助我們矯正認知偏誤，所以正確答案是 (D)。

Step 8 模擬測驗

■ 解答

A. 1. cocksure　2. fallen victim to　3. the odd one out　4. turned a blind eye to

B. 1. (B)　2. (C)　3. (D)　4. (B)　5. (A)

文章中譯

　　有個與一般常識相反的論點：人類並非一直都是邏輯與理性的。事實上，人會做出錯誤的解析及不當的決定，這並非是少見的。造成這問題的主要因素之一是推理和判斷上的缺陷。人們根據自己的偏見 — 通常是無意識地 — 去察覺資訊，一般稱這樣的傾向為認知偏誤。諸如此類例子不勝枚舉。舉例來說，儘管許多人會用 Google 進行事實核查，但多數人對於與其信念不一致的資訊視而不見，所以會無意識地只尋求可以強化其信念的來源。換言之，他們更可能去關注能夠證實其想法或他們已經知道的事物。這種尋求有利證據但避開來自另類觀點的資訊傾向，我們稱之為「驗證性偏見」。這可能發生在我們任何人身上。

　　另一個常見的認知偏誤是從眾效應，它指的是人們「因為大多數人都這麼做，所以跟著做」的傾向。舉例來說，有家餐廳裡面人比較多，所以覺得進去吃東西不會踩到地雷。就政治層面來說，大多數人都不想被當成異類，且往往把票投給民調領先的候選人。人們「渴望跟多數人在一起」的想法，讓他們容易受到潮流效應的影響。這樣的效應也可見於金融界。當人們看到別人正將資金投入股市時，他們也很可能被驅使去做同樣的事。大家可能只是跟進，而不會對於投資項目進行獨立性的評估，只因為不想錯失良機。

　　當提及自己本身的知識與能力時，人們也可能出現盲點，此即所謂

「達克效應（DK Effect）」。這樣的認知偏誤指出，在特定領域能力較不足者，更可能自以為是地充滿信心，而知識與技能較豐富者，有時反而內心充滿疑慮。也就是說，對於一項主題僅有的一丁點知識，往往可以讓人錯誤地認為他們已了解所有該知道的事情。然而，事實上一個無所不知的人也可能是一無所知的。這種毫無理由的自信，源自於一個「不讓人看見自己哪裡有錯」的盲點。對抗認知偏誤的一個辦法是，敢開心胸面對建設性的批評以及培養思辨能力。能夠以評論的態度評估我們的選擇，會讓我們免於成為認知偏誤的受害者。

NOTE

國際學村 LA PRESS 語研學院 Language Academy Press

語言學習NO.1

學英語

讓日常生活成為你的文法老師！
〔實境式〕
生活大小事
文法這樣用
徹底融合情境，學會真正用得上的實用英文文法
作者 Joseph Chen

學韓語

韓語學習必備教材
我的第一本
韓語語源
記單字
外交官的韓語老師教你
用50個語源輕鬆記住2000個韓語單字
作者 朴鎮權

KOREAN 한자어

學日語

「沉浸式學習法」
我的第一本
觀光·遊學
日語課本
從日本生活學好對話、文法、單字，教學有效率，自學最實用！

JAPANESE
TRAVEL MADE EASY！
藤井麻里/著 楊詩蕓/譯

第二外語

從新開始
學法語文法
FRENCH GRAMMAR FOR EVERYONE
發音及連音規則×組字規則×語序結構×陰陽性規則×
動詞類型及變化×時態 通включно有！
適合大家的法語初級文法課本。基本認識，基本詞性，全方位活用句全
★全教MP3 ★全書音檔下載QR碼
王柔� 著

考多益

[HACKERS] × 國際學村
新制多益
全新！TOEIC
單字大全
Vocabulary
備考多益唯一推薦權威單字書！
David Cho 著

考日檢

N5-N1
新日檢
單字大全
精選出題頻率最高的考用單字，
全級數一次通過！

適合任何級別的日檢考生
循序漸進、任意跳級，準確滿足各種日檢考前準備
經20餘年研析統計結果，精選各級測驗必考單字
金星坤、徐暘折、丹桐凱/著

考韓檢

國際學村
New
TOPIK II
新韓檢
寫作應考
祕笈
中高級
唯一最齊全
繁體中文版

考英檢

[HACKERS] × 國際學村
全新托福
TOEFL
單字大全
Vocabulary
最新托福單字資訊完全掌握！
徹底分析最近10年考題，
針對托福測驗量身打造的單字書！
4種版本音檔，配合各學習需求
David Cho 著

想獲得最新最快的
語言學習情報嗎？

歡迎加入
國際學村&語研學院粉絲團

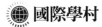

台灣廣廈 國際出版集團
Taiwan Mansion International Group

國家圖書館出版品預行編目（CIP）資料

英文閱讀技術／周昱翔 著; -- 初版 -- 新北市：國際學村, 2023.01
　面；　公分
978-986-454-258-1（平裝）
1. 英語學習. 2. 英文閱讀

805.18　　　　　　　　　　　　　　　　　　111018851

國際學村

英文閱讀技術

台大名師最強高理解速讀課！養成大量接收資訊與抓住關鍵的能力，大幅提升英語閱讀力！

作　　　者／周昱翔

編輯中心編輯長／伍峻宏
編輯／許加慶
封面設計／林珈仔・內頁排版／菩薩蠻數位文化有限公司
製版・印刷・裝訂／皇甫・秉成

行企研發中心總監／陳冠蒨　　　線上學習中心總監／陳冠蒨
媒體公關組／陳柔彣　　　　　　產品企製組／顏佑婷
綜合業務組／何欣穎

發　行　人／江媛珍
法律顧問／第一國際法律事務所 余淑杏律師・北辰著作權事務所 蕭雄淋律師
出　　版／國際學村
發　　　行／台灣廣廈有聲圖書有限公司
　　　　　　地址：新北市235中和區中山路二段359巷7號2樓
　　　　　　電話：（886）2-2225-5777・傳真：（886）2-2225-8052

代理印務・全球總經銷／知遠文化事業有限公司
　　　　　　地址：新北市222深坑區北深路三段155巷25號5樓
　　　　　　電話：（886）2-2664-8800・傳真：（886）2-2664-8801
郵政劃撥／劃撥帳號：18836722
　　　　　　劃撥戶名：知遠文化事業有限公司（※單次購書金額未達1000元，請另付70元郵資。）

■出版日期：2023年5月初版3刷　　ISBN：978-986-454-258-1
　　　　　　2024年4月4刷　　　　版權所有，未經同意不得重製、轉載、翻印。